Spinners' Wharf

Spinners' Wharf

IRIS GOWER

St. Martin's Press
New York

Library of Congress Cataloging in Publication Data

Gower, Iris.
  Spinners' wharf.

  I. Title.
PR6057.0845S65   1986   823'.914   85-31729
ISBN 0-312-75237-7

First published in Great Britain by Century Publishing Co., Ltd.
First U.S. Edition

10   9   8   7   6   5   4   3   2   1

With love to
Luther and Hilda

Chapter One

The train twisted and turned through the Welsh hills, spitting out steam and cinders in great gusts like a monster sensing its prey. Small fires began softly in the grass bordering the track before bursting into flames and marking the progress of the iron beast with irregular pyres which were quick to die. For a fine rain had begun to fall, misting the narrow windows, a million tears slipping along translucent cheeks, grieving.

Imprisoned within the carriages as though inside a gigantic glass necklace were men in flat caps and white scarves with lean, blue scarred faces – the stamp of the miner. From along the corridor came the singing of soldiers freshly clasped to the bosom of Kitchener's Army. They sang bravely and cheerfully, 'Goodbye Dolly, I must leave you,' for war was not yet a reality.

In one of the dusty plush seats sat a girl who seemed unaware of the people around her. She wore thick boots and from beneath the hem of her flannel skirt peeped the edges of a coarse calico petticoat.

She leaned back, her face hidden by the shadow of her bonnet, apparently reading an advertisement for Fry's chocolate cakes at 3d each as though it was of the utmost importance to her. No one would have guessed that because of her mixed emotions she fought a constant battle with the tears that threatened to spill down her cheeks.

Rhian Gray was coming home and as the train clattered remorselessly against the lines, she seemed to come alive, turning to look at the now familiar countryside on the outskirts of Sweyn's Eye. When she saw the low, dark stone sprawling buildings of the copper works lying along the banks of the river that was dull red, the colour of old blood, she shivered.

As it entered the station, the train jerked and shuddered as though in its death throes. Rhian rose shakily to her feet, brushing at her skirt, knowing she must look crumpled and untidy. She picked up her bag, clutching the handle with fingers that trembled; she was back in Sweyn's Eye, yet there was no happiness in her homecoming.

Yorkshire had been left far behind and the new life she had made there seemed a distant dream. At the Mansel mills where she had worked for almost two years, she had been sharp and quick to learn. She knew how to weave thousands of threads together into a colourful pattern; she had even designed turnovers, the small shawls which were worn by the women of the Yorkshire mills just as they were by their counterparts from the Welsh valleys. And in Yorkshire she had regained her pride.

Rhian walked quickly along the platform, flinching as the acrid smoke from the engine burned her eyes. She could taste the ashes and she coughed as she rubbed dust from her skirts, straining to see a familiar face in the throng of people at the station gates.

'Rhian! Come here, *merchi*, let me look at you. *Duw*, there's a lovely young woman you've grown up to be, proud of you I am!'

'Carrie, I'm glad you could come to meet me.' She hugged the older woman, warmth sweeping through her for it was Carrie who had cared for her as a child. Carrie was the one who had mothered her when Aunt Agnes was too tired; she had been part of the household, coming in each day to light fires, to clean and cook – yet there was more to Carrie than met the eye.

'How's auntie? I came as soon as I got your letter,' Rhian said and Carrie's face fell into lines of sadness.

'There's a terrible change in Agnes,' Carrie said softly. 'She won't eat anything, gone as thin as a bird and her face pointed, the bones standing out sharp – but her eyes are seeing everything as usual, mind.'

As she left the bustle of the station at Carrie's side, Rhian became aware of the silence that hung over the town. There

8

were no bakers' vans or horse-drawn milk-carts creaking along the roads. She stared round in amazement and paused as she saw a bill posted in one of the shop windows:

WE ARE AT WAR. GREAT BRITAIN'S FATEFUL STEP.
FIGHT FOR
NATIONAL HONOUR AND SAFETY.

Beneath the banner headlines was printed a story of a German cruiser being sunk. And the Kaiser's troops had been repulsed by the Belgians. Rhian turned away, her heart beating swiftly in fear. The poster crystallised the fact of war which, engrossed in her own problems, she had almost dismissed as being scaremongering.

'There's terrible, isn' it?' Carrie caught her glance. 'The damned war has changed everything, factories shut down, copper works silent and even the docks are at a standstill; like a dead town Sweyn's Eye is – and all because of them foreigners.'

As Rhian walked towards her home along achingly familiar streets, she saw men standing on corners talking in hushed tones, eyes lowered and faces solemn. There was no flashing of sparks from the copper works, no glare as the blast furnaces were tapped; it was as Carrie had said, a dead town.

'Even the pawnshops are closed,' Carrie said with a trace of humour. 'Comes to something when you can't hock your best pair of boots. There's soft men are, wanting to fight each other.'

Rhian's throat constricted, her eyes clouding with tears as she drew nearer to the neat row of cottages. She saw them as if through a haze and painful memories pressed on the edges of her mind . . .

Sharp images of a man with ugly tufts of hair and ugly hands. Gerwin Price had torn and plundered, violating her soul as well as her body. She pushed the agonising thoughts away, but she was trembling.

'Come on, *merchi*, no good standing out by here, let's go in and have a nice cup of tea, shall we? I've made some nice *teisen lap* for you.'

As Rhian followed Carrie indoors, the aroma of the cake – rich with fruit and baked flat on a plate – filled the house.

'I'll just run up to see auntie and then I'd love that cup of tea,'

Rhian said cheerfully.

It was just as well that Carrie had warned her of the change in Aunt Agnes, for she was nothing but a pale shadow of the strong woman she had once been. She lay huddled in her bed, as thin as a child beneath the sheets, and only her eyes held anything of her former spirit.

'Auntie, there's good it is to see you!' Rhian kissed the parchment-thin cheek, half afraid to touch lest she damaged the frail bones.

'She's been talking to you, hasn't she?' Aunt Agnes stabbed a thin finger towards Carrie. 'Told you I'm losing my brains, I'll warrant, just because I want to die out of it all.' She lifted her head and for a moment she was the old Aunt Agnes. 'And die I will, so don't try your wiles and weepings on me, my girl.'

Rhian sat carefully on the edge of the bed. 'Now, auntie, why talk like that? There's plenty of spirit in you, anyone can see that, and what would I do without you? If only you'd eat sensibly, you'd be back to your old self in no time.'

Aunt Agnes sighed. 'You'll do very well without me, you've proved that. Anyway, you don't get my meaning, do you girl? I want to go, I've had enough of life – and don't pity me because I know full well what I'm saying for all that Carrie tells me I'm deranged. There's this war – do you think I'm going to endure seeing our young men go to shed their blood in some foreign land? Oh no, I'm better out of it.' She looked at Rhian imploringly. 'Try to find your brother Billy, that's all I ask.'

Rhian nodded her head. 'Of course I will, auntie – and just think, the war may not last long, everyone is saying it'll be over before it's really begun.' Her aunt simply turned her face to the wall and Rhian sighed softly.

'I'm going to unpack my things and then perhaps we can have tea together. Draw the curtains, Carrie, will you? And put more coal on the fire, it's chilly in here.'

Rhian was unconscious of the air of authority she had assumed, nor did she notice the quick deferential glance Carrie gave her. She followed the older woman and stood on the landing a moment, staring at the closed door of her own bedroom.

'What do you think?' Carrie asked, her voice trembling. 'Should we have Dr Thomas to look at her? She goes mad if I

10

even suggest it, but you're here now, perhaps she'll listen to you.'

Rhian shook her head. 'I'll talk to auntie later,' she smiled. 'If I threaten to send for Bryn Thomas, that may be enough to do the trick!' She brushed back her hair wearily, 'And if it isn't, then I'll decide what's to be done in the morning.'

Carrie looked at her with new respect. 'You've grown up,' she said quietly and Rhian allowed herself a small smile.

'I suppose I have.' In her heart she knew her childhood had ended a long time ago. Her thoughts veered away sharply; one indulgence in unpleasant memories was enough for anyone.

'I'm going home now,' Carrie said. 'I've spent more nights by here than under my own roof lately.'

'There's good of you, Carrie.' Rhian's tone was warm, 'I do appreciate your kindness. I seem to have taken you for granted all these years, but I won't make that mistake again.'

'*Duw*, don't you go praising me, mind. I've got to have something to fill my days, haven't I?'

Later as Rhian sat alone in the silence of the familiar living-room, she acknowledged that it was good to be home. The fire glowed behind black-leaded bars, the kettle was singing on the well-polished hob. And yet strangely there was a home-sickness within her for the things she had left behind.

She thought nostalgically about the craggy, rugged hills of Yorkshire, where nothing grew except the tough grass that fed flocks of thick-coated sheep. She had severed herself abruptly and with difficulty from the satisfying life she had made there, for the simple reason that Auntie Agnes needed her.

Rhian slipped from the chair on to the mat in front of the fire and covered her face with her hands. She thought of Mansel Jack with a sense of loss, even knowing that she had not the right. Yet she had found herself so drawn to the man whose very presence in a room made everyone stop and stare. He was her boss, owner of the small woollen mill where she had learned her trade. He had wrested a living from wool, pitting himself against competition from some of the biggest mills in the land, and making a success out of a venture which had appeared to be doomed to failure.

Yet it was not his success that impressed Rhian so much as the man himself. There was a steeliness about him, a quiet strength and the feeling he imparted that Mansel Jack could cope with fire and flood and come through smiling and victorious.

Moreover there was an unexpected softness in him that seemed to be only for her – or had she imagined the overt liking that shone from his eyes whenever he looked at her? When the letter had come from Carrie, it was like tenuous fingers of love and duty drawing at her soul and she knew there was no other choice but to return home to Sweyn's Eye.

And now that she had given up the trade she loved and was so proud of, would she simply sit here along with her dying aunt and become old and sere herself? Feeling tears burn against her closed lids, she was angry. She rose to her feet and with fierce jabs of the twisted poker riddled the fire so that the ashes fell sparkling into the grey dust beneath.

'Turning into a cry-baby already and only home two minutes, there's daft!' Her voice sounded strange in the silent room; she lifted her head and the ticking of the grandfather clock in the corner seemed unnaturally loud. It was about time she stopped feeling sorry for herself, so she resolutely turned and went upstairs to bed.

Yet she could not sleep but tossed and turned, trying to ease the tempest of thoughts that rushed through her mind. She saw behind closed lids the shadowy figure of her brother Billy. He had been the talk of Sweyn's Eye once, the subject of avid gossip over silver teapots and fine bone china cups.

The entire town seemed to believe he was a man who had got away with murder and then had run off with a married woman who was far above his station in life. Yet Rhian knew that Billy was innocent of any crime except that of loving Delmai Richardson.

Rhian wished her brother could be here to help her cope with the awful dogged determination to die which gripped Aunt Agnes. But God alone knew where Billy had fled when he left Sweyn's Eye behind him.

She turned over in her bed and closed her eyes tightly, ashamed of the tears that burned behind her lids.

*

Heath Jenkins walked through the narrow streets of Sweyn's

Eye, his step eager, his spirits high. He had heard that Rhian Gray had come home and was on his way to see her. At the edge of the harbour he paused and stared at the sailing ships lifting and rising on the tide, his thoughts drifting and a smile curving his lips.

She had chased him shamelessly once, but Rhian had been a young girl then and perhaps she had changed. Yet his feelings for her had grown, fed by her absence, and love for her burned deep in his gut.

He watched the gulls wheel and curve overhead; as they called raucously to each other, they reminded him of flurries of rice thrown at a wedding. He might bring Rhian here when the time was right and propose to her. The edge of the sea would be an ideal setting and he knew that to women, such things were important.

Heath felt he had a great deal to offer Rhian now. She would have her own comfortable house on the lower slopes of the hill near the sea and a fair bank balance to go with it. For the last year or more he had been manager of Brandon Sutton's steel works and had put the increased wages to good use. Some said his rise in position was due to the fact that his sister was married to the owner, but Heath had worked damned hard for promotion and he felt he deserved it – not that he intended to remain at the steel company much longer.

He could scarcely remember the hovel where he and his sister had been born. Mary was bitter about it still; it had marked her life, made her strong and independent. She was a successful business woman and no one could attribute her achievements to anything other than her own iron will.

Heath wondered how Rhian would feel about being the wife of a soldier, for against all advice from Mary and from Brandon he had decided to enlist in the Army.

He was well aware that steel-making was an occupation that would be more necessary than ever now that the country was at war, and there would be no shame attached to him if he remained in Sweyn's Eye to work the steel. But his young blood called out for combat; he needed to be at the heart of the conflict, he'd not be content with being on the sidelines.

Rhian would be proud of him, he felt sure of that, and he was sure too that she would agree to be his wife. She had come

13

home with no ring on her finger, still the same Rhian Gray who had left town nearly two years earlier.

Heath had understood her need to leave Sweyn's Eye; she had to renew herself, find inner peace after the terrible thing that had happened to her.

His hands clenched into fists at the thought of the barbarism of Gerwin Price, who had taken away Rhian's innocence in the most cruel and defiling act which it could be any woman's misfortune to bear. Rhian had felt unclean, degraded and Heath could understand that too. But he loved her and he wanted to marry her, for her past was dead and gone just as was Gerwin Price himself.

He was about to move away from the harbour when he caught sight of a slim figure, dressed in a light cotton skirt and blouse, dark red hair peeping from under a stiff calico bonnet. He knew even from a distance that it was Rhian – he loved every inch of her, she had been part of his pulse since he was a boy and he had always known that one day she would come back to him.

Slowly he moved towards her, noticing the tilt of her head, the grace of her movements, the precise way her small, booted feet touched the ground. She was more beautiful than ever, a woman now and no longer a light-headed young girl.

'Rhian, *cariad*, you've come home!' They stared at each other for a long moment and her eyes were alight as they looked into his face. He held out his arms and she came into them as though she had always belonged against his heart.

'Heath, I'm so glad to see you, let me look at you properly.' She held herself away from him, the palms of her hands cool against his cheeks. Unable to prevent himself, he leaned forward and kissed her and, startled, she drew back.

'Rhian, my lovely, I won't hurt you.'

'I know.' She held his hand and smiled at him, colour tinging her cheeks. 'You look well and so handsome it takes my breath away!'

She was more poised, Heath thought. Rhian had learned to conceal her feelings. Her dark eyes were clouded, as though to deter anyone from knowing too much about her.

'And how's Mary?' she asked lightly. 'Has your sister got any children yet?' Her face softened. 'I'm going to have such a

14

lovely time meeting up with my friends again.'

Heath shook his head, smiling. 'No, she's far too busy for motherhood – you know Mary. Anyway, I think she must have had enough to do bringing me up, I probably put her off for life.'

'I doubt that.' Rhian removed her hand from his and sat on the sea wall, tucking her fingers beneath her skirts, sitting on them – he wondered if this was to stop him from taking her hand in his once more.

'What brought you home, Rhian?' he asked quietly. 'I doubt if it was my baby blue eyes. In fact, I doubt if you even gave me a thought all the time you were away.'

'There's nasty you are, Heath Jenkins.' Rhian smiled enigmatically. 'I haven't asked you how many girls you've taken up to Ram's Tor in the past two years, have I?'

'Only because you know I'll lie through my teeth.' He rested his arm around her shoulder and could feel her withdrawal even though she scarcely moved. She sighed heavily and her face was grave as she looked up at him.

'I came home to see auntie. She's telling me she's going to die – now what do you do with an old lady like that who has a will of iron?'

He hardly heard her words, he was totally captured by the beauty of her eyes, the fine cheek-bones and full lips. She was a desirable woman and he could not believe that some man hadn't made advances to her during the past two years.

'Auntie Agnes will live for ever,' he said abstractedly. 'Tell me the truth, Rhian – has there been anyone else since you've been away?'

She lifted her chin and her eyes were suddenly cold. 'You've no right to ask anything of me, Heath,' she said quickly. 'I don't have to answer to you or to anyone else and I'll thank you to remember that.' Her shoulders relaxed a little and she sighed, shaking her head. 'But don't worry, no man's promised me his undying love and devotion. I'm the same Rhian Gray who left Sweyn's Eye, more's the pity.'

'You were waiting for me,' he said gently. 'We were meant for each other, Rhian. I'll show you what real love is all about and make you happy to be a woman; it's time, past time, that you learned about a man's passion.'

15

Rhian rose to her feet and stared down at him with a haunted expression on her face and he cursed himself for his clumsiness.

'Just don't say any more, not now, Heath. I must be getting home. Carrie will be growing anxious – she can't leave auntie alone, you see, and I told her I was going out for a breath of air.'

'I'll walk with you. Now don't go making a fuss, let's just be friends the way we always were, that's a good enough start for me.'

The day was sultry, airless and Rhian untied the ribbons of her bonnet, letting it trail; it hung half-way down her back, the calico stiff and unyielding.

'It looks as if you've developed a hump!' Heath couldn't keep the laughter from his voice and Rhian turned and kicked out at him playfully.

'Making fun of me now, is it? Well, you just watch yourself, Heath Jenkins. You're not too big to get a clout around the ear, mind!'

They walked the rest of the way in companionable silence and Heath, trying to match his long stride with Rhian's dainty footsteps, felt as though he was suddenly ten feet tall.

*

As the summer days passed slowly, Rhian found that Agnes became steadily weaker. She had called out the doctor, but old Bryn Thomas had told her quietly that there was nothing he could do.

'She's an old and frail lady,' his tone had been hushed, 'and if she wants to depart this world, my dear, then nothing on God's earth will prevent her. I've seen it happen many times before.'

Rhian had been impatiently angry, but there was no point in venting her feelings on the doctor. If Agnes refused to eat – and she did – there was nothing he could do. Rhian pleaded and coaxed and at last quarrelled with her auntie, telling Agnes that she was selfish and uncaring, but none of it weakened her aunt's resolve.

'I've had my day and now it's over. I want to go, Rhian – let me die in peace, I beg of you.' Her voice was gossamer, her

16

breathing ragged. Defeated, Rhian turned away, hiding her tears.

'Oh, auntie, I can't bear it when you talk like that,' she said unevenly.

She was relieved to hear the familiar knocking on the door and with a quick look at Agnes, who smiled encouragingly, she hurried downstairs thankful to Heath for his constancy. He had come to sit with Rhian most evenings and she found that she was comforted by his presence, fearing to be alone, dreading the moment which must surely come when her aunt finally relinquished her feeble hold on life.

'There's tears in your eyes,' Heath said, putting his arm around her shoulders. 'I wish there was more I could do, *cariad*.' He took her hand, touching her finger-tips, studying each nail as though it was a precious pearl. Rhian was touched by his devotion even though she couldn't return it, and she smiled, pushing a curl of hair from his brow.

He was a handsome man, tall and slim but with good shoulders and the strength that came from working the tinplate. His face was strong, his eyes clear.

'You're doing just what I want you to do, keeping me company.'

She moved away from him, her movements brisk. 'You're not growing soft now that you're a manager, are you?' she asked gently and Heath leaned towards her, his eyes saying the things she had forbidden him to speak.

'Soft where you're concerned, Rhian. I wish ...' He stopped speaking as Rhian put her hand over his lips.

A small sound from upstairs alerted her and with a quick, frightened look at Heath, she hurried along the passageway.

'I'm coming, auntie,' she called, hearing the breathless panic in her voice. In trepidation she ran upstairs and entered the bedroom, her heart racing. Aunt Agnes was leaning against the pillows, her eyes more clear than they had been for days. There was even a little colour in her cheeks.

'Auntie, I was so frightened.' Rhian sat at the side of the bed and Heath stood over her protectively. Agnes reached out a thin hand and clung to Rhian's arm and it was clear she was trying to speak.

'What is it, auntie?' Rhian could feel her aunt's strength

17

draining away and knew suddenly that she had been fooled by appearances and that Agnes was trying to say goodbye. The lips moved, the voice whispery and barely audible, and Rhian leaned closer. 'It's the house, girl. It's no longer mine, I've nothing to leave you and there's sorry I am. Thought you'd stay in England, I did. Oh, Rhian, what have I done?'

She closed her eyes wearily and it was clear that the effort to speak had taken what little strength she had.

'Please, don't die, Auntie Agnes,' Rhian said, closing her eyes in pain, telling herself that it was all a horrible nightmare. She looked down at her aunt's closed lids; they were shadowed violet, the lashes long and unusually full, curling on the parchment skin.

There was a sudden silence in the room, an unearthly stillness. Rhian stared at the pallid face of her aunt, unwilling to believe what her mind was telling her.

'Come away, Rhian, *cariad*, she's gone.' Heath drew her to her feet. 'Let me take you downstairs. I'll see to everything and get the nurse. Mrs Benson will know what must be done.'

Rhian had lost her bearings and she obeyed Heath blindly, grateful for his protective arm supporting her. She clung to the strength of him as he led her down the stairs and paused in the passageway, steadying herself, taking deep breaths of the dreamy summer air drifting in from the open door.

With sudden cruel clarity, she realised that she belonged nowhere; she had no home, no roots in the town where she had grown up. Fear for the future for a moment superseded even her grief. Her mind cried out a name – Mansel Jack – and with a flash of insight she realised that she ached to feel his arms around her, holding her, comforting her with his unfaltering strength.

The realisation brought fresh anguish and Rhian shuddered with hopelessness. Disengaging herself from Heath's gentle hands, she turned and walked heavily into the kitchen, the silence of the house pressing around her and feeling inside nothing but a cold emptiness.

Chapter Two

The air was soft, the early morning mists like jewels on the grass. The sound of Sunday church bells began to peal out over the English countryside, a harmonious reminder that it was time to begin the day for, as yet, the war had not touched the rolling Yorkshire hills.

Mansel Jack rose from his bed in one swift movement, pushing aside the patchwork quilt and heavy woollen blankets, standing birthday-naked in the chill of the morning. He dressed as he did everything – with smooth, unhurried efficiency, buttoning his waistcoat over the crisp linen shirt. His suit was of good woollen cloth, dark and neat, and as he saw himself in the mirror over the washstand he felt he looked nothing like his thirty-seven years.

His sister was downstairs before him, as was her custom, organising a hearty cooked breakfast of devilled kidneys and salt lean bacon. She looked up at him fondly as he entered the dining-room and a sudden frown creased her brow.

'You're dressed to go out!' Her mouth fell open in astonishment. 'Haven't suddenly got religion, have you?'

He smiled without humour and seated himself at the table as Lizzie brought in the tea-tray. The young maid's eyes were downcast; she looked sleepy and heavy-eyed, although she must have been out of her bed for more than an hour.

Doreen sat at the table and lifted the heavy silver teapot and Mansel Jack smiled inwardly. His sister liked to have fine possessions around her, enjoyed playing the gracious lady. Anyone would think she had been born to it!

Their origins had been humble by any standards. Mansel

19

Jack senior had been a scholar, making a meagre living at tutoring the children of the gentry. Sometimes, Doreen and Mansel Jack were taken along to the big houses, left to while away the time in elegant but chilly hallways, and it was from these visits that Doreen had found her taste for another way of life.

Fortuitously and not by luck alone, Doreen had married into money. Young and beautiful and with a gift for absorbing facts and presenting them intelligently, folk took her for a scholar like her father, but in reality Doreen had only a spurious intelligence. It had been a release for her when her elderly husband died and she had wasted no time in returning to her home.

'Penny for them,' Doreen said softly now. 'Thinking about the past, by the look in your eyes.' She smiled warmly. 'I'm glad we were able to help each other after mammy and daddy passed on.'

Mansel Jack hated euphemisms, but he put down his napkin and refrained from correcting his sister.

'Aye, lass, with your husband's money and my know-how we've made something of ourselves, haven't we?'

Doreen looked down at her hands. Mansel Jack was her life, the only living being she cared about. She was more than a little in awe of him, for he had a quality of hardness in him that made her feel no one, not even she, dare stand in his way. But then he had needed to be hard to survive in the world of commerce. She thought of the success of her little plan for him and smiled. She must be very careful and he must never be allowed to feel she had manipulated him, yet Charlotte Bradley was such a catch for him!

It had been a wonderful day for Doreen when her brother had become engaged to Charlotte, for the girl's family had a very high position in the county. Not only was she every inch a lady, full of character and verve, but more importantly Doreen felt that a marriage between Charlotte and Mansel Jack would raise their stock considerably.

Mansel Jack rose to his feet, shaking his head at Doreen; she was day-dreaming again and that look meant she was probably trying to make him do something he had no wish to do. He smiled inwardly, for she had very little chance of success. He was quite aware of her machinations where Charlotte was concerned; Doreen fondly imagined she had brought them together, but in reality Mansel Jack had intended to propose to Charlotte anyway. The girl had breeding and strength of character and he admired her greatly; she would make an excellent wife.

When he left the house, he decided to walk the short distance to the cluster of buildings clinging low on the river-bank where his mill was situated. He paused for a moment on a ridge, looking back at the tall elegant building he now called home and feeling the sweet thrill of achievement.

The house was not large by some standards, but it was built of solid stone. Its rooms were high-ceilinged, cool in summer and warmed by fires in huge grates in the winter. It was a symbol of what he had worked for all these years since he was nothing but a young lad.

As he climbed the steep rise, he acknowledged that it was the injection of Doreen's money which had built the mill into the thriving business it was today, but he would have succeeded anyway – it might just have taken a little longer.

He began to stride out, his long legs covering the uneven ground quickly. The row of cottages where his workers lived was in sight now, lying flat beneath a ridge and curving along the line of the narrow road. The doors were built low, the windows of the upper storey so near that Mansel Jack could touch them if he so wished.

On an impulse, he rapped loudly on one of the small doors and it was opened almost immediately.

'Morning, sir. Come on in, though the fire's not lit yet.' The woman was flustered as she backed away to allow him entry.

'It's all right, Mrs Fisher, I just want to know why Rhian Gray hasn't been at work these last few days. Is she sick?'

She pursed her lips, peering up at him with faded blue eyes – as though afraid he might bite, Mansel Jack thought in irritation.

'Rhian Gray, she's gone,' Mrs Fisher said slowly. She backed along the narrow passageway and flung open a door. 'See for yourself, sir, she's not here no longer.'

Mansel Jack could hardly conceal his surprise as he stared into the bare, impersonal room that was innocent of any

21

trappings of habitation. He turned to Mrs Fisher, impatient at her slowness.

'Do you know where she's gone and why?' he asked abruptly. 'Surely she didn't just vanish off the face of the earth – she left an address, I imagine?'

The woman made no reply; she simply stared at him dully.

'Think, Mrs Fisher! What did she say when she paid you her rent, she must have told you something?'

'Her auntie took sick, Rhian said she must go home to see her.' Mrs Fisher's forehead was a patchwork of lines as she struggled with her memory. 'Sweyn's Eye, that's the name of the town, sounds an outlandish place and I don't know owt else about her.'

As he stood in the narrow dingy passageway, Mansel Jack thrust his hands into his pockets, wondering at the sense of dismay he was feeling. He could talk to Rhian Gray, he had admired her quickness of wit and the sparkling intelligence that lit up her eyes, animating the delicate features whenever she spoke of the weaving which had become part of her life. He would miss her and the knowledge came as a surprise to him.

*

Warm soft breezes drifted in from the calm crystalline sea that lapped at the shore with the delicacy of a kitten's tongue. Fruit began to thrive amongst the rich foliage of the trees on the hills to the west of Sweyn's Eye and the summer days were breathless.

But Rhian saw none of it; she was closeted indoors behind curtained windows, for the sun had no place in a house where the spectre of death stalked the rooms. Her mind was still clouded and her entire being seemed to ache. It pained her so much to think of the nightmare events of the day her aunt had died, yet the memories crowded in at every unguarded moment.

Rhian still found it difficult to believe that the house that she had looked upon as home ever since her childhood was no longer hers. Aunt Agnes had believed – and with some justification – that she would remain in England. And yet, to let her house go must have cost her a great deal and Rhian punished herself with the thought that had she been closer, in

22

spirit as well as in flesh, her aunt might have confided in her.

And now she was homeless and, worse, without direction. She could return to England to the mill where Mansel Jack was, but every instinct warned her against such a move. She rubbed her hand across her eyes, weary of thinking futile thoughts while over all like a black bird of prey hovered the loss of Aunt Agnes who had seemed so indestructible.

The days had seemed to pass in a cloud of unreality and when Rhian walked trembling up the stairs to pay her last respects before the coffin lid was closed, she could not believe that the strangely set features, coloured with all the undertaker's skill, were those of her beloved aunt.

She felt a sense of loss that was more than grief. Part of her life had vanished – the childhood days when she and Billy had played together, secure beneath Agnes's iron will laced with the gruff kindliness that was the order of their days. And where was her brother now, when she most needed him?

After the first few hours she shed few tears; they solved nothing – Rhian had learned that lesson a long time ago. Crying merely exhausted, drained the will. Yet the days until the funeral seemed to drag interminably.

The service was simple as Aunt Agnes would have wished. She was interred beneath the soil of *Dan y Graig* cemetery, ashes to ashes, dust to dust – the words ringing in Rhian's mind had no meaning.

'Come on home, *merchi.*' Carrie ,was at Rhian's side, drawing her from the flower-strewn grave and away down past the gracious Richardson vault where the rich were laid to rest. The sun dipped, clouds slid over the skies and a swift shower sent the mourners hurrying from the graveyard.

Rhian had not wished for the traditional Welsh funeral which was a hearty celebration of death. She could not bear to have people invading the silent house, eating cold ham, women drinking tea and their menfolk becoming jovial on ale. She realised she offended the proprieties, but that was unimportant; Rhian wanted only the peace and tranquillity of an empty parlour.

'I hope you're not going to sit around here like a drowned kitten and mope.' Carrie removed her good black shawl, shaking it free of rain, and the wool exuded the smell of the

23

sheep from which it had come.

'No, I'm not going to mope,' Rhian said firmly. 'I mean to find work.'

'Work?' Carrie's dismay was almost comical and Rhian smiled. 'Don't make it sound as though I'm going out on the streets as a shilling flossie,' she said. 'I've worked in a Yorkshire mill these past two years and I'm not about to let all that experience go to waste.' Her own words brought vividly to mind the memory of the long narrow mill with its clatter of looms. And she saw Mansel Jack, strong and massive, his presence shedding a radiance which warmed her . . . but that was in the past now, something else to be forgotten.

'But what will you do?' Carrie's voice interrupted her thoughts.

'Anything I can lay my hands on. I've heard that Mr Sinman from Spinners' Wharf needs a worker.' She didn't add that what he wanted was someone to clean the house and help his wife, who was expecting her first child. But at least she would be near a mill and perhaps, sometimes, she might be allowed to work on the looms.

Rhian suppressed a sigh. 'I'm going to change out of my good clothes and then I'll make us both a nice cup of tea.' At the doorway leading to the stairs, she paused. 'We both know the grief of losing Aunt Agnes,' she said softly, 'but there's no point in dwelling on it, she wouldn't have wanted that.'

Carrie paused a moment and then nodded, but there was a troubled look in her eyes which puzzled Rhian. She stared down at the apron she had just wrapped around her waist, tying and untying the strings, then sighed softly. 'I 'spects you won't be needing me any longer.' Her voice was low and empty and in a swift movement, Rhian crossed the room and hugged her tightly.

'Of course I'll need you; how can I go out to work and come home to a cold empty house?' She smiled and tweaked Carrie's cheek. 'I'll depend on you more than ever now, can't you see that? With Billy away, you are the only family I have left.'

Carrie turned and rubbed at her eyes. 'Go and get out of those damp clothes before you catch a chill, there's a good girl.' She sniffed derisively. 'And don't forget you have to visit that Mr Irons as soon as you can.'

Once in her room, Rhian's cheerful pose disappeared and her shoulders slumped as she leaned on the sill staring out of the window. The clouds had dispersed, the sun was shining once more and the pavements outside were drying a bluey grey. Rhian took a deep breath, knowing that she must make yet another new beginning. She sank on to the bed and closed her eyes and though there were no tears, there was a silent weeping deep inside her.

*

'Spinners' Wharf.' The sign was faded, the painted wood scored and scratched. The round windows like so many eyes were grimed with dirt and the entire building had an unused look about it.

Rhian knocked on the door, her heart beating rapidly in apprehension mingled with excitement. She could almost hear the clatter of the willowing machine and the hum of the mule and she could taste the raw wool. Somehow the particulars of spinning and weaving had got into her blood, she had known it from the moment she first took up a piece of soft thread and witnessed how strong and firm it became when twisted between her fingers.

The man who opened the door was tall and barrel-chested, his round face seeming to dip into a point in a prickly, greying beard.

'Vot can I do for you, missie?' he asked and Rhian smiled, noting the trails of fluff in his hair.

'I'm Rhian Gray,' she said warmly, for she liked the big man on sight. 'Are you Mr Sinman?'

'Yes, I Mr Sinman. You haf business with me?'

'I hope so. May I come inside?'

'You come to the house with me.' He led her up the sloping yard and through a long passageway into a stone-floored kitchen. The room was warm and cheerful and at the fireside a woman, heavy with child, was stirring a pot.

'This is Gina.' Mr Sinman's voice was full of pride. 'She good Welsh girl, makes me a fine wife.'

Rhian took the chair that was offered and smiled warmly at the woman.

'I want to work for you,' she rushed the words, her tongue

25

tripping over them in her nervousness. 'I'm not very experienced at housework or with children, but I can learn.' She
smiled. 'And I could help out in the mill sometimes, if you
like.'

Heinz Sinman looked at her doubtfully. 'It is hard work in
the kitchen, but even worse in the mill.' He paused for a
moment, rubbing at his plump cheek. 'Handling the wool is
something that grows with you, not easily learned, you
understand.'

'I've worked for almost two years in a Yorkshire mill,'
Rhian said quickly. 'I know how to make up patterns, how to
handle the machines – and I will be reliable, really I will!'

Heinz Sinman looked at his wife and she sat down on a stool,
her bulk overflowing the seat.

'Well, Heinz,' she said slowly. 'There's nothing to lose if
you ask me. I'll only need a little bit of work done by here, just
until I've had the baby – and it would be good for you to have
help in the mill, wouldn't it?'

He nodded his large head. 'Well, we can give it a try, I
suppose.'

Rhian felt a dart of triumph; the first hurdle was over. 'I
would like to try to find new customers,' she spoke eagerly.
'I'd have to be cautious at first, but I think I could be quite
good at the selling side of the business.'

'Maybe, but my darned machines break down all the time.
What we do about that?'

'Heinz, language!' Gina Sinman admonished sharply and
Rhian hid a smile as she rose to her feet. 'I'll find someone to
repair them, don't you worry.' She held out her hand. 'Do we
have an agreement Mr Sinman?' she asked and he nodded,
shaking her hand vigorously. 'You moving so fast, you take me
over if I not careful.'

Gina smiled at Rhian warmly. 'Been working too hard
lately, he has, mind.' She looked down at her hands. 'And all
this talk of war doesn't help, what with people suspicious of
my man because he's a foreigner. We'll be glad to have
someone on our side to tell the truth.'

Outside, Rhian took a deep breath of the soft summer air,
but it was not the rich bush of wild roses that held her
entranced, it was the scent of raw wool in her nostrils evoking

26

memories of Mansel Jack so crystal clear that she felt she could reach out and touch him. 'Forget Mansel Jack!' she told herself harshly.

She took a tram to the centre of Sweyn's Eye, and sat in the hard wooden seat gazing unwittingly at a woman opposite her; she wore an ancient battered velvet hat and continually tugged at her unfashionably long gloves. The woman sniffed and turned away and Rhian realised that she had been staring.

When she alighted from the swaying tram, Rhian walked purposefully along the streets down towards the heart of the town. A baker's cart jogged along in the gutter, the horse's head dipping as the animal strained between the shafts, glinting shoes slipping on the dusty, dry cobbles. A cockle-seller jostled Rhian out of the way, her basket of sea-food resting on her flat basket hat. Her thick Welsh shawl was pulled tight around ample breasts in spite of the pleasantness of the day and Rhian's spirits rose – there would always be a market for wool.

She paused outside the offices of Gregory Irons. The lawyer had sent for her and she had decided to get the interview over as quickly as possible; she had a feeling it was not going to be pleasant.

'Good morning, Miss Gray.' Gregory Irons was seated behind a large polished desk; his soft hands moved an ink-tray an inch further to his right before his eyes met hers for an instant. 'I should have dealt with this matter sooner, but you're here now.' His tone suggested that she had inconvenienced him.

Rhian forced herself to relax, though it was difficult in the circumstances for she was seated in a stiff high-backed chair. It seemed that Mr Irons did not intend his clients to be too comfortable.

'Perhaps you would explain what it is you want to see me about?' she said abruptly.

Mr Irons put his finger-tips together and stared at her over his spectacles. She didn't remember him wearing spectacles, Rhian thought fleetingly.

'It's about the cottage,' he said flatly. 'We must come to some arrangement about it.' He paused and shuffled a handful of papers in front of him.

'The cottage?' Rhian was aware of a sudden panic rising

27

within her and she clenched her hands together, trying to control the impulse to get to her feet and rush out of the office, like a penny chicken tucking its head beneath its wing.

'The deeds of the cottage were sold some time ago. I warned your aunt that she was being foolhardy.' He pressed his thin lips together. 'She wanted money, you see, and apparently she gave it all to your brother.' His clipped tone told Rhian exactly what he felt about that. 'The building now belongs to the Richardson estate, part of the property purchased to house the copper workers. These last two years your aunt has been simply a tenant.' He paused. 'It was only through the goodwill of Mr Sterling Richardson that she was allowed to stay on there.'

Rhian sat in the still, hot room listening to the drone of a bee engaged in a futile attempt to penetrate the glass of the windows.

'There are a few bits and pieces of furniture and some jewellery,' Gregory Irons continued remorselessly. 'You are at liberty to take these things away with you of course, when you move out.'

Rhian stared at him in speechless despair, swallowing the tears that constricted her throat.

He regarded her coolly, his eyes fathomless. 'Let's be reasonable about this. We will say that you are free to live at the cottage for two months, but then Miss Gray, I'm afraid you must vacate the premises.'

Rhian was trembling. 'Thank you for your time, Mr Irons.' She left the office with her head high but her mouth was dry and she had an ache in the pit of her stomach.

She made for the long stretch of golden beach, hardly aware of her surroundings. The water was a clear blue and the edges, pearly with foam, laved the shore but Rhian was staring out to where the horizon met the sea in a hazy mist. She had realised she would have to leave the cottage, of course, but not yet – surely not yet.

'Aunt Agnes, what am I going to do?' she whispered. She sank on to the warm stone wall and untied the ribbons of her bonnet, allowing the cool breeze to run through her hair. She felt alone in the world, isolated in a small oasis of time with only the wash of the sea and the calling of the gulls to disturb the silence.

Her hands lay still in her lap but her mind was racing. Perhaps she could sell Agnes's furniture, but she didn't have the heart for it and anyway, who could afford to buy it in these difficult times? She would need to find lodgings – perhaps Carrie would take her in.

Rhian kicked off her shoes and felt the softness of the sand beneath her stockinged feet, experiencing the old childlike wonder at the largeness of the sea, the glory of the arching bowl of the sky above her. It was as if she was a young, carefree girl again. It had all been so simple then, she was in love with Heath Jenkins and knew what her future would hold: marriage and children and happiness ever after. But much had happened to change her.

She breathed deeply. If she were to be honest with herself, she would remember that the physical side of love was always a mystery, something to avoid thinking about too deeply. She had seen the apple blossoms and the gold of the ring, but had never thought beyond the walk down the aisle of a church.

'Rhian, my lovely girl, why are you sitting here alone?' The deep masculine voice was close, startling her and she looked up quickly, colour rising to her cheeks.

'Heath.' Had some thread of thought brought him to her side, she wondered, and she shivered as he reached out to her. Glancing up at him and seeing the tenderness in his eyes, she looked away again. 'There's a fright you gave me.' He settled himself beside her and as she breathed in his familiar scent she felt a kind of love for him – something she couldn't explain even to herself.

'Oh, Heath,' she said as he took her hand in his strong fingers. He drew her slowly forward and for a moment he was poised above her, the crispness of his hair like an aura in the sunlight. She trembled as he moved nearer, then his lips touched hers and her heart fluttered frantically as though trying to escape from the feelings that were racing through her.

Deliberately he held her closer, his mouth seemingly on fire. Rhian wanted to drown in the sensations he was rousing, yet at the same time something within her was telling her that this was all wrong.

She shook back her hair, her thoughts so confused she could

29

not answer him. He must have wondered about the time she had spent in England, but he had asked her few questions and she was grateful; she could not begin to explain the sensations that gripped her whenever she thought of Mansel Jack.

Heath rested his hand lightly on her shoulder then, like a friend. 'Come with me, let me show you my new house,' he said. 'I told you I've gone up in the world since you went away.' He paused, waiting for her to turn to look at him. 'I won't harm you, I would never do anything to hurt or frighten you.'

Rhian nodded. 'I know,' she said, her voice sounding insubstantial against the wash of the waves and the calling of the gulls.

Together they left the beach and Heath led her across the road and towards the western slopes of Sweyn's Eye.

'You have become posh,' Rhian forced a smile, 'living among the toffs up on the hill, indeed.'

'I have to keep up appearances now that I'm a boss instead of a worker.' Although there was humour in his voice he could not conceal his pride. 'Good at the job I am, too.'

'I'm sure you are, Heath,' Rhian said quickly, sensing a chink in his armour. 'You always did put everything into your work; even when your chest was bad, you went to the mill and handled the pieces of eight like they were paper.'

'Oh, so you haven't forgotten your origins, then?' Heath tweaked her hair playfully. 'And yet subtly you are altered, Rhian. What has your life been like since you've been away?'

Rhian's heart missed a beat. 'I've been learning the wool trade,' she said evasively. 'I'm very good at making up patterns for weaving.'

Heath turned her to face him, his hands on her shoulders. 'I didn't mean that and you know it,' he said gently. 'You told me you weren't promised to anyone, but I'll ask you again – have you had a lover, Rhian? I think I've a right to know?'

'Why is everyone nosey-parkering into my life?' Her voice shook. 'I've had no lover, I told you I'm still the same as when I left here, the Rhian you always knew.'

'I doubt that,' Heath said soberly. 'All right, don't talk about your past now, perhaps later on you'll want to tell me.' He smiled at her. 'Something I do know is that you've grown into a very lovely woman.'

Rhian pushed him playfully, wanting to break his serious mood, but she caught him off-balance and he fell into the softness of the grass.

'Well, you're wrong, then,' Rhian said. 'I'm still a child at heart!' She ran from him as he lurched to his feet and with his hands hanging apelike down to his sides, began to follow her with mock menace.

He grasped her around the waist and lifted her off her feet, swinging her around until the sky and sea and land merged into a dizzy pattern, then he set her down carefully and held her close as the laughter disappeared from his eyes.

'I love you, Rhian,' he said urgently. 'I think I've always known it. Even when I was with other women, it was you I was waiting for.'

Her face was against the linen of his shirt and she breathed in the masculinity of him, knowing only that she liked being held close in his arms.

'But Heath, how can you ever forget the dreadful thing that happened to me, for I can't!'

Heath caught her chin in his hand and forced her to look at him. 'Listen to me, Rhian. You are a lovely, a very beautiful woman. What happened all that time ago was not your fault. Price hurt and humiliated you, but he's dead and gone and so should the memories be. Come on, *cariad*, you can't punish yourself for the rest of your life.'

She looked up at him pleadingly. 'Can you help but think of me as second-hand, spoiled like shop-soiled goods?'

He kissed her eyelids gently. 'No, Rhian. I'm thinking that I'm the luckiest man in the world to be holding you like this.'

His words warmed her so that she felt light-headed. Heath would accept her, flawed as she was, but then he was a man who had lain with many women old and young, so perhaps he was not so discriminating as some might be. A man like Mansel Jack, an inner voice said. But she hugged Heath and kissed his cheek, feeling the bristles of his moustache tickle her face.

'Let's see this lovely house of yours,' she said with forced cheerfulness. 'I haven't got all day, mind.'

Pen y Bryn was a tall narrow structure built on the lower slopes of the hill and Rhian loved it on sight. The odd-shaped house was haphazardly constructed, the front appearing Grecian in design with elegant mock pillars. The rest of the building sprawled backwards into the curve of the hill as though added as an afterthought. Within, it was comfortable and warm with a cheerful fire in the grate and Rhian could see that a woman's hand had been at work.

'I know what you're thinking and you are wrong,' Heath said, slipping his arm around her waist. 'Mrs Greenaway, who used to work with Mary in Sutton's Drapery – well, she keeps house for me and keeps me in order too.'

'I've no right to ask you any questions, Heath,' Rhian said softly and he smiled down at her.

'You're a funny, proud little thing and I love you.' He kissed the tip of her nose just as the door from the kitchen opened.

'Hello there, Greenie, how about some tea for my visitor? You remember Rhian Gray, don't you?'

The older woman's eyes were shrewd. Like everyone else in Sweyn's Eye she knew the sister of Billy Gray, the man who was thought to have murdered and got clean away with it. Then to cap it all he had run away with a married woman, one of the gentry at that. Rhian could almost read her thoughts, but then Mrs Greenaway smiled with genuine warmth.

'I've made some lovely Welsh cakes for your tea, Mr Jenkins – and there's more than enough to go round, don't you worry.'

It was pleasant to sit in the window-seat and stare down at the sea below. Rhian felt more at peace than she had done for some time. Since Agnes had died, there seemed no one left she could think of as her own kin and it was a strange, rootless feeling.

Mrs Greenaway brought in the tea-tray and the mouth-watering aroma of freshly baked cakes filled the room.

'Looks after me well, doesn't she, Rhian?' Heath said, helping himself to a cake from the plate. 'And I'm very good to her too, though she doesn't deserve it the way she treats me like a little boy.'

Mrs Greenaway tapped his hand playfully. 'I've got to admit that he is good to me, mind. Took me in when I didn't have a job. Folks said I was too old to work, but I didn't want to spend the rest of my life chewing my gums, did I? And anyway, you got the best of the bargain, didn't you, Heath

Jenkins?'

'All right, I'll give in and agree I got the best of the deal.'
Heath held up his hands in mock resignation.

When the door closed behind the old housekeeper, there
was silence in the room except for the shifting of coals in the
grate and the ticking of the clock. Rhian sipped her tea, feeling
the warmth of the sun through the window and closing her
eyes as she imagined herself living here as Heath's wife. Then
the mists of dreaming vanished as behind closed lids she saw
the image of Mansel Jack, his dark features and deep eyes.

'What's the matter, Rhian?' Heath's voice intruded on her
thoughts and she looked at him quickly.

'Nothing, just enjoying the peace of your lovely house,' she
replied carefully.

'You're a liar,' Heath's voice was soft, 'but then you are
entitled to your own thoughts, though I'd give anything to
share them.'

He sat beside her on the window-seat and took her hand in
his. 'Rhian, I'd be patient with you, I promise I'd teach you
what happiness can be found from loving. I would take my
time, not rush you – please let me try.'

She leaned against his shoulder, closing her eyes, and as his
fingers brushed her breasts she forced herself to remain still.
He slowly undid the buttons of her bodice and gently caressed
the warm flesh beneath the linen camisole. And after a time she
relaxed, enjoying the feel of his fingers teasing her nipple. But
when he would have leaned over her, she pushed at him in
panic.

'You said you would not rush me, Heath, remember?'

'All right, perhaps it's time I took you home,' he said easily.

She felt suddenly disappointed as he moved away. Frightened as she was, she had half wanted him to continue arousing
strange and wonderful sensations within her.

It was cooler as they strolled hand in hand down the hill
towards the roadway and Rhian felt grateful to Heath for
caring about her.

'You needn't come all the way – just take me as far as the
tram terminus,' she suggested, but Heath shook his head.

'I said I'd take you home and so I will. I'm not risking
anyone else snapping you up on the way!'

33

He laughed, but Rhian sensed a seriousness behind his words that disturbed her. Heath was already looking upon her as his property, but was that what she wanted?

'Look, there is something I must do,' she said quickly. 'Carrie suggested I go to visit Mr Richardson, see if he knows where his wife is. If I can find her, I can find our Billy and he must be told about Aunt Agnes's death.'

She paused. 'And please don't come with me. I am capable of doing things on my own, you know.'

'Hey!' Heath laughed. 'All right, I shan't come with you – don't be so defensive, I'm on your side, remember?'

As Heath left her, giving her a light kiss on the cheek before striding away, Rhian watched him go with mixed feelings.

The sun was warm as she made her way up the hill. Roses blossomed, gentle among sharp-tipped thorns, and low in the grass daisies opened white petals to the sky.

Standing on the imposing doorstep of Rickie Richardson's house, she felt nervous and uncertain but knocked loudly, determined not to go away without at least trying to see him.

'Yes, what is it you want?' A maid with wide blue eyes was staring at her curiously and Rhian returned her look defiantly.

'I want to see Mr Richardson and it's important, so I suggest you fetch him at once.'

Greatly daring, Rhian stepped into the hallway and waited expectantly. The maid bit her lip and glanced around worriedly. 'Best wait here, I'll see if the master will talk to you.'

Rhian couldn't help but be impressed with the graciousness of the hallway and she wondered that Delmai Richardson – a woman who had all this – would give it up to run away with a gaol-bird – for that was how the townspeople thought of Billy.

She became aware that Mr Richardson was standing in the doorway, staring at her, his eyes cold. 'Do I know you?' he asked pompously.

Rhian shook her head. 'No, I used to work for Mrs Richardson and I'd like her address so that I can ask her for a reference,' she improvised quickly.

'The devil you would!' He looked as though he was about to tell her to leave, then he paused! 'Well, I think I do have her address somewhere; I'll get it.' He disappeared into a book-

34

lined study and Rhian felt excitement grow; she was about to find out where Billy was!

'Here!' Rickie Richardson handed her a torn piece of paper. 'When you contact Mrs Richardson, perhaps you could tell her that I'll take *her* back but not her bastard?'

Rhian's face burned as she hurried away from the house and her mind was racing. It was obvious that Delmai Richardson had asked her husband if she might return to him. And what's more, she had borne Billy a child – what a tragic mess it all was. But at least now Rhian could see Billy, talk to him and be with him.

She felt warmed as she tucked the scrap of paper into her bag and quickly made her way to the tram terminus. But as soon as the swaying car took her towards the eastern part of the town, and the rows of cottages came into sight, Rhian was suddenly dispirited. The house would be empty without Aunt Agnes's forceful presence to cheer it and soon Rhian would have to leave the only real home she had ever known.

It was dark and cool in the long passageway, but Rhian could hear the kettle singing on the hob and knew with a sense of gratitude that Carrie had been at work. She entered the kitchen and sank into a chair, brushing her hair away from her face with a hand that trembled.

'What's wrong with you, girl?' Carrie asked as she poured water into the teapot. 'You look as if you'd lost a sovereign and found a farthing!'

Rhian attempted to smile. 'I've just found out where our Billy lives and it sounds as if that woman is thinking of leaving him and coming home to her husband.'

Carrie looked at her shrewdly. 'You've seen Mr Richardson, then?' She didn't wait for a reply, but went on, 'Well, I think that's the best thing that could happen – gentry and workers don't mix.'

'You're right, I suppose,' Rhian said softly, but why did she feel like putting her head down on the table and crying as though her heart would break?

Chapter Three

A haze of fog hung over the small mining valley of Carreg Fach and a spiteful drizzle was falling, drenching the solitary main street that lay like a grey ribbon between the hills.

Delmai Richardson lifted the heavy bag higher on her arm and adjusted the position of the small child on her hip. The baby was asleep, unaware of anything but the comfort and security of being in her mother's arms.

Delmai pushed open the door of the dingy, coal-dust-covered cottage with her shoulder and, sighing with relief, allowed the bag to sink to the table. She sat before the fire and hugged her child close, tears slipping down her cheeks as she looked into the small dimpled face.

Not for the first time, she wished she was out of this hell and back home in the elegance of her house in Sweyn's Eye, or even in the small house on Canal Street where she had gone when first she left her husband, while Billy Gray was still in prison and before her affair with him began. She had run away so willingly with Billy, heedless and falsely optimistic, greedy for the passion he gave her so readily.

And he could offer her little else, for Billy was not only a convicted felon, he was far beneath her in station. At first everything had been wonderful for, furnished with the small amount of money his aunt had provided, they had managed to live quite well. And Billy still appeared to be happy with the situation – but then he was used to small houses and few amenities. She on the other hand had been brought up to a different way of life and she was finding the harshness of her surroundings too much to bear.

It had been all right before little Cerianne had come along. Delmai and Billy had been like children; he had taught her the joys of the flesh, which to a woman who had believed herself cold and passionless had been a wonderful awakening. But he had taught her the meaning of poverty too and now black dust ruled her life, for Billy worked the coal-face as a miner.

Delmai, who had never needed to wash her own clothes, found the task of keeping the family supplied with clean linen almost beyond her. She could not achieve the lines of clean washing which were so ordinary a sight in her neighbours' gardens, however hard she tried.

Suddenly the hooter from the pit tore at the silence, penetrating the cottage and filling the kitchen overwhelmingly. Startled, Delmai sat up straight in her chair, a sense of fear running through her veins. She felt chilled as she wrapped a shawl around her shoulders, tucking the baby in its folds; then she flung open her door and hurried out into the street, her heart pounding.

'*Duw*, there's been an accident at the pit.' Mrs Jones was white-faced, her hands trembling as she tied the ribbons of her bonnet. 'I'd get along down to the gates if I were you, *merchi* – see if your man is all right.'

Delmai heard the woman speak, yet her words seemed not to have any meaning. 'Yes, I'm going now, Mrs Jones,' she mumbled through lips that seemed frozen.

The woman's face softened. 'Poor dab, not used to any of this, are you? I'll come with you for company if you like.'

Delmai was only partly aware of Mrs Jones beside her as she hurried along the cobbled streets, but her neighbour was talking incessantly.

'My Sam's in bed, he came off shift an hour ago, thank the good Lord. But you mustn't take fright, mind, there's most likely nothing much wrong – a bit of gas or some water perhaps.'

Delmai didn't hear her, her mind was racing with fears and unimaginable horrors. What if Billy was maimed, how would she care for him and the baby too? She recognised that she was inadequate, that she had not the strength of will or body that was needed to live as the woman of a working man. She was not even Billy's wife, so there would be no compensation for her as there was for pit widows.

Most of the women of the village were gathered at the pit gates. They stood silent, heads covered with shawls against the rain, faces long, enduring familiar fears with stoicism. A baby cried miserably and then was hushed into suckling contentment. Delmai lifted Cerianne higher in her arms, easing her aching back and trying to see over the heads of the women in front of her.

Mrs Jones was more forceful. 'What is it?' she asked loudly. 'What's happened here, anybody killed?'

There was a murmur of voices speaking in Welsh and Delmai bit her lip in frustration, unable to understand. She found herself praying that Billy was safe.

'It's only a little bit of a roof fall.' Mrs Jones intended her words to be reassuring, but Delmai shivered. 'A few miners are trapped, but it's nothing to get all fretful about . . . yet.'

Delmai hugged the baby closer to her breast and as Cerianne stirred and whimpered, she smoothed back the baby-fine hair absently.

The rain had stopped and a pale sun shone through the clouds, but nothing seemed to be happening at the pit-head. Delmai stared at the winding gear rearing up into the sky, and fell to brooding about the letter she had sent to her husband. A feeling of guilt washed through her as she remembered that she had begged Rickie to take her back. This life here in the valleys was no way for her to spend the rest of her days. Not even for the wonderful nights spent in Billy's arms could she endure the dirt and the never-ending work that turned her hands red and her skin coarse.

Rickie had not so far made any reply and Delmai didn't know whether to be glad or sorry. She knew that she would never love her husband – indeed in some ways she despised him – yet he could give her comfort and silk clothing and in his gracious elegant house she would never need to clean or scrub again.

There was a movement at the pit-head and the wheel turned against the sky as the men were lifted from the bowels of the earth. Delmai held her breath – she loved Billy and even though she wanted to leave him, she did not wish him dead.

The men were pouring from the pit-head now, most walking

but some being supported by friends. All were black with coal-dust and it took Delmai a few agonising minutes to recognise Billy's tall frame as he pushed his way through the throng of women.

As she moved instinctively towards him she wondered what she was doing to them both. She was condemning Billy to the life of blackness and fetid air and cold water that threatened to extinguish him. And herself . . . well, drudgery had become her middle name, she thought helplessly.

'Oh, Billy!' She was in his arms, uncaring of the dust that clung to him like a second, abrasive skin. 'I've been so worried.'

'Come on, girl, let's get home,' he said. 'My mouth feels as dry as an old bone.'

In the privacy of the small cottage, Delmai wept in Billy's arms. 'I can't take much more of this,' she said brokenly. 'It's not fair to any of us to live this way.'

'Get the bath from the back door, Delmai, and let me wash the dirt and stink off me – then I'll show you what life is all about.' He forced a smile and pulled playfully at her apron strings, though his eyes white against the black of his face were filled with anxiety.

She obeyed him, wondering afresh at the lackey she had allowed herself to become. Anyone looking at her now would not take her for a lady at all, but a serving wench or a kitchen-maid.

The baby slept as Delmai washed Billy's fine young body. But already he was marked with tell-tale blue lines where the coal-dust had entered wounds and refused to be washed away. There was a scar across his nose and another along his neck, and as Delmai scrubbed at them she felt like dissolving into tears of hopelessness.

Billy took her in his arms and unbuttoned her bodice, kissing her breasts, his mouth warm with tenderness and passion.

'Come to bed with me, girl,' he said softly, 'now while the babba's asleep.'

She went upstairs undoing her clothes, as eager as he was to lose herself in passion. Billy was naked and his arousal was plain to see. He was a magnificent man, Delmai thought with pride – strong as a stallion and gifted with sensitivity so that he knew just what pleased her.

They lay together in the bed beneath the brightly coloured quilt and Delmai shuddered delicately as Billy's hands roved over her body . . . touching, seeking, pleasing.

'Oh, my love, come to me.' She moaned the words softly and Billy kissed her neck.

'Not yet, I want to tease you into such passion that you'll never want to leave me.'

While she was like this, spellbound, entranced with the sensations he aroused within her, Delmai could not believe she would ever bring herself to part from him. He worked his old magic, bringing her to a crescendo of love that was almost painful in its intensity. They moved together in an age-old rhythm and she heard her sighs like the wash of the ocean. She was lifted high on a crest of delight and her own voice was far away and unrecognisable as she cried out in pleasure.

They lay for a long while in each other's arms and Delmai clung to the moment, for such times were becoming rarer. Perhaps even now it had only been the fear of losing Billy which made the ecstasy so great. The hardness of her life was grinding her down, wearing her spirit so that she no longer laughed. Deep creases were forming on her forehead and she believed there was a tinge of grey in her hair.

Billy fell into an exhausted sleep at her side and with a pang of impatience, she heard the baby begin to whimper. She loved the child, of course she did, Cerianne was part of herself and of Billy. But Delmai was not equipped for motherhood. Cerianne should have a nanny and be reared in a nursery, just as Delmai herself had been.

She slipped from Billy's side, hating herself for resenting his ability to sleep. He was always the same; if the baby cried during the night, it was invariably she who was disturbed.

Cerianne was wet through and with disgust, Delmai changed the child's clothes. The baby gurgled and smiled winningly and for a moment Delmai responded, laughing and cooing with Cerianne. Then she sighed; the dinner must be started, for when Billy woke he would be hungry.

She had made soup, *cawl* as the local people called it. She had bought a piece of bacon, for it was cheap and the joint could be taken out of the liquid and served cold for another meal. Delmai was not a good cook, but necessity had taught her to be stringent.

At first when she had left Sweyn's Eye in the full flush of her love, she had considered such matters unimportant, but now she realised that simply to exist she needed to be thrifty to the point of meanness.

There was a loud rapping on the door and before Delmai could open her mouth to speak, Mrs Jones was in the kitchen. This was another habit of the lower orders which Delmai did not like and could not understand; it seemed there was no such thing as privacy.

'Mrs Jones, what can I do for you?' she said evenly, concealing her irritation.

'A bag of flour, *merchi*, can you lend me one just 'till tomorrow. Got visitors coming, I have, all the way from Sweyn's Eye, and me not prepared.'

Delmai's heart began to beat rapidly, though as she went into the cool pantry and picked up a bag of flour she was keeping her feelings tightly under control.

'From Sweyn's Eye you say, that's interesting.' She spoke casually. 'A relative, is it?'

'Yes,' Mrs Jones nodded. 'My sister, Doris. There's a good worker, she is, used to stoke boilers in the Canal Street Laundry till they had a terrible explosion there. She'll be here come morning and you must take a sip of tea with us – being from Sweyn's Eye yourself, you might know her.'

Delmai nodded. 'That would be lovely, Mrs Jones, and please don't worry about returning the flour; I've more than enough until shopping day.'

She saw her neighbour's face flush with pleasure. '*Duw*, there's kind of you, but I'll give it back of course. See you in the morning, then!'

When she was alone Delmai sank into a chair, her hands trembling. What if she were to write a letter to Rickie, begging him once more to take her back – could she not ask this Doris to deliver it personally, make sure that her husband received her message this time?

She clasped her hands in her lap, tasting the bitterness of her disloyalty to Billy. But, she reasoned, this way of life was

41

going to kill her and if she remained in the valley any longer, she would end up hating him.

Looking at her work-roughened hands, she sighed. It would take months of creaming to bring them back to their former softness and beauty. Quickly she brushed the thought aside as unworthy and trivial. Her heart would be broken at leaving Billy, she told herself, and of course planning to leave him was an agonising decision to make, but she was sure it was the right thing for both of them.

Billy loathed the pits and the small valley so far away from the sea. And he missed his home and his family. He could be comfortable back in Sweyn's Eye in his aunt's nice little cottage.

She fed Cerianne a little of the soup and the baby gurgled happily on her knee. Delmai studied the child, loving her and yet feeling as though she belonged to someone else. She had never felt the overwhelming sense of mother love that others seemed to enjoy – perhaps her own childhood had been too austere.

Delmai had been brought up by a strict father who had never hidden the fact that he wanted a son. She sighed, impatient with herself. She could not blame her father or her past life, the fault lay in herself – was she capable of loving, really loving any other mortal on this earth? She admitted that she was selfish, she wanted the old days back again when she was a lady and treated as such. She wanted silk next to her skin and fine airy, high-ceilinged rooms in which to live. Not even the love and the joy Billy gave her could compensate for all that.

She heard Billy moving about upstairs and rose quickly from her chair, stirring a little more pepper into the soup and then awkwardly lifting out the bacon to put it on a plate. She trimmed the excess fat with disgust, hating the whiteness and the softness of it. At home, she hardly ever saw food in its raw state and found that now she often lost her appetite after cooking a meal.

'Hello, *cariad*, something smells good.' Billy had entered the kitchen and he slipped his arms around her waist from behind, drawing her back against him.

'You're beautiful, have I ever told you that?' he whispered softly, nuzzling her ear.

42

'Let me go or your dinner will be burnt,' she said with mock severity. 'Go and wash your hands now while I put the soup out.'

Billy stared at her thoughtfully. 'You are happy, Delmai, aren't you?' he asked softly, but her eyes refused to meet his.

'Of course I am, stop asking foolish questions and eat your meal before it goes cold.'

He came to her and tipped up her face so that she was forced to look at him. His eyes were penetrating and Delmai was uncomfortable.

'I have felt a restlessness in you, girl,' he said. 'I know you find the life of a collier's wife a hard one, but *duw*, don't the love make up for it all?'

Delmai was saved from replying by the sharp crying of the baby and thankfully she hurried to take the child in her arms.

'There, there,' she soothed, 'let your mother see what you've done to your hand, then. You mustn't play with the fire-irons, Cerianne, I've told you before. You're lucky you didn't burn your little fingers.'

Billy took his seat and leaned on the table, studying Delmai closely. She was changed from the eager young woman she had been when he first met her and there was fear in his heart that perhaps she would just up and leave him one day.

'Why are you staring at me?' Delmai demanded. 'For heaven's sake eat your soup, I've spent hours making it and I don't want it to be wasted. Can't afford to throw it away, so if you don't feel like it now put it back in the pot and have it later.'

She was aware of Billy's scrutiny and it made her uneasy, but she forced herself to begin her meal, avoiding his gaze.

'Delmai,' he persisted, 'tell me what's wrong, *cariad*. You're changed, somehow.'

Suddenly a fierce anger flared within her. She threw her spoon on to the table and her chair screeched against the stone floor as she pushed it back.

'For God's sake, Billy!' she cried. 'Do you wish to turn my head inside out and examine the contents? Can't I have any privacy even in my thoughts?'

Rage grew and burgeoned as her pent-up frustrations rose to the surface. 'Isn't it bad enough that I have to scrimp and save

43

in order to make ends meet? I'm chained to this filthy hovel all day and I can't stand it, Billy – do you understand that? I'm not born to this sort of existence. I hate every moment of the dirty life we lead – there, is that plain enough for you!'

As she turned away from him, hiding her face in her hands, she heard the door slam behind him and knew Billy would be on his way down to the public bar in the village. There, she thought savagely, he would be able to drown his sorrows in a glass of ale while she was left at home to clean up yet again. She boiled a kettle of water ready to wash the dishes and the baby grizzled sleepily. Cerianne was lying on the rag mat near the fire, her thumb in her mouth and with a pang of guilt, Delmai took the child in her arms.

'Let's leave it all and go to bed,' she said softly, kissing Cerianne's flushed cheek. The child was teething and that doubtless meant another restless night.

Delmai pretended to be asleep when Billy came home smelling strongly of beer. She turned her back on him, feeling like a traitor. But her mind was made up: she must leave him before she destroyed them both. She was just slipping into the comfort of sleep when Cerianne began to whimper. 'I just can't stand any more of this,' Delmai muttered into the darkness, tears of self-pity misting her eyes. Even though she recognised her weakness, there was not a thing she could do to control her emotions and she wept.

The next day was bright and sunny and Delmai's spirits rose as she thought of meeting the visitor that Mrs Jones was expecting from Sweyn's Eye. She dressed carefully – almost as though she was about to take tea with one of her own kind, she thought ruefully – and a wave of nostalgia swept over her as she remembered lavish food served in high, elegant dining-rooms. But impatiently she forced her thoughts back to the present, telling herself sternly that she had indulged in enough self-pity during the night.

She moved excitedly to the window as she heard the clip-clop of a pony and the creaking rumble of a trap stopping outside the cottages.

Peering from behind the curtain, Delmai could see little, but anticipation was a sweet wine to her senses as she waited impatiently for Mrs Jones to knock on the wall as a signal for her to go next door. Delmai's fingers trembled as they closed over the letter she had hastily penned to Rickie. She was glad Billy was on early shift, because he was too sensitive a man not to notice her agitation. She knew she would never have the courage to tell him to his face that she was leaving; she was too much of a coward to witness the hurt bewilderment that would surely appear in his eyes.

There was a muffled knocking on the wall and although Delmai was expecting it, the sound startled her. Quickly she picked up the baby and hurried outside, blinking at the bright sunlight.

Immediately she entered the small neat kitchen, she realised she had made a mistake in dressing so carefully. Mrs Jones's visitor was short and rather plump, fresh-faced enough but without any refinement of feature, and her dress was ordinary to say the least.

'This is Doris, my sister,' Mrs Jones said, smiling. 'There's a great family likeness, don't you think?'

Politely, Delmai nodded. 'Yes, indeed, you both have such fine dark eyes.' She was not being false, she told herself, just diplomatic. As she took a seat Doris leaned forward eagerly, touching Cerianne's round face with real delight.

'What a lovely babba! Makes me feel bad about leaving my own little boys at home and them pleading to come with me.'

'Nonsense!' Mrs Jones said quickly. 'Deserve a rest, so you do, working hard cleaning other folks' mess up after them, as well as carrying that no-good man of yours around in a shawl.'

'Oh, hush now, Jessie. Don't you start on me or I'll be sorry I came.' Doris took the baby from Delmai's unresisting arms, obviously captivated by the little girl.

The effort of making polite and meaningless conversation was a strain and Delmai sipped her tea, trying her best to be pleasant, but she had the uneasy feeling that Doris could see right through her. It took a great deal of courage to bring up the subject of the letter, but at last she managed it.

'I wonder if you would do me a small favour?' she asked with false brightness. Doris hardly looked up from the baby, but the quick glance from the girl's narrowed eyes was enough to show Delmai that she was no fool. Delmai decided it was politic to tell at least some of the truth.

45

'I need to get a message to my former husband, Mr Richardson. Perhaps you know him?' She spoke haltingly, knowing how foolish she must sound. Of course Doris would not know Rickie, they hardly moved in the same circles!

'I've heard of him, yes,' Doris said warily. 'Do you think he'd take kindly to me treading dirt on to his fine carpets?'

'I'm sure you could persuade him to see you.' Inside Delmai was trembling; she half wished she hadn't begun all this, but she was committed now so might as well continue.

'I realise you would have to go out of your way and I'd gladly reimburse you for your trouble,' she said, but slowly Doris shook her head.

'All right then, give the letter here, but I don't need no bribe, thank you.' She pushed the letter carelessly into the cloth bag that lay beside her on the floor and Delmai's heart sank – would Rickie ever get her message, she wondered doubtfully.

Mrs Jones sensed the uneasiness that was almost tangible and rose to her feet quickly.

'A nice cup of tea, that's what we all need,' she said brightly. 'Would you like a few Welsh cakes, Mrs Gray? Freshly cooked, they are!'

Delmai nodded, though her mouth was dry and she had never felt less hungry in her life. Doris was ignoring her, playing with Cerianne, and Delmai sank back in her chair with the colour rising to her cheeks. It was obvious from her attitude that Doris understood her relationship with Billy. She was quite clear in her mind that the girl had little regard for her or her problems. It was humiliating, Delmai thought angrily, more than ever determined to leave this life behind her and return to the comfort of her home in Sweyn's Eye.

She took a few shillings from her pocket and put them on the table beside Doris, who glanced up briefly and then turned her attention to Cerianne once more.

'Well, come on then, Doris, what's going on in the town? Let us into all the gossip, won't you?' Mrs Jones said quickly, seating herself at the table. She offered a plate of flat round cakes that smelled deliciously of fruit and spices and Delmai politely took one.

Doris shrugged her shoulders. 'Not much to tell really.' She paused with her eyes on Delmai. 'I'm working for Mr Gregory

Irons the lawyer now, cleaning and polishing his offices – not a bad job and you do get to hear a lot of things you shouldn't ought to.'

'Tell us then. I shan't coax you any more, mind,' Mrs Jones said tartly.

'Well now, there was a little something that might interest . . . Mrs Gray,' Doris said slowly, her gaze insolent. Delmai felt her shoulders grow tense, though she tried to appear unaffected.

'Oh, and what would that be?' she asked mildly.

'Poor old Mrs Gray passed away, dead and buried she is, God rest her soul,' Doris said solemnly. 'That's Billy's auntie, you know – called for him till the last she did and him not coming even to the funeral.'

'*Duw*, there's bad news indeed.' Mrs Jones broke the silence which was charged with hostility. 'Nice lad is Billy, always liked him from the first time I set eyes on him.'

Doris nodded. 'Me too and he's no murderer, is Billy Gray – a lovely man, deserves better than what he's getting.'

Delmai swept the baby from Doris's arms and stood trembling as she faced her. 'You have made it clear what you think of me, but I'll tell you this – we knew nothing about Billy's aunt; he would have gone home if he'd had any idea that she was ill.'

She made her way towards the door, shaking with anger. 'You are determined to think the worst of me, so I won't inflict my company on you any longer. If you'll just give me back the letter, I'll be on my way.'

Doris's hand closed over the bag in a protective gesture. 'Not if hell takes me. I think I can guess what you're up to; you want to go back to that husband of yours and if you ask me, I think that would be the best thing that could happen to poor Billy Gray.'

Delmai faced her squarely, 'How dare you talk to me like that?' she said sharply.

'Why shouldn't I?' Doris replied laconically. 'You're living tally just like I am. You're not a respectable married lady now, mind, just a loose woman who's had two men between her legs and is the mother of a by-blow! Not that I blame this lovely little babba here – don't deserve a mam like you, she don't.'

47

'Now, Doris, you've said enough.' Mrs Jones put her hand on her sister's arm, restraining her as she would have said more. 'What Mrs Gray does is no one's business but her own, so just you cool that tongue of yours.'

'Well, there's no good in her, it's not right her puttin' on airs and graces, who does she think she is?' She turned her back on Delmai. 'But I'll give this letter to Mr Richardson if it kills me, then Billy will be free to find himself a nice respectable little wife.' She raised her voice. 'There's a lovely life he had before she came along, Jessie. Going to wed Mary Jenkins, he was, and her set up proper now with a big shop and so rich that even the toffs respect her. Ruined Billy's life, this woman has, so don't ask me to give her any respect.'

'I think it best if you go home now, *cariad*,' Mrs Jones said quickly, turning to Delmai. 'Now don't go upsetting yourself, there's nothing to be gained by tears.' She opened the door and Delmai stepped out into the sunshine, almost tasting the coal-dust that covered the valley like a shroud.

She burned with anger as she let herself into her own kitchen where she stood staring around her, seeing everything through a haze of despair. She could not endure this life any longer, she *must* leave the valley before she lost her mind.

Delmai settled Cerianne in her bed and then sat for a long time staring out of the window. She missed the soothing calm of the waves lapping the shore, and the cool curved splendour of the bay, just as she missed everything connected with her former life. She closed her eyes wearily. Was it true, she wondered, that she had ruined Billy's chance of a happy marriage with Mary Jenkins?

While Delmai had been falling in love with Billy, she had not stopped to consider anyone else's feelings, which was yet another good reason for leaving him to get on with his own life. He would soon forget her, indeed he would be better off without her as Doris had so bluntly pointed out.

Her head slowly sank on to her hands and she closed her eyes wearily. She would wait a while, see if Rickie responded to her latest appeal and if he did not, then she would go to Sweyn's Eye and confront him and if necessary beg him on bended knees to take her back.

Chapter Four

Spinners' Wharf nestled in a small valley within the boundaries of Sweyn's Eye, close to the dust and smoke of the copper and yet sheltered from the larger industries by the gentle fall of the hills. The woollen mill itself was long and low, squatting beside a stream that ran rust-coloured over stones turned green with verdigris, a bequest from the works higher in the valley. And it was this swiftly-flowing brook, parallel to the river, that drove the machines housed in the old grey building.

Rhian breathed in the atmosphere of the mill as she worked at the smaller of the two looms, triumphant at the complexity of the patterns in the turnover she was weaving. The shawl was almost ready to come off the 56-inch loom, the thousands of threads married together as though magically by the clattering machine.

At the other side of the long room, Heinz Sinman was working on the carding engine that was continually breaking down. Watching him, Rhian felt a warm gratitude that he had so readily offered her a home.

'I need a woman round at nights, what with Gina near her time,' he had said, but Rhian knew he was being kind.

When she had left the cottage, Carrie too had warmly offered her a home and in response, Rhian had given her some of Aunt Agnes's good old furniture.

She bit her lip now, staring at Heinz as he threw down the oily rag he had used to wipe his hands.

Rhian felt sorry for him these days, for he was constantly being harassed by the local ruffians. His forehead still bore a bruise where a stone had caught him, yet he was so kind and honest . . . how could anyone mistrust him, Rhian thought angrily.

Yesterday a window had been broken in the house, startling Gina so that she had screamed out loud. Heinz had been angry then, but it seemed there was nothing he could do about it. If the situation did not improve, for the Sinmans it would mean ruin.

'That will haf to do.' Heinz rubbed the grease from his hands with a piece of rough wool, his big arms glistening with sweat.

'Tell me, Rhian,' he said worriedly, 'what 'appen to women when they go shopping? My Gina left over an hour ago and she not back yet.'

Rhian was fond of the big, gentle Austrian and she hated to see him fretting. 'There's a lot of gossiping to be done down at the market,' she said. 'It's the best place I know for meeting your friends.'

Heinz frowned. 'Friends, eh?' His tone was sceptical. 'Well, it must be nearly time for my dinner; my big belly tells me that!'

Rhian watched as he left the mill and strode up the yard leading to the house and suddenly she shared his unease. She switched off the loom and brushed the fluff from her hands; Gina shouldn't really be out so long, it couldn't be good for her to be on her feet all day with the baby due at any time. What if she started labour and was unable to return home?

In the kitchen, Heinz stood staring at the coals dying into greyness in the grate. He had a perplexed expression on his open face and rubbed his hand through his hair like an anxious little boy. It was Rhian who took up the small shovel and began to mend the fire.

There was a sudden noise outside the door and Rhian's heart missed a beat. The sound of human voices baying like hounds after a fox penetrated into the silent room, filling it, growing louder, more menacing.

Heinz moved quickly. Snatching up a knife from the table, he hurried to the front door with a lightness of foot that was surprising in such a heavy man. Rhian faltered to a stop behind him, her eyes widening in dismayed disbelief. Crouched against the wall of the house was Gina Sinman, her hands wrapped around her body and her head bent as though to

50

protect her unborn child.

Even as Rhian stood horrified, a stone whirled past her face, catching Gina a blow on the shoulder that sent her staggering to her knees. She looked up appealingly, her face deathly white, her eyes starting from her head and Rhian melted in pity. Another stone found its mark and Gina began to cry helplessly.

'What do you women think you're doing?' Rhian hurriedly stepped in front of Gina's crouched figure, holding out her hands appealingly. 'Have you all gone mad?'

'She's a *bradwr*!' a voice cried. 'A traitor, and bearing a traitor's spawn.'

Rhian stared in the direction from which the voice had come. 'Is that you, Sally Benson?' She felt anger rise like a sickness, pounding in her head so that she could scarcely control her voice. 'What gives you the right to pick on Gina Sinman – won't your mam be there at the birth and glad to take her shillings, mind?'

'My mam may be a midwife, but she don't have nothing to do with the likes of this slut!' Sally Benson shouted. 'Everyone knows that Gina's man is a German and most of us have got menfolk joined up in the Army to fight the Huns.'

Rhian took a deep breath, suddenly at a loss, and it was Heinz who took command.

'I no German, I from Austria,' he said with painful slowness. 'I haf lived with you all and worked with you ever since I was a young boy. How can you think of me as an enemy now?'

'Austrian is the same as German – they're all against us,' Sally Benson called loudly. 'What's to stop you spying on us? I saw you with my own eyes down at the recreation ground, watching the soldiers marching. Come on, you women, let's get them!' Her voice rose to a screech.

Heinz held up the kitchen knife, his face white and a dogged set to his lips. 'I show you I'm on your side, that I do anything not to fight the people I grow up with. After today, I shall never be able to pull the trigger of a rifle.'

Before Rhian could guess his intentions, Heinz had placed his hand on the pavement, square fingers outstretched. The blade gleamed in the sunlight as it swished downward, then

51

there was a sickening thud and blood was streaming into the gutter.

Sally Benson started back in consternation. '*Jawl!* He's cut his fingers off!' she said in disbelief.

Gina staggered towards her husband, tears coursing down her cheeks. 'Heinz, my lovely, what have you done!' She knelt beside him, wrapping his hand in her apron and clinging to him in desperation.

'Perhaps you'll all go home now that you've done your worst.' Rhian's words fell into the shocked silence. 'And I hope that you're all proud of yourselves!'

Gina was leading a white-faced Heinz indoors while Rhian took his other arm, her whole being dissolving into pity as she felt him trembling.

'I'll boil the kettle while you find some clean linen, Gina.' She spoke calmly, though the raw pain reflected in Heinz's face made her feel ill.

'Oh, Heinz, what are we going to do?' Gina asked as she bound his hand carefully. She was trying to hold back her tears as he held her against him, his usually ruddy cheeks pallid.

'We are going to live here as always and do our work and pray that the people of Sweyn's Eye will forget this madness.'

Rhian steeped a pot of tea with hands that were unsteady. 'Don't think that everyone is against you,' she said softly. 'There's daft those women are, like sheep following Sally Benson – want their heads knocking together they do.'

Gina shuddered. 'I'll be afraid to go out,' she said, covering her face with her hands as she began to weep afresh. 'My poor Heinz, you're so brave and there's me blubbering like a babba.' She kissed his cheek softly. 'We'll be all right, won't we? You, me and our little one will be happy together and to hell with the rest of the world!'

Rhian left them and returned to the mill. The long room was empty and silent, the loom and carding machine crouching in the shadows like animals about to pounce.

She shivered. Until now she had not taken the war seriously; it was something that didn't affect her, a silly quarrel over territories. She had seen the advertisements in the *Daily Post* telling the menfolk that Lord Kitchener needed them to add to his already considerable Army, but after the initial announcement of war little had happened to disrupt the normal flow of life in Sweyn's Eye.

The attack on Heinz brought home with chilling emphasis the fact that the stories told of the war might not be gossip spoken by a few idle women, but a dreadful reality.

She looked round her at the darkening shadows in the mill and wondered if she should light the gas-lamps and do a little more work, yet somehow her heart wasn't in it. She turned her back on the silent looms and carefully locked the door.

*

Carreg Fach was a small village hidden among a circle of hills which were almost indistinguishable from the towering slag-tips. Winding gear rose like a sentinel against the sky and everywhere was the taste and smell and feel of coal, for the pit was the life-blood of the valley.

As Rhian left the tiny railway station a man in a cloth cap touched his brow to her. 'Pony and trap is it, gel?' he asked. But she shook her head and began to walk towards the rows of dusty cottages clinging to the hillside. She glanced ruefully at her boots, highly polished when she had left Sweyn's Eye but now coated with gritty coal-dust.

Her steps faltered as she drew nearer the cottages. They were cramped, the door built low as though for people not used to walking upright, and Rhian's heart ached for her brother. She took a torn piece of paper from her pocket and looked at the address on it.

Delmai Richardson answered her knock and as she was admitted into the tiny kitchen, Rhian was aware of the net curtains moving on the windows of the house next door.

'I've come to see our Billy.' She felt uneasy, for Delmai was staring at her as though she couldn't believe her eyes.

'How did you know where to find us?' she asked quickly, breathlessly, her cultured voice sounding strange against the backdrop of the sparsely furnished room. 'Did my husband send you?' The question seemed almost eager.

Rhian shook her head. 'No, though he did give me your address.' She wondered if she should repeat his cryptic message, but for the moment she decided to hold her tongue.

Delmai sank into a chair. 'Billy's not off shift yet, but he

53

shouldn't be very long. Perhaps you'd care for some chicken –
I've just taken it out of the oven?'

Rhian shook her head politely, seeing that the meagre bird
would not be enough for three. 'I've got bad news for Billy,'
she said gently. 'Our aunt, the one who brought us up, has
died.' It was a bald statement but she could think of no other
way to say it.

'I'm sorry.' Delmai spoke without any real interest and
Rhian felt her hackles rise. Delmai Richardson was not and
never would be one of their kind, however much she looked
the part in her stained apron.

Rhian glanced round, wondering if she could ask Delmai
about the baby. A crib stood in the corner, but it was empty.
Delmai saw her look and pushed back a strand of hair wearily.

'Mrs Jones next door is looking after Cerianne for a few
hours,' she said quietly. 'If you like, I'll go and fetch her.'

There was such a world of reluctance in her voice that Rhian
shook her head politely. 'No, I can see her later.'

Thankfully, Delmai sank into a chair. 'Tell me about
Sweyn's Eye,' she said hungrily. 'What's been happening
there? Nothing goes on here in this God-forsaken place.'

Rhian took a deep breath. 'It's the same as ever really, there's
the constant talk of the war and many of the young men have
enlisted.' Her voice faltered into silence. There seemed
nothing she could say to this woman who sat proudly in her
flannel skirt and calico blouse as though she was wearing the
finest silks. Delmai suddenly leaned forward.

'You said my husband gave you my address – did he say
anything about me?'

Rhian looked at Delmai askance. 'I came here to see Billy,
not to talk about your husband,' she said evasively.

'Well, there is no need to be hoity-toity with me, girl.'
Delmai rose to her feet, her chin in the air. 'I was only trying to
make conversation.'

Rhian shook her head. 'Are you stupid or something?' She
spoke abruptly. 'Here are you living tally with my brother and
having the nerve to ask me about your husband. You want to
go back to him, don't you?' She could not prevent a note of
accusation from creeping into her voice. 'I know it's true, so
don't bother to deny it.'

54

Delmai pounced on her words eagerly. 'Then he did talk about me! Tell me what he said . . . please,' she added more humbly.

'I only saw him for a few minutes,' Rhian said, then she sighed in resignation. 'All right, he told me to say that he'd take you back but not your bastard. I'm sorry.'

Delmai sank back into the old rocking-chair placed near the fire and rubbed at her cheek with her fingers as though trying to erase the shock of Rhian's words.

'He'll take me back?' she said. 'I can go back?' She spoke as though she could not believe the evidence of her ears.

'I've just told you his exact words,' Rhian said more firmly. 'He was adamant that you can't take your baby with you.'

Delmai waved Rhian away impatiently as though what she had said was of no consequence. She stared into the flames of the fire as though lost in thoughts of her own and Rhian moved uneasily towards the window, staring out at the bleak landscape. Her heart leapt with joy as she saw the tall rangy figure of her brother toiling up the hill. It was his build and his walk that helped her to recognise him, for he was blackened with coal-dust.

He laughed when he saw her, his teeth unnaturally bright against the dust on his skin. 'Rhian, *cariad*, there's good it is to see you, and kiss you I would if I was a bit cleaner,' he said in delight. 'Go and fetch the bath, Delmai girl, let's get a bit respectable like to welcome Rhian properly.'

Delmai looked uncertainly at Rhian and Billy laughed out loud. 'Don't mind her, she's my sister isn't she – she don't care if she sees me naked.'

Rhian rose to her feet hurriedly. 'I'll go next door and fetch the baby, let you have a bath in peace,' she offered.

'Our Cerianne is with Mrs Jones again, is she?' Billy frowned. 'I swear that woman minds her more than you do, Delmai.'

'Only so that I can have a rest,' Delmai said defensively. 'Anyway, Mrs Jones loves having her.'

Rhian closed the door of the cottage tightly and stood in the sunshine, tasting the coal-dust as the breeze drifted towards her. She was angry; Billy deserved better than a woman like Delmai – she obviously begrudged every little task she did, even palming off her baby on her neighbour.

Mrs Jones smiled broadly as she led Rhian into the spotless kitchen, so different from the muddle next door, and gestured towards a comfortable armchair.

'Sit by there, *merchi*. *Duw*, there's like your brother you are! Here, I'll hand your little niece over to you. A right beauty, isn't she, and so sweet-natured like her daddy.'

Cerianne lay in the shelter of Rhian's arms – her eyes wide, blue and curious. She reached up a chubby fist and touched Rhian's face and it was as if they recognised each other.

'*Duw*, taken to you she has and her never set eyes on you before, there's marvellous it is.'

Rhian felt inordinately pleased. Impulsively she kissed the firm round cheek and with a laugh, Cerianne pulled at her hair.

'Beautiful little thing, isn't she?' Mrs Jones was warming the brown china teapot, swirling the water round with quick easy movements of her hands, and Rhian felt much more at home in the small neat kitchen than ever she could in her brother's house.

The tea was fragrant and refreshing and Rhian smiled gratefully. 'It's very good of you to mind Cerianne like this,' she said, careful not to reveal any criticism of Delmai in her voice.

'No trouble at all. I love having the little girl by here with me – lonely I get sometimes, see. You got no babbas of your own, then?'

Rhian shook her head. 'I'm not married, just a working girl not long come home from Yorkshire where I've been learning to spin wool.'

'Well, and isn't that interesting, then?' Mrs Jones looked at Rhian with admiration. 'I used to spin my own wool on a hand loom, but got in a terrible muddle with all them threads; 'tis work for deft fingers and my hands are peasant hands, no getting away from it.'

Rhian smiled. 'I'm working at Heinz Sinman's mill, not far from the copper works. Perhaps you know it?'

Mrs Jones shook her head. 'No, bless you. I don't get into Sweyn's Eye much. But my younger sister Doris would know it, I expect. Used to work in the Canal Street Laundry, stoking boilers, till it closed. But a cleaner for Mr Gregory Irons she is now.'

'I know Doris,' Rhian said eagerly. 'I used to work at the Laundry myself – see that faint scar there on my arm, that's where I was burnt in the explosion.'

'Bless me, will you just look at that!' A silence fell over the small kitchen. There seemed nothing left to say and the ticking of the grandfather clock sounded loud but somehow comforting. Rhian was not at all uneasy; she felt peaceful and most welcome in the warmth of the spotless room.

'I suppose I should be going,' she said, almost reluctantly. 'Shall I take Cerianne with me?'

Mrs Jones shook her head. 'No, leave her by here, *merchi*. I'll give her a bit of something to eat and fetch her back later.'

Rhian stood for a moment in the silence of the valley, staring at the towering slag-heaps, knowing that the moment had come when she must break the news of Auntie Agnes's death to Billy. She saw that the sky was blue above the hills and the sun warm and golden, highlighting the man-made ugliness of Carreg Fach.

Delmai was sitting near the fire, her hands clasped in her lap, her mouth set in a straight line. From the almost tangible atmosphere of hostility, it seemed that there had been a quarrel. Billy was seated at the table; his skin shone and he had a fresh, scrubbed look. His hair lay flat around his face and Rhian was reminded of the time when he had been in prison with his head shaved. She swallowed hard.

'Billy, I've got something to say to you, boyo.' She sat on an upright kitchen chair beside him and rested her hand on his. 'It's auntie, she's dead. I'm sorry, there's no other way to say it.' She saw the changing expressions on his face and longed to put her arms around him and hug him close. But Delmai was watching and there was an almost disdainful look on her face, as though any display of emotion was the height of bad manners.

Billy looked at Rhian in disbelief. 'How could that be and me not know anything about it?' A muscle worked in his cheek and he looked down at his big hands; they were heavily scarred, the creases ingrained with coal-dust, and he gazed at them as though seeing them for the first time.

'I would have come running, you know that, Rhian,' he said

57

slowly. 'Why couldn't you have found me sooner – come to that, how did you find me now?'

Rhian was suddenly angry, for it seemed that Billy was blaming her in some way. Delmai looked up, her face flushed, her eyes imploring, and Rhian bit her lips, not knowing what to say.

'Come on, what's going on here, I want to know?' Billy was looking from Delmai to Rhian, his body suddenly tense. 'Rhian, where did you get our address? No one in Sweyn's Eye has it.'

'I went to see Mr Richardson,' Rhian blurted out the words. 'He'd had a letter from Delmai, that's all I know.'

Billy's huge fist crashed down on the table and the wooden salt cellar bounced and then tipped, sending a shower of salt over the scrubbed surface.

'*Duw*, don't lose your temper, Billy, there's a good boy!' Rhian said in a low voice.

'Writing letters to that man, are you? Well, I'll want an explanation from you, my girl,' Billy said. 'I've had my share of bad luck over the past years, more than any man should put up with.' He looked straight at Delmai. 'I'm not a violent man, but *jawl*, I'd like to wring your neck.'

Delmai rose to her feet, her eyes bright. 'Don't you dare scold me!' She lifted her head haughtily. 'Just what do you think I am, a drudge? I've lived here in this hovel, scrimping and struggling to make ends meet.' She glanced around her scornfully. 'I think you should go down on your knees in gratitude to me for remaining with you all this time.'

Rhian picked up her bag. 'I must get back to town,' she said flatly, 'I've got work in the morning and this is a private argument after all.'

'Wait, I'll come down to the station with you.' Billy took a white silk scarf and hung it round his neck, opening the door without another word to Delmai.

'God, there's sorry I am about all this,' he said, the harshness in his voice revealing the depths of his feelings. 'I'm that mad with Delmai I could kill her – have it all out with her I will later. And I'm sick to my gut about Agnes.' He rested his arm on Rhian's shoulder. 'Thank God you were there with her, otherwise she would have died alone.'

58

'You couldn't help it, Billy, it wasn't your fault. You would have come home like a shot if you'd known.'

Billy looked down at her steadily, his eyes meeting hers. 'Try not to blame Delmai too much,' he said softly. 'She is a strange girl, full of uncertainties – not used to our way of life, see?'

'I suppose you're right, Billy,' Rhian said doubtfully. 'You know your own business best.'

He hardly heard her. '*Duw*, I wish I'd gone to see Agnes once in a while, I feel so bad about it all now.' He sighed. 'But to be in Sweyn's Eye would bring back all the unpleasant memories I've tried so hard to forget.'

Rhian deliberately changed the subject. 'Anyway, you've got a lovely little girl. I think Cerianne is the sweetest little baby I've ever seen.' She smiled. 'I admit I'm biased, mind, being her auntie. *Duw*, there's strange the word sounds!' She pulled a long face and stared at Billy as though over the top of a pair of spectacles. 'So no cheek from you, my man, I'm a respectable maiden aunt now.'

Billy took her arm and tucked it through his own. 'You don't look like anybody's maiden aunt, you're far too beautiful for that.' His eyes were warm. 'And I mean it, Rhian, you've grown into a lovely young woman.'

She flushed with pleasure. 'Well, what's come over you then, giving me compliments? Grown a silver tongue you have, Billy *bach*.'

At the tiny station, Rhian kissed Billy's cheek. 'Go on home, make your peace with Delmai. I'll be all right, I can see myself on to the train.'

'Are you sure?' he asked and seeing doubts reflected in his eyes, Rhian nodded emphatically. 'Of course I am. But before you get off home, I'd like you to know I've been walking out with Heath Jenkins, so don't you go worrying your head about me.'

Billy appeared relieved. 'Well, that's good news then, we'll have one decent marriage in the family at least.'

Rhian hugged his arm to her side. 'You sound bitter, Billy – you're not happy, are you?' She saw him frown and knew the truth in the darkening of his eyes.

'She's an outsider, like,' he said at last. 'However hard

59

Delmai tries, she can't fit in with the valley folk. They don't take to her because of her snooty ways and it's only Mrs Jones who bothers with her at all. And it must be lonely for her while I'm at work.' He sighed. 'She'll leave me one day, I'm sure of it. She'll take Cerianne and go home to Sweyn's Eye, perhaps live with her father for all she says he was strict with her.'

Rhian remained silent, unable to shatter her brother's few remaining illusions about Delmai. And yet the knowledge that she was trying her best to get her husband to take her back rankled.

'See that poster on the wall there?' Billy said suddenly. 'It's an invitation to enlist in the Army. That's where I'd go if Delmai left me; I wouldn't put up with life at the coal-face a moment longer if it wasn't for her.'

Fear washed over Rhian in waves as she stood on the draughty platform looking up at her brother. She hadn't found him again just to lose him to the war, had she?

'But Billy, people are saying it will all be over in a few months; Lord Kitchener has got such a big army that the Germans will be easily defeated.'

'Maybe, maybe not, but don't you go worrying your head about it. Look, there's your train coming and thank God for that. I'm dying for a pint of ale down at the Colliers' Arms.'

Rhian watched the steam from the train form patterns against the blue of the sky, she heard the clickety-clack of the wheels, almost felt the rhythm in her pulse and her heart was heavy.

'See you soon, Billy.' She kissed him hurriedly on the cheek and he smiled down at her cheerfully. 'Too true, *merchi*, we've hardly talked about you and here I am wallowing in self-pity, there's a brother to have. But I'll make up for it, you'll see!'

As the train drew slowly out of the station, gradually gaining speed, Rhian sat in a corner staring out at the blackened hills that seemed to glide past the narrow windows. She felt saddened; Billy was far from happy and there was nothing she could do about it.

Becoming aware of a young soldier seated opposite her, she smiled, sensing his pride in the stiff new uniform and guessing he was no more than sixteen years of age. He saw her look and leaned forward, eager to talk.

'Going to war I am,' he said proudly. 'My mum said anything is better than the pit. My dad and my brother got killed in a fall last year, see, put her off coal-mining it did.'

'Do you think it will be over soon – the war, I mean?' she asked and the boy's eyes were bright with enthusiasm.

'*Duw*, I hope not. I want to give those Huns a bashing, show them they can't run roughshod over us Welsh.'

Rhian was silent, wondering at the way the soldier treated going to war like a game.

'Joined the Sweyn's Eye battalion, me,' he said, his young face alight with enthusiasm. 'Got to do some training first and then I'll be off to foreign parts. Can't tell you where, because it's to be kept a secret.' He smiled disarmingly. 'To tell the truth, I don't know where I'll be posted, but they'll tell me once I arrive at the barracks.'

'Are you from Carreg Fach?' Rhian asked and the boy nodded.

'Yes, lived there all my life and my father and grandfather before me. Dai Jones, I am.' He looked at her expectantly.

'Rhian Gray,' she said, feeling a hundred years older than the young soldier. 'Are you related to Mrs Jones who lives in the pit cottages?'

'*Duw*, course I am. Most everyone in the valley is related in one way or another.'

Rhian was silent, wondering what the boy and his family made of Billy and Delmai. No doubt the couple stood out like a sore thumb.

'Well, Dai, I wish you all the best of luck in your new career,' Rhian said and there was a note of finality in her voice that brought the conversation to an end. To underline the point, she settled back in her corner and closed her eyes.

Suddenly she remembered the other train journey when she had been travelling home from Yorkshire, and the image of Mansel Jack came vividly into her mind. She could picture him as clearly as if he stood before her now – tall and strong, with crisp dark hair that grew in unruly curls on to his collar. He had keen eyes and a sensitive mouth, yet there was a quality of steeliness about him that marked him as a powerful man with a great strength of will.

His eyes used to grow warm when he looked at her, she

61

mused. But perhaps she had only imagined that look, she told herself sharply. In any case, the sooner she put him out of her mind, the better. And yet the memory of him clung to her and though they had never even touched, she knew that there would never be another man on earth who would move her as did Mansel Jack.

Chapter Five

Slowly the town of Sweyn's Eye was settling into the state of war, the citizens accepting with stoic pride the privations forced upon them. Even with stock running low, shops still opened their doors and were bent on making a living. Harries the Greengrocer self-consciously placed boxes of underripe fruit and sparse garden-grown vegetables on a trestle table outside his door, while Gwyn the Baker doled out the bread fair and square, disdaining favouritism.

Davey the Boots was better placed, for he had plenty of stock in his dusty back rooms and had he not always said to his wife that the boots and shoes he kept in abundance didn't eat anything? So it was with a sense of triumph that he continued to hang strings of leather footwear along the outer edges of his coffin-shaped doorway and ignored Mrs Davey's taunts that he was what the good book would call a wise virgin, filling his lamp with oil so to speak.

But it was the re-opening of Brandon Sutton's steel works that caused the biggest stir, for the American had decided not to enlist but to stay at home and make steel for shells that would destroy the Kaiser's army.

Mary Sutton sat in the conservatory and the scent of wild roses was fragrant, filling the summer air. 'I don't know why you are so unhappy, *bach*,' she said softly. Her husband thrust his hands into his pockets, staring down at her, his eyes unreadable.

'I just feel I'm not doing enough,' he spoke impatiently. 'My every instinct tells me to get out and fight. It seems I'm the only able-bodied man left in Sweyn's Eye.'

'Come and sit down by here and don't talk so soft,' Mary said gently. 'There has to be steel and who will produce it if you don't? And of course there will be other men left at home; you're making a fuss about nothing, Brandon.'

He gave her a quick look. 'You're a woman – you just don't understand.' He took her hand. 'It's freedom, that's what the fight is all about,' he said reasonably. 'The Germans have invaded Belgian territory and if we let that pass, how long will it be before they send troops here?'

Mary was out of her depth and she knew it. She leaned her head against her husband's shoulder, breathing in the clean scent of him, loving him even more than when they had taken their marriage vows in the tiny chapel on top of the hill.

Brandon moved away from her and stared out into the garden that stretched away into the distance. 'At least I can make some sort of financial contribution,' he said with a tinge of satisfaction in his voice. 'For the wives of my men who have enlisted, I've decided to give an allowance of ten shillings, plus an extra shilling for every child under fourteen.'

Mary felt a lump rise to her throat. 'There's generous of you, *cariad.*' She spoke softly, her heart contracting in pain, for she had no child. There would be no continuation of the Sutton family name, for Mary feared she was barren.

She looked down at her clasped hands, her thoughts drifting to the problem that worried her like a bad tooth. Perhaps it was time she consulted Dr Thomas. It was true he was growing old now, but he inspired trust in her and she felt he would give her a sympathetic hearing – not like the new young man with his neat clipped moustache and slicked-down hair who had recently come into the practice.

She had visited him once and Dr Soames had regarded her steadily, listening with attention to what she had to say, and then told her simply that there was in all probability nothing wrong with her except an over-eagerness to become a mother.

'But I am past thirty!' she had protested. 'If I don't conceive soon, it will be too late.'

His reply had been brusque. 'Nonsense, women ten years older than you are giving birth every day. Now go home and try to rest easy. Anxiety itself will make you infertile if you let it.'

His views were strange and new and Mary felt that they did her no good at all. She did concede she might be over-anxious, for some nights when Brandon came to her bed she thought more of conceiving his child than of enjoying their union. And dimly, she realised her attitude was the wrong one, for she was slowly driving a wedge between herself and her husband.

'I can see you are not with me.' His voice drew her back to the present. 'Don't worry, it wasn't important. I just said that I'm going back to the foundry and will see you later. By the way, isn't it about time you opened your store? Most of the shopkeepers are trading again.'

His words made Mary feel guilty. She had neglected the emporium for some time, leaving a great deal of the adminis- tration to Katie Murphy – which wasn't fair, for the Irish girl had her own life to lead. Mary sighed; sitting here breathing in the scent of the roses was not going to solve anything. She rose to her feet and kissed Brandon's cheek, walking arm-in-arm with him to the front of the house. Outside on the dusty driveway stood the gleaming new Austin car in all its splendour.

'Take care driving that thing,' Mary said, glaring at the shining machine with dislike. 'I'd much prefer you used the pony and trap, Brandon.'

'Don't be silly, honey. Everyone has an automobile these days; you worry too much, I'm tired of telling you that.'

There was a decided edge to Brandon's voice and Mary stepped back from him, retreating as a snail glides back into its shell.

'See you later, Mary – and think about getting back to work. It's not good for you to be sitting around doing nothing all day.'

When the sound of the car's engine had died away, Mary returned to the house and stood looking at herself in the mirror. Her hair was swept up into a glossy bun at the back of her head and the style was becoming, fining out the slight roundness of her face. She didn't look like an old woman, she thought ruefully. Her gown was of softest georgette in pastel blue edged with navy and a huge bow decorated the back which otherwise was plain, falling in soft folds to her feet.

She moved restlessly into the drawing-room, standing

before the window, wondering once more if she should pluck up the courage to visit the old doctor. Yet the thought of facing his wife's inquisitive eyes was not something she relished. Bryn Thomas was kind enough, but Marion was another matter; she needed only to catch a hint of Mary's problem and she would be gossiping over the teacups from one end of Sweyn's Eye to the other.

But she could not bear to remain in the house alone and so she threw a light silk shawl around her shoulders and made her way slowly down the hill and towards the town.

A breeze was drifting in from the sea that was lying calm in the basin of the harbour. The water seemed tinged with gold on an azure blue background, reflecting the sun's rays. Ships rose and fell on the gentle waves as the tide washed into the docks and it seemed that Sweyn's Eye had come to terms with the sword of war and was a bustling seaport town again.

In the heart of Sweyn's Eye, the streets were busy and Mary began to catch the fire of the old excitement. The challenge of running her store returned in full measure. Tomorrow, she decided, she would take up the reins again, for the housewives of the town needed cheap food and clothing more than ever now.

She paused, her heart beating quickly as she found herself outside the doctors' surgery. The building was dulled by the grime of years, the façade chipped and blackened with the smoke and cinders from the nearby railway.

Her heart began to beat faster. Was she here by accident or design, she asked herself. Should she go inside on the offchance that the old doctor would see her?

As she stood hesitating, the door opened and to her chagrin Dr Soames stood facing her. She stepped back a pace, but it was obvious that she had intended to ring the brass bell.

'Can I help you, Mrs Sutton?' Dr Soames spoke civilly enough, so why did she have the feeling that he didn't like her? She searched her mind for some excuse for her presence on the doorstep, but could find none.

'I was hoping to see Dr Thomas,' she said breathlessly, 'and I see you have no time to spare if you're going out. There's nothing urgent, so perhaps another day?' She would have left but his words stopped her.

'Do come in, I can't afford to turn patients away.' There was a hint of laughter in his voice and Mary's embarrassment grew.

He left her alone for a moment in the surgery that smelled of old leather and wintergreen oil and Mary stared round her curiously, trying not to dwell on the forthcoming interview. High on a shelf were stacks of medical books and in one corner of the room a skeleton was hanging from a hook in the ceiling. Mary shivered. The new doctor didn't believe in herbs and potions, as did Dr Thomas; indeed it was difficult to understand what he did believe in, for he sold hardly any elixirs or remedies.

When Dr Soames returned, he was wearing a neat white coat over his dark suit and Mary, glancing up at him, saw that he really was quite a handsome man.

'Now, tell me what's wrong with you?' He leaned across the desk, not touching her and Mary was perplexed; Bryn Thomas always listened to her heart and lungs or took her pulse, establishing a pattern in an orderly manner and setting her at ease.

'Well, that's what I hoped you would tell me,' Mary said quickly, wondering why she felt on the defensive. 'I still haven't . . .' Her words trailed away and he stared at her, his dark eyes revealing amusement.

'You haven't conceived a child – don't be afraid of the words, Mrs Sutton; I assure you I won't be shocked by anything you say. Now, I'll explain one or two things which might help you.' He paused, watching her so intently that to her annoyance Mary felt her colour rising.

'There is a pattern you experience each month, in common with most women, and it is at the middle of this cycle that you are at your most fertile. You do understand what I mean, don't you?'

'Of course I do, I'm not an imbecile!' Mary found herself retorting quickly. 'And I'm not a rich pampered woman crying for the moon, as you seem to imagine. I am a wife who has passed her thirtieth birthday and is anxious to give her husband a child – is that so strange?'

'On the contrary it is perfectly natural, but as I tried to explain before, the more worried you are about these things the more difficult you make it for yourself.' He stood up and moved round the desk, righting a bony hand on the skeleton with a wry smile. 'Why is it that no one believes a physician when he tells the truth? Would you be happier if I gave you some harmless pills and called them a miracle cure?' He shook his head. 'I think you are far too intelligent a woman for that, Mrs Sutton, so I will simply reiterate what I've said before: that you must give nature a chance. You have been married just short of two years and that isn't very long, you know.' He paused, his eyes running over her. 'And as regards to your age, I shouldn't give that another thought, for nature is obviously being very kind to you.'

To Mary's consternation she found that she was blushing. Was the upstart doctor paying her a compliment or making fun of her? She rose to her feet.

'Well, thank you for nothing,' she said breathlessly. 'There's a few shillings for your advice, though I don't think it's worth a bent penny.'

He didn't even bother to reply and as she let herself out of the house, she felt his laughter as though it was something tangible.

She walked down to the old harbour and stood staring out to sea, feeling as lost as the small boat that bobbed on the waves, mooring rope dragging behind it. Why could she not be content with her life as it was? She had Brandon and he was all that mattered to her, surely? She also had her store and made a good living for herself, so why did she feel this continual sense of loss?

She was becoming obsessed with the idea of having a baby and for all she knew, the young doctor could be right – perhaps she was defeating nature by being too eager. And yet the dreadful fear that she might be barren persisted.

She sat on the sea-front for a long time and it was almost dusk by the time she returned home. The dining-room lights spilled out on to the lawn and the house had an unreal fairy-tale look about it. She had not been born to all this, she told herself fearfully. Was childlessness the price she had to pay for rising above her station?

Brandon rose briefly when she entered the room and then resumed his seat without another glance in her direction and finished his meal in silence. At last he threw down his pristine damask napkin and spoke to Mary in tones that she hardly recognised.

'When you have eaten, come to the study. I want to talk to you,' he said. Irked by his tone Mary pushed her plate away with the food untouched, and followed her husband into the book-lined room. She waited impatiently as he poured himself a drink from a gleaming glass decanter, her heart beating fast, her anger growing. What right had he to issue orders as though she was a child, and in front of the servants too – what on earth had come over him?

'Well, what is it you want to talk to me about?' Mary demanded and Brandon's eyes were suddenly hard.

'I do not like your tone,' he said deliberately. 'Remember that you are my wife and I expect a certain respect from you. Now sit down!'

Surprised at the command in his voice, Mary obeyed him at once, clasping her hands together in her lap to prevent them from trembling.

'Where have you been until this late hour, and wearing only a flimsy gown? Have you taken leave of your senses, woman?'

'There's no need to shout at me, mind, I'm not deaf.' She held her head high. 'I've been giving myself time to think, sitting in our old spot on the harbour. That's where I've been – no harm in that, is there?'

Brandon's anger dissolved. 'Why don't we talk any more, Mary? We've become like strangers. Oh, we touch and we lie together but in your thoughts you are always far away from me.'

Mary could not meet his eyes; she longed to tell him what was in her heart and yet how could she broach the subject of her childlessness – might he not think it was a reflection on his manhood?

'You see?' he said softly. 'Even now your thoughts are secret from me, I can tell by the way you avoid my eyes.'

'There's soft you are. I've nothing to hide from you, Brandon.'

He sighed and shook his head. 'You are doing it again, Mary, keeping me at a distance. I just fail to understand you.'

'Is that so surprising?' Mary was stung into anger once more. 'I'm just a working girl and you're a toff, remember?'

Her cheeks burned and tears threatened to spill over as she stared into the flames of the fire, feeling the warmth of them but not seeing the coals glowing in the ornate grate.

'I will get to the bottom of this!' Brandon said fiercely. 'Mary, look at me, I want to know what's wrong – is it that there's another man in your life? I want the truth, now!'

Aghast, Mary turned to face him, suddenly feeling drained as though the blood had flowed from her veins.

'How could you speak to me so cruelly?' she whispered. 'Do you think of me as a flossie, then?'

'What am I to think when you come home here late at night, dressed only in a flimsy gown and with your hair disarrayed? In the circumstances, any man would ask himself what his wife might be up to.'

'Up to? How *dare* you!'

'I dare because I'm your husband and I mean to know what's going on.' He grasped her by the shoulders and shook her. 'Speak, damn you!'

'I'll speak all right, if only to tell you that I hate you, Brandon Sutton!' Mary's voice was hoarse. 'I can't believe I'm really hearing these awful things. Hurt me deep, you have, and forgiveness won't come easy.'

He seemed to withdraw from her then. 'You talking of forgiveness – that's rich, that is. It's not me running round the town like a wild thing; haven't you stopped to consider how foolish you must look?'

'I won't listen to any more of this; damn you to hell, Brandon!' She hurried from the room and stumbled up the wide staircase, her eyes blurred with tears. What was happening to her marriage? What had she done to deserve Brandon's mistrust?

She fell on to the bed, bitter tears tasting salt on her lips. This was their first quarrel, she and Brandon had not so much as raised a voice against each other before. And it was clear that she was to blame. It was her unremitting desire for a child that was turning her heart inside out, souring her relationship with her husband – and even worse was her inability to talk to him about it.

She heard him come into the room and turned, holding out her arms beseechingly. 'Brandon, my love!' He held her close, murmuring her name, kissing her neck, his mouth hot with passion.

'Love me, Brandon,' she whispered, clinging to him tightly and feeling the hot surge of blood in her veins.

His hands were tender as they removed the flimsy gown and he caressed her proud breasts, his eyes dark with passion.

'I love you so much, Mary, it's like a sickness. I can't get enough of you and I'm insanely jealous – without cause, I realise that.'

'Hush, don't blame yourself, I'm a vixen to turn on you so and you know I love you more than my life itself.'

He laid her gently against the pillows and as he drew her close, she felt the lean hardness of him against her and gloried in his strength. Brandon was a fine man and any woman would be proud to have him as a husband.

His hands were touching, delighting her, bringing sighs of joy from her . . . and Mary closed her eyes, surrendering to the love which was like sweet wine to her.

But as Brandon came to her, she could not help the thought which crept unbidden into her mind, growing into an all-important desire which overwhelmed any other. Perhaps now, tonight, lying in Brandon's arms and full of love for him, she might conceive his child.

Chapter Six

The autumn sun shone brightly as though reluctant to accept that summer was past. A drowsing heat hung over Sweyn's Eye, turning the parks and gardens of the western slopes into a blaze of colour. Late roses rioted in lush grass and the fruits of autumn grew in abundance. Blackberries bursting with juice stood proud on prickly thorn and wild white bryony lingered amongst leaves that spread upwards like open palms. An air of peace hung over the hot streets where tar turned to acrid liquid and war was a distant threat, an unreality except for the continued announcements in the pages of the *Daily Post*.

Rhian was seated in the low grey building of the mill on Spinners' Wharf, unaware of the haze of heat outside the high round windows. Deftly she placed bobbins on the twister, bringing two threads together to make double ply for knitting. But her thoughts were not on the wool that slipped easily between her fingers. She sighed softly, stretching her arms upwards and easing the ache in her back. And she wondered with a trace of impatience why Mansel Jack's dark features still haunted her.

She allowed memories to revolve in her mind, a multi-coloured kaleidoscope of emotions falling into a pattern as sure as the wool beneath her fingers. She had chosen to leave Yorkshire without a word, unable to face the strain of saying goodbye. They had become close in an inexplicable way. She had listened to him talk with enthusiasm about the mill, witnessed the ambition in his eyes and marvelled that he even saw her, so high were his sights set.

But she had worked hard at Mansel Jack's mill and it was not long before he began to notice her. He had been amused by her flair for making patterns and had eventually given her a free hand, much to the chagrin of the other women.

On more than a few occasions he had called her into his office – the little room standing in the corner of the mill where the clatter of the carding engines receded to a distant hum. There Mansel Jack had talked to her about her background, his dark eyes appraising and with such an air of authority that she had felt compelled to answer him.

She had described the humdrum parts of her life in Sweyn's Eye, had even mentioned Heath Jenkins and that as a young girl she had fancied herself in love with him. But she did not speak of the secret that lay dark and coiled snake-like in her being, though his shrewd eyes missed nothing.

When, as he sometimes did, he paused at the loom to talk to her, the other women winked at each other, mouthing words over the noise of the machinery. Rhian knew exactly what they thought of her.

Once Mansel Jack had arrived unannounced at her mean lodgings; she had just washed her hair and it hung curtain-like, dark chestnut over her shoulders. He filled her room with his presence, touching the damp strands of her hair with the gesture of a lover. And she had felt her face burning.

'I've admired you for some time now, lass.' He leaned closer, his mouth curving in a smile, the strong line of his jaw emphasised by the dark hair that curled around his face. 'You've a fine mind and nimble fingers and I like that.'

There was no time for false modesty. 'I know.' She had smiled up at him and he had leaned back in his chair, laughing.

'There, you see, you don't dissemble or giggle behind your hand, you come straight out and say what you think. You're a perfect woman, Rhian Gray.'

Rhian had sighed inwardly, for she was far from perfect. A great fear gnawed at her in her nightmare: the dread of a man's hand touching her intimately. This was the legacy left her when Gerwin Price had torn and plundered, leaving her for ever scarred. Slowly she shook her head. 'No, I'm not perfect, not by a long chalk.'

Mansel Jack had not tried to pursue the conversation, for he had a fine sensitivity and realised there were matters which

73

must be secret. He had simply smiled down at Rhian, his eyes soft, his mouth turning up at the corners, treating her with warmth and friendship. Now she could not erase the image of him from her mind.

The sound of the door opening startled Rhian. Once more she was at Spinners' Wharf, working the small loom, and she felt like a sleepwalker waking in a strange place. She looked up to see Heinz framed in the doorway. His mutilated hand was bound in a swathe of cloth and his hair stood on end. Rhian hid a smile, he was so like a big innocent baby sometimes.

'What's wrong, Mr Sinman?' she asked, setting the twister into movement. The bobbins turned in unison on thin spindles, winding wool more quickly than the eye could see.

'We haf lost another order.' He came towards her, rubbing his uninjured hand against his apron. 'The shops up in the High Street say they want no more blankets from us.'

Rhian felt anger run like wine through her veins. 'There's daft of them! But don't worry,' she said stoutly, 'I'll find us some new markets. I'll go further afield if necessary.'

'Good honest words, Rhian, but you know the bad feelings the people haf for me now.' He shook his head. 'I think I must give up the mill and go away like the townspeople tell me to.'

Rhian shook her head. 'No, don't give in, we're not beaten yet.' She drew off her apron. 'I know just where we can get a good order for our wool – you depend on me, Mr Sinman.'

She washed her hands free of the grease from the wool at the deep sink in the Sinmans' kitchen, rubbing angrily at her fingers while Gina Sinman poured her a cup of tea.

'*Duw*, if my belly grows any heavier I swear I'll go pop – and me got to go down to the market for potatoes and I don't think I'll make it back up the hill.' Gina eased herself into a rocking-chair and brushed back a damp curl from her forehead. Rhian stared down at the swollen figure with compassion; Gina still bore the bruises from the stoning, though they were fading a little now.

'You can't have long to go and the baby will come when it's ready, you'll see.'

Gina smiled dreamily. 'It's going to be a boy, a fine son for Heinz, I can tell by the lazy way he sleeps all the time. Used to kick me to pieces he did, but now he's saving his strength to come into the world.'

'Yes, and you need to save your strength too,' Rhian said firmly. 'Look, if you want potatoes I can fetch them. I've got to go out anyway.' Neither of them mentioned the incident of the stoning, but both recognised the need for Gina to stay out of harm's way.

'There's kind of you, Rhian. Get me a piece of boiling bacon as well – if you don't mind, that is.'

'I've said I don't mind, haven't I? Now why don't you go and lie down on the bed for an hour, you look all in.'

'Oh, I don't know about that. There's lazy it seems to be, lying down in the middle of the day.'

'You do as you're told,' Rhian insisted. 'Go and tell that husband of yours that you mean to rest and I'll see you later. Don't worry about supper, I'll put the bacon on to boil if you're not up when I come back.'

The streets shimmered in the heat of the sun and Rhian felt breathless, her skin was beaded with perspiration in a matter of minutes. But as she strolled downhill towards the town, her spirits rose. It was good to be alive on a day like this, when even the bees hung lazily over the hedgerows, cells overfilled with honey.

The birds sang in the high leafy branches of the trees and as she neared the sea a fragrant breeze drifted towards her, caressing her face, lifting her hair from her neck, and she felt as though the gods were smiling on her.

She paused for a time on the edge of the golden bay, staring out at the clear horizon where a sail-ship was outlined against the backdrop of the Devonshire hills. Such clarity of sky and sea and mountains was a sure sign of the soft rain of Summer.

At last she turned towards the town, the streets seeming hard beneath her feet. A milk-cart rattled past, the horse between the shafts moving reluctantly, head drooping. The milk churns clanked, spilling frothy liquid along the metal sides like pearly tears.

Outside Mary Jenkins' store, Rhian paused, staring at the display of fine gowns in the windows. She sighed heavily; in such fine weather it was difficult to sell heavy woollen shawls, yet she was bound to try her best. That's why she was here, to ask her old friend for help.

The inside of the store was large and impressive and Rhian had to summon up all her courage, putting confidence in her voice as she asked to see Mary Jenkins. But she need not have worried, for her welcome was warm.

'There's a nice surprise, Rhian! I've hardly seen you since you came home, where have you been hiding?' Mary was genuine in her delight and Rhian smiled in response.

'Mary, I should have come to see you before this, but I do have an excuse. I've been working at Spinners' Wharf.' She shrugged. 'Times are hard, Mary, and I won't deny that Heinz being a foreigner doesn't help. That's the reason I'm here, I might as well be honest.'

'Right then, what can I do for you?' Mary led the way across the store and Rhian, following her, felt dwarfed into insignificance by her stature.

'I want you to give us an order for woollen goods, Mary.' Rhian spoke appealingly and Mary turned to look at her, shaking her head.

'*Duw*, there's nothing I can do for you and there's sorry I am. Come with me, I'll show you what I mean.'

Mary led Rhian along a passageway to the back of the store. 'Look, *merchi*, there's my stock of wool blankets and shawls – not moving in this heat, see?'

Rhian stared at the shelves full of woollen goods, her heart sinking. She moved closer, lifting the edge of a shawl and staring at it in bewilderment.

'How is it you buy your wool from Yorkshire then, Mary?' she asked in surprise. 'Should be supporting local trade, for shame on you!'

Mary stared at Rhian, her eyebrows raised. 'What do you mean? I don't buy wool from Yorkshire at all, but from Alfred Phillpot who is an official of the Sweyn's Eye Cooperative.'

Rhian fingered the blanket, shaking her head in determination. 'I don't know what this Alfred Phillpot is telling you, Mary, but I know the Yorkshire patterns when I see them – didn't I make up most of these myself? This man is buying his wool from the mills belonging to Mansel Jack – the same mills where I used to work.'

Mary turned over one end of the blanket and studied the label. 'Well, look, this says "Welsh wool" clear enough. Are you sure you're not mistaken, Rhian?'

'As sure as I'm standing here.' Rhian spoke so positively that after a moment Mary nodded.

'Right then, that man is cheating me yet again. He's always been a thorn in my flesh and now he's taking me for a fool into the bargain.'

Rhian frowned. 'But Mary, I'm not saying there's anything wrong with Yorkshire wool and I don't see that you can lose anything by this strange carry-on.'

'Well, I can!' Mary said angrily. 'The Yorkshire mills produce goods in such large quantities that the prices are lower than for Welsh wool and it's Welsh wool I've been paying for, do you see?'

Rhian nodded slowly. 'I suppose the trick is to prove all this,' she said uncertainly. 'I know my own patterns sure enough, but it's only my word against that of Alfred Phillpot.'

Mary smiled suddenly. 'Not if Mansel Jack can confirm what you say, *merchi*. You must give me his address; come on up to the office with me, this is too good a chance to miss. I've been wanting to give Alfred Phillpot his come-uppance for a long time.'

Rhian felt her heart beat faster; she didn't want Mansel Jack to be involved, but how could she explain that to Mary?

'Well, I'll give you his address, but keep my name out of it, mind,' she said quickly.

Mary stared at her with a puzzled expression on her face. 'Why, Rhian, don't look so frightened – you won't be called upon to face Alfred Phillpot, I'm capable of doing that alone.'

Rhian bit her lip. It must seem to Mary as if she was a coward without the courage of her convictions, yet there was nothing she could say to excuse her attitude without going into complicated explanations.

'Don't look so worried, Rhian. I promise I'll not even mention your name if it bothers you.'

Rhian held her head high. 'I'm sorry, Mary, but I have my reasons, believe me.'

Mary rested her hand on Rhian's shoulder. 'There's soft you are, you don't have to tell me anything you don't want to. Now I'll say this: if what you claim is proved to be true, Alfred Phillpot can have all his woollens back and then I'll deal with your Mr Sinman. There, does that please you?'

'That's very good of you, Mary.' Rhian felt at a disadvantage, reading something like pity in Mary's eyes and wondering what she must be thinking. But she had no need to justify her actions, she told herself firmly.

'I must get back,' she said quickly. 'Mrs Sinman isn't well and there's such a lot of work to be done at the mill.'

Mary walked to the door with her and paused for a moment. 'I've had an idea, Rhian – why don't you come to my house and have Sunday dinner with me? I feel that I haven't really seen a great deal of you since you came back to town, and it really is too bad of me to neglect you so.'

'If you're sure it will be all right, then I'd love to come – but what will your husband say?'

'He'll welcome you as warmly as I do. Brandon isn't a snob, I'll say that for him.'

'Then that settles it,' Rhian smiled. 'It'll be a treat for me.' Her thoughts flew unbidden to the last time she had eaten dinner with Mary. It had been a Christmas time and Rhian had been as numb as the ice that settled on the pond in the cottage garden. Still in a state of shock, unable to shake loose the memory of the horrors inflicted on her by Gerwin Price, she had wanted nothing more than to drown herself in the glassy waters of the pool, for the scars of her ordeal went deep.

'Are those bad memories I see in your eyes, Rhian?' Mary asked gently. 'If so, forget the past. You're a young and lovely woman and you have your whole life in front of you.'

'Too clear-sighted for comfort you are, Mary,' Rhian said, forcing herself to speak lightly. 'I'll see you Sunday then and thanks for everything.'

She moved away briskly down the street that shimmered with heat. It would be good to leave the humid air of the town behind and make her way back along the beach road and up the hill towards Spinners' Wharf. There the stream would be gurgling past the long low building and the birds singing their tribute to the sun while sheltering in the shadows beneath the eaves.

She had almost forgotten her promise to do some shopping for Gina, and with a sigh she turned towards the market. The square was quite deserted, the air was hot and dust lay thick between the stalls. The mingling odours of meat and huge chunks of country butter gone rancid were almost too much to bear.

Rhian declined to take any ham, for flies crawled over the stained wooden chopping-block where the butcher set up his meat ready for cutting. Instead she bought fresh vegetables and a smooth round cheese covered in mutton cloth, kept cool in an old wooden barrel filled with water.

She was pleased when she was able to leave the market square behind. Ruefully, she noticed that her dress of soft cotton trimmed with hand-sewn rosebuds had become crumpled and grimy at the hem. Her hair was escaping from the confining pins and she felt she could do with a good scrub.

In the Sinmans' household there were few amenities. Heinz allowed the women the privacy of the kitchen sink in the morning and conducted his own ablutions in the yard, working the pump with gusto and singing out loud in his own tongue that was strange to Welsh ears. But now even a splash of cold water from the kitchen tap would refresh her, Rhian thought wistfully.

It was good to see the low building with twin windows like a pair of eyes beneath the gables and she sighed with relief. The kitchen was dim and empty and she wondered if Heinz was working at the mill which was separated from the house by a stretch of rough ground. She put her purchases away in the cool of the pantry and rubbed her hand wearily over her eyes. Gina must still be asleep up in her room – the best place for her in such heat, Rhian thought absently.

She was about to put coal on to the dying fire when a sound from upstairs attracted her attention. It was soft, almost indistinguishable and Rhian straightened with the shovel in her hand, her neck arched as she strained to hear if the noise was repeated. It was. Low guttural moans were coming from the direction of the bedroom and Rhian felt cold with fear.

'Gina!' She hurried up the stairs, her heart beating fast, her mouth dry. 'Gina, is everything all right?'

The question was absurd, as Rhian realised when she entered the room where Gina was crouched on the bed, knees drawn upwards, mouth shaped into a silent call for help.

'Is the baby coming?' Rhian felt panic rise within her. She

79

must get help, but she couldn't bear to leave Gina alone.

'Where's Mr Sinman?' Rhian was astounded by the apparent calmness in her voice. Gina bent her head, overcome with pain once more. 'In the mill, is he? Well, don't worry, *cariad* – I'll call him right now.'

Rhian was not familiar with the process of childbirth, yet she felt in her bones that all was not well with Gina Sinman's confinement. She leaned as far out of the window as she dared. 'Mr Sinman! Come here quickly!' she shouted.

After what seemed an eternity Heinz appeared from the coolness of the mill. Strands of wool fluttered in his sideburns and he was open-mouthed in astonishment.

'Is the baby coming?' he asked. 'But it is not due until the day after tomorrow.'

Rhian smiled at him encouragingly. 'You'd better tell your son that. Go on with you now, Gina needs a midwife,' she urged as Heinz stood in bewilderment, fleeting expressions of joy and fear passing like shadows over his face.'

'You'd better fetch Mrs Benson and I shall see to my Gina.'

Rhian paused for a moment to watch him stride stolidly towards the house, his big back straight, his thick legs set down firmly with each step as though walking the deck of a ship in high seas.

He was right, the midwife might not come if Heinz showed his face on her doorstep. In spite of the heat, Rhian found herself running along the road that led uphill from the mill, wishing fruitlessly that she had not dallied so long near the beach.

Canal Street lay along the line of the brackish strip of water that gave the cobbled roadway its name. A barge moved silently through the waving fronds of the brown rushes with an old mare pulling at the rope, head nodding, ears forward as though seeking shelter from the sun.

The animal paused on the towpath to stare at Rhian with rolling eyes and the bent figure of the old man holding the reins seemed to merge into the muddy colour of the water.

'*Bore da* to you, miss.' He raised his cap and Rhian saw that his white hair was streaked with green, the verdigris from the cargo of copper ore in the barge. 'If it's the midwife you're looking for, I saw her not ten minutes ago, rushing to a birthing – didn't even have time to talk to old Will the Copper.' He moved away and ghost-like the barge slid silently through the murky water behind him. Rhian stood for a moment, wondering what to do. In panic she knocked on the door of the Bensons' neat house in the faint hope that she might find someone in.

The lace curtains of the neighbouring houses twitched and Rhian felt as though many eyes were boring into her back. She held herself straight, rapping on the door once more, and to her relief it swung open.

'What do you want here, Rhian Gray?' Sally Benson stood with hands on hips, her pebble-dark eyes hostile. 'Don't want no foreigner's skivvy at our door, so go away, right?'

'I want to see your mother, where is she?' Anxiety lent Rhian's voice a sharp edge. 'Move, Sally Benson, before you feel the back of my hand.'

'Well, she's not here.' Sally's voice was less belligerent as she stepped back into the safety of her doorway. 'So that's just hard cheese on you, isn't it, 'cos I don't know where my mam is gone.'

Rhian bit her lip in panic. 'You must know where I can find her?' she said and Sally half closed the door, peering insolently round it.

'Fish and find out!' she said nastily.

'Look Sally, Gina Sinman is sick, she needs a midwife. Stop being so childish and tell me where your mother's gone.'

'There's a cheek, talking to me like that!' Sally's face, already flushed with the heat, grew even redder. 'I don't know where my mam is, see, and if I did I wouldn't tell you. That Gina Sinman is living with a *bradwr*, a traitor, don't you understand that much? He's probably sending off messages to the Huns, telling them all about us.'

Defeated, Rhian turned away just as Sally slammed the door. She hurried back the way she had come, knowing that she must help Gina herself. She was so ignorant of what needed to be done, she thought desperately, but she would do all that she could.

As she neared the mill, Heinz leaned out of the bedroom window and gestured to her frantically. 'Come, Rhian Gray, we need you at once!'

81

Rhian hurried up the stairs, her heart beating swiftly. Heinz had the bedroom door open for her and his face was filled with apprehension as he ushered her into the room. 'You will haf to deliver the child; it is coming, you can see the head.'

She felt a moment of blind panic as she stood staring at Gina, who with knees drawn up was toiling in an effort to give birth to her child. Her face was crumpled in pain, sweat running down her forehead and into the creases around her mouth. She opened her eyes and stared imploringly at Rhian. 'Help me, please help me!' she gasped.

Rhian rolled up her sleeves and, taking a deep breath, approached the bed.

'You must try to pull him free of me,' Gina said in a voice ragged with pain. 'Grasp his head and ease him out.'

Rhian obeyed, knowing instinctively that Gina could stand no more of the pain that was sweeping over her in waves.

The head of the baby was moist, the dark hair flattened to the skull. Rhian felt a sudden surge of power and her hands moved with a skill she didn't know she possessed, grasping firmly and drawing the tiny head towards her. Then the face of the child was clear, the eyes closed, the small features without animation. The baby was like a doll, Rhian thought, still and lifeless.

'You must turn the shoulders,' Gina said breathlessly. 'Go on, I'm depending on you.'

Rhian became totally immersed in her task. She forgot Heinz standing anxiously behind her, even shut her mind to Gina's groans. This was a battle between herself and nature and it was one she meant to win.

The shoulders emerged at last with a swift smoothness. One more thrust and the child was born. The umbilical cord lay across the small body, twisted snake-like around the infant's neck.

'Tie the cord in two places and cut it,' Gina said, her head falling back weakly against the pillow.

Rhian obeyed instinctively and felt tears sting her eyes as she held the baby close. 'It's a boy,' she said softly. 'You've got your son, Gina.'

He was big of head, with a broadness of body inherited from his father. His eyes were still closed, the mouth and cheeks tinged with blue. Rhian held the baby away from her, slapping him hard, but there was no response.

'My babba, is he all right?' Gina was straining to sit up, her eyes meeting Rhian's imploringly.

'Fetch me some cold water!' Rhian spoke sharply to Heinz who was standing wide-eyed, staring at her. Knowledge came from somewhere deep in the recesses of Rhian's mind, a wisdom that was as old as time.

Heinz hurried to do her bidding and Rhian opened the child's mouth, clearing it of mucus. When he returned she doused the child in the cold water, but it seemed as if nothing was going to revive the baby. He lay inert, his perfect features waxen.

In desperation Rhian began to press the tiny boy's chest, softly, rhythmically. 'Please breathe, please breathe.' She said the words over and over again like a chant, unaware that her back was aching and her eyes brimming with tears.

'My boy is dead.' Gina's voice was flat, as though all her strength was spent, and Heinz awkwardly took her in his arms, his eyes turning to Rhian in desperate hope.

As Rhian continued to press the small rib-cage she saw a fleeting movement, so small that she thought she had imagined it. Like a butterfly opening its wings, a finger stirred on the tiny hand. She continued to massage the boy's chest and with a shock saw that his eyes were open and he seemed to be staring up at her.

He cried, short and sharp, then the sound of the infant's voice soared into the rafters, filling the room like a triumphant song.

'Praise be to God!' Gina said hoarsely. 'My baby is alive.'

'Praise be to Rhian Gray!' Heinz laughed out loud, watching as Rhian wrapped the boy in a piece of clean linen. She felt light, lifted out of herself, knowing a deep joy that her stubborn refusal to accept defeat had saved the baby's life.

'Is anyone up there?' The voice floated upwards, to be followed by hurried footsteps on the stairs as Mrs Benson panted into the room, her round face flushed.

'Duw, you've managed without me then?' She smiled a little sheepishly. 'There's sorry I am that I wasn't here sooner – been delivering Dai-End-House's first grandchild, I have. Now

83

let's see this baby and then, mother, I'll attend to you.'

She gave Rhian a quick look. 'Seems like you'd make a fine midwife, Rhian Gray! Strange how a woman knows what to do in times like this.'

'Saved my son's life, she did,' Heinz said warmly. 'If we didn't haf Rhian Gray with us, my son would now be dead.'

'The cord twisted around his little neck,' Gina added weakly, lying back against the pillows. 'Wouldn't breathe until Rhian got to work on him, wonderful she is and I'll never be able to repay her.' She began to cry, large silent tears that she brushed away quickly as though ashamed of them.

'Well, then, it's good you were on the spot, Rhian. But now get out of here, all of you, this little mother is in shock and I have business to do with her. And you, Rhian Gray, look as if you could do with a cup of tea.'

Thankfully Rhian left the room and hurried downstairs, running her hands under the tap in the kitchen. Heinz lumbered into the room behind her and stood looking at her, gratitude in the wideness of his eyes.

'If ever you haf need of me, Rhian Gray, then I am willing to lay down my life for you.'

Rhian touched his arm lightly. 'There's no need to say anything.' She smiled up at him wryly. 'But do you think you could manage to make a cup of tea with that one good hand of yours? I'm parched!'

She sank down in the rocking-chair and leaned back against the smoothness of the wood, closing her eyes, but the tears of relief forced themselves from behind her closed lids and poured unchecked down her cheeks.

Chapter Seven

The morning air was cool and misty with a hint of rain, for the clouds were grey and heavy above the town. The twin hills of Kilvey and Townhill were ghostly, insubstantial, the tips had vanished as though sliced away by a giant knife.

The cobbled streets were dull and dour as Morgan Lloyd walked quickly away from the small overcrowded house in Green Hill and made his way towards the wide pewter line of the River Swan.

He walked quickly, with the easy stride of the young. His head was bare to the elements, for he eschewed the wearing of a cap. His eyes were bright and shrewd and he appeared to possess an inner strength unusual in a man so young.

He walked through Copperman's Row and even at such an early, ghost-ridden hour, Dai-End-House was playing a haunting tune, the notes of the accordion rising and falling like ripples through the silence. A cat screeched loudly like a human in pain and Morgan frowned. '*Duw*, there's no peace round here at all.'

He moved downhill towards the copper works, wondering if his decision to move from the coal-black valleys to the copper town had been the right one. But there had been little choice. The air in Carreg Fach carried the black plague of coal-dust and it was this dust that was insidiously killing his father.

Morgan had seen his dad change from a man big of frame and strong of arm to a thin, wasted shadow. And so, with anger burning in his gut, Morgan had brought him to Sweyn's Eye, where there was work for a man willing to put his back into it and fresh sea air.

Some days Morgan would take his father to sit on the golden curving beach, where the air was free from the stink of the copper. But now, even the tram journey was getting too much for the old man. Not that dad was that old, Morgan reasoned; he must be rising forty years, but his teeth were gone and there was a parchment-like quality to his skin that worried Morgan.

He moved in through the gate of the Richardson Copper Company and raised his head as he caught the eye of the boss. Some men doffed their caps, but not Morgan Lloyd; he was his own man, worked hard for his money and was beholden to no one.

Inside the sheds, the furnaces belched and bubbled like a witches' stew. The heat was almost a tangible thing, around and above and within him, bringing the sweat to Morgan's brow. He thought that Hades must be like a copper shed.

'*Bore da*, Morgan boy, there's bright and early you are then.' The furnaceman stepped away from the cauldron of molten metal that shimmered like gold, wiping his face with a damp mutton cloth.

'Morning, Peter Harries. Resting again, is it? Getting too old for the job you are, man.'

'Aye and you are a young cock without a hen, strutting all over the place showing off that hairless chest of yours. Button up your shirt, boyo and hide your youth from me, for it's jealous I am.'

Morgan smiled and put his tea-can on the ground, the handle clanking against the chipped enamel sides.

''Bout ready for ladling now, Morgan.' Peter was peering into the glowing mouth of the furnace where the heat was cruel to the skin, his eyes narrowed almost into slits.

'What's this lot of copper for?' Morgan was rolling up the sleeves of his striped navy flannel shirt and Peter glanced over his shoulder.

'Fire boxes for locomotives mainly, boyo.' The furnaceman lowered his voice. 'Though there's talk that we're rolling plates for shell bands. It's supposed to be secret, mind. Hush now, the rest of the boys are here.'

Morgan took his ladle and dipped it swiftly into the hissing stew of the metal, withdrawing it smoothly though his muscles strained at the weight of thirty pounds of molten copper and his sinews stood proud. He tipped the copper into the mould, falling into line with the other men of the gang, moving in the familiar round of activity.

The dip of the spoon-like ladle into the copper, the endless walk over the few yards to the top-hat moulds and then the releasing of tension on muscle and sinew as the load was shed – all this was performed mindlessly. Was this any better than crouching in some dark watery pit wresting coal from the ground, Morgan wondered briefly.

There was no time for talking now, no breath either; the moulds standing like sentinels around the mouth of the furnace were ravening hungry beasts, needing to be filled time and time again. Morgan worked as hard as any of his fellows, though when he had joined the gang some months ago he had been teased unmercifully because his sixteen-year-old body was then slim and unmuscled. He had developed strength soon enough, he thought ruefully, and now he had the power to fill his ladle to the brim like the best of them.

The grub-break was a welcome rest from the backbreaking work and as Morgan rubbed the sweat from his eyes, he felt thirst gnaw at his throat and his belly. He took up his can and drank deeply of the tea kept warm by the heat of the furnace.

'What do you reckon on this war, then?' Peter crouched on his haunches just as the miners did back home, Morgan thought. 'Would you like to go off to fight the Hun boys?'

'*Duw*, there's a soft question, man!' Frank was a lean man with a worried frown perpetually creasing his forehead. 'I got a young wife and four children. Anyway, they don't want men above thirty – says so in the *Daily Post*.' Frank grinned at Morgan. 'We're both out of it, boy; you're too young and me, well, I'm past my thirtieth birthday two year ago. Anyway, in a special occupation we are.'

'Well, I think a lot of us will have to enlist before long. It's early days yet and Lord Kitchener can be fussy but wait you – take the ruddy lot of us before the end he will.' Peter spoke mournfully.

'*Jawl*, stop being so cheerful, man,' Frank said impatiently. 'I hope that this little lot will be over and done with in a few months. Told us it would only last a year, that's what all the big-wigs are saying.'

'They're talking about making Mr Lloyd George Minister of Munitions,' Morgan said soberly. 'So the government must think it'll be quite a long job beating the Kaiser.'

'Aye well, they would,' Frank said laconically, disposing of the entire Cabinet with a sweep of his hand – a hand that was missing two fingers, the price sometimes paid for carelessness in the face of molten copper. 'Money in it for them, see. And I can't see Lloyd George giving up a cushy job as Chancellor – a sensible Welshman, isn't he?'

'Well, I wouldn't mind going into the war,' Morgan said, deftly sidestepping Frank's question, for once started on politics he would talk tirelessly and endlessly on the subject.

'You!' Peter laughed out loud. 'God, you're still wet behind the ears, not even a bit of bum-fluff on your chin – no danger of them mistaking you for an eighteen-year-old.'

Morgan was not the least affronted. 'Well, it would be something to see a bit of the world, wouldn't it?'

'All you'd see, lad, is the mud of a battlefield.' Peter was determined to fulfil his role of pessimist. 'If the Germans didn't kill you, the foreign muck they call grub would. No, you stay by here, boy, where you're safe.'

Peter rose from his hunkering position and stretched his arms. 'Well, back to the job in hand now is it, boys, or it'll be the order of the boot for all of us. Then we'd have to join Kitchener's Army whether we liked it or not.'

Later, as Morgan made his way from the works towards Green Hill, he felt weariness drag at him as though he was carrying a physical burden on his shoulders. His arms ached with the pain of a rotting tooth and his legs were trembling with fatigue.

The roadway was shiny with rain and children playing in the street splashed murky water over thin legs. Morgan felt pity gripe at his stomach – little babbas needed fresh air and sunshine, not smoke and dust and grime.

Six months ago, when he had searched Sweyn's Eye for a home to rent for himself and dad, the only people who offered him a roof over his head were the O'Connors in Emerald Court.

The houses were small and crumbling, the roads unmade

and unlit. The Irish were the descendants of those come over as ballast on the coal-ships to settle in a land that seemed free of famine and blight. But they had been forced to accept lower wages and a poorer standard of living than the Welsh. And so they had clung together, making their own communities around the churches of St David and St Joseph, and to Morgan and his sick father they had been kindness itself.

He moved indoors past the youngest of the O'Connor girls, all of them drawn from the same mould with light ginger hair and a sprinkling of freckles over snub noses – and not a boy to carry on the name, which was a great trial to Brendan O'Connor who kept trying to rectify nature's mistake.

'Your daddy's been bad today.' Mrs O'Connor rubbed her hands on her apron and stared up at him sympathetically. 'I've tried giving him a bite of stew, but sure he won't be after eating anything.'

Morgan rested his hand for a moment on Stella O'Connor's shoulder. She was a beautiful woman, robust and healthy in spite of being constantly full with child. 'I know you're doing your best and all I can do is say thank you.'

'Oh, stop your blarney, your dinner's ready, hot rabbit pie and tatties. I'm sure you're good and hungry, so come down to the kitchen when you've seen your daddy.'

In the room up the stairs and at the back of the house, John Lloyd lay asleep. His thin frame made hardly any impression as he lay huddled beneath the blankets.

'Dad, how are you feeling?' Morgan sat on the bed and took his father's thin hand between his own strong fingers.

'Oh, it's you, Morgan. I'm fine, boyo, there's good it is to see you home!' He struggled to sit up against the pillows and the effort made him cough, the harsh dry racking sound filling the room.

'Can I get you a good strong cup of tea, dad? Hot as hell and sweet as sin, just as you like it,' Morgan said brightly.

'That would be a treat, boy, a right treat, but don't be long.'

Morgan hurried down the stairs, pain gnawing at him. It was lonely for his father in that one room with only a view of the wall of the house next door, but once he had enough money saved Morgan meant to find a nice airy house to rent, preferably with a garden so that dad could sit outside on sunny days.

'Dad would like a cup of tea.' Morgan smiled, catching the glance of Honey O'Connor, fifteen and beautiful with hair so golden and thick that a man knew at once why she had been so named.

'You go and wash, boy,' Mrs O'Connor said quickly. 'Get all that copper dust off you and I'll make the tea, so I will.'

The pump was in the yard and Morgan stripped off his shirt and rubbed at his body with the bar of home-made soap that smelled of carbolic. The abrasive copper dust stung like a hundred wasps, clinging to the skin as though in rebellion against the coldness of the water. But it was good to feel clean again. Morgan glanced up at the sky where grey clouds lay low like a roof over the buildings, and the green of the copper smoke spiralled upwards insidiously, pretending innocence. He sighed; it must be good to live away from the stink and fumes of the town, to walk in soft country meadows and smell wild flowers instead of sulphur.

He took his dinner upstairs. Dad was alone long enough and found pleasure in talking to Morgan about the old days when mam had been alive and when he himself had worked, strong and young, down the blackness of the pits.

'Started as a boy, I did,' he said as Morgan settled himself beside the bed. John Lloyd's eyes were distant, as though seeing other things beyond the faded peeling wallpaper of the little room. 'Didn't know where to go to piss I didn't, so asked where the lavvie was and everybody laughed. Right here, boyo, I was told. Never did like that, a man wants his private moments after all.'

Morgan was only half-listening. The story was a familiar one and he had heard it many times before. And the rabbit pie was good and hot, covered with mouth-watering gravy.

'Don't you want anything to eat, dad?' he asked as he put down his plate at last. 'You know there's always plenty to go round in this house.'

John shook his head. 'Not now, son, this cup of tea is all I want, lovely it is.' He smiled, a wicked light appearing in his eyes. 'I wouldn't say no to a drop of whisky if you're going to the public, though.'

Morgan groaned inwardly, for he had been looking forward

90

to getting his feet up and perhaps sitting outside enjoying the impromptu concert that usually took place at weekends. Mrs O'Connor would play on the battered piano that stood in the corner of her front parlour and folks would gather round the open window and doors and sing of the Emerald Isles whence they came, so different from the dusty roadway in the shadow of the copper works as to be another world.

'How can you bear it here?' Morgan had asked once and Mrs O'Connor had shaken her head. 'Oh, Ireland is lovely sure enough, but there's children with empty bellies and hunger in their eyes and I wouldn't go back to that for anything.'

Morgan moved to the window. The light was fading, the sky mottled like the underbelly of a fish – green, grey and with a smoky blackness that dragged at the spirit of a man. Perhaps war would not be such a bad thing if it took him away from the poverty and stink of Green Hill.

John began to cough again, spilling some of the tea on the thick calico of his nightshirt. Morgan took the cup from his father's shaking hand and set it on the table. How could he think of leaving when he was all his dad had in the world?

'Never mind about an old cup of tea,' he said, smiling down into John's drawn face. 'I'll go to the Dublin and get you a real drink!' He took a clean shirt from the drawer, silently giving thanks for Mrs O'Connor's immaculate housewifery. For the ten shillings he paid her she was washerwoman and cook, aye and sometimes nurse, and Morgan thanked providence for leading him to her door.

Honey O'Connor was leaving the house just as Morgan hurried down the stairs. She smiled up at him, shy and sweet, and blood pounded in his ears.

'Where are you going?' he asked and the question fell flat and hard into the coldness of the misty evening.

'To see my friend.' She lifted her head and the soft honey hair washed in waves over her shoulders. Morgan felt a constriction in his throat – why was he so tongue-tied now, when usually he could talk with the best of them? A trickling of unease made him stumble on.

'What friend is this, then?' He waited breathlessly for her reply, his shoulders tense, his fingers curled into fists in the darkness of his pockets.

'Maureen, you know her for sure, the girl with the beautiful black hair.' There was a note of wistfulness in her voice and along with the rush of relief that she was not walking out with some man, Morgan felt a strong sense of protectiveness rise up within him.

'Can't be as beautiful as yours, Honey.' He lifted a curling strand and watched as the evening light turned it into spun silver. Honey blushed hotly and Morgan pushed his hand back into his pocket, wondering if he had offended her.

The silence lengthened as both of them stood on the corner of Green Hill. Below them in the docks, a ship was moored; it rose and fell on the tide, high masts pointed like fingers towards the sky. To the west, the towering Kilvey Hill rose dark and somehow threatening against the stormy sky and in the silence Honey sighed softly.

'Can I walk with you to Maureen's house?' Morgan asked quickly, fearing she might fade away into the darkness.

'You can if you want.' Her reply was not exactly full of enthusiasm, but at least she had not flatly refused him.

'Going to get your daddy a jar, is it?' Honey spoke slowly as though having difficulty with the words and Morgan searched her expression, but her golden lashes were lowered and her mouth was small, a rosebud ready for plucking. He pushed the thought aside as irreverent.

'Aye, a drop of whisky sends him off to sleep like a babba.' He thought with a pang of guilt that he should be hurrying down to the public bar at the Dublin, not fecklessly walking the streets with Honey O'Connor whose mam would not approve of him because he was a Protestant.

'Here's Maureen's house, isn't it fine an' big?' Honey sounded so impressed that Morgan longed to give her a house just like that of her friend Maureen.

'In summer she has roses over the door, isn't that lovely? 'Tis only a short walk away from Green Hill, yet here 'tis like the country.'

They stood for a moment, staring at each other in silence, and Morgan searched his mind for a polite way of taking his leave. It was Honey who moved away.

'Well, good night to you then, Morgan Lloyd. Give my regards to your auld fella when you go home.'

He watched the swish of her skirts as she crossed the lane and a soft feeling that he did not understand lay in the pit of his belly. Long after the house had swallowed Honey into its depths, Morgan stood staring at the lighted windows and the door which was closed firmly against him.

The Dublin was crowded as usual, men scuffing the sawdust on the floor with heavy boots, sporting fresh white silk scarves as a disguise for coats grown shabby. The sound of a tenor singing 'The Mountains of Mourne' with sadness and longing lifted the hairs on the back of his neck as Morgan pressed himself towards the long glass-lined bar.

He caught fragments of conversation and a mingling of Welsh and Irish accents.

'How can this be Irish stew, boyo, when there's so much Welsh beef in it?' The voice was strong and filled with laughter and Morgan, recognising it, glanced over his shoulder. Crouched at a table in the corner of the bar was Peter Harries. For a moment, Morgan was tempted to join the furnaceman over a jug of frothy ale, then he thought of his father sitting alone.

'Bottle of whisky by here,' he said loudly and the barman rubbed his hand on his apron and turned to reach up to the shelf behind him. The liquor gleamed gold in the lamplight just like Honey O'Connor's hair.

Morgan sighed as he left the smoke-filled bar and turned to make his way back up to Green Hill. His father would be glad of a good slug of whisky to take away the pain. God forgive him, Morgan thought unhappily, but sometimes he wished he was free. He heard the hum of an automobile engine and saw an Austin Ascot being driven along the roadway at a spanking pace. The driver he recognised as Mr Sterling Richardson, his boss and owner of the copper works, and for a moment envied him. But only for a moment . . . turning, he stepped into the dark courts and dusty roads of Green Hill, content now to be going home.

*

Mali Richardson was seated in the pale blue of the drawing-room, sewing rosebuds on the petticoat she was making for her baby daughter. She glanced up at the clock a little anxiously,

93

wishing that Sterling would not work so hard. She knew that he needed to spend time over his books, yet recently she sensed that something was troubling him.

Now she put down her sewing and moved towards the window as if the strength of her thoughts could reach out and bring him to her. She was an old married woman now, with a son and a daughter, yet she still longed for her husband's touch and for the reassurance of his presence.

She could never forget that she was once Mali Llewelyn, copperman's daughter, born and bred in the ugly sprawling streets that gathered around the works like a gaggle of chicks around a mother hen. Her marriage to Sterling Richardson, copper boss, had shaken Sweyn's Eye to its foundations, and even now she knew she was not entirely accepted by some of the older people of the town. None of that mattered to her just so long as she and Sterling were happy together, and they were.

Her heart lightened as she heard the sound of the Austin's tyres crunching on the gravelled driveway. She smiled softly, touching her hair into place and smoothing down the skirt of her gown, her heart beating swiftly like that of a young untried girl.

He stood in the doorway for a moment just looking at her, then he held out his arms and she went into them, clinging to him and breathing in the scent that was all his own. How she loved this man!

'Give your husband a kiss and tell me what sort of day you've had.' He tipped up her chin and his mouth was strong and tender, reaching into her soul.

'I've been busy as usual; your son has been a naughty boy, refusing to eat his greens; the baby's teething, so you see there's nothing new to tell. What about you, aren't you a little later than usual, *bach*? Getting anxious, I was.'

He sat in the chair near the fire, for the evening air was growing chill. 'My men are enlisting in droves,' he said softly, his head back, his eyes closed. 'Being in a reserved occupation, they don't have to join the Army, but how can anyone blame them for wanting to fight for their country? I certainly don't.'

Mali felt a knot of apprehension grip her, but she forced herself to be calm and to take the chair opposite him, smoothing her gown now but not seeing the delicate pink

94

velvet.

'I know the way your thoughts are running, Sterling, for Mary's told me she's been through this with her husband. Brandon would love to go to war but like you, he's needed at home. There are our children to consider, mind, and who would run the copper works if you went away?' She spoke pleadingly and he looked into her eyes, his own almost violet.

'My brother Rickie could manage the works, you know he won't enlist and someone has to preserve the honour of the family name.' He smiled wryly. 'You know I must go, don't you, Mali?' He didn't touch her, but his words reached out like a caress. She forced herself to be calm, wanting to scream that he couldn't go for a soldier – the unknown forces of war were too terrifying. 'Why?' The word was tight and hard as she strove not to cry.

'Officers are needed to lead the men, you must see that.' He rose and moved towards the window, but she knew he was not seeing the gardens nor the sea far below, but was caught up in his own conscience where she could not reach him.

'There's a Sweyn's Eye battalion being formed as a division of the Welch Regiment. If my men are willing to go to the front, then how can I stand aside and do nothing?'

She wanted to go to him and bury her head against his shoulder – tell him she couldn't think of a life without him. Yet she knew that if she prevented him from doing what was right, he might never forgive her.

To Mali, war was a silly game – men fighting over a parcel of ground – but to her husband there was a principle involved and though she could not understand it, she must accept that to him it was vitally important. She sighed softly. 'Well then, you must follow your own instincts, my love.'

He took her in his arms then and it was all she could do not to cry out her pain and fear. She clung to him, her arms around his broad shoulders, thinking of her children asleep upstairs.

'How did we become involved in this war in the first place?' she asked bitterly.

Sterling led her to a chair and sat facing her; his eyes were alight, his face eager and it was obvious that he had given the matter of the war his full attention.

'Mr Asquith's government felt threatened when Germany,

in spite of the treaties that were signed, violated Belgian neutrality. An appeal was made to King George to intervene, but the Germans took no notice of the King's ultimatum and so Britain declared war.' He smiled. 'There's a lot more besides, but it's too long a story to go into now.'

'So all this is for a foreign country then?' Mali could not help the note of anger which crept into her voice and Sterling smoothed back her hair tenderly.

'My dear girl, the consequences of Germany's actions are far-reaching. If we allowed them to terrorise and subdue Belgium they might send troops into our own country.'

Mali opened her mouth to speak and then closed it again. What did she know about the ways of war? It was man's territory and she loved and respected Sterling enough to know that he believed in the fight for freedom.

'Come on, Mali, there are shadows under your eyes. Let me take you to bed and show you how much I love you.'

She rested her cheek against his, feeling the prickling of his beard, and resisted the longing to beg him to stay at home with her. Instead she smiled up at him, touching his face with her hand, tracing the outline of his lips with her fingers.

'There's a way for an old married man to talk to his wife – take me to bed indeed – for shame on you, Sterling Richardson!' She took his hand and pressed it to her breast. 'What are you waiting for, boyo? Not all tongue and no strength, are you?' She moved away from him, giggling as he reached out to cuff her playfully.

'I'll show you my strength now, young lady; just let me get my hands on you!'

Mali hurried out of the drawing-room and oblivious of the servants, lifted her skirts and ran up the stairs, closing the door of her room and pressing herself against it in a half-hearted attempt to keep Sterling out. With one push he had the door open; then he swept her off her feet and carried her towards the bed where he set her down gently. He drew her close, his hand light and caressing on the nape of her neck.

As soon as his mouth touched hers, laughter fled and Mali felt the same old sweet thrill run through her. She was as roused as any young girl on her first encounter and her arms encircled her husband's broad shoulders, holding him lovingly, her eyes closed as her very pores seemed to open to his embrace. Sterling meant more to her than life itself and mingling with Mali's passion was the underlying fear of the separation that must surely come. How could she bear not to see him and touch him and hold him? Her days would be lonely, her nights empty, her whole being would be suspended in a state of waiting.

His kisses were sweet, his hands tender as they undid the bows on her gown. They were together as one flesh, but even at the height of her pleasure Mali's heart was heavy. Sterling was used to her tears of joy so how could he know as he lay so contentedly at her side that now her crying had the bitterness of gall?

Chapter Eight

The sprawling dry-stone buildings of the Mansel Mill stood gaunt and grey in the early morning light. The clatter of the machines sent a lone robin twittering angrily upwards, abandoning its retreat beneath the eaves. And the ruggedness of the Yorkshire hills was enhanced by a coating of frost.

In his small dusty office, Mansel Jack fingered the letter that had reached out to touch him with prying fingers all the way from Sweyn's Eye. He had put Rhian Gray out of his thoughts with great difficulty and it irked him somewhat to be reminded of her now. Her small, vivid face and the dark red of her hair came so easily to mind that he wondered at its own absorption with her. She was the antithesis of Charlotte Bradley, who was tall and delicate in a bone-china kind of way. And Charlotte was every inch a lady, fragile to the touch and yet with great strength of character, which was the way Mansel Jack liked his women to be.

He would in all probability marry Charlotte quite soon and there were practical reasons for his decision intermingled with his sense of what was right and proper. He was no social climber, but his mill needed an influx of money if it was to survive and Charlotte had money in plenty.

He sighed and his hand clenched into a fist, crushing the pages of the letter as he moved towards the small window. But he did not see the hazy blues of the hills and the glittering icing of frost; he was seeing the lovely face of Rhian Gray, her lashes long and tinged with gold, her eyes when they met his filled with mysteries that he longed to unravel.

It was a long time since any woman had attracted him in the

way Rhian Gray did. Young and full of life, she had a quick wit and ready tongue and between them there had grown an unmistakable bond. But at thirty-seven years of age Mansel Jack had sown all his wild oats and in any event, Rhian Gray was not the sort of woman who would agree to a roll in the hay. Despite her youth she had dignity and pride and though she treated him with deference, he wouldn't put it past her to administer a sharp rebuke if he stepped out of line.

But the letter had not come from Rhian and it mentioned her only in passing. A business woman, Mary Sutton, had asked for patterns of Yorkshire wool to be sent to her, specifically those designed by Rhian Gray.

He moved impatiently. What he needed now was a good woman to bear his children and warm his hearth – a role which Charlotte Bradley would fill admirably.

He smoothed out the letter and re-read it, his brow creasing into a frown. It seemed that some jackanapes was passing off the Yorkshire wool as Welsh – even going so far as to replace the labels – and Mansel Jack itched to get his hands on the man.

He banged his clenched fist on the smooth surface of his desk. If there was one thing he detested it was being taken for a ride. This fool would soon learn that he couldn't put anything over a hard-headed Yorkshireman, Mansel Jack would see to that personally.

There was a knock on the door, moderate, deferential and Mansel Jack returned to his desk and seated himself behind it, consulting his watch and then tucking it back into the pocket in his waistcoat before responding.

'Come in,' he said at last, the leather of his chair creaking as he settled himself against the curved back.

'Good morning, sir. I need to have a word with you.'

Mansel Jack's eyes were shrewd as they rested on Collins, an intelligent young lad born and bred in the Yorkshire woollen industry. Would it not be just as well to send *him* to Sweyn's Eye? He stared for a long moment at Collins and the lad fidgeted uncomfortably. Mansel Jack inclined his head, indicating that he was ready to listen.

'I'm enlisting in the Army, sir.' The words fell from Collins' lips as though he was half afraid to speak them. He stood tall, his shoulders straight as though he was on parade already;

Mansel Jack could almost hear the ring of the bugle and the roll of the drums.

He coughed, hiding his surprise, for Collins was a lad who had appeared too malleable for his own good. What chance would he stand against the hardened soldiers of the Kaiser's army?

'Well, lad, that's very admirable of you, but are you sure you want to go to war? Why not wait a bit longer and see which way the wind blows?'

Collins lifted his chin, his eyes clear and blue and full of the fervour of patriotism. 'I'd like to go now, sir.'

Mansel Jack sighed. 'Very well, if you must leave then go with my blessing.' He had seen the propaganda in the newspaper too. Pictures of 'Tommies' smiling as they stood alongside a locomotive – eager, apparently, to give their life for Britain.

'Thank you, Mansel Jack.' Collins stared at his boss, aware that he had stood up to the big man for the first time in his life.

'Don't look so frightened.' Mansel Jack allowed himself a smile. 'Keep your fear for the Germans, you'll need all your wits about you when you're at the front.' In an uncharacteristic gesture, he held out his hand. 'Good luck, Collins, in some ways I wish I was in your shoes.'

Long after Collins had gone, Mansel Jack stared at the rough wooden panels of the door, deep in thought. He was too old for the Army, yet if the war continued to drag on he would have to do something other than work at the mill.

Wool was in his blood, he knew by touch if the warp and weft of a pattern were coming together in harmony. The Mansel Mill had been in production for nearly twenty years, ever since as a boy of seventeen Mansel Jack had bought the run-down building with his father's burial money – saved in an old tea-tin and made worthless by the fact that Mansel Jack senior had died at sea.

From the first, Mansel Jack had loved the smell and the feel of the wool, the satisfaction of seeing the finished goods as perfect as they could be. And yet he recognised that to strive to help the country which had given him life was a deep primaeval instinct in a man.

A vague feeling of unrest hung over him for the rest of the

day. He couldn't tell if it was because of the letter from Sweyn's Eye or Collins' decision to enlist, but dissatisfaction with his life continued to plague him.

Later, as he walked the short distance from the mill to his home, he felt the cold of the winter air on his cheeks and his breath hung in puffs on the frosty air. Winter, creeping over the countryside, had stripped the leaves from the trees so the branches pointed like skeleton fingers towards the overcast skies.

He climbed the soft slopes, his feet slipping on the frosted grass, and paused at the front door. His large old house was a source of pride, sold cheaply because of draughty rooms and dry rot. But the building was gracious to look upon. The windows were lit from within and sent out a welcome glow which warmed Mansel Jack and lifted his spirits.

Dusk was settling over the roof-tops, blurring the edges of the chimneys and softening the outline of the ornate façade, and he felt pleasure in his possession of the house. He let himself in to the hallway and stood for a moment breathing in the familiar scents. Beeswax worked lovingly into the wood panelling vied with the smell of the meat roasting and Mansel Jack smiled. Here was where he belonged, in the rough-hewn Yorkshire hills with the harshness of the mills a strange but lovely contrast. What reason would he have to leave all this – and even if he were young enough, he'd be a fool to join in the war fever that was sweeping the land. Furthermore, he would be all sorts of a fool to travel to Sweyn's Eye himself.

'Mansel Jack, you're late this evening. I was quite worried about my little brother.' Doreen was full-bosomed and plump, a warm motherly sort of a woman but widowed before she could bear her old man of a husband any children.

Older than her brother by five years, her chances of marrying again were remote and it was a situation that seemed to suit her. Her husband had left her comfortably provided for and she was sensible enough to know that together she and Mansel Jack might accomplish great things. Since she had come to live beneath his roof, she had taken the place of their mother who had died shortly after Mansel Jack's birth, expending her considerable mothering instinct on her brother.

He smiled at her, resting his hand for a moment on her

101

shoulder. 'Something smells good and I'm famished!'

'Roast saddle of beef, darling, I know how you like to get your teeth into some good red meat.' She tucked her arm in his. 'I hope you don't mind, but we have visitors coming to supper – now before you scold me, let me tell you that Charlotte Bradley and her dear mother are giving us the pleasure of their company.'

'And if you think I don't know what you're up to in that quarter, then you think me dafter than I am, lass.' But Mansel Jack smiled warmly, not minding at all that there was to be company. Perhaps with a beautiful woman to admire his restlessness would ease.

'Now go to your room and change, dear boy. There are fresh clothes laid out for you and hot water for your bath, so don't dally round in the hallway.'

He smiled indulgently. Doreen said exactly the same words every night when he returned home from the mill; he could recite them by heart if he so wished.

In his room, he stripped off his clothes and climbed into the enamel bath which had been placed before the roaring fire. He enjoyed washing the smell of the wool from his body and as he stared down at his lithe frame he wondered why men past thirty were not required to go for soldiers. At thirty-seven he was a man in his prime; his belly was flat, his chest broad and he was well-muscled with no superfluous fat.

The door opened and the maid stood staring at him with bold eyes though she feigned shyness.

'Sorry, sir, I didn't know owt about you being in the bath. I've brought clean warm towels for thee.'

He smiled. 'Shut the door, Lizzie, and come here.'

She obeyed him willingly, for they were old friends in the game of sensual enjoyment.

'Shall I dry thee first?' she asked softly. Mansel Jack smiled and pushed the towels aside, stepping out of the water unaware of the beads like jewels that gleamed on his skin in the firelight. He needed soft arms around him to reassure him of his masculinity, he thought with wry self-knowledge. The war and Rhian Gray had a lot to answer for!

The supper party was pleasant and Mansel Jack ate his beef with a hearty appetite. Seated opposite him, Charlotte watched him continually and as her eyes met his the expression in them was enough to convince him that he had only to name the date and she would be happy to agree.

She was quite a catch, was Charlotte, he mused. The fortune her father was rumoured to have left from his overseas enterprises was enough to attract any man. He smiled at her and her eyes were suddenly lit from within; she seemed quite unable to conceal her love for him.

Sons born from a woman like Charlotte Bradley would have breeding and strength of will – he was one hell of a lucky man, he told himself.

When they had eaten, the women left him to drink his brandy. Mansel Jack smiled wryly, knowing there would be a great deal Charlotte would wish to teach him about manners. He could hear bubbles of laughter from the drawing-room as the women talked together and it was a good feeling to be master in his own house.

Doreen had been very much taken with Charlotte Bradley and if she found Mrs Bradley was rather overbearing and pompous, at least the older woman had impeccable manners. It seemed that a union between Mansel Jack and Charlotte would satisfy everyone concerned.

Then why was he hesitating to name the day, Mansel Jack asked himself impatiently? He tipped up his glass and looked into the glowing liquor; his hand remained steady and his pulses did not race whenever he thought of lying with Charlotte. Even little Lizzie had more power to rouse him, he thought almost angrily.

He rose to his feet and put down his glass, feeling weary of his own company. The women would lighten his mood and make him laugh and he felt in need of some distraction. Charlotte's blue eyes turned towards him as soon as he entered the drawing-room; she looked radiant when he smiled at her and soft colour rose to her cheeks as he sat near her. She was so beautiful, he thought admiringly, and there was a serenity about the smoothness of her forehead which made her appear almost nun-like. He brushed the disquieting thought aside and gave her his full attention, well aware that Mrs Bradley and his sister were exchanging delighted glances and revelling in the fact that their efforts at match-making had borne fruit.

'What do you think about the war?' He heard his words fall abruptly into the sudden silence of the room and Charlotte looked up at him with a troubled expression.

'I think it's dreadful that a man like the Kaiser can create such chaos in the world.' She leaned forward earnestly and he saw that her blue eyes had darkened. 'I sometimes wonder if I should become a nurse and play an active part in the war,' she continued.

Mansel Jack looked at her in surprise; it seemed his bride-to-be had the virtues of the missionary in her. Then Doreen spoke: 'Mansel Jack, don't you think the subject of war a little too distressing for a young lady like Charlotte?'

'Well,' he said, not without humour, 'what does my dear sister think of world affairs then?'

'I don't know anything about the war and what's more I don't want to,' Doreen said acidly.

Mansel Jack smiled and took Charlotte's hand, playing with her fingers, lifting them one by one as though they were of intense interest to him. 'I should have known better than to ask you ladies your views on such a matter.'

Charlotte moved as though she would protest, then she fell silent. The light bubbling mood of the evening had vanished for good and shortly afterwards Mrs Bradley rose to her feet, swishing her soft velvet skirts with an impatient gesture and making her intention to depart quite clear.

After his guests had gone, Mansel Jack took a glass of brandy to his room and sat staring into the fire, his brows drawn together in a frown. And in the flames of the fire, he saw the vivid eyes and dark red hair of Rhian Gray.

*

Mansel Jack was not the only man to be haunted by the dark eyes and oval face of Rhian Gray. In his bed, listening to the cheerful throaty song of the robin on the cold sill outside his window, Heath Jenkins was thinking of her soft skin and the way her hair shone darkly red, framing the vividness of her face. His love for her went deep and though it had taken him a long time to realise it, no other woman could fulfil the role of wife to him.

He did not fool himself that he would be eternally faithful;

he was the sort to like variety, but then that was true of most men. But to think of her at his hearth and tending his children made him feel warm inside. His decision to enlist in the Army might seem paradoxical to some but to Heath, the desire to fight for his country was all mixed up with his love for Rhian. This was the war to end all wars – wasn't that what the politicians and the Army generals were claiming?

Heath had spoken to Brandon and with an expression of envy, his brother-in-law had wished him well. 'Though I don't know what Mary will have to say about it.' Brandon's smile was good-humoured. 'She'll doubtless try her best to talk you out of enlisting.'

Heath had returned Brandon's smile. 'Aye, she will that, but she'll be wasting her time.' He grimaced. 'But I'm glad she's your wife and only my sister, for her tongue's as sharp as a viper's sting when she's roused!'

A cold north wind was gusting around the house and reluctantly Heath pushed back the bedclothes and stood staring out at the mauve hills of Brecon in the distance. It would be hard to leave Wales, but it was a decision he had taken only after a great deal of thought.

Downstairs Mrs Greenaway was busy over the fire and the mouth-watering smell of bacon filled the room.

'*Duw!* Up before you're wise and this your day off – not ailing, are you?' She poured strong fragrant tea from the large brown pot. 'Here, drink this. It will chase the sleep from your eyes.'

'You're a dragon, do you know that?' Heath sat down, tucking his long legs beneath the table.

Mrs Greenaway glowered at him in mock anger. 'Got to be,' she said fiercely. 'Need keeping in check, you do, boyo.'

Heath ate heartily of the bacon, eggs and lavabread she set before him. He felt good, for his future was decided and strength seemed to flow through his veins.

Later, he would go into town and be at the recruiting office early. Then he would walk over to Spinners' Wharf, call for Rhian and take her somewhere nice, perhaps the Mackworth Arms in Wind Street. There, over a fine dinner, he would ask her to marry him.

Anticipation made his blood tingle. He had not seen a great

deal of Rhian since she had come home, but she must know in her heart how he felt – hadn't she been in love with him when she was just a girl? And now he hoped she would smile and melt into his arms and promise to wait for him until the war was over.

'*Duw*, there's dull you are, boyo, spoken to you three times I have and you far away with dreams in your eyes. In love, are you?'

'You could just be right, Greenie,' he said softly.

'Well, give me your cup and I'll pour you some more tea. Still got to eat and drink whatever, mind.'

Heath stared at Mrs Greenaway thoughtfully. 'I've decided to go for a soldier,' he said, suddenly serious, 'and I want you to look after the house for me while I'm away.'

Mrs Greenaway set down the teapot and sank heavily into a chair. She raised her apron over her face as though by the action she could erase the blow of his words.

'Come on now, Greenie, there's no need to go all awkward on me.' Heath spoke impatiently; he didn't know what reaction he had expected, but it certainly wasn't tears.

'You'll be killed by them awful Huns, for sure.' Mrs Greenaway's voice was muffled. 'They don't have no mercy, cruel they are. I've heard tell they eat their own babies! Don't go, Heath – you haven't got to join up, have you?'

He rose from the table and took his scarf and coat from the peg behind the door. 'No, I don't have to go as I'm in the steel business, but what would the country do if we all refused to fight?'

'That Lord Kitchener, he's got a proper Army. They're used to wars and guns and all, leave it to them.'

Heath sighed. 'I'll see you later, Greenie. Meanwhile keep what I've just said to yourself, right?'

It was cold on the hill with the wind blowing rough coming in from the sea. Pausing to look down into the valley, Heath felt a tug of pride. Sweyn's Eye was ugly with the fumes and the stink of the copper works, yet the curving gracious bay stretching a full five miles was unspoiled and lovely.

He moved towards the town, ignoring the tram that swayed to a stop on the roadway alongside him. It would do him good to walk. Above him the sky was overcast, with clouds drifting

106

like grey sheep. The tangy smell of tar and fish from the docks was carried towards him and he felt the old familiar excitement that the ships in the harbour always gave him.

The town seemed more than usually busy. Pavements were crowded and bands of men stood on corners – faces wan with worry, white silk scarves worn like badges of hope, for unemployment was rife.

There was a sudden crashing of glass and the sound of angry voices and Heath watched, startled, as a man scrambled through a shattered shop window and began to throw tins of food to a small boy standing on the pavement.

'Run, Dewi, get off home to your mam!' the man called and as a constable appeared, pushing his way through the throng of people, he gave himself up without resistance.

'My children are hungry,' he spoke simply. 'Got to eat, haven't they?'

The constable deliberately turned his back and unbelieving of his good luck, the man disappeared into an alleyway. Someone began to cheer and then white scarves were being waved like banners. Heath found himself joining in, his voice hoarse for there was a lump in his throat. He realised quite suddenly that not everyone was as fortunate as himself. Many of the townspeople had been thrown out of work as firms closed their doors. War fever had broken out and over the months the epidemic had spread.

The recruiting station was crowded with eager young men and first in line was the eldest son of the mayor, who signed his name with a flourish to the sound of cheers from his friends. Heath bided his time, waiting in the background until the crowd thinned out.

'*Bore da.* Heath Jenkins, what are you doing standing here by my desk then?' The sergeant was a man who had lived all his life in Sweyn's Eye; too old now for active service himself, he was set the job of inspiring others to enlist.

'Come to join up, what do you think?' Heath moved to take up the wooden pen with the nib twisted from too much pressing against paper, but the gnarled hand of Sergeant Meredith stopped him.

'No, boy *bach*,' he said softly. 'The Army isn't for you, not with your bad chest and all. You'd be living in trenches neck-deep in mud and water – kill you off in no time, it would. Anyway, you're in a reserved occupation.'

'Are you telling me you don't want me?' Heath felt the heat rise to cover his body; the rejection bit deep and he could scarcely conceal his anger.

'Look, it's not me personal like – got to pass the doctor, you have. Don't you understand they won't enlist anyone with bad health? Just turned away a boy with poor eyesight – got to be fit for to be a soldier, see?'

As he left the recruiting office, Heath felt the stinging smart of humiliation; now he hardly saw the busy street he was walking along. He moved past the railway station and up the hill, striding out quickly as though to prove to himself that his lungs were as good as ever.

Breathless he was, but surely that didn't mean he wasn't fit to fight? He stopped at Spinners' Wharf, the silence telling him that there was no work being done that day. Had the world gone mad, he asked himself in sudden despair.

He paused, wanting to see Rhian and speak to her, yet knowing that the impetus had gone out of his wish to make her his wife. How could he expect any woman to marry half a man who wasn't considered strong enough to go to the front?

'Heath, what are you doing here?' Rhian was leaning out of one of the windows, waving her hand to him. Her hair drifted across her face and she laughed as she brushed it away. 'I'll be down now. Don't go,' she added urgently as he half turned away.

He thrust his hands into his pockets and kicked at a loose stone, his mind in a turmoil. He had never thought of himself as anything but a strong man. Hadn't he worked the tinplate, and done so from a young boy, so he couldn't be the weakling the sergeant made him out to be.

'What's wrong, Heath? There's a terrible glower on that handsome face of yours!' Rhian was at his side, her soft eyes filled with concern. He walked away without answering and almost running to keep up with him, Rhian grasped his arm.

'Been turned down for the Army.' The words came out short and sharp and he was aware of Rhian taking a deep breath.

'Oh, Heath, you're not thinking of going to war, are you?'

108

She dragged at his arm, forcing him to a halt, her cheeks flushed with exertion. 'But everyone is saying it will be over before long, so why bother to enlist anyway?'

'Because I don't think it *will* be over quickly,' Heath said. 'Nothing as big as a war can be settled that easily; it's just propaganda put about by the politicians to keep us quiet.' He stared down at her angrily, somehow blaming her for his rejection which was totally absurd.

'I wanted to fight for my country, is that so difficult to understand?' he asked. 'The mayor's son was enlisting – two years younger than me, his is, and him fit enough to fight on the front line. But me because of an illness I had years ago, I get turned down flat.'

'Look Heath, if you really mean to go, then don't give up so easily,' Rhian said. 'From what you say, the war will go on for some time and more men are bound to be needed. Leave it a little while and then try to enlist again.'

Heath laughed bitterly. 'You're right Rhian. If the war continues, men will die and then perhaps the sergeant won't be too particular who he sends to the front.'

'I didn't mean it like that.' She hung her head. 'And don't talk that way, it frightens me.'

Suddenly Heath put his arm around Rhian's shoulder – it was wrong to punish her for his own disappointment. He hugged her close and led her slowly downhill towards the docks.

'Let's go and watch the ships coming in,' he said softly, liking the feel of her slight body against him.

The tide was high and a sailing ship rode majestically on the water, given precedence by the steam-ships which waited offshore. The sea was pewter in the cold winter air and wind-lashed waves beat against the wooden struts of the pier.

'I was going to ask you to marry me,' Heath said wryly. 'I thought the sight of me in uniform would soften your heart so that you'd say yes.'

'There's daft you are sometimes, Heath Jenkins.' Rhian spoke sharply to cover her embarrassment. 'Sinful it is to tease a girl, mind.'

'I'm not teasing.' Heath looked down into her face, trying to read her expression, but she avoided his eyes and he sighed.

109

'You are not going to reject me too, are you?' He knew he sounded self-pitying but could not help himself.

'I'm not saying anything to you when you're in such a nasty mood. Talk to me another time, ask me proper like and I might agree to listen to you.'

She withdrew herself from the shelter of his arm and Heath sensed she was already regretting her words. She was a strange woman, he thought, so changed from the eager young girl he used to meet outside the Canal Street Laundry. But now she was far more interesting and doubly desirable.

'I'd love and cherish you, Rhian,' he said. 'I'd give you a nice home and children of your own – and I'm fit enough to work, whatever the old buffer Meredith says.'

'Give me time to think,' Rhian said gently. 'It's not every day a girl gets an offer of marriage.'

'Don't you feel anything for me, Rhian?' Heath asked and she smiled up at him, her eyes bright.

'There's a daft thing to ask of the girl who once chased you shamelessly.'

Heath touched her cheek gently with his fingers. The skin was soft like the petal of a rose and the urge to love and protect her was fierce within him.

' "Once" was a long time ago,' he said.

'Come on, let's walk by the sea and climb through the dunes and enjoy a bit of freedom while we can,' Rhian suggested. 'We'll talk no more of marriage or of war, do you understand?'

Smiling, Heath allowed her to lead him away from the docks and towards the curving stretch of sand that edged the water. She was right, he decided, he would enjoy today and think of tomorrow later.

Chapter Nine

The town of Sweyn's Eye smouldered beneath a blanket of freezing fog. The smoke from the plethora of works on the banks of the river Swan lay heavily beneath the clouds, smothering Green Hill and the cottages of Copperman's Row in a green mist that stung the eyes and irritated the lungs. But at Spinners' Wharf the air was clearer, though the river, moving swiftly past the low grey building, had turned the colour of copper which stained the banks and choked the rushes.

Rhian worked at the larger of the two looms, passing threads of wool through the eyes of the heddles which, when lifted, formed a triangular space through which the shuttle moved with lightning speed.

Deftly she reversed the movement of the heddles, locking the weft thread into place, but it was not the patterns of the wool she saw for in her mind's eye was a sparklingly clear picture of Mansel Jack. It seemed his image was imprinted on her mind – the crisp hair, the eyes so shrewd and knowing. She had held him in awe at first, hardly daring to open her mouth when he was around, but slowly she had come to like and admire him. Her feeling might have gone deeper, but Mansel Jack was unnattainable, a man about to be married to a rich and beautiful woman.

Heath Jenkins on the other hand was one of her own kind – young and vulnerable and very dear to her. Over the Christmas season he had been constantly with her, buying her small gifts and taking her out to the Mackworth Arms; in short, he was wooing her. And she was confused by her own mixed feelings – did she love Heath enough to marry him?

'Well, Rhian, you haf worked hard today, now you must eat before you fall sick.' Heinz had come into the mill without Rhian noticing; startled, she pulled at the thread so that it snapped between her fingers.

'*Duw*, there's careless of me.' She halted the loom and stared at the broken ends of wool knowing she would have to work them together, a tricky and tiresome task.

'Leave it all for now,' Heinz suggested. 'You haf tired eyes and you be no good to me if you are not strong, so come and eat.'

Heinz wore an apron which was covered in stains from the wool dyes; he looked like a great gaudy, genial clown and Rhian smiled.

'You're right, I am tired.' She straightened and rubbed at the small of her back with her hands, trying to ease the ache. As she followed Heinz from the mill and towards the house, the appetising smell of steak and kidney pie drifted towards her and she realised quite suddenly that she was hungry. Heinz saw her expression and smiled.

'My Gina, she is a good cook, her pastry is so light.' He pushed the door open, allowing Rhian to enter the welcome warmth of the kitchen where Gina was sitting near the fire suckling her son.

Rhian sat at the white scrubbed table and wondered if she would ever feel maternal the way Gina did. Her face was alight with love as she looked down at her child and Rhian felt a sudden sense of envy.

It seemed that all the normal womanly emotions had been left out of her character, for when she was a young girl she had never sought to lie with some boy beneath the stars on Ram's Tor. Not even in the flush of her first love for Heath had she overtly desired him. And now, watching Gina, she could not imagine the ties that bound her to the small gurgling creature in her arms.

'There's pale you're looking, Rhian,' Gina said suddenly. 'Now when you've had your dinner, you take the rest of the day off and get out for a bit. It looks as though the rain is going to clear.'

Before Rhian had time to reply, Heinz bellowed in mock rage, 'Listen to this woman of mine giving the orders!' His

112

beard bristled. 'I not the boss in mine own house no more.'

'Shut up your nonsense!' Gina said quickly, her entire body shaking with laughter so that the baby in her arms, deprived of her nipple, set up a loud wailing.

'You haf made my son cry now.' Heinz took Gina's face between his hands and kissed her mouth. 'Come on, woman, no more fooling about. Mine belly thinks my throat's cut, so where is the pie I've been waiting for all morning?'

Gina rose from her chair and handed him his son. 'I'll get it for you now if you'll stop nagging.'

Together, in the warmth of the kitchen, the three of them ate hungrily. Rhian was more than welcome in the Sinmans' household, she knew that, but at times like this she couldn't help feeling like an interloper.

By the afternoon, a watery winter sun was breaking through the clouds. Rhian took a deep breath, pleased to be leaving the mill and strolling along the street towards the town. She had no idea what she would do with her unexpected free time, but she was grateful to the Sinmans for seeing her restlessness and not asking any questions.

She moved along the Strand towards the docks and the pungent smell of fish lingered on the breeze, for the sea-food market was open for business. She nodded to Bryn The Fish and he grinned at her from behind his stall, holding up a dead fish entreatingly.

'Will you buy something, for pity's sake? There's no one wants even a nice bit of cod this morning.'

Rhian saw the scales of the flaccid fish gleam in the sunlight and shivered at the gaping mouth and dead eyes which seemed to pin her with an unnerving gaze.

Cockles, still encrusted with sand, lay in enamel bowls; they would need to be boiled quickly at the peak of freshness to bring out the full flavour.

Lavabread made from seaweed, thick and black, clung to the sides of a zinc bucket. Looking at it, no one would guess how delicious the food would taste when fried in oatmeal and with a few slices of bacon.

Suddenly there was the sound of shouting and the peace of the afternoon was abruptly shattered. Soldiers were running through the docks with bayonets fixed and Rhian crouched

113

back against the stall, her heart beating rapidly in fear.

'It's the men of the 6th Welch,' Bryn said excitedly. 'Come in by here, Rhian. You'll be out of harm's way then.'

Hastily Rhian obeyed, scrambling over the boxes of fish, careless of her shawl catching on a nail. Soldiers continued to swarm over the dockside looking frighteningly businesslike – faces grim, gleaming blades flashing in the sun.

'What's happening?' Rhian's voice shook and the fact of war was suddenly a vivid reality. Bryn The Fish wound his scarf more tightly around his neck and pushed the cap to the back of his head.

'There are two German ships in port – had to come in I suppose, because of the bad weather last night. The *Serak* and *Brema*, two fine ships and no one knowing what's to be done about the crews until now. *Iesu Grist!* Here they come.'

Rhian shrank back as the pounding of soldiers' feet against the cobbles echoed in her ears. The prisoners were a dispirited lot, faces long with worry and not at all the demons that Rhian believed the Huns to be. They were men, just ordinary men, and she could not help but feel sorry for them.

'Where are you taking them, boyo?' Bryn called loudly and one of the younger soldiers was surprised into replying.

'To Rutland Street School. We're locking them up there until we decide what's to be done with them. Going to round up all the other Germans in the town too, while we're at it.'

A kick from one of his fellows silenced the soldier and Rhian bit her lip, unable to believe that this was really happening in the normally peaceful streets of her home town.

The pleasantness of the afternoon was shattered for Rhian as she wandered aimlessly into *Stryd Fawr*, where the shops were open and people going about their business unaware of the drama unfolding near the docks.

'Rhian, don't walk past your old workmate then!' The voice was familiar and Rhian turned to see Doris Williams hurrying towards her, clutching a woollen turnover around her shoulders, her bonnet falling over her eyes. Rhian smiled. The last time she had seen Doris was when she was black from the coal used to stoke the boilers at the Canal Street Laundry.

'There's lovely to see you, Doris, you haven't changed a bit.' The girls had never been good friends, but it was a relief to

Rhian to be communicating with another human being instead of wandering around alone like a lost soul.

'Isn't it strange, then? I was only talking to your brother the other day,' Doris said breathlessly. 'Went up to see my sister in Carreg Fach, I did and your Billy is living next door to her. Lovely babba he has, too.'

'Yes, Cerianne is beautiful. I haven't seen her for some time; I suppose I should go to visit our Billy again soon,' she said, feeling suddenly guilty.

'There's a favour I want to ask of you, Rhian Gray.' Doris rubbed at her cheek with her finger. 'Got to register at the Borough Treasurer's office, I have, see? That's if I wants to claim benefit from the Prince of Wales Fund.'

'And you'd like me to come with you? Yes, of course I will,' Rhian said quickly and Doris sighed in unmistakable relief.

'There's good of you, scared I am. Can't write my name proper-like and they frighten me to death, all them men sitting behind a counter frowning at me.'

Rhian allowed Doris to take her arm, guiding her away from the main street and into a small cobbled lane. 'Had a job I did, cleaning for Mr Gregory Irons, but he gave me the order of the boot and got himself a pretty young girl now and she'll do more than sweep his floors, I'll bet a shilling.'

As soon as she entered the office at Doris's side, Rhian knew the reason for the girl's timidity. A row of men sat at a long table with lists of names on a pile of papers in front of them.

'*Duw*, they look like a lot of St Peters on the day of judgement,' Doris whispered. 'Quick, get in this queue,' she urged. 'It's shorter than the rest and the man at the desk don't seem so bad – see, he's got nice kind eyes, blue they are though his thick spectacles do hide them a bit.'

The wait was a long one and Rhian moved restlessly, staring around her, hearing the low hum of voices and wondering what had happened to her afternoon off.

'Came in here once before,' Doris whispered. 'Sent me away they did, and me not knowing what for.'

Rhian smiled reassuringly. 'We'll see if we can get some sense out of them today.' She was aware that her voice lacked conviction. Getting anything out of the awe-inspiring men seated at the long table was not going to be easy.

'What's the fund for, Doris?' Rhian asked and Doris made a wry face. 'It's been set up for the poor and it's been put into the hands of men who don't know what it's like to go short of a bit o' bread to put into their bellies.'

The bedraggled queue of women moved forward. A child began to wail and one of the men behind the table raised his spectacles as though to question the sound.

'*Duw*, who does that old goat think he is? I suppose he don't even smell when he breaks wind!'

It was an hour later when Doris reached the head of the queue where she bobbed a curtsey to the old man in spectacles. He looked at her without a change in his expression, gruffly demanding to know her name.

'Doris Williams, sir,' she said slowly. 'I got no job and 'as two children, if it please you, sir.'

He frowned, reading through the lists before him. After a moment, he removed his spectacles and looked at her coldly.

'But you've been here before, haven't you?' The words were almost an accusation and the colour rose in Doris's cheeks.

'Yes, sir, but they didn't give me no money, see? Got to feed my babbas, haven't I?'

'But you were refused aid because you are not legally married – it was all explained to you.'

Doris looked at him in surprise. 'But I still got to have food to put in the bellies of my children; they feel hungry just like you do, sir.'

Rhian moved closer. 'Is there any provision for orphans in the fund?' she asked and the man glanced at her over the top of his glasses.

'There is provision for children born in wedlock, but nothing written here says we have to support immorality.'

'Have you never heard of charity?' Rhian asked angrily and Doris, emboldened, spoke up quickly.

'The good book tells us that there is faith, hope and charity and the greatest of these is charity,' she said, nodding her head emphatically.

The man replaced his spectacles, quite unmoved by Doris's outburst, and gave his full attention to Rhian.

'The good book also tells us that marriage is an honourable estate.' He sat back in his chair as though triumphant. 'Now, if you are not here to make a claim, then I suggest you leave at once.'

'So that you can browbeat people like Doris?' Rhian said flatly. 'You are a hypocrite, do you know that?'

'If you don't leave, I'll send for a constable,' the man said coldly and it was Doris who took Rhian's arm and drew her out into the paleness of the afternoon sunshine.

'The old bugger!' Doris was near to tears, her lip trembled and she brushed at her eyes in embarrassment. 'I could stick him like a pig, that I could.' The defiance vanished and her shoulders slumped. 'What am I going to do now?'

'Look, I'll lend you a few shillings,' Rhian said quickly. 'Now don't refuse, I know you'll give it back when you've got it.'

'I'll get myself another job, don't you fret,' Doris said, her spirits lightening. 'There's a munitions factory starting up soon; it's supposed to be a secret, but I'll be the first one in the place when it opens, don't you worry.'

Rhian looked at her doubtfully. 'But it will be dangerous work, won't it?'

Doris shrugged. 'Aye, it'll be packing shells with TNT, but someone's got to do it and I haven't got much choice, have I?' She placed her hand awkwardly on Rhian's arm. 'Well, thanks for trying to help, anyway.'

Rhian watched as Doris walked away, still burning at the injustice meted out to her, feeling hopeless and inadequate – a fat lot of help she'd been! At last she turned and retraced her steps back to the *Stryd Fawr*; the afternoon was nearly over and the clouds were forming again, racing across the sky and blotting out the sun. A spot of rain fell on to Rhian's face, running like a tear down her cheek. It would be good, she thought, to get back to the comparative peace of the mill where she could weave her patterns and operate the looms and lose herself in her work.

*

The days seemed to run into each other as Rhian found herself increasingly busy at the mill. She worked long hours at the loom, repeating the patterns she had invented herself while she was in Yorkshire. Biscuit-shaded wool, a traditional colour for the base, she blended with browns and pinks and hues of blue as the mood took her.

She spent some of her evenings carrying hanks of good Welsh wool in a basket, selling to housewives on the doorstep. She tried all the harder for knowing that Heinz had become very quiet of late, scarcely venturing outside the mill, and that his big-hearted smile had disappeared.

Rhian burned with anger at the ignorance of the few townspeople who in their panic branded the genial Austrian a traitor.

One day as Rhian threaded the heddles, Heinz entered the long room with his arms full of deep blue wool ready for carding. He wore a woebegone expression and Rhian sighed, knowing she must not show him pity even though she wanted to take him in her arms and comfort him.

'Come on, Heinz, stop being so long-faced. No one is going to bother you now. The search parties have all given up and surely all of Sweyn's Eye know you as a friend.'

Heinz shook his big head. 'It not so, Rhian Gray, what about those women who stoned my Gina and her big with child? I worry sometimes in the night that they will come for me, take me away to the camps like they did with the sailors off the *Brema* and the *Serak*.'

Rhian suppressed a shudder. 'That'll not happen here, Heinz, don't you worry.' She pushed the lever and the belt running the loom moved from the loose wheel to the fast wheel, setting the shuttles into movement. Over the clatter she was aware of Heinz working at the carding machine, his big shoulders stooped; in spite of her optimistic words, she too feared that the hotheads of the town might turn violent and come for the Sinmans one dark night.

By the time Rhian left her loom, her back was aching from bending and her eyes felt full of dust. The evening air was crisp and cold and frost hardened the ground, crunching underfoot. It would be good to sit in the warmth of the kitchen and rest, she thought wearily.

Gina was placing shawls over a series of wooden rails behind the house; they had come off the loom and were freshly washed.

'I'm hoping they might dry a bit,' she said to Rhian. 'I can

118

hang them on the rack in the kitchen later on.'

She fell into step beside Rhian. 'Got rabbit stew for supper,' she said brightly. 'Put it on hours ago, so it should be simmered nicely by now.' She sighed as a piercing wail came from the kitchen. 'Our little Dewi wants his supper too, by the sound of it!' She touched her breast, wincing a little. 'The milk comes flowing in the minute he cries,' she said in wonder.

The warmth of the house seemed to envelop her as Rhian stepped inside. The oil lamps cast shadows over the scrubbed white table and the fire glowed warmly behind the brass fender as she sank into a chair with a sigh of relief.

'Got something to tell you.' Heinz Sinman entered the room and stood rubbing his hand against his apron. 'Got to let you go, Rhian.' His voice was low, his eyes avoiding hers and Rhian felt the shock of his words as though someone had poured a bucket of cold water over her head.

'*Duw*, there's a clod you are sometimes, Heinz!' Gina said angrily. 'Why didn't you let the girl eat her supper before you broke the news?' She sat down and stared at Rhian worriedly. 'I know you've got no home and you can stay here just as long as you like; while I'm alive there'll always be a roof over your head. But what Heinz is trying to say is that we've got no money left to run the mill.' She shrugged and sank back in her chair, then as the baby's wails grew more vociferous she manoeuvred him against her breast.

'If it wasn't for you, Rhian, we'd never have kept our lovely boy; but there's no money, see, not even enough for food let alone for buying more wool.'

Rhian felt as though the ground had been moved from beneath her feet. She heard the tick of the clock on the mantelpiece as though the sound was magnified. A coal shifted in the grate and she stared round the small kitchen which had become like home to her.

'You mustn't think of leaving, mind.' Gina stressed the words. 'You are to live with us for as long as you like – you're one of the family.'

But how could she stay, Rhian thought sadly – she would just be a liability, another mouth to feed.

'Let's have our supper,' she said brightly. 'That rabbit stew smells too good to waste.' She glanced through the window; it was dark outside and she shuddered. She would not dare venture through the streets with only the gas-lights for company, but tomorrow at first light she would look for a job and then she would see Mary Sutton again – plead with her if necessary to buy wool from Heinz.

She went to bed early, lying wide-eyed and staring at the low ceiling which in the moonlight was full of cracks like a crazy paving. She tried to suppress the waves of panic that swept through her. What would become of her if she left the mill, she wondered fearfully. And yet she could not stay and be a burden to the Sinmans. At last she fell asleep, but her dreams were haunted by visions of Mansel Jack laughing at her, holding out his arms and commanding her to come back to Yorkshire and to be with him.

The streets of Sweyn's Eye were silent next morning as Rhian walked in the cold winter air towards Mary Sutton's emporium. It was so quiet that a tram rolling past seemed like thunder and she shivered, drawing her shawl more closely round her shoulders.

Rhian was aware of curious glances following her progress as she crossed the red-carpeted floor of the store and made her way up the darkly-varnished stairs towards Mary's office. Glancing down at her plain flannel skirt and heavy boots Rhian smiled grimly, aware that ladies in soft satin pumps and good woollen coats were more the kind of person to be visiting Mary Sutton.

'Rhian!' Mary rose from her seat behind the imposing desk and held out her hand. 'Sit down, *cariad*, there's strange you should come to see me today. I've had a letter from Mansel Jack in Yorkshire. You're quite right, he does recognise the scraps of patterns I sent him as his own.' She sighed. 'Though quite what I can do about it, I'm not sure.'

Rhian's hands were suddenly trembling and she looked longingly at the letter in Mary's hand, resisting the desire to snatch it and devour the words Mansel Jack had written.

'Well, you can buy wool from Heinz Sinman for a start.' She spoke decisively. 'Poor man is worried to death wondering where the next penny is coming from.' Rhian shrugged. 'The people are against him because he's a foreigner but he can't help that, can he?'

120

Mary shook her head. 'I know how you feel, Rhian, but folks can't help being afraid either. Just this morning I've heard there's a German destroyer lying off Lundy Island – don't know if it's true, mind.'

Rhian stared at Mary with a lump in her throat. 'You're not backing out, Mary?' she asked in a small voice. 'You said you'd buy wool from Spinners' Wharf.'

Mary shook her head.

'*Duw*, when have I ever cared a jot about what folks thought of me?' she asked. 'I'll buy Mr Sinman's wool all right, but will the people of Sweyn's Eye?' She brushed a hair neatly into place. 'But I'll tell you this much, Rhian, I'm not the rich woman I was,' she said softly. 'So many people owe me money that if things don't change soon, I'll have to stop giving goods out on tick.' She sighed heavily, adding, 'And Brandon is feeling the strain of making allowances to the families of his men who have gone to war. Times are bad for everyone, Rhian.'

Rhian bit her lip, feeling defeated, and Mary reached out to touch her hand gently. 'Now don't look so downcast. I've told you I'll buy wool from your Mr Sinman and I will, just this once, but then I can't help any more. I must go where the wool is cheapest and right now that means trading with Mr Mansel Jack in Yorkshire – offered me a cut in price, he has.' She paused. 'I'm a business woman, Rhian, and I need to make some profit if I'm to survive – you must see that?'

'I'm sorry to be a trouble to you, Mary, but the Sinmans are important to me.' As Rhian thought of Heinz, his multi-coloured apron stained with dyes and the trusting smile on his big honest face, she felt near to tears.

As she left the store and stepped out into the cold of the day, she shivered. Her great hope that Mary Sutton's orders would save the Sinmans from ruin had been dashed and there seemed nothing more she could do. She was defeated.

She wandered past the line of the shore and stared at the sea merging into the pearly sky so that there was no visible horizon. Were there German ships out there in the Channel just waiting to attack Sweyn's Eye, Rhian wondered?

She returned to the mill almost reluctantly, for she knew that Gina and her husband would be eagerly waiting for her return.

121

And she would have to tell them that Mary Sutton would take the stock already in hand, but then there would be no further need for production.

In the cosy kitchen where the brasses gleamed brightly and the table shone white in the flickering flames, Gina Sinman was nursing her baby son. She looked up at Rhian and her face was shadowed. 'There's sad you look – does that mean bad news?' she asked softly.

Rhian sank into a chair and stared into the flames. 'Mary Sutton will buy our existing stock, but after that she must deal with the Yorkshire mills, for they can sell their goods more cheaply than us.'

Gina stared at Rhian, her eyes steady. 'And the folks of Sweyn's Eye don't want to put shawls on their backs which were made in the mill of a foreigner, is that right?'

Rhian looked down at her hands. 'I suppose that's about the size of it and in a way you can't blame the people. They don't understand Heinz; they are panicked by all the war stories we're forever hearing.'

She closed her eyes and leaned back wearily in her chair. 'They are afraid, Gina – wanting to strike out at something and Heinz is a convenient scapegoat, so . . .' Rhian never finished the sentence, for there was a loud crash at the front door and the mad calling of angry voices like the baying of an animal.

'*Iesu Grist!*' Gina rose to her feet, clutching her son close to her breast, and Rhian moved in front of her protectively as the door of the kitchen burst open.

'Where is the *bradwr*?' a voice demanded. 'Find that traitor, men, even if you have to take the place apart.'

'There is no need of that.' Heinz moved into the room, his round face sombre, rubbing his injured hand against his apron in a familiar gesture. In the surprised silence, Rhian took Heinz's bandaged hand and held it high.

'Look at this!' she said loudly. 'Heinz Sinman cut off his own fingers so that he would not have to go to war against the people he has lived among most of his life. You, Dai-End-House, what are you doing here with this gang of hooligans? Get off home, the lot of you!'

There was an uneasy stirring among the men like the sound of the sea rippling over stones and Dai-End-House threw down the pick-handle he was carrying.

Rhian's eyes searched the room in the hope of seeing another familiar face, but most of the crowd were strangers, come in from the valleys no doubt.

'Are you men or not?' A harsh voice shattered the silence. 'We know that the soldiers of the 6th are rounding up all the damned foreigners in town and we must do our bit to help. This Sinman fellow might be sending out messages to the Huns. There were two German ships in our own docks and how did they come here? Ask yourselves that!'

'Stop!' Rhian commanded. 'Mr Sinman is no traitor and if you boys are so eager to help, why aren't you in uniform yourselves?'

The leader of the men moved forward; he was a tall man with curling hair and the look of the gypsy about him.

'Are you this man's wife?' he demanded. 'For we will take you too, mind.'

Heinz spoke up quickly. 'I haf no wife,' he said thickly. 'I will come with you, but leave the women alone, they haf nothing to do with me.' His eyes met Gina's, begging her to be silent. In her arms the baby cried out as though in protest.

Aware that attention had been drawn to his son, Heinz lunged forward, throwing himself heavily against the leader. His huge weight bore the man to the ground and for a moment Rhian watched helplessly as they struggled together. And then, like the slow silent pictures that haunt a nightmare, Rhian saw clubs raised, blows being rained down on Heinz's unprotected head and body and in the background Gina's voice rising to a scream.

It was all over in seconds, though it seemed like an eternity, then Heinz was being dragged, half-conscious, out into the street.

'I must go with him,' Gina said brokenly, but Rhian grasped her tightly around the waist, holding her back.

'Not now, *cariad*, wait until morning and then we'll find out where they are being taken. Think of Dewi and what that crowd of animals might do to him if they find out he's a foreigner's child.'

Gina sank into a chair and covered her face with her fingers, trying to stem the tears. On her lap the baby cried too, as

123

though his mother's unhappiness had communicated itself to him.

Rhian walked cautiously along the passageway and found that the front door had been completely torn from its hinges. She tried to lift, it but it was too heavy and with a sigh she gave up the struggle. The street was empty and silent now, the gaslights from the road shimmering over the waters of the river that ran dark red, like blood. Rhian shivered and went back into the house.

Chapter Ten

The copper sheds were steaming, the heat shimmering the air so that the eye was tricked into believing that the very ground wavered. Molten copper hissed and spat as green saplings were pushed into the fiery glow, sending up gushing clouds of steam.

Morgan Lloyd had just finished his shift and stood for a moment with his mutton rag over his face, fighting a losing battle to stem the sweat that darkened his hair and ran in rivulets on to his eyebrows.

'Have you heard the news then?' Peter Harries was fresh and clean, just come in to begin his shift; he hunkered down beside the furnace to take the enamel top from his tea-can, thirst already gnawing at his throat.

'What news?' Morgan rubbed at his neck with the sodden cloth and particles of copper stung his skin.

'Sterling Richardson is going to war – our boss is enlisting in the Sweyn's Eye battalion, got to admire him.'

'Aye, I suppose so,' Morgan conceded, 'though I'm sick of the war and of seeing the town filled with Territorials. Camping out in the streets, some of them are.' He didn't add that his feelings were heightened by the fact that he longed to enlist – he wanted to be a soldier, to be fighting the Hun, but with his dad sick it was out of the question.

'Well, needed here we are, boyo, everyone knows that. Got to have copper for shell bands, so we're doing our bit – don't you fret.' Peter knew a little of Morgan's circumstances and was making a clumsy attempt to be comforting.

Morgan smiled at him gratefully. 'Here, give us a drink,

125

boyo,' he said lightly, and at once Peter handed him the rounded enamel lid of his can filled to the brim with tea.

Morgan drank thirstily, his own brew having been finished a long time ago.

'Get off then, you lucky bugger,' Peter said good-humouredly. 'Wish I was ending a shift instead of just starting.'

The air outside was cold in spite of the pale spring sunlight, and though Morgan shivered it felt good to be away from the searing heat of the sheds.

He was looking forward to a thorough scrubbing and then a hot meal cooked by Mrs O'Connor, who was a wonder at conjuring up a satisfying dinner out of little more than a few potatoes and some scraps of meat. The O'Connors were finding it difficult to make ends meet, for Brendan had lost his job – through drinking too much, it was said, but Brendan O'Connor insisted that a Welshman had taken his place and he was furiously bitter about it.

Morgan had increased his rent of his own accord, giving Mrs O'Connor twelve shillings instead of ten, for he needed little for himself – just enough to keep dad in a small amount of comfort.

He strode uphill with his hands thrust into his pockets, the sweat drying rapidly as the chill air encompassed his body. In time working the copper must take away a man's strength, he mused, but for now his blood was young.

As he passed the towering slag-tips, he caught sight of a sun-yellow daffodil – the first mark of spring – and his spirits lightened. Dad had been bad of late, his cough worsening, but surely with the coming of the milder weather he would take a turn for the better?

'Hello there, sure it's yourself, Morgan Lloyd, catching me at my prayers.' Mrs O'Connor looked up at him as he entered the house and placed her rosary on the small altar she had erected in the parlour.

'*Duw*, don't stop because of me,' he said quickly, embarrassed for he had no religion. 'I'll just get the bath, rub some of this copper dust from my skin before I go up to see dad.'

'That'll be fine,' Mrs O'Connor smiled at him. 'You'll have the privacy of the kitchen, 'tis nice and warm in there,' she

126

said. 'The three youngest girls are out with their daddy and Honey is gone to work.'

Morgan felt his heart sink. 'Work – does that mean that she's been taken into service then?'

'It does, so.' Mrs O'Connor's sad eyes belied her cheerful tone of voice. 'And to be maid to Mr Richardson in that big house is a good chance for her. At least she'll have her own little bedroom and plenty to eat and . . .' her voice trailed away and Morgan saw a tear glint in her eye.

'Don't cry then,' he said awkwardly and Mrs O'Connor shook her head.

'I know it's foolish, but I just don't want to part with my sweet girl. My first-born, Honey is, and I do hope they'll treat her right.'

'Why shouldn't they?' Morgan felt his hands gripped together into fists as he waited for Honey's mother to continue.

'I don't know, I'm being a silly old woman I expect, but there's been talk about Rickie Richardson – him whose wife ran off with a gaol-bird. One for the girls he is, by all accounts.'

Morgan's hair seemed to rise on the back of his neck. 'There are other servants, surely. She won't be up at the big house alone, will she?' He was relieved when Mrs O'Connor shook her head.

'Oh no, not alone, her daddy wouldn't have that. Don't like to think of her going at all, he don't, but we need the money, what with himself being out of a job now.' She sighed. 'Away with you now and have your bath, for your old fellow will be looking to you for a bit of company, sure he will.'

The warmth of the kitchen was welcoming as Morgan pushed the big kettle on to the fire. He took the zinc bath from its hook outside the back door and set it in front of the gleaming brass fender. The silence of the house seemed strange, almost oppressive.

It took several kettles of water to cover the ridged bottom of the bath and even then there seemed more steam than anything else, but Morgan stepped into the warmth and sighed with the pleasure of it. He had no room to sit, for he was a big fellow and it was with difficulty that he settled himself on his knees.

127

He scrubbed at his skin with the bar of carbolic soap, feeling the particles of copper sting his flesh. If he remained in the trade, eventually he would become bronzed because of the copper dust impregnated into his skin. It was not only the trade folks referred to when they called the men 'copper boys'.

Morgan heard a small sound in the doorway and looked up, astonished, to meet Honey O'Connor's startled gaze. For a moment their eyes locked and he saw with a quick beating of his heart how the delicate colour rose to her creamy skin.

She made no move and as though frozen they remained motionless, neither knowing how to break the spell. They stared at each other and Honey slowly lowered her eyes, but not before he saw a glow in them. It was a sound from the parlour which galvanised them into action and Morgan reached for a towel as Honey pushed the back door shut with herself on the other side.

'Are you decent yet, Morgan?' Mrs O'Connor called. 'I need to see to the meal if we're not to starve to death.'

Morgan wrapped the towel round his body and stepped out of the cooling water. 'I'm decent enough, Mrs O'Connor.'

She came into the room, scarcely giving him a glance as he moved to the door awkwardly. 'There's a fool I was not to get my clean clothes ready, like. Upstairs they are – I hope you don't take offence at me being half-naked in front of a lady.'

Mrs O'Connor laughed out loud. 'I may have all girls, but I was brought up with six brothers, so don't think you've got anything I haven't seen before. Get upstairs with you, talk to the old man for a bit and I'll see to the supper, sure I will.'

'Give me a few minutes to dress and then I'll empty the bath out the back; now don't you go trying to lift it, Mrs O'Connor.'

'Oh, away with ye, boy, 'tis like a horse I am.'

Morgan hurried up the stairs and into the room he shared with his father. The old man was asleep and as Morgan dressed he stared anxiously towards the figure in the bed. His father's cheeks were not quite as pale as usual and his breathing seemed a little easier. Hope began to flicker inside him and Morgan's spirits rose – perhaps with the coming of spring, his father's health was going to improve.

'What you looking at, boyo?' His father chuckled, '*Duw*, a

man can't even sleep in private without waking to find his son staring at him, gives a man a turn it does.'

Morgan buttoned up his trousers, 'You're feeling better then, dad?' He sat at the side of the bed. 'Have you eaten anything today? Now tell me the truth, for I'll only ask Mrs O'Connor.'

'Don't bully me, boyo, or I'll fetch you a clout around the ear. Yes, Mr Nosey-Parker, I did eat today – some nice red beef that Mrs O'Connor got me special, like.'

Morgan felt gratitude run like fire through his veins. The Irish family were treating dad as one of their own; they could scarcely afford to eat, yet they were giving him the best. Morgan could never have expected such kindness as he had found at Emerald Court.

'What's the latest talk about the war, boyo?' John Lloyd settled himself more comfortably against the pillows. 'Is it true that all the Germans been rounded up and packed off on the train to an internment camp?'

'Aye,' Morgan sighed. 'The war sounds glorious according to the newspapers, with the British fighting like ten men against the Germans, but it hasn't done Sweyn's Eye much good.'

'From what I read in the *Daily Mirror*, this Captain Grenfell belonging to the 9th Lancers was saved by the Duke of Westminster. Look, it says so here on the front page.'

Morgan took the newspaper and glanced at it quickly. 'Aye, right enough, but this paper's more than six months old; I expect a lot has happened since then.'

'Well, try to get me some new papers then, Morgan, so I can keep up with things. It's the only bit of life I get, lying by here.'

'I know, dad,' Morgan sighed. 'I'm working such funny hours though – I hardly get to the shop in time for papers. What if I give one of the O'Connor girls a halfpenny to fetch the *Mirror* for you tomorrow?' He moved from the bed, sniffing appreciatively. 'I think the supper's nearly ready. Good thing too, I'm starving.'

'You go down and get your grub then, boy. I'll have mine later, after I've had a tot of whisky.' He winked at his son. 'Fine stuff this, Morgan, keeps the old spirits up.' He laughed. 'Spirits, boy – joke, see?'

129

'Aye, I see, and a bloody awful joke it was too – think you're a music-hall turn now, don't you?' Morgan ruffled his father's hair in an awkward gesture of affection.

'Aw, get out of here before I throw you out, don't appreciate wit when you see it.'

Morgan left the bedroom, his throat thick with emotion. His father was a sick man, yet still he found the courage to make jokes.

'Well then, Morgan, good to hear you and your dad enjoying a laugh.' Brendan O'Connor sat at the head of the kitchen table, now neatly covered with a cloth and with the food set out appetisingly.

'Aye, dad seems to be more himself today.' He seated himself next to Honey with a quick glance in her direction, but all he could see was the golden tips of her lowered eyelashes.

'Honey's come home for some more of her things,' Mrs O'Connor said quickly. 'Perhaps after supper you could walk back with her to Mr Richardson's house.' She pushed a plate towards her husband. 'Brendan here's got to go down to the Dublin as soon as he's finished his meal – heard of a job going – well, that's what he says.' Her eyes rested for a moment on her husband, who carved the meat in stubborn silence.

'Yes, I'll walk with Honey, glad to,' Morgan said casually, though his tongue almost refused to form the words.

'Right, 'tis settled now. Let's give thanks to God for our bread and get on with our meal before it's cold.'

Morgan sat back in his chair and let the excited chatter of the younger girls flow around him. He felt warmed by the thought of walking with Honey O'Connor in the night air. She didn't reveal anything of her own feelings, for she kept her face turned away from him. He wondered if she had thought him ugly, catching him in the bath the way she had. She was well brought up and not used to boys; it was doubtful if she ever saw anyone except her father even without a shirt. Well, she had seen enough of him, Morgan thought ruefully.

'A gang of ruffians went down to the Sinmans' place,' Brendan said, glancing in Morgan's direction. 'Dragged that poor Austrian bugger away from his own hearth. Don't know what the world is coming to – did you hear anything about it in work?'

'Aye, heard a bit of it. Rhian Gray was there and tried her best to speak up for Heinz Sinman, but the men were armed with pick-handles, knocked three kinds of . . .' He stopped, aware that there were ladies present. 'Beat him bad anyway, they did.'

'Scared, folks are,' Mrs O'Connor said shortly. 'Afeared of anyone different and who can blame them with this stupid war going on? Saw a soldier the other day without a leg, hopping on two sticks so he was – didn't take long to send him back from France and him half the man he was before.'

'Hush, mammy, don't talk so in front of the children,' Honey O'Connor said softly.

Stella shook back her hair defiantly. 'The saints be praised – will ye listen to the girl? What do you think the little ones got eyes and ears for, then? Aren't they going to see it all for themselves before long?'

'Well, let's talk no more of it in our own kitchen.' Brendan wiped the gravy from his plate with a chunk of bread and Mrs O'Connor sighed.

'There's no pleasing men. All they think of is war – bite their gums over it all night they would – but let a woman join in and it's all wrong, so it is.' She moved from the table. 'Well, all I can say is that I thank God for my girls – they won't have to go to the front and throw their lives away for nothing.'

'You don't know what you're on about, woman,' Brendan said angrily. 'The war has got to be fought whether you like it or not. Can't let them Huns get away with anything or they'll be on our shores taking everything from us, making us slaves – is that what you want?'

'And what do you think we are now, Brendan O'Connor?' Stella sounded angry and Morgan rose to his feet quickly. He was used to the eruptions which flared up in a moment and were as soon forgotten.

'I'll get my coat, shall I?' he said. 'That's if Honey has finished her supper.'

'Aye, go on, you.' Mrs O'Connor was distracted from her row with her husband just as Morgan had known she would be. 'Come on, Honey,' she added. 'Get your bag and be quick, you don't want your new boss to think you unwilling.'

The air was soft, the clouds drifting like dark lace over the face of the moon. Morgan took a deep breath and glanced covertly towards the girl at his side. Honey O'Connor was beautiful, there was no denying that. Her hair, slipping free from the ribbons that held it back, was spun silver, her eyes were large and heavily fringed with golden lashes.

'Good of you to see me back to *Plas Coch*, so 'tis.' Her voice was soft, as though Honey was afraid of shattering the fragile mood that encompassed them both. Morgan longed to reach out and take her hand, but he was wary of offending her.

'Are you happy to be working for the rich folks?' he asked and she shrugged her slim shoulders.

'Not happy, no. But my mammy needs the money and I'd be wrong not to help out now that I'm grown-up.'

Morgan swallowed hard. Honey was only fifteen, a lovely girl who should never have to scrub floors or stand for hours peeling vegetables in someone else's kitchen. He wished fiercely that he could protect her from the hardships that must surely be ahead of her, but he had no right to think that way, no right at all.

'I suppose being in service is better than working the tinplate.' Honey was determined to be cheerful. She hugged the cloth bag containing her few possessions close to her, as though for comfort. 'But 'tis hard to leave home.' Her voice trembled and Morgan kicked viciously at a stone lying in his path.

Together but not touching, they passed the tram terminus and began to walk up the hill away from the town. Glancing back over his shoulder, Morgan could see the sweep of the bay and the sea silver-grey in the moonlight. 'At least you'll be away from the stink of the copper works,' he said in a low voice.

Honey sighed heavily. 'Green Hill is my home, it's all I've ever known and even though me mammy talks about Ireland and the beauty of it, I wouldn't leave the house in Emerald Court for anything, not if I had my way.'

Morgan stopped walking and stared down at her. 'You're growing up, Honey and one day you'll find a follower, a good Catholic who'll marry you and make a home for you.' His voice cracked as Honey stood quite still, her hands grasping the bag tightly.

132

'That's not what I want, Morgan Lloyd.' The words were almost a whisper and for a moment he wasn't sure if he had heard right. What was Honey saying? Hope flickered inside him even as he told himself he was a fool.

'Then what do you want?' The words came out stilted and harsh and Morgan wondered what had happened to his usual easy manner. His emotions were so near the surface that he couldn't think straight.

'I can't tell you what I want.' Honey's voice was still low. 'It wouldn't be proper.'

As her eyes met his Morgan felt a lightness swelling his lungs, rising to his head so that it swung like a carousel with music ringing in his ears. He swallowed hard and tentatively held out his hand. Honey smiled shyly, her fingers slipped cool and trembling into his.

As he moved up the hill with Honey at his side, Morgan felt as if he owned the whole world.

*

Within the elegant building of *Plas Coch* Rickie Richardson was again reading his wife's latest letter. He experienced an immense feeling of satisfaction in knowing that Delmai had become heartily sick of her bid to live on love and wanted to return home. He would let her, of course, but she would never be allowed to forget the humiliation she had heaped upon him by leaving him in order to live on her own in Canal Street and then running away with that gaol-bird Billy Gray.

As for the brat she had borne, he would never consider having it near him. She would have to shake off her sordid past and try to become the respectable Mrs Richardson again. And when she bore him a son, which would be soon if he had his way, Rickie would be a rich man – hadn't Delmai's father promised him that? Glynmor wanted a grandson more than anything on earth and was prepared to leave his considerable fortune in Rickie's charge if he got himself an heir.

Rickie rose from his chair and moved to the window, staring out into the darkness. He would send Delmai a letter telling her of his decision. To travel to Carreg Fach himself would be a mistake; the last thing he wanted was a confrontation with Billy Gray. The man was a maniac, capable of all sorts of

133

violence.

Once Delmai was safely beneath his roof, Rickie would make sure she didn't make a fool of him again. He would fill her with child as often as was possible, give her a real family and then she could forget she had borne the bastard of a criminal. If she was amenable to his wishes he might put her indiscretion out of his mind and treat her as a proper wife, at least outwardly.

He sighed with relief. Of late he had been troubled lest Glynmor, who had aged over the past years, might make his will in favour of some distant cousin or other. However, perhaps now was the time to see Delmai's father and acquaint him with the facts, tell the old man that he intended to be magnanimous and take Delmai back into the fold. Glynmor would certainly feel obligated to him and the thought was a pleasant one.

Rickie poured himself a drink and returned to the window, a feeling of restlessness gripping him. He had taken his fill of women, whores the lot of them, but his life lacked bite. Delmai would provide just that, he thought in surprise. His days – and more importantly his nights – had seemed empty without her. Could he actually be a little in love with his wife?

But that was absurd, for she was cold, distasteful of anything to do with the marriage bed. At least, she had been so before her escapade with this Billy Gray. Perhaps now she had grown up a little, suffered the hardships that came hand in hand with poverty. She might be chastened and so be more eager to please him. The thought gave him pleasure as he tipped the smooth brandy into his mouth.

The crunch of footsteps on the gravel of the driveway caught his attention and he leaned closer to the window. As his eyes became accustomed to the moonlight, he took a deep hissing breath. The young girl coming towards the house was slight of build and daintily proportioned, but what caught his attention was the hair uncovered and swinging loose like an aura of light around her head. She disappeared from sight and with a quick movement, Rickie crossed the room and pulled on the satin bell sash. He stood with his back to the fire, glass in hand, as the parlour-maid responded to his summons.

'That girl – the one who just arrived – who is she?' he asked

134

briskly. As Jinny bobbed a curtsey, the lace on the young maid's cap fluttered like butterflies around her face. She was almost the twin of Letty, the maid who had warmed Rickie's bed years ago in his youth. But although she had a fresh country bloom to her cheeks, so far Jinny had escaped Rickie's attentions. She was a little too subservient and he liked to see a show of spirit.

'She's called Honey O'Connor, a Catholic girl from Green Hill, sir.' Jinny did not look up at Rickie, nor did her facial expression change, but her tone was an indication of the low opinion she had of anyone coming from Green Hill.

'Send her to me,' he said briefly and with another bob, Jinny left the room. Rickie replenished his drink and swirled the liquid round, watching the patterns of light which glinted in the cut glass. 'Honey', that was an unusually poetic name for a girl come from poor Irish stock, he mused.

When she entered the room with her hair tied back from her face, he took a deep breath. She was even more beautiful than he had thought, with fine high cheek-bones, vivid blue eyes and skin like cream.

'I always like to make my staff feel welcome,' he said easily. 'Come along in and close the door.' He waved his hand to Jinny who hovered in the background, and with a quick look she disappeared.

Honey moved with grace, her absurdly small boots peeping from under her long skirt. She was tiny and so lovely – almost a porcelain doll except for the animation in the clear eyes.

'What are you going to do in my house, Honey?' Rickie asked as she shook back a stray hair that had fallen across her serene forehead.

'I'm to be kitchen-maid, if it please you, sir.' Her voice was light and breathless with just a trace of her Irish ancestry, enough to make it charming.

'Oh, dear, that means scrubbing floors and peeling potatoes. Let me look at your hands, my dear.'

She obeyed him without question, turning her palms upward, and Rickie ran his finger lightly over them. 'Far too nice to be spoiled,' he smiled. 'Tell the housekeeper that you're to be put to work as a chamber-maid – that way you'll only need to make beds and dust and that sort of thing.'

135

Honey looked at him in wide-eyed innocence as Rickie lifted a strand of her hair. 'Beautiful,' he said, almost to himself. She fidgeted, uneasy for the first time.

Rickie moved away from her. There was no point in making the girl nervous when there was nothing to stop her running off home to the bosom of her family. Let her become accustomed to the good living she would enjoy at *Plas Coch* and then she would be more malleable.

'Very well then, Honey, off you go back to the kitchen.' He smiled in amusement as she curtsied to him awkwardly; it was quite obvious that she had never been near gentry before.

When the door had closed behind her, Rickie returned to the window and stared out into the garden. The moonlight was brighter now and the trees and bushes seemed silvered as though with snow. Matters were improving for him, he thought in satisfaction; not only was he going to have his errant wife back under his roof, but also a new little amusement to while away any spare time he might have. In any case, it would be good to play Delmai off against a young fresh girl and might make his wife more responsive.

He sank into his chair and stared into the fire that was falling low into the grate. There was only one irritant left to bother him now, he thought with a taste of displeasure – and that was this blasted war. Rickie had imagined it would be over in a matter of months and there seemed no need to put his patriotism to the test.

Unfortunately, the battle had not been so easily won. But there was a spark of hope, for he had heard from his mother that Sterling was going to enlist in the Sweyn's Eye battalion and was thinking of asking Rickie to run the copper works. Trust Sterling to play the hero, Rickie thought bitterly, as he remembered the way his mother had eyed him in her usual disapproving manner.

'You should join up too, Rickie,' Victoria had said. 'You know I want to be proud of both of you.'

Rickie had been tempted to tell her that she had never given him half the devotion she showered upon Sterling, who had always been her favourite son – probably because he was born of her scandalous affair with her lover. It was an old grievance, but it never failed to rouse Rickie's anger and resentment.

His brother had inherited the copper empire left by Arthur Richardson while he, Rickie, the true heir, had been forced to take the crumbs. He filled his glass once more and took a deep draught of the amber liquid, pushing the memories away. At least now, he told himself, he had a good chance of inheriting a fortune from Delmai's father.

Suddenly he felt a sense of wellbeing creep over him. It would be pleasant to have Delmai under his control once more and in the meantime, he could find some amusement with little Honey O'Connor.

Chapter Eleven

It was raining heavily; the sulphurous smoke from the copper works blended with the mists and the stink of it was the first thing Mansel Jack noticed when he stepped from the train on to Welsh soil.

He found a cab waiting just outside the station and climbed into it with a sigh of relief, giving the driver the address written at the head of the letter he held in his hands.

Mrs Sutton had offered him hospitality while he was in Sweyn's Eye and he had accepted readily, hating the thought of a bleak hotel room even though his stay would be a short one.

The correspondence with Mary Sutton had been useful and interesting; he had elicited the information that a munitions factory had been proposed and the land and buildings were ready for leasing. Though he had come to the town first and foremost with a view to dealing with Alfred Phillpot, the idea of settling in Sweyn's Eye at least for the duration of the war was beginning to grow on him.

He was not seeing the town at its best now, he decided, for the sea was obscured by mist and the houses on the western slope of the hill loomed ghost-like through the gloom. But his welcome into the Sutton household was more than warm – indeed, it appeared there was something of a busy social evening waiting for him.

Mary Sutton was a fine proud-looking woman with an honest face and clear eyes and he liked her on sight.

'I hope you'll make yourself at home while you're here,' she said in a soft lilting voice and he returned her smile with genuine liking.

'I feel at home already,' he said quickly.

He had little time to enjoy the warmth of the fire in the large, elegant bedroom, since from the sound of voices rising up from the drawing-room it seemed the soirée was in full swing.

Mansel Jack found himself introduced to so many people that he had little hope of remembering any names. Though one tall, handsome man who gripped his hand warmly made quite an impression on him.

'I'm Sterling Richardson,' he said genially. 'If I can ever be of help, just let me know.'

After a time, Mrs Sutton came to his side and discreetly drew him away from the noisy, crowded drawing-room and towards a book-lined study.

'I thought you would like to talk to Rhian Gray,' she said, smiling. 'After all, it was she who drew my attention to the tricks Alfred Phillpot was getting up to.'

He found his eyes drawn to the slender figure standing near the desk; her eyes met his as though with a challenge and there was a proud lift to her head.

'Rhian, it's very good to see you,' he said as he moved forward impulsively and took her hands in his. Her small fingers curled warmly against his skin and washing over him was a sudden sensation that he could not describe.

She drew away and as she sank gracefully into a chair, he tried to read her thoughts – but as always, she was an enigma to him.

'I'm sorry you had to come all this way,' she said gently, 'but that Alfred Phillpot does deserve to be taught a lesson.'

'Yes, indeed.' He seated himself opposite her. 'Though that's not the only reason I'm here, as it happens.'

'Oh?' Clearly she wanted to know what his reasons were, but she was too polite to ask. He found that he wanted to confide in her, she had always been a sensible, sharp-witted girl.

'I'm going to look at a factory on the outskirts of the town,' he said slowly. 'I've had a very good offer for my mill and I feel it's time I moved on to something new.'

'Oh, but you can't leave the wool trade – how could you be happy leaving it behind?' she asked quickly.

'You did,' he pointed out, but she shook her head.

139

'No, not completely. I'm working at Spinners' Wharf, doing my best to keep it going for the owner – Heinz Sinman – to come back to after the war is over.'

He admired her spirit and her capacity for hard work, running a mill was no easy task especially for a woman.

'And how are your sales?' he asked, leaning forward genuinely interested.

She shook her head. 'Not very good at the moment.' Then she straightened her back. 'But I intend to improve the business, however long it takes.'

Mary Sutton appeared in the doorway, an apologetic smile on her face. 'I'm sorry but there are so many people who want to meet you, including the agent who is leasing the land occupied by the factory buildings – I think perhaps you should meet him first.'

Reluctantly Mansel Jack rose to his feet. 'I'll doubtless see you again before I leave, Rhian,' he said quietly and she inclined her head.

In the event he did not see her again, for the winding-up of the deal for the factory took longer than he had anticipated. And then he felt free to deal with Alfred Phillpot. The following morning he found the man standing behind a counter in the large Cooperative Stores in the middle of the town and for a time, he studied the shifty eyes and restless hands which betrayed Phillpot's character.

'I'm Mansel Jack,' he said at last, leaning forward so that instinctively Phillpot drew away.

'You've been buying my wool, I hear?' His tone was deceptively mild and the man chanced a nervous smile.

'I don't know about that,' his tone was reedy, ingratiating. 'I buy from so many companies, as I'm sure you are aware.'

'But you'll remember my goods better than most.' Mansel Jack paused, folding his arms across his chest, swinging back on his heels with a thoughtful look on his face.

'Oh, why?' Alfred Phillpot was becoming increasingly uneasy.

'Because they're the goods you've been buying cheap, changing the labels and reselling at a greater price as Welsh wool – now do you remember?' It was clear that his words instilled the fear of God into Alfred Phillpot and Mansel Jack

140

leaned closer. 'I haven't finished with you yet, but I'll be back,' he said evenly.

He left Sweyn's Eye almost at once, for there was a great deal of business for him to wind up at home.

Doreen was anxiously waiting for him. 'My dear, you were away so long I was becoming quite worried.' She petted and fussed him and he smiled at her a little ruefully, seating himself near the fire burning in an ornate marble grate.

'Come and sit down, Doreen,' he said calmly. 'There's something I want to tell you.'

She obeyed at once, her eyes wide and Mansel Jack felt himself soften towards his sister. It was not her fault that she was capable of forgetting there was a great big world outside the four corners of her house.

'I'm going to move to Wales, at least for a time.'

'Move to Wales, indeed? I never heard such nonsense!' The words exploded from Doreen's lips.

'Will you listen to what I'm saying, lass?' He tried to keep the edge of impatience from his voice. 'The country is at war and if I were a few years younger I'd be in the thick of it. As it is, I'll be running a munitions factory.' He paused. 'It'll be a challenge, lass. I'll be making shells, which at least is more like war work than weaving wool.'

'But Mansel Jack, why can't you run a factory here in Yorkshire?'

He rose to his feet, sighing in exasperation.

'The factory in Wales is built and ready to go into production, also the place is reasonably cheap.' He regarded her steadily. 'In any case, Doreen, I've had a very good offer for the Mansel Mills and I'm prepared to take it. If I don't, a newer and larger mill will be built on our doorstep and then we'll be finished anyway.' He smiled. 'I'll not be leaving the wool trade entirely; I might buy myself a small run-down mill in Sweyn's Eye as a sideline – something to be built up from nothing, just as I did with our own mill. It's a good business move – trust me Doreen.'

When she did not reply he shook his head impatiently. 'I've made up my mind to go, Doreen. You may stay here in Yorkshire, if that's what you want.'

She put her hand to her mouth, her eyes wide with distress.

141

'I don't want you to live alone and yet to move away from my friends, live among strangers – it's too much to ask.'

Mansel Jack rested his hand on her shoulder comfortingly. 'It won't be for ever, so don't be distressed.'

Doreen began to cry, pressing a linen handkerchief to her face. She was a sorry sight, her eyes red, her usually neat hair falling free of the restraining pins.

'And what about Charlotte, your wife-to-be, have you considered her feelings?'

Mansel Jack realised with a flash of surprise that he had not. But Charlotte was a sensitive woman, she would understand his need to be involved in the war in the best way he could.

In his mind's eye he suddenly saw an image of Rhian, her vivid face so full of character and beauty and the soft loveliness of her voice which seemed to haunt him.

'I'm going upstairs to change,' he said with forced calmness. 'I'd like supper on the table by the time I'm washed and ready.'

In his room he stared out at the gardens, shadowed and dark now that the weak sun was dying so that the thick oak trees bordering his grounds seemed flat and dead. Why did Rhian Gray continue to come into his mind, he asked himself. She was so different, beautiful and fiery but certainly not a lady in the way that Charlotte was. The two women were poles apart, yet the fire in his belly told him which one he desired.

*

The mill at Spinners' Wharf seemed to slumber in the swirls of mist that rose up from the river: there was no chattering of looms to break the silence in the low buildings. Rhian sat in the kitchen staring into the fire, feeling lost and alone.

There was the sound of light footsteps on the stairs and she forced herself to smile as Gina came into the kitchen, her baby wrapped in a shawl Welsh fashion.

'I'm all packed,' Gina said softly. 'You know why I have to go – say you understand, Rhian.'

'There's a soft thing to say, of course I understand. I'd do the same thing myself if I was in your shoes.'

Gina sighed. 'I'm not sure if I shall be able to find my Heinz, I only know that all the prisoners have been sent to an internment camp at Camberley. But I must try to find him,

142

there's nothing to be gained by sitting here moping.'

Gina handed Rhian the keys of the mill. 'It's yours, for as long as you want it,' she said gently. 'We may be back one day if God is willing, but you will always be part of the mill and part of our family.'

Rhian felt tears burn her lids and her lips trembled even as she smiled.

'Let me come with you to the station, Gina – that's the least I can do.'

Gina shook her head. 'No, I don't want you to come with me, Rhian. I'd only blubber like a child when the time comes to leave. Better if we say goodbye now, isn't it? Come on, give Dewi a kiss and wish us well.'

As the door closed behind Gina, Rhian stared into the fire. The coals shimmered through the black-leaded bars of the grate and she rubbed at her eyes impatiently. The silence was almost tangible and the building seemed empty of life. Was this to be her future, this silent loneliness?

She sighed. At least there was work for her to do and she must not waste time in self-pity. Now she must be responsible for everything from the dyeing of the wool to the final wash. She would have to put her heart and soul into it, she told herself fiercely. But doubts teased the edges of her mind, for who would buy from her?

Well, it would do no good to sit around and stare into the fire, she chided herself. She must stir herself out of her apathy, for there was no other way she could earn her living except by weaving – not unless she went with Doris to the munitions factory.

Suddenly she felt overcome with emotion and couldn't bear to sit in the silent kitchen haunted by the shadows of Gina and Heinz Sinman. She needed to be among people so, drawing a heavy woollen shawl around her shoulders, she let herself out of the house.

The mists were clearing from the river and the red swift waters roared between the banks, for the tide was high. Rhian stood staring into the murky depths for a time, searching her mind for a way out of her problems. She would break her back producing wool, but that was not the trouble – she must find customers. Perhaps the townsfolk would buy from her now that Heinz was gone.

She walked on past the river and made her towards the heart of the town. The copper works spewed forth green smoke and noisy gushing sparks which intermingled with the greyness of the skies and at first glance everything appeared to be normal. Yet subtly it was all altered. The war had touched the town with harsh fingers, throwing many out of work. Men of the Territorial Army filled the streets – peacetime volunteers who now, confronted with the realities of war, swilled ale and laughed loudly to cover their fears.

As Rhian walked past the Flint Mill, she heard through the open window the rise and fall of raucous voices. The smell of stale beer swept up at her from the doorway and the sawdust that covered the floor trailed out into the street.

She seemed to be surrounded by bustling busy people who had purpose, a destination, yet she felt more alone than ever. It was as though she had no form or substance, was a ghost moving unseen among the living.

Leaving the busy streets, she made her way uphill to where the serene houses of the rich of the town perched on the hillside facing the sea. She stood for a moment outside *Pen y Bryn*, wondering if Heath might be home. The need to be with and talk to another being who cared that she was alive was strong, so Rhian swung open the large gate, making her way steadily along the pathway.

She stared at the windows, looking at her as though they were blank eyes, and had to force herself to lift the brass knocker. The sound reverberated through the house and she suddenly felt self-conscious about her appearance. Wearing her thick dark flannel skirt and a heavy shawl, and with a faded bonnet covering her hair, she looked like someone begging at the doorstep, she thought ruefully.

'There's a fright you gave me, Rhian Gray, banging on the door like the bailiffs come to take away the furniture!' Mrs Greenaway opened the door wider. 'Come on in, you. Heath Jenkins is not home yet, mind, but he would want you to wait, I know that much.'

Gratefully Rhian stepped into the hallway. It was a modest house by the standards of the others on the hill, but gracious and elegant in comparison with the cottages of the workers.

Heath Jenkins could be proud of his achievements, Rhian thought warmly.

'There's sad about that nice Mr Sinman being taken off to an internment camp – don't seem right at all.' Mrs Greenaway moved towards the kitchen and not knowing what else to do, Rhian followed her.

The room was mellow as though filled with sunlight, the white scrubbed table gleamed with cleanliness and on the stove against the far wall, a conglomeration of heavy black pots simmered and danced.

'Sit down by here and we'll treat ourselves to a cup of tea.' Mrs Greenaway pushed the kettle on to one of the hobs and smiled easily at Rhian. 'There's pale and peaky you look, not eating enough I'll warrant.' She rubbed her hands against her spotless white apron. 'Well, stay and eat with Heath Jenkins. I know he'll insist on it and so will I.'

Rhian seated herself in one of the kitchen chairs and leaned forward, hands supporting her chin. 'I'm all right, Mrs Greenaway, it's just that I'm worried about Gina and her son. Worried about myself making some sort of living too, if the truth be told.'

Mrs Greenaway warmed the brown china pot and spooned tea into it with generosity. 'Likes my brew strong,' she said with a smile. 'Now, tell me all about it.' She seated herself and placed the cups in position, pouring the tea quickly with the deftness of long practice.

'Gina Sinman gave me complete charge of the mill,' Rhian said softly, 'but the trouble is – where can I sell the woollens? Toil like a slave I will, doing the job that really is the work of two people, but what's at the end of it when no one wants to buy from me?'

Mrs Greenaway scratched at her greying hair beneath the crispness of her starched cap. 'Aye, I see the problem, *merchi*.' She frowned pensively. 'What about Mary Sutton – can't she be persuaded to buy from you? Heath would surely put in a word with his sister.'

Rhian shook her head. 'Mary's done all she can, but times are difficult for her too because of the war.'

'It's a puzzle then, isn't it? What about giving up your work in the mill? Don't you think you could find a job somewhere

145

else?'

Rhian shook her head, a set expression on her face. 'I must make a success of it for the Sinmans' sake if not my own. Anyway, the only jobs about are those in the munitions factory and I wouldn't do that for all the tea in China.'

The sudden sound of the outer door opening startled the two women. '*Duw*, there's Heath Jenkins home for his dinner and me not half-ready yet.' Mrs Greenaway swept the teacups into the sink and rubbed at the white table with a cloth. 'Go on you, Rhian Gray and keep the man company. Talk to him until I get myself organised or it's the boot for me!'

Heath was hanging his coat on the stand in the hall and his face lit up when he saw her. He came towards her and put his arm around her shoulders, drawing her close.

'There's a lovely surprise to walk into my house and find you here! It would always be like that if I had my way.'

His love was like a balm and Rhian closed her eyes, leaning against the young strength of him. The fondness that had been with her since her childhood rose up now and swamped her, so that she felt in herself a longing to cling to Heath and have him take away all her troubles.

'There's a light in the your eyes that gives me hope,' he whispered. He bent from his great height and kissed her eyelids gently and Rhian responded by putting her arms around him and burying her head in his shoulder.

He led her into the drawing-room and together they sat on the big comfortable sofa, hands entwined.

The silence surrounding them was an oasis of peace and Rhian wanted to cling to the moment. Her loneliness had vanished and she felt warm ar.d secure.

Mrs Greenaway smiled as she stepped into the room. 'The supper will be ready in a couple of minutes – lovely onion stew it is and mutton pie cold to follow. I bet you're starving, Heath Jenkins?'

He relaxed against the cushions, still holding Rhian's hands. 'Sounds nice enough to eat!' he joked and Rhian felt lightness and laughter bubbling through her. She had always loved being with Heath; even as a young spoilt girl who thought of no one but herself, she had enjoyed his gift for humour.

The meal – taken in the small dining-room lit by a chandelier blazing with candles – had almost a festive air. Rhian found herself forgetting her worries and laughing for the first time in what seemed an eternity.

'Why not stay here tonight?' Heath asked as he poured her a glass of porter. 'We've a spare room and there's nothing to take you back to the mill, surely?'

Rhian pondered for a moment, tempted by the offer, for the house on the wharf would be cold and silent. But finally she shook her head.

'I'd better get back,' she said. 'I wouldn't like to leave the building empty, there's no knowing what might happen.'

Heath frowned. 'Well, that makes me more uneasy about you staying there alone, Rhian.'

'Don't worry about me, I'll be all right. Anyway, the mill's my home and I won't be driven out of it.'

The moon was silvering the trees when at last they left the house and began the journey downhill towards the town. Once or twice Rhian turned to look over her shoulder, troubled by an uneasy feeling that they were being followed. The street-lamps shone in pools of brightness and she tried to shrug away her worries, telling herself she was probably nervous and overtired. But the feeling persisted and as Heath led her into a grove of trees Rhian felt a prickling of fear. She stopped walking and grasped his arm.

'There's someone behind us, I'm sure of it,' she whispered and Heath looked down at her, his eyes unreadable in the darkness.

'I think so too, but keep on walking and don't panic – it's probably nothing to worry about.' His voice was curt as he took her hand and began to walk rapidly towards the clearing.

The bushes rustled and a twig snapped and as a shaft of moonlight penetrated the branches of the trees, figures came silently out of the darkness. Heath drew Rhian close, his arm protectively around her.

'What do you want?' he demanded in a strong voice. 'We've got no money or valuables if that's what you're after.'

As the men moved closer Rhian could see that there were four of them, their faces covered with white silk scarves.

'It's not money we want, boyo, it's your hide!' The voice reached out sinuous and snakelike in the silence and Rhian felt

Heath stiffen at her side.

'Well, if your business is with me then the lady can go.' He spoke harshly, pushing Rhian away from him. She had almost reached the clearing when a hand caught her by the hair and held her fast.

'That's not what we want at all, is it, gel? There's daft you must think us, you'd be back with a constable before we could start on our business with Mr Jenkins.'

He took off his belt and dragged Rhian's arms around the trunk of a tree, tying her wrists together with the leather so tightly that the buckle bit into her flesh. But her fear was not for herself as she watched the men advance towards Heath.

A fist lashed out and Heath dodged it, turning to trip his assailant who fell heavily on to the ground, groaning in pain.

'The bastard, I think he's broken my leg.' The words were spoken in small gasps of pain. 'Give it to the coward, boys – and one for me as well.'

Heath fought valiantly, hitting out with all his strength, but he was outnumbered. Yet it still took a mighty blow with a branch of a tree to put him on the ground. Rhian screamed as she saw a boot swing towards his head and connect with a sickening sound that brought from him a hissing sigh.

'You'll kill him!' she cried out, anger chasing away her fear. 'You mad dogs, you're too cowardly to take him on in a fair fight – there's scum you are, the lot of you!'

Her words seemed to strike home and one of the men motioned the others back. 'That's enough to teach him a lesson. Leave him his present, boyos, and let's get out of here.'

Rhian watched as a small box was laid beside Heath's unconscious form and then the men were stumbling away into the darkness carrying their wounded companion between them.

As she struggled against the cruel leather which held her wrists, tears of frustration and pain clouded her eyes. But she must free herself, for Heath was still lying silent on the ground. She tugged at the belt with her teeth, ignoring the bitter taste of the leather, twisting her head and worrying at the buckle until at last she felt it loosen.

With a cry of relief, she ran towards Heath and crouched beside him on the grass.

'Heath, oh God Heath, what have they done to you!' She rubbed at his hands, seeing with despair the way his eye had swollen to the size of an egg. His mouth was cut and there was blood on his shirt. Rhian lifted his head and cradled it against her, wondering frantically if it was best to stay with him or leave him to find help.

He stirred in her arms and moved awkwardly and Rhian felt relief pour through her like a stream of pure joy. 'There, there, *cariad*, don't you try to move now, just lie still a minute and get your breath back.'

'At least I put one of them out of action.' He mumbled the words through swollen lips. 'And when I find out who's done this, I'll have the bastards' guts for garters.'

'Hush now, just rest a minute and then I'll help you back to the house.' Even as she spoke, Heath was stumbling to his feet.

'What's this?' Rhian picked up the box and held it out to Heath and he took it, staring at it for such a long time that she wondered if he was still dazed.

'I recognise it,' he said at last. 'Boxes like this have been given out to several of the younger men of the town.'

'What do you mean?' Rhian asked, putting her arm carefully around Heath's waist. 'What's it supposed to be for?'

'Here, take it and look inside,' he answered, leaning heavily against her.

She stared in puzzlement at the contents of the box. 'There's stupid, it's just a white feather.'

He took the box and threw it to the ground, grinding it into the earth with his heel. 'It's the feather of cowardice, Rhian – it's because I'm not in the Army. If only the fools knew that I tried to join up and the sergeant turned me away.'

'It's so unfair.' Rhian spoke in a low voice. 'I know better than anybody that you're not a coward. Come on, *cariad*, let's get you home and clean you up and then we can see what damage has been done. We may need to get a doctor out to you.'

Heath paused and looked down at her; his puffy, bruised face looked strangely boyish in the moonlight.

'Does the way you're looking at me mean you could bear to be the wife of a man branded a coward?' he asked softly and Rhian felt a thrill of anguish run through her.

149

'It means that I care very much about you, Heath Jenkins. Let that be enough for now, is it?'

But as she steered him back uphill towards his house, her heart was beating swiftly and her thoughts were far away . . . and the image in her head was not of Heath Jenkins but of a man called Mansel Jack.

Chapter Twelve

The sea whispered softly on the curving shoreline, rippling inwards before sucking at shells and tiny pebbles, the waves chattering on the ebb. The sky was streaked with red, merging with the bloody ocean and dazzling the eye.

Heath stood tall, very conscious of his uniform which was warm to his skin – but it made him even warmer inside to know that now he was a fighting man. He could cast aside the white feather which had taunted and nagged at him, lying on his bedroom table lifting and fluttering with every breeze, coquettish like a lady's fan.

He had taken Rhian's advice and returned to the recruiting office, making sure that the sergeant on duty was a man who did not know him. This time he had been accepted without question, for the war was a devouring, insatiable monster.

Now Heath became aware of Rhian watching him and he smiled at her, placing his arm on her slim shoulder.

'How does it feel to have your sweetheart go for a soldier then, *cariad*?' he asked softly. Rhian's eyes slid away from his and he was puzzled, unable to understand her mood. 'I shan't be killed, I'm too wily for that, there's soft you are to be so downcast.'

Rhian's expression did not alter as she moved away from him, staring down into the rippling waves that laved her shiny boots.

'The war has taken so much from Sweyn's Eye and now you're leaving too. Soon there'll be only old men and boys left, it's a frightening thought.'

Heath caught her slim waist in his hands and drew her to

151

him. 'Good, then you won't fall into temptation while I'm away, will you? In any case, you can depend on the older men to look after everything until we soldiers return.' He was unconscious of the pride in his voice. 'Come on, let's walk.'

He took her hand, leading her to the higher dunes, standing for a moment to look at the golden sand that stretched into an enormous curve around the town. To the east the bay ended in the docklands and to the west was the rocky outcrop of the Mumbles Head. The bay was sheltered as though in curving arms and the breezes coming off the water were soft and salt.

It would be a wrench to leave it all behind and he was taking the chance that on his return there would be no steel works to give him the security of a job. He might return maimed or crippled, but that was a risk he was also prepared to take for he was eager for the battle. His young blood sang as he thought of the conquests he would make. Cowardice had never been part of his being and it had distressed him more than he could bear to be branded with the white feather.

'You are already far away from me.' Rhian spoke softly and the words which from another woman might have been an accusation from her were a simple statement. He swept her into his arms, feeling the smallness and softness of her, wanting what he had never yet tasted – her sweetness.

'*Cariad*, let me take you home, I want you so much.' He whispered the words in her ear and felt her stiffen. He knew her fears, the dreadful memories that plagued her, but he needed to make her his own before he went into battle.

On the tram that swayed and bucked its way up the hill, he sat close to her, holding her hand, his blood singing. She was pale, her eyes shadowed and he loved her so much that all he wanted to do was to take away the ghosts that haunted her.

The house was empty and Heath was relieved, for the presence of old Greenie would have made things difficult.

'Look, Rhian, you must trust me. I would never hurt you – you know that, don't you?' His hands cupped her cheeks so that she could not turn away; her eyes were dark with fear.

'Heath, I don't think I can . . .' The whisper trailed away as he touched her soft lips with his own. The blood rose in a blinding heat within him and he wanted to crush her against him, but his clear mind urged caution.

He took her upstairs and into his room and she came gently – a lamb to the slaughter, he thought, pitying her. When he laid her on the bed she stared up at him, trembling like a frightened animal. He lay beside her and cradled her and she lay still, obedient, cowed. And yet he would be making her whole again, he told himself; he would teach her that loving was good and clean, a part of life that was meant to be beautiful.

'There there, *cariad*.' He hushed her as though she was a baby, opening her bodice and lightly touching the firm young flesh . . . teasing, gentle. He must take his time and not give in to the agony of desire that brought his senses tinglingly alive. He had experienced many women, but never one that he loved more than life itself.

'Try to be easy, my lovely,' he whispered in her ear and she clung to him, burying her face in his neck.

'I'm frightened, Heath.'

He smoothed back her hair, kissing her eyelids and then her mouth. 'I will take care of you all my life. I'll worship you always, Rhian, and I want to know you're truly mine before I go to war.'

He felt her relax a little and with a flash of insight realised that his words had broken down the last of her defences and that now he could teach her the beauties of love.

When he moved above her she was pale, her face taut, her eyes tightly shut. He kissed her eyes, her mouth, taking his time, exerting all his powers of restraint. When she moaned in fear he was almost tempted to let her be, sorry in his heart for her, yet if he left her now she might never know the joy of loving.

She cried out, a small animal sound and he quickly covered her mouth with his own. 'My darling sweetheart, I love you,' he whispered, gentling her, his hands stroking softly. His kisses were tender and with mighty self-control he moved slowly in the rhythm of the waves that gently invaded the shore.

And then he sensed a change in her. The coldness of fear was melting, her arms reaching round him to hug him close. Jubilantly he kissed her with more passion, parting her lips with his tongue. He held her tightly against him as though he could truly make her one flesh with himself, his heart soaring

153

in happiness because she loved him in return.

She cried when it was over and the tears misted her beautiful eyes, but Heath was happy because the biggest hurdle of her life was over and now she would know now that physical love was not the nightmare which had haunted her memories these past years.

'Are you content, *cariad*?' he asked softly, kissing the salt tears from her cheek. She turned to look at him and there was tenderness in her gaze that warmed him.

Silently they lay together on the bed with arms entwined and Heath felt a closeness with Rhian he had never known with any other woman.

After a time she sat up, shyly covering her breasts. 'There's grateful I am, Heath. You were so sensitive, I feel as if I never knew the real you before.' She leaned against the warmth of his shoulder, her hand moving over his skin so tantalisingly that he turned to her with a question in his eyes. After a moment she nodded, looking steadfastly at him even though the heat rose from her proud young breasts up through her neck and coloured her cheeks.

Heath took her more fervently and his heart beat with hers as one. He had never felt such joy in his life; even if he died in the trenches he knew that God had been good to him, giving him all he had ever wanted.

The beach was lit only by a silver moon as Heath took Rhian home. He walked with his hand around her waist and stopped to kiss her warm soft mouth, love melting his being.

'Stop it, Heath,' she chided gently, 'someone might see us.' She tried to pull free, but he held her fast.

'I don't care who sees us, tomorrow I'll get a licence and we shall be married.' He held her close to him for a long moment. 'Though you couldn't be more truly my wife than you are now at this moment.'

She reached up to caress his cheek and then spun away from him, running down the hill with hair flying and skirts swishing around her ankles.

He caught her easily and drew her breathless into the shelter of his arms.

'Heath, do you really love me?' she asked, her voice like the whisper of the waves on the shore. He sensed her uncertainty and kissed her full on the lips.

'Would Heath Jenkins have anything but the best? You're going to be my bride – I shall put a ring on your finger and everyone will know that I couldn't live without you.'

'I love you Heath, really I do,' she whispered and for a brief moment he wondered why she was being so vehement – was she trying to convince him or herself? He brushed the thought aside and caught her hand in his. 'Come on, let's get you home.'

The streets of the town were deserted. The hill rose in a gentle incline towards Spinners' Wharf and the gurgling of the ruddy waters could be heard clearly as they neared the buildings. Above them shimmered the lights from the houses in Green Hill and further along the banks of the river the works lay in shadow, except for the belching of sparks and smoke that intermittently lit up the night sky.

Over all, the moon lay a silver shroud that beautified the ugly, turning the town of Sweyn's Eye into a fairy-tale land. Heath's heart swelled with pride; he was going to fight for all this, for his home town and for Rhian, for all he held dear in the world.

At the door of the mill, he took Rhian in his arms. 'Shall I stay with you tonight?' he asked softly but she shook her head.

'No, best go home, have a proper night's sleep.' She smiled wickedly. 'For if you stay with me, there'll be little enough of resting. Even in my inexperience I can see what a devil of a man you are, Heath Jenkins!'

He kissed her tenderly, his hands caressing her shoulders with gentleness rather than with passion.

'Tomorrow I'll see about our wedding, my lovely. Good night and God bless you.'

He turned once as he walked away and saw that she had lit the lamp and was framed in its light, waving to him. His heart was full and in spite of the manliness of his stride and the crackling of his new uniform, he had to admit there were tears in his eyes.

Rhian slept little that night. She lay staring at the ceiling in the flickering light of the candle . . . wondering, reliving the moments when she had lain in Heath's arms. She had made love with him and he had been kind, teaching her gently as he had promised that human contact was not the ugly thing she had believed it to be. For that she felt a deep gratitude to him, for now she was a woman and knew she was capable of passion.

At first she had resisted him and the pain had enveloped her body and mind but he had been careful, restraining himself for her sake. Gradually her emotions had emerged like a beautiful butterfly opening its wings.

She sighed softly, feeling a mingling of joy and sorrow as she hugged her pillow to her. Before slipping into bed, she had stood naked before the full-length mirror in her bedroom and had really stared at her reflection for the first time. She knew that she was desirable and felt a voluptuous sense of pleasure at the creamy flawlessness of her skin. Her breasts were full and high and her belly unmarked. And she wept because now Mansel Jack would never look upon her.

The thoughts which had been tormenting the edges of her mind all night would be denied no longer and Mansel Jack's image pressed behind her tightly closed lids. She had told herself that there was no future for any kind of relationship between them yet the knowledge that one day the situation might change had given her a kind of perverse comfort.

Now there was no going back, for she had committed herself to Heath Jenkins and she was his. In a few days' time she would be his wife in law as well as in deed, put beyond the pale of Mansel Jack or any other man. The brief happiness she had felt in Heath's arms vanished as Rhian turned on her side and bitter tears soaked into her pillow.

Her first feelings on waking were a mingling of elation and sadness. She turned over on her back and stared up at the ceiling, thinking about the happiness she had found in Heath's arms. He had brought her the gift of her womanhood and she owed him her loyalty – if she could not give him her love, it would not be for the want of trying.

But why was there the sadness and a longing for Mansel Jack? That part of her life was over and done with; she would only hurt herself and tear her emotions to pieces if she constantly harked back to the past.

She ate a solitary breakfast of bread and cheese, deciding not to light the kitchen fire until later in the day; she needed to save coal, for the stocks were getting low.

In any case, she couldn't linger in the house when there was a great deal to do in the mill. She dressed warmly in a stout calico camisole, covered by a thick blouse and a warm turnover. Her flannel skirt swung to her ankles as she combed her hair quickly.

The air outside was filled with the scents of the town. The sulphur from the copper works lay heavily on the air, the clouds were low and glowering. Rhian could smell the dampness of the freshly washed wool that hung outside on wooden rails and cursed her foolishness in not taking the turnovers into the house last night.

She rubbed her fingers against the wool and found it was soaked with dew, then glanced up at the sky hoping for a brisk wind to blow away the storm clouds.

The rushing waters of the tributary that branched off from the main source of the river ran gurgling alongside the low mill building, turning the wheel that produced the power for the machinery.

At Mansel Jack's mill there had been water turbines, but then he had been more successful than Heinz Sinman. Just before Rhian had left Yorkshire he had been talking of installing gas turbines, which would be even more efficient.

'Stop it, stop thinking about him!' she said fiercely, her words sounding unnaturally loud in the stillness of the morning. She moved nearer the bank and stared down at the stream, marvelling at the rush of water which served the mill so well.

The wheel rods ran the length of the long building, suspended from the ceiling. These rods were rotated continuously and each machine was attached by a belt to a pulley on the overhead line shafting. To switch the machines on and off, the drive belt was slipped from the drive pulley to the adjacent free-running one and it was second nature to Rhian to operate the fast and loose pulleys.

She set the 'willy' into operation, feeding the raw wool into the body of the machine where a large roller studded with long teeth chewed and gnawed at it. As she brushed stray pieces of wool from her hair, her thoughts turned to Heath and she wondered what he was doing this morning – was he arranging

157

their marriage? She viewed the prospect with mixed feelings and decided not to dwell on it.

Rhian watched the 'willy' as it performed its dual function of blending two different colours of wool and opening up the matted fibres, breaking down the woollen mass into smaller pieces.

She felt tired before the day was half begun and unaccountably there were tears in her eyes as she stared around the lonely mill. The only company was the clatter of the machines and she had never felt so lost in all her life.

She longed to ask advice from someone wise, to be told which direction she must take. And yet she knew the answer already. She was bound now to Heath Jenkins, she had given herself to him, allowed him to think he was the only man for her and so he was. If only the memory of Mansel Jack's dark, handsome face wouldn't keep creeping into her mind . . .

'There's daft you are, Rhian Gray!' she told herself fiercely. 'Get on with your work, girl, or there'll be no food to put in your belly come tomorrow.'

She brushed back her hair and straightened her shoulders. However momentous the events of last night had been, she must concentrate on her work. Wool-making was too dangerous a job to do with only half a mind on it.

It was while she was eating a meal of cheese and cold ham that Heath came to the mill to see her. One look at his face told her that all was not well. He took her in his arms, held her close and smoothed back her tangled hair.

'Tomorrow I'm to go for training in North Wales, *cariad*,' he said gently, 'there's no getting out of it.'

Rhian touched his cheek with her fingers. 'It will be all right, Heath, I'll wait for you – don't look at me like that.'

He buried his face in her neck, his body trembling. 'I wanted to make you my wife, I'm afraid of losing you.'

'Hush now, of course you won't lose me. Who will be here to look at me unless I suddenly take it into my head to fall for Dai-End-House and him with no teeth in his head!'

Heath moved away from her. 'There were practical reasons for marrying you too; as my wife, you would have the security of an allowance from my pay. But as soon as I come back we'll be wed, Rhian, I promise you that.'

158

'I know that, love. It's all right, I tell you. Don't worry.'

'But I do worry, my lovely girl, I can't help it.'

'Now how do you think I've managed on my own these past two years? I'm no longer a baby; I'm all grown-up, especially now!'

A smile lit his face. 'Come on, let me take you to bed,' he said softly.

Rhian kissed his mouth, longing to protect him; he was like a lost boy and she needed badly to comfort him.

'I love you, Rhian, so much that it hurts me in my gut. When this war's over we'll never be parted, you'll see.'

She took his hand and led him towards the narrow twisting staircase. 'Don't talk of war, not now, talk to me only of love.'

He was gentle and held her with a tenderness that was enough to break her heart. His approach to her was subtly altered, it was as if she was the teacher now and he the pupil and Rhian found great joy in her role as protector and comforter. She closed her eyes but, to her shame, saw Mansel Jack's face above her in place of Heath's. Thrusting his image aside together with her guilty thoughts, she clung to Heath's shoulders. 'I love you, my darling boy,' she whispered, but she knew that it was like a candle to the sun compared with her feelings for Mansel Jack.

Later, when Heath had gone and Rhian was alone in the silence once more, she stared at the greyness of the unlit fire and tears formed a hard lump in her throat. It was as if something was telling her deep down in the secret places of her heart that she would never see Heath Jenkins again.

Chapter Thirteen

The sun brushed light and shade over the twin mountains of Townhill and Kilvey, revealing on the eastern slope the stricken scars where nothing would grow on land devastated by copper blight. And on the western side of the river were the gaping-tooth wounds of Townhill where the bright new housing estate was meant to be, the project halted by the war.

The sea ran high, in full flood, eroding the dunes of Brynmill and – further along the five-mile stretch, towards the docks – punishing the arms of the piers with thunderous blows.

And Mr Walter Long had introduced the National Registration Bill into the House of Commons . . .

Katie Murphy sat in the untidy kitchen of her father's fresh-fish shop in Market Street, staring at the registration form in despair. "Tis a barrack-room lawyer you have to be to fill in this damn paper!' Her young brothers looked up at her briefly and then returned to the more important task of playing soldiers with wooden pegs painted with moustaches and red cheeks, each one of them a general in Kitchener's Army.

'Jesus, Mary and Joseph! Will you listen to the girl!' Mrs Murphy poured a full measure of gin into her glass. 'You, with all your brains, finding a little piece of paper difficult! That's not like you, Katie. Come on, what really ails you?'

Katie brushed back her red-gold hair and leaned forward on her elbow. 'I'll have to leave Mary's shop, mammy, can't stay there any longer – it appears that being a shop-girl is not doing my duty.'

Mrs Murphy's eyes became sharp. 'What is it you're gabbling on about now, child? Leave Mary's shop, indeed –

and where else would you get paid such good money?'

'Sure and don't I know all that?' Katie stared down at her finger-tips. 'But mammy, serving in a shop isn't helping the war any and I'm going to have to work in the munitions factory. They need all the young, strong women they can get, for the work is . . .' she paused, 'well, it's very hard.'

'I've had one of them forms too, so has your daddy – anyone between fifteen and sixty-five has had one, it don't really mean nothing.'

Katie sighed. 'You won't have to work, mammy, you've got the boys to look after – and daddy's too old. I'm the only one in this house who will be affected by the Registration Act.'

'I don't see that it means you *have* to change your job at all. Where does it say that?'

Katie held out the form. 'See, mammy, it asks: "Are you willing to serve your country in national service for the army or in the manufacture of munitions?" '

''Tis a foine thing when folks are told what they can and can't do.' Mrs Murphy drank deeply from her glass. 'I'm only glad that me boys are still too young for any such nonsense.'

'So am I,' Katie said softly. 'Before they grow up it will all be over, please God.'

She rose and moved restlessly to the window. A pale sun was breaking through the clouds and the harsh winds that came in off the sea were easing. She was tired of being cooped-up indoors; she would take a walk down to the front and watch the ships, ignoring the fact that they carried more sinister cargo now, and try to forget the war and all its ramifications.

'I shan't be long, mammy. Going to get a bit of peace away from these noisy brothers of mine.'

'Aren't you going out with Mark today?' Mrs Murphy asked quickly and Katie smiled.

'No, didn't I tell you he has to work an extra shift? There are so many men gone away that he's short-handed. See you later, mammy.'

Outside, Katie took a deep breath and looked up towards the sky. There was little to be seen except for the smoke that gushed and spat from the chimneys of the works on the river-bank.

She walked through Green Hill and smiled warmly at

Honey O'Connor who was just emerging from her house.

'Well, Honey, I haven't seen you at mass for a long time. Where have you been keeping, then?'

Honey's friendly smile lit up her face. She was a sweet, beautiful girl, Katie thought with a trace of envy, untouched as yet by the harsh side of life.

'I'm in service now up at the Richardson house.' She fell into step beside Katie, a wry expression on her face.

'Nothing wrong in that – is there?' Katie asked and Honey glanced quickly away.

'It's Mr Rickie, he's too familiar, I mean, I don't like the way he puts his hands on my shoulders and such.' She sighed. 'But then perhaps that's the way with the gentry.'

Katie stopped in her tracks. 'Now don't you be takin' any nonsense from that man,' she said firmly. 'They all try it on a bit, specially with a new young maid like you, but don't be havin' any of it, do you understand.'

Honey's eyes were troubled. 'I don't know what to say to him, he's not doing anything wrong . . . well, not really.'

'Tell your mammy if he does then and get yourself out of his way. There's more than one young girl been ruined by her master – don't think of us as people at all, some of them.'

They walked a short way in silence and Honey brushed back the trailing tendrils of hair that escaped from under her bonnet. 'Anyway, now I'm sixteen it looks as if I'll end up working the munitions,' she said. 'I've just been filling in that form they sent us – did you get one, Katie?'

'Sure enough, everyone is getting one except the very young or very old,' she smiled. 'We might find ourselves working together, then.'

Honey smiled ruefully. 'It can't come quick enough for me, anything to get out of Mr Rickie's way.'

'Well, it's not going to be any picnic in the munitions, I don't suppose,' Katie said doubtfully. 'Don't really know what we'd be doing, but I'm sure it will be dangerous.'

Honey paused. 'Enjoyed my day off, so I did, but I'm not looking forward to going up to the big house. A good job it is, so my mammy says, but she doesn't have to do it.'

Katie watched the slight figure of the young Irish girl as she turned to climb the hill towards the west, where the fine houses stood facing the Channel. Poor Honey, she was such an innocent and it didn't seem right for her to be in the charge of a man the like of Rickie Richardson. Rich he might be, but he was no gentleman, for Katie well remembered the gossip that swept Sweyn's Eye when as a young boy he had got a maid into trouble and then had her packed off somewhere, never to be seen again.

She moved on towards the docks, where fussy tugs hooted protests at the larger ships, dipping and bowing in the swell, chivying them into place like sheep. There she sat on the dry-stone wall and stared out at the ocean which lashed the shore as though to smash all before it.

It was difficult to believe that the country was at war, for merchant ships still berthed at Sweyn's Eye. Indians rubbed shoulders with Chinese, walking the docklands under the heavy skies as though without a care in the world.

And yet Katie had seen evidence of the war, for wounded and maimed soldiers were becoming a more frequent sight in the old town. They wore the blue of the hospital uniform so that others would know they had been injured fighting and were not cowards; men could be so child-like at times, Katie thought.

A warm feeling swept over her as she allowed her mind to dwell on the hours she had spent with Mark the previous night. He was a fine strong man, fit for a soldier but held in Sweyn's Eye by the necessity to produce steel and tinplate. He at least was safe from the battles which were being fought on foreign soil.

Sometimes she sensed a restlessness in him, a feeling that he wanted to be where the action was taking place, yet common sense told him that some had to remain in the town and work the metals that were the lifeblood of the nation.

At last she turned her back on the sea which always brought her a sense of calm. It was time that she spoke to Mary and told her that she would soon be leaving the store. Katie couldn't help feeling sad – she and Mary had been friends for a long time – but the shop didn't really need her and it seemed that the munitions factory did.

The emporium was busy in spite of the inclemency of the day and as Katie moved through the crowds of shoppers, she wondered that the rich still had money to spend. The goods Mary sold were of a high quality and reasonably priced, but what she had originally intended to be a store for the poor of the town had become a fashionable place where the gentry sat for afternoon tea in the new lounge with its potted palms and oak panelling.

'Katie, there's nice to see you! I thought when you didn't come into work this morning that you were sick.' Mary smiled over the top of her polished desk and Katie, shaking her head, stood near the window watching the people below hurrying through the narrow streets like ants.

'I must give in my notice, Mary,' she said gently. 'Got to work on munitions, there's no choice – can't exactly call shopkeeping a reserved occupation, can I?'

Mary looked down at the nib of her pen thoughtfully. 'Had your registrations form, have you?' she asked, her face troubled. 'Katie, if you leave me I won't have anyone I can trust to carry on when I'm not here.'

'It's not up to me, though; there'll be a lot of changes now, Mary,' Katie said ruefully. 'Looks like you'll be taking on older women to do the work, for us younger ones must serve our country. Jesus, Mary and Joseph, where is it all going to end!' Katie felt anger run though her veins, for she loved her work in the store – loved the smell of the bolts of cloth, the scent of lavender polish on the furniture, the gracious elegance of the emporium and the nice clothes she wore to work. It would be a vastly different proposition when she was in the factory.

'You're right. It's going to affect us all,' Mary said in a low voice. 'This war has a lot to answer for, mind. There's Mali crying her eyes out last night because she hasn't heard from her husband for over a week – breaking her heart she was, half angry with Sterling Richardson for enlisting and yet proud to the point of bursting at the same time. And don't I just know how she feels?'

Katie sank into a chair. 'The war is something we can't see and don't know anything about, yet it reaches out with greedy hands to take what we love best.'

Mary bit her lip. 'My brother Heath was set upon by thugs, beat him sore they did, gave him the white feather . . . and that

164

hurt Heath more than the bruises. Wanted to enlist ages ago and they turned him down because of his bad chest. They're not so fussy now, snapped him up like a dog with a bone the second time he tried.' She sighed. 'Well, let's forget about the war and I'll treat you to a cup of tea and a Welsh cake in my new restaurant, is it?'

Katie forced herself to smile. 'Right then, Mary, it's about time you put your hand in your pocket, for sure 'tis mean you're getting in your old age!'

*

The train stood in the station puffing and blowing, the steam issuing forth in frightening intensity with sparks falling like stars to burn out before they touched the platform. Katie tucked her grub-pack more firmly under her arm. She felt almost as though she had been taken backwards in time, for she was wearing thick boots on her feet instead of light pumps and her flannel skirt was covered by a coarse apron.

'*Duw*, Katie Murphy, what are you doin' here?' The voice was a familiar one and she turned to see Doris standing beside her.

'Same as you, sure enough,' Katie smiled warmly. 'Doris, I hardly recognised you without coal on your face. Had good times when we both worked in the Canal Street Laundry, didn't we? But that's a long time ago now. So you're working the munitions too? Thanks be to the saints that there's one familiar face here this morning!'

'I am that,' Doris said gleefully. 'Be like the old days, won't it, and I wonder how many of the crowd will be working in the factory with us?'

'Well, I know two who won't be,' Katie said, 'that's Mary Sutton and Mali Richardson.'

'Aye, I suppose Mali has to look after her babbas, and her husband away doing his bit an' all. And there's Mary in her shop – can't leave that to anybody else. But me, glad I am to have a job, mind – starving I'd be if it wasn't for the munitions factory.'

The train swallowed up the crowds of women, sucking them into dusty carriages. Slowly it began to move out of the station and Doris sat beside Katie, clutching her arm in fear.

165

'*Duw*, don't fancy doing this every day. I never did like trains, last one I went on was going to Carreg Fach to visit my sister. Is it supposed to make that awful row, do you think?'

'Trains have been running in Sweyn's Eye for more than sixty years, Doris, so don't worry about it, you'll be quite safe.' Katie settled herself back in her seat and looked around her. The carriage was occupied mostly by working girls like herself, but two well-dressed women were sitting near the window, faces turned away as though unwilling to recognise the lower orders with whom they were forced to travel.

'I bet them two won't be packing shells like us,' Doris whispered, following Katie's glance. 'Office toffs they'll be, I bet a pound to a penny.'

'I think you're right, Doris.' Katie hid a smile.

Doris pushed at her arm. 'It's a wonder they'll put themselves out to sit in the same train as the likes of us. Don't like it though – you can tell by the tilt of their noses, can't you?' Her voice was loud.

'Hush, Doris!' Katie said, biting her lip to prevent herself from giggling. 'They're doing their bit sure enough and they can't help the way they're made, I don't suppose.'

'Well, they'd better not look down their noses at me,' Doris continued. 'Give 'em a swipe, I will – good as them any day, me.'

The factory was like nothing Katie could ever have imagined. The vast room was filled with tables upon which shell-cases stood, stiff and military, innocent enough without the packing that would turn them into harbingers of death.

Down the centre of the room like sentinels stood the lathes, silent now but waiting to spring into raucous life. The women stood in little crowds, anxiously wondering what was expected of them, for the practice of filling shells was not like any other occupation they had ever known.

The noise of chatter ceased as slowly the groups of women became aware that someone else was present. Katie looked up and nudged Doris into silence as a man came forward into the body of the factory. He was tall and ruggedly handsome but more than that, he had a presence that was indefinable.

'I think it's God come down from his heaven,' Doris whispered in awe and Katie frowned at her.

'Hush, don't blaspheme like that, you heathen!'

Doris was not in the least offended, she gazed in open-mouthed admiration as the man's eyes roved over the women who were waiting for him to speak.

'The work you are about to do is dangerous.' His voice fell clearly into the silent factory, strong and masculine and with the hardness of the North country giving it zest. 'None of us yet realise exactly what the dangers will be, but we will learn together.' When he smiled not one woman in the factory was left unmoved by the raw animal quality of the man.

'I'm Mansel Jack. I won't ask for quarter or give any, but I *will* be fair. Any grievances must be brought to me. And I shall expect ideas for improving the work conditions from you. Now, I suggest you go to your tables and then I'll come round and show you what is to be done. One last word: we are handling explosives here, so it is essential to have respect for your own safety and that of your workmates.'

'Isn't he the giddy limit!' Doris giggled excitedly. '*Duw*, what would I give to have a man like that in my bed!'

Katie smiled and linked arms with her, leading her towards one of the tables. ''Tis mad you are, girl – and what would the likes of him be looking at us for when he could have any fine lady in the land?'

'Aye, you're right, but a girl can have her dreams, can't she?'

Katie led Doris to the nearest table, smiling at a young girl who stood alone and was embarrassed by her loneliness.

'Going to be part of our gang?' Katie asked easily and the girl smiled in relief.

'*Duw*, I was beginning to feel there was something wrong with me.' Her voice was light and breathless, tiny as was her physical stature. 'I'm Janey Jenkins from Landore near the copper works – and there's daft I feel, standing here not knowing what to expect.'

Doris put her head on one side. 'Are you kin to Heath Jenkins and his sister Mary who is gone all posh now?'

The girl's colour rose. 'Yes, I am – and not posh at all is Mary, still one of the workers in her heart. Just good at making money she is, mind.'

'No offence meant,' Doris said a trifle huffily and Katie hastened to smooth over the awkward moment.

'Mary is a real friend, sure enough, always fine to me and to you, Doris -- didn't she lose her job in the laundry rather than put you out of work?'

'Aye, she did that, I'll give credit where credit's due.'

Mansel Jack moved easily towards the table, the force of his personality reaching out and silencing the women although he had not spoken. For a moment he studied them individually and Katie felt he was memorising their faces.

'Your job will be to fill the gaines,' he said at last, holding up a tube. 'This is a gaine and it is to be pushed into the TNT. Its purpose is to ensure that the fuse in the nose-cap effectively detonates the contents of the shell.'

He stared around the small group, waiting to see if they understood what he had said, his glance resting on Katie for no more than a moment but filling her with a tingling sensation she could not explain. All she knew was that this Mansel Jack was a man of power and the like of him she had never seen before.

His face relaxed into a smile. 'You, Katie Murphy, will be in charge of this table. You may all come to me at the end of the week and collect the uniforms you will be wearing.' As he moved away the girls stared at each other in silence for a long moment.

'Isn't he a lovely-looking man – and how did he know your name, Katie?' Doris asked.

Katie shrugged. 'I've no idea, but it's my guess that there's not much that one doesn't know about any of us. Come on then, we'd better start work or we'll be out of a job before we've begun.'

At first Katie – along with the other women – handled the explosives with timidity as though packing eggs. But soon familiarity with the job took over and she found herself singing along with Doris, wondering if perhaps Mansel Jack had been over-cautious in his warnings.

By the end of the day, Katie was so tired that she could hardly stand. The shift had lasted twelve hours with short breaks for dinner and tea, and her arms felt as though they were no longer part of her.

'I'll have just enough strength left to fall into bed,' she said, her voice cracking with weariness.

168

Doris turned, a wry expression on her face. '*Duw*, you're lucky. I got to go home and feed my kids; me mother will have had a guts-full of them and that's for certain. Still, got to do your bit in this life, haven't you – and when I think of my man gone to fight the Huns I'd do anything to help the war effort.' Tears trembled on Doris's lashes and she brushed them aside impatiently. 'There I goes, blubbering like a babba myself, don't take no notice of me.'

On the train journey back into Sweyn's Eye, Katie leaned back in her seat too weary to talk. Her wrists ached with the effort of holding and filling the gaines and her skin tingled. She examined her hands – they seemed to be tinged with yellow but it must be a trick of the light, she told herself.

'There's a strange day it's been,' Doris said in a low voice. 'What do you think of the boss then, Katie? Isn't he the finest, handsomest man you ever saw?'

'*Duw*, I could lay down and die for him.' The small voice of Janey Jenkins broke the silence and Doris turned to look at her disapprovingly.

'I wasn't speakin' to you, *merchi*, so don't stick your nose in where it's not wanted, right?'

Katie sighed and roused herself. 'Hush now, Doris,' she said wearily. 'We've got to work together for the saints know how long, so don't let's quarrel amongst ourselves. Come on, give Janey a chance – she's done a good day's work today, you must admit that.'

'Aye, all right,' Doris said reluctantly. 'A good worker she is an' all, can't say no different.'

'Then that's settled,' Katie sighed with relief. 'Perhaps now I can have a bit of peace.'

She closed her eyes, realising she had not answered Doris's question. What did she think of Mansel Jack? she asked herself. Well, one thing was sure: if she had not already been so much in love with Mark, she might have fallen head-over-heels for her new boss!

The grey of night greeted her when she stepped off the train, the platform suddenly filled with women who walked wearily towards the entrance, a silent stream of humanity thankful to return home.

'Jesus, Mary and Joseph, I don't know how I'm going to

make my way up that hill,' Katie said, sighing as she leaned on the fence that bordered the railway line. 'I must get some new boots, the floor of the factory is as hard as flint and cold with it.'

'Come on,' Doris took her arm. 'Lean on me – I'm like an ox, my man always says so.'

Katie brushed back her red-gold hair and forced herself to move forward. 'I'm going to get my mammy to bring in the tin bath and fill it to the brim with hot water, and then I'm going to soak for hours and hours.' She smiled, though every part of her seemed to ache. 'Working in the shop was like playing a game compared with the munitions factory,' she said wryly.

'Well, I'm glad of the money I'll be getting,' Doris said eagerly. 'The work's hard, right enough, but no worse than humping coal scuttles in the Canal Street Laundry. Soft you've gone, Katie Murphy, you'll soon toughen up and then you'll enjoy yourself, see if I'm not right.'

At the foot of Green Hill Katie paused. 'Well, it's different roads for us now,' she said. 'I'm going to miss leaning on your strong arm, sure enough. See you tomorrow at the station . . . and Doris, don't be too hard on Janey. She can't be more than seventeen and she's got a lot to learn yet.'

Doris nodded. 'Aye, you're right, and she's not such a bad sort really. Just there's some people you takes to and some you don't, can't be helped.'

As Katie trudged wearily up the hill towards Market Street, she could hear the mournful notes of Dai-End-House's accordion drifting on the silent air. She paused and bent down to rub at her ankles in turn, but her feet seemed to be swollen to twice their normal size. 'Gone soft, just like Doris says,' she told herself and with an effort covered the last few yards to her home.

It was almost midnight by the time Katie was ready for bed. She brushed back her hair with long sweeping strokes, almost too tired to lift her arms, then sat on her bed staring at the flickering light of the candle, her eyes misting with fatigue. She had spent only a short time with Mark and when he had laughingly complained about the acrid smell that clung to her, she had bitten his head off.

He had been wonderful, so kind and understanding; he had

taken her in his arms and kissed her gently, cradling her as though she was a baby. How she loved him! Yet his visit had left her with a tinge of unease, for he had talked a little about the war and the urge he had to enlist. She had taken great pains to point out that he was needed at home working in the copper and he had readily agreed. But there had been a restlessness about him which had frightened Katie.

She snuffed out the candle and lay back against the pillows, her eyes burning as though covered in sand. She longed for sleep, yet it was as elusive as the shadows that stalked the room when the moon slid silently through the clouds.

With a sigh, she pushed back the bedclothes and got up to stand near the small window, staring down into the street. The town of Sweyn's Eye slumbered like a beast beneath the skies marred by the ever-present copper smoke. What did the future hold, Katie wondered fearfully. The war had altered the even tenor of the town; shops sported posters of Lord Kitchener pointing an accusing finger at the young men, telling them their country needed them. Factories now produced the trappings of war: the shells, the copper bands, the weapons that would be used to bring death to ordinary soldiers.

Katie shuddered and took her rosary from the shelf, running the beads through her fingers and muttering prayers with an urgency that had not possessed her since she was a child. At last she climbed into bed and lay wide-eyed, staring up at the ceiling, giving up the unequal struggle to find release in sleep.

*

Mansel Jack stood in the window of the modest house he had rented on the sea-front and stared at the smooth waters that flowed out into the Bristol Channel. Sweyn's Eye was a beautiful place and he felt sure he had taken the right decision in coming here.

His second meeting with Alfred Phillpot had been fruitful. The man was so frightened at the thought of being exposed as a cheat that he would have paid any price for his silence. He smiled grimly; it was poetic justice that the profit Alfred Phillpot had made on the woollens should go towards leasing the munitions factory.

Mansel Jack had received a gratifying price for his mill in

Yorkshire and though it was a wrench parting with the business, the excitement of the move he was making had been adequate compensation. Doreen had decided to remain at home, keeping the house like a shrine waiting for his return. He smiled – she would wait a long time, for he fully intended to buy Spinners' Wharf and make a success of the little mill.

Restlessly, he thrust his hands into his pockets. He was having difficulty in tracing the owner of the mill, but then difficulties had always made him more determined. His face softened as he thought of Rhian Gray, struggling to keep the place going, slaving from morning till night for a business that was not hers.

He moved from the window and jerked the curtains together. What was wrong with him? he thought impatiently. The girl was becoming an obsession.

Turning out the gas-light, he stood for a moment in the darkness. Soon he would go to see her, but he would wait until the time was just right.

Chapter Fourteen

The train swayed and groaned as it wound slowly between the folding hills into the town of Sweyn's Eye. A mist was rising from the turgid waters of the river, mingling with sulphurous smoke from the copper and tinplate works that presented to the newly-arrived the ugliest face of the town.

Delmai sighed and lifted the baby higher in her arms, grasping her bag awkwardly, her mouth dry and her heart beating uncomfortably fast as she peered through the narrow begrimed window of the carriage.

The platform was thronged with people. A farmer leaned heavily on a shooting-stick, his flat cap shadowing his face, his wide-legged trews tucked into heavy riding-boots. A girl – small and pale, dressed in a frilled apron and woollen turnover – stared eagerly into the train, her eyes wide. Delmai shuddered – would her own daughter wear that look several years from now? She shrugged the uncomfortable thought aside and pushed her way out of the carriage towards the open door, a sudden feeling of fear gripping her. And then she saw him . . . her heart lurched and she trembled as though she was physically ill.

Rickie was standing aloof from the crowds on the platform and as she watched, he took out a watch and consulted the ornate face before tucking it away into his waistcoat pocket once more with a deliberate movement that betrayed his impatience. It seemed he might stride away at any moment and, panicking, Delmai forced her way through the throng of people.

'Rickie!' She waved her hand in a wild gesture that almost

knocked the bonnet from her head. He turned, staring at her coldly as his eyes lit on the child in her arms. Then he took a few steps away from her and she hurried towards him desperately.

'Rickie, wait a moment, please wait!' Delmai hastened to his side, grasping his arm, but he averted his gaze.

'Get rid of that child and then you can come up to the house and we'll talk.' He pulled away his arm roughly and the next moment had disappeared into the crowd.

Delmai wanted to weep. She had cherished a small hope that he would look at Cerianne and relent, that he might accept the little girl into his home and into his life, but she realised now that she had been deluding herself.

She sank on to a bench and stared around her, wondering in desperation what would happen if she left the baby here alone on the station platform. Would she be cared for or would she simply remain alone for ever with people constantly passing by and looking the other way until, half-starved, she was put behind the grim walls of the workhouse?

Delmai lifted Cerianne higher in her arms and left the station, standing in the *Stryd Fawr* and wondering where she could turn. When she looked up the slope towards Green Hill a thought tingled on the edges of her mind, gaining strength even as her feet led her upwards away from the bustling shops as hope blossomed anew.

The hill seemed to grow more stony and steep with every step, and her shoes slipped against the hard rocky surface. Delmai was breathless and when the child in her arms began to cry, she shook her angrily. 'Be quiet! I'm doing my best for you, aren't I?'

At the brow of the hill she paused, leaning against a dry-stone wall, resting Cerianne on the hard rock and struggling to regain her breath. A young girl with honey-gold hair was coming towards her, staring curiously, and Delmai drew herself upright.

'Can you tell me where Rhian Gray lives?' she asked without preliminary and the girl answered in a soft Irish brogue.

'She'll be at Spinners' Wharf – it's down there by the stream, not very far.' The girl held a finger tentatively towards Cerianne and the baby gurgled with pleasure, her blue eyes

174

wide, her lashes curling upwards so sweetly that Delmai felt tears constrict her throat.

She turned quickly and hurried in the direction the girl had indicated. As yet she had no idea what she would say to Rhian, or how she could convince her that she must take Cerianne, but convince her she must – there was no other way.

The house was small and behind it stood the long building of the mill. When Delmai knocked at the door, it swung open under her touch. The kitchen was empty but a cheerful fire glowed in the grate, so Rhian could not be far away. Then she heard the clatter of the loom and sighed with relief.

Delmai put Cerianne on the rug and looked down at her with tears trembling in her eyes. 'Now don't you touch anything, be a good girl!'

Biting her lip, she left the house and hurried towards the roadway. Her hands were trembling and her eyes misted with tears. But Cerianne would be safe with Rhian, who would have to keep her now.

Her arms felt cold and empty and Delmai paused for a moment, tempted to turn back and to go to her child. She stood in the mean cobbled street with its small cottages crouched drunkenly together; this would be her life for evermore if she didn't show some spirit now. 'I'm sorry, baby,' she whispered and then with renewed determination hurried away from Green Hill.

Afterwards she did not remember the journey up the western slopes to the big house on the hill. She was faintly aware of the surprised stare she received from the young maid who opened the door to her, and realised she must look like a peasant dressed as she was in a rough flannel skirt and heavy boots, her hair covered with a harsh calico bonnet.

'Go upstairs for God's sake and get yourself scrubbed clean,' Rickie said in disgust and ashamed, Delmai hurried up the wide staircase towards her room. Even in her confusion and despair, she felt the warmth of the house fold around her with comforting arms. The light shone through the huge window and in the ornate grate a fire glowed with warmth. She took a deep breath, knowing that never again would she forsake all this, no matter what happened.

The bath was prepared and as the soft scented water flowed

175

over her skin Delmai felt renewed. She rubbed briskly at her naked flesh, as though to remove the long months of grinding poverty and dirt. Briefly she thought of Billy, for the perfume drifting from the water was making her feel voluptuous. She closed her eyes, trying to imagine him here in the gracious bedroom and her heart sank.

He could never be part of her life again – her time with him was an episode best put away from her. Now she must be a dutiful wife to Rickie Richardson and please him in all things.

Rickie would take the money and lands which her father would leave her and make them his own, then she would have nothing except what her husband provided by his goodwill. Yet if she could bear him sons that would satisfy him and he would find release with his whores as he had always done. That was the answer then – she must get with child as soon as possible.

Dinner was a strained affair. Rickie sat staring down the long length of the polished table, the glitter of lamplight on the silver cutlery reflected up into his face. He had scarcely glanced at her as she came down into the dining-room, but Delmai knew she looked well in the rose-pink velvet dress that was gathered into a series of tiny bows at the back, falling softly to her satin pumps. But she was ashamed of her hands. They were rough and red like those of a kitchen-maid and she hid them swiftly in her lap.

Rickie ate his meal in silence and Delmai simply picked at her food, unnerved by him and almost wishing that he would rant and rave – anything but stare about him as though he was alone. He had not asked about the baby and Delmai did not expect him to, yet her heart felt as though it was being squeezed inside her as she imagined Cerianne's soft warm arms winding around her neck.

She glanced quickly at her husband, afraid that he would read her thoughts, but he was helping himself to more meat and seemingly engrossed in his task. He was fuller of figure, Delmai realised – manly and almost handsome – but there was a coldness about his features which marred his looks.

'Well, Delmai.' His meal finished, Rickie turned to look at her and her heart beat faster even as she tried to compose herself. 'So you've come home?'

Delmai hung her head. 'Yes, Rickie, and I'm grateful to you.' The words stuck in her throat and her husband laughed knowingly.

'Yes, so you should be.' He leaned back in his chair and stared at her through half-closed eyes and with such intensity that she shifted nervously in her chair. 'You've changed,' Rickie said thoughtfully. 'I think, my dear wife, that you may have learned the meaning of humility.'

Delmai kept her eyes lowered, clasping her hands nervously in her lap. She remained silent, not knowing what he expected of her.

'I trust there will be no childish scenes when it's time to go to our matrimonial bed?' He was being deliberately provocative and she glanced up at him with a little of her old spirit.

'There's no need to play cat and mouse with me, Rickie,' she said shortly. 'I fully intend to do my wifely duty and provide you with sons.' She glanced away from the scorn in his eyes, her heart fluttering in her breast.

'I'm very pleased to hear it,' he said dryly. 'If that oaf Billy Gray can sire a child on you, then I'm certain that I can.'

Delmai felt the colour rise to her cheeks. Was she going to be subject to her husband's cruelty all her life, were even her creature comforts worth the loss of her pride and spirit?

'Rickie, don't treat me like an imbecile,' she said in a low voice. 'I know I have wronged you and I'm grateful that you are taking me back, but we must come to an amicable agreement. I won't and can't put up with your taunts and cruelty. I'm a woman with feelings and I have given up my child in order to please you – what more can you ask?'

He studied her in silence for a moment and in spite of the colour hot and stinging in her cheeks, she did not look away. He nodded. 'Very well, we shall forget your misspent and lowly past and you shall be treated with every respect as my wife, but you must do your duty without making me feel like a leper each time I take you to my bed. If you can lie with a gaol-bird – and a man from the lower orders at that – then you cannot find me repulsive.'

On impulse Delmai rose from her chair and leaned over her husband, running her finger along his cheek. 'I don't find you repulsive at all, Rickie. Indeed, I've been thinking what a

177

handsome man my husband has become.'

He took her hand and drew her close to him and she felt his kiss with a sense of surprise. There was nothing unpleasant about the touch of his mouth on hers – perhaps there was even a tingling of sensuousness, knowing she was to sleep with her husband again after such a long time.

Rickie rose to his feet, scraping his chair against the polished floor. Then he took her in his arms and held her close, and breathlessly she melted against him. His skin smelled fresh, without the acrid tang of coal-dust and sweat that clung to Billy.

He was not so aggressive in his approach either; had he changed or was it her own experiences which had altered her response to him, Delmai wondered curiously? She was not unwilling when he led her upstairs to the master bedroom where fresh flowers stood in the cut-glass vase near the bed and a fire burned cheerfully in the grate and she felt welcome.

'Help me with these fastenings,' Delmai said, her voice almost a whisper. She felt a strange, heady excitement as though she was indulging in an illicit affair rather than going to bed with her own husband. She had forgotten the silky feel of a gentleman's skin and as Rickie lay beside her on the bed, her hands were caressing his shoulders and drawing her to him. Why had she ever found him distasteful, she wondered in surprise? It must have been her own naïvety, her innate sense of false modesty which lying with Billy Gray had torn asunder. But she should not be thinking of her lover . . . not with her husband's arms around her.

Comparisons were invidious and yet inevitably must be made. Billy was a born lover who held sensuousness in his fingers, able to raise her to the point of ecstasy with a touch. And yet Rickie was in his own way an accomplished lover too. He was more gentle, sensitive even. Perhaps he had learned a great deal about relationships during the long months they had been apart? Or was it that she had entirely misjudged him?

'There you see, Delmai, aren't I better than some ape-man?' He tipped her face up to his. 'Go on, my sweet wife – tell me I'm better than your gaol-bird lover.'

Suddenly an imp of mischief lit up Delmai's mind. She moved sinuously against Rickie, pressing herself close, feeling her nipples begin to harden.

'I'm waiting for you to prove it.' Her voice was a hoarse whisper.

With a low animal growl, Rickie arched himself above her and like a hoyden she lay back, her hair spread fan-like over the pillows, her eyes misted with passion. But even as her husband took her, one small corner of her mind was cold and clear. 'Thank you, Billy Gray, for the gift you gave me that nothing and no one can ever take away.'

*

In the morning, Delmai was awake early. She stared up at the high, ornate ceiling and felt the comfort of her bed and for a moment experienced a sense of peace. Then came the thought of her child – Cerianne, with her large innocent blue eyes and soft rose-petal skin – and she longed to hold the little girl in her arms. She told herself to be calm, for Cerianne was safe with Rhian Gray who was a flesh-and-blood relative. Billy's sister would be well able to care for a child – women like Rhian Gray were bred to it.

She became aware that Rickie was awake and staring at her; she smiled at once and touched her fingers to her lips in salute. As he sat up against his pillows, she was unsettled slightly by the look of amusement in his eyes.

'You won't have a life of ease for very long, you know, so make the most of it,' he said dryly.

She leaned towards him, allowing the sheet to slip away from her body. 'What do you mean?' she asked provocatively and he laughed.

'It's clear you have not heard of the new Registration Act, under which we are all obliged to fill in a form and state our willingness to work for our country while we are at war.' Turning over to face her, he explained, 'People of all sorts are being asked to work in the munitions factory or do active service; times have changed, Delmai, and I can't have my wife lagging behind, now can I?'

He was talking nonsense, she decided, pressing herself against him, not unaware of her nakedness and the light that was growing in her husband's eyes.

'By God, you've changed,' he said, his mouth resting against

179

her shoulder. 'I think it was almost worth the humiliation of losing you to that no-good gaol-bird.'

For a moment Delmai was uneasy at his reference to her past, then she remembered that she had the key to this man now and that her own sexuality was all she needed to enslave him.

Perhaps she should put it to the test once more, just to reassure herself that she could control Rickie. She snuggled down under the bedclothes and giggled as her hand reached towards him – one thing her husband could not hide was his need for her.

And if Delmai's first flush of desire for her husband was diminishing, she was far too clever to let him know it.

Later, she went down the flight of stone steps that led into the kitchens, for she meant to take over the reins of the household and make the servants accept her again by sheer force of will. She wondered with amusement if there was more of her father in her than she had realised, for he had a way of issuing orders which had people obeying him instantly.

The familiar smell of carbolic greeted her as she entered the warmth of the kitchen. Cook looked up from her chair near the fire with surprise and a certain amount of hostility, for this was her domain. Slowly she placed her cup of tea on the gleaming table.

'I was just about to bring you the menus for today, Mrs Richardson.' She tucked her hair neatly into place and Delmai watched her for a moment in silence.

'Well, go on, Mrs Cunningham. I have come to you, so tell me what you have planned and then I'll tell you if it is what I want.' Delmai watched with a feeling of satisfaction as cook, flustered, took up a piece of paper and coughed to clear her throat.

'Well, madam, I thought we might have mutton cutlets with sieved boiled potatoes and onions.' She looked at Delmai as though waiting for some response and when none was forthcoming, she hurried on.

'Then cod slices in sherry, garnished with pickled walnuts, followed by stewed beefsteak. And perhaps a fig pudding, if that is acceptable to you?'

Delmai stared at the cook's red face, well aware of the veiled antagonism behind her bland expression. Anger poured through her like wine. What right had this old woman to pass judgement on her betters? Delmai could well imagine her gossiping to the servants just as soon as her own back was turned.

'I presume you are discussing the dinner menu?' Her voice was cold, laced with scorn. 'Do I have to remind you that I – and more importantly, Mr Richardson – have not yet breakfasted.'

Cook's eyes flashed defiance, her pride stung. 'I don't think master Rickie is ready to eat just now, not with Honey O'Connor being so long at her duties.' The woman's face flushed even redder and it was quite obvious that she regretted her hastily-spoken words the moment they had left her lips.

'Honey O'Connor – and who is she?' Delmai's voice was like a whiplash and Mrs Cunningham flinched visibly.

'I'm sorry, madam. I spoke out of turn. Honey's new here – chamber-maid she is, see, and a good Catholic child.'

Delmai turned on her heel and made her way up the stone steps, pausing for a moment in the hallway. A watery sun slanted in through the stained-glass windows, casting coloured reflections on the polished floor. More quietly, she approached the wide staircase, making her way cautiously towards the master bedroom. It was empty and of Rickie there was no sign.

Anger grew and burgeoned within Delmai's breast; she could scarcely believe that her husband was already up to his old tricks of seducing maids again. Slipping off her shoes, she padded up the curving staircase to the servants' sleeping quarters, knowing that if she could catch Rickie in a compromising situation his taunts about her past would be silenced for good. She stared down the long dim corridor, wondering which bedroom belonged to the young chamber-maid. She was not left in doubt for very long, for a low cry suddenly cut off drew her forward.

She listened for a moment, head resting against the wooden panel, then she pushed at the handle so that the door flew from her grasp, crashing open.

Rickie sprang away from the maid, who was clearly distressed with large tears welling in her eyes. Her blouse was

181

open, revealing barely-formed breasts, but it seemed that no great harm had been done.

'Get about your duties, you little slut!' Delmai said angrily, scarcely sparing the girl another glance.

'Get about my duties, is it?' The soft Irish voice startled Delmai and she looked at the maid in surprise.

'I'm going to leave this house – and right now!' The girl's eyes were afire. 'I think you're evil, both of you, and I wouldn't stay here any longer if you paid me double.' With a strange sort of dignity she moved to the door, buttoning up her blouse with trembling hands. 'I'll tell my daddy about you, Mr Richardson, and he'll take a shotgun to you for sure!'

In the silence the sound of the maid's footsteps faded away and Delmai flung Rickie an accusing glance.

'I'll try to placate the girl, though why I should bother I don't know,' she said angrily. 'And don't think I'll forget this little episode, for I won't.'

She hurried away along the corridor and down the stairs, catching up with Honey just as she was flinging wide the front door.

'Wait a moment!' She caught the girl's arm. 'I'm sorry about what happened and I don't blame you for leaving – anyone can see you are a nice young lady.' Honey tugged her arm away and Delmai hid her irritation.

'Look my dear, if you tell your father and he comes up here to cause trouble, Mr Richardson will simply say you're a liar. Even if you were believed, folk would think you'd led the master on, so best if you keep quiet.' Delmai paused as a mixture of emotions flitted over the girl's face, then continued, 'Better to be sensible, and I'll send you the money you're entitled to and a little more besides.'

Honey looked at her scornfully. 'Keep your money, 'cos you won't stop me speaking out if I so wish.' As she hurried away, Delmai resisted the urge to run after her and slap her face.

Slowly she returned indoors and made her way into the dining-room where breakfast was already laid. Cook – perhaps in order to redeem herself – had made egg kedgeree with bloater toast on the side. Delmai glanced up as Rickie came into the room and he looked away sheepishly.

'I hope we'll not have a repetition of this morning's little affair,' Delmai surprised herself by saying coldly. 'I have no intention of lying with a man who takes women from the lower orders into his bed. Are you not aware that such people can bring sickness and vermin into the house?'

He sat down and unfolded his paper and his eyes slid away from hers. 'Don't you think that's something you should bear in mind, too?' he said calmly.

Delmai felt her colour rising – she had asked for that, she realised with a sinking heart. 'We'll say no more about it then.' Her tone softened and she leaned across the table to touch his hand. 'I'm sorry to be so harsh Rickie, but I can't help thinking you should keep all your strength for me – after all, you do want a legitimate son, don't you?'

He glanced at her briefly and gave a curt nod, but Delmai smiled to herself well-satisfied. Rickie Richardson was going to be more easily handled than she had thought; much easier than ever Billy Gray had been.

*

The house in Carreg Fach was chill, with the cold wind sweeping down from the mountains finding every crack and crevice. Billy Gray shuddered and cursed the fire that would not light. At last he sank into a chair, his large hands hanging between his knees in a gesture of helplessness. Why, he asked himself for the hundredth time, why had Delmai run out on him?

God, how he was going to miss her soft body next to him in the nights. He had come home weary to the bone from hacking at coal in the bowels of the earth, only to find her gone. Well, no more! He would leave his job and never work the coal-face again. The only answer was for him to join Kitchener's Army. He would leave the valleys and return to Sweyn's Eye – but stay there only long enough to enlist in the Sweyn's Eye battallion.

He realised clearly enough that Delmai must have gone home to her husband – he'd seen it coming, hadn't he? But what of his baby, he thought miserably – would she now be brought up in a big house with a strange man for a father?

Yet she was too young to grieve, he consoled himself, and

183

moreover, his daughter would grow up a lady. She would have the finest of everything that money could buy, including a nanny to take the worry of her off her mother's hands; for Delmai was not the maternal type – indeed, it was the coming of the baby which had altered their idyllic way of life.

He pushed himself upright and stared around the cottage in disgust. It was dusty now and dirty, the tin bath still before the dead fire, covered in grime. He kicked out at it in anger before hurrying up the stairs. He would pack up his few belongings, then turn his back on the valley and all it had meant to him.

Chapter Fifteen

In the chill grey dawn, fog hung shroud-like above the town of Sweyn's Eye. The river ran swiftly over rust-red stones, the only sound in the silence of the morning.

Within the house on Spinners' Wharf Rhian was crouched beneath the bed covers, hugging the warmth of the child in her arms and studying the plump tear-stained cheeks with a feeling of anger. Cerianne had cried most of the night, grieving for the mother who had abandoned her so heartlessly.

Rhian had been puzzled and then outraged when she had come into the kitchen and found the little girl sitting on the floor weeping. Still she hadn't known what to do, didn't know where Delmai Richardson could be until at last she realised that Delmai wasn't coming back. How dare she just walk away from her responsibilities?

Rhian sighed softly and the bright curls on the baby's head fluttered like golden butterflies. One thing was certain, she couldn't keep Cerianne here. The best step would be to take her to the Richardson house on the hill, for it was almost certain Delmai had gone back to her husband.

Cautiously Rhian moved from beneath the patchwork quilt, fearful of disturbing Cerianne. The little girl had cried herself to sleep, her small rosebud mouth repeating the word 'Mamma' over and over again until Rhian almost cried with her.

In the kitchen, Rhian quickly lit the fire for the morning was chilly. She stood with hands black with dust and watched as the sticks caught fire, licking round the pieces of shiny coal. Then she glanced out of the window towards the mill – there would be little work done today.

But at least now trade was picking up. The town had come to terms with the war and had returned almost to normality. Indeed the war was providing work . . . and fat profits for some.

Rhian had found that the thick woollen blankets she made were being sent to the front by the more patriotic ladies of Sweyn's Eye. It was not the quality of her work or the way she blended her colours which made her work so popular, Rhian thought ruefully – it was the price, the cheapest in town, that attracted customers.

Rhian washed her hands quickly, flinching at the coldness of the water. From upstairs she heard the sound of Cerianne's voice and sighed softly, pushing the kettle on to the weak flames and longing for a hot cup of tea. In the bedroom Cerianne was kneeling on the bed, her eyes filled with tears, her face flushed and Rhian's heart contracted in pain.

'Come to your auntie, then,' she said softly and the child leaned against her breast, tears still flowing. Rhian carried the little girl downstairs, where the fire burned cheerfully now and the kettle had started to sing.

'Shall Rhian make you some nice porridge, then?' She tried to soothe Cerianne, but her crying didn't falter. Rhian admitted to herself that she was clumsy with her niece, but then she had had little experience with children.

She smoothed back Cerianne's hair, but the little girl looked up at her pitifully. 'Mamma,' she said and Rhian knew there was nothing she could do to pacify the child. Rhian bit her lip; she was at the end of her tether and felt like standing in the middle of the kitchen and screaming for help – but what good would that do?

Spooning the lumpy porridge into the baby's mouth was a work of art, and at last she flung down the spoon in exasperation. 'Come on then, little girl, let's take you to your mammy.'

At just over a year old, Cerianne was small for her age, but even so carrying her to the tram terminus was something of an ordeal. As Rhian waited patiently in the queue, her anger was increasing until she almost felt she could physically attack Delmai Richardson. She was irresponsible and cold-hearted.

Rhian heard the hum of the tram before it came into sight, feeling the vibration of the wheels on the rails near her feet. It was a relief to sink on to the wooden slatted seat and she sighed heavily, hoisting Cerianne higher and tucking the small turnover more firmly around the little girl. Cerianne whimpered and Rhian felt herself grow tense, praying that the baby would not set up a wailing. The woman in the next seat glanced at her sympathetically.

'There's red the little one's cheeks are, teething is she?' The voice was kindly and Rhian smiled gratefully.

'I suppose so. Poor Cerianne!' she whispered against the soft cheek.

'Rub in some witch hazel, girl, it'll do the trick right enough – used it on all my babbas, I did.'

The tram jolted to a halt and Rhian rose unsteadily to her feet, smiling her thanks. She stepped down into the roadway and sighed in relief – not far to go now.

She knocked on the door of the imposing house with a feeling of apprehension, but the sounds of life from within cheered her and she smiled as a young maid opened the door and looked down at her from the high steps.

'I'm here to see Mrs Richardson,' Rhian said forcefully and the young girl's eyes flickered over her even as she shook her head.

'Madam is not up and about yet, she can't see anybody.'

'But this is urgent,' Rhian spoke quickly. 'I *must* see her. Tell her it's Rhian Gray and I've got her baby with me, then she'll come.'

The door was closed in her face and Rhian sank down on the step prepared to wait all day if necessary. She was not about to leave without seeing Delmai, even if it meant causing a scene.

After a long pause, during which Rhian could hear voices rising and falling within the big house, the door was flung wide and a man stood there, eyes hard, face set and angry. He was unshaven and wearing only trousers and an open shirt, but it was clear he was master of the house.

'Get away from here before I set the dogs on you,' he said fiercely. 'We want no gaol-bird's kin on our doorstep.'

Rhian rose to her feet and the baby started to cry. 'This is Delmai's child.' Rhian was equally angry. 'Cerianne wants her mother – can't you see that?'

From behind Rickie Richardson came a small sound. Delmai was white-faced, her large eyes filled with anguish as she stood close to her husband. She made as though to move forward, but one look from Rickie stopped her in mid-stride.

'I'm telling you for the last time – get off my property and don't come back here or I'll inform my solicitor that you are attempting to blackmail us. Now go! Don't you understand plain English, you ignorant peasant!'

The door was closed with such violence that it shuddered on its hinges and Rhian moved back a pace, frightened by the man's anger.

This was ridiculous, people couldn't simply abandon a child and get away with it. Perhaps it was she who should see a solicitor? She was so dispirited that she hardly noticed the long journey home and when she opened the door of the old mill house, she sensed rather than saw another presence in the warmth of the kitchen.

'Rhian, it's me, Billy.' The tall figure unwinding from the armchair was unfamiliar in a neat suit. 'I've done it, girl, I've just enlisted!' Then he noticed the baby and held out his hands. Cerianne laughed excitedly and snuggled into her father's arms and Rhian felt tears burn her eyes.

'My god, Rhian, what's Cerianne doing here?' Billy asked shakily.

'Sit down while I make us a cup of tea, it's a long story.' She looked at her brother with shrewd eyes. 'Joined the Army to get away from it all, have you, boyo? Don't really blame you – that woman was never any good – but what am I going to do? Delmai won't have Cerianne, Mr Richardson turned me away from his door.' She sighed softly. 'And I know nothing at all about children.'

'What do you mean, he turned you away?' Billy asked with an edge to his voice. 'Cerianne's place is with her mother.'

Rhian hauled the kettle on to the flames and picked up the teapot, staring into its shiny surface as though she could read answers in the hard china.

'It's like this, Billy,' she said in a low voice. 'Mr Richardson says he won't have Cerianne in the house – "gaol-bird's kin", that's what he's just called me to my face. I tried to get Delmai

188

to take Cerianne back, I did, but it's no use.'

'Christ almighty!' Billy thumped his fist against the table. 'I didn't know she'd sink so low as to give up our child.' He rubbed one hand through his hair in a distracted gesture. 'And I shouldn't have acted so hastily, I realise that now.' He looked down at his polished boots and frowned. 'I must go to war, Rhian, there's no getting away from it . . .' He paused. 'I'd rather Cerianne stay with you than with anyone else. I could send you money and perhaps you could get someone in to mind her while you're working in the mill!'

'You don't know what you're asking, Billy,' Rhian said reluctantly. 'Cerianne has cried all night for her mamma, so how can you expect her to settle down with me when I'm practically a stranger?'

Billy looked lost and Rhian's heart went out to him. 'Billy, you surely won't be going away just yet, will you? Why not stay here for a few days and we can see how things work out.'

'That's the best idea I've heard yet,' Billy said in relief. 'I'm waiting to be told where I start training, and I'll be based near here for a while anyway.'

Rhian forced herself to smile. 'Now don't you go worrying your head about us, we're family and we'll be all right.' In spite of her optimistic words Rhian dreaded the moment when Billy would walk through the door, leaving her to cope with Cerianne alone.

A sudden sound outside made her pause in the act of pouring tea; she looked at Billy and both of them turned expectantly.

'Who's that?' Rhian asked and the latch was lifted, the door swinging open.

'Gina!' Rhian said in delight. 'Come in out of the wind, cariad.' She caught Gina's arm, drawing her in from the greyness of the day. 'Sit by the fire, you look frozen and so does that son of yours.'

Billy moved quickly from his chair and Gina Sinman took his place gratefully.

'I'm that tired,' she said, staring up at the tall man with wide eyes.

'This is my brother Billy,' Rhian said, 'and Cerianne's his little girl. Going for a soldier, he is.' She paused. 'But what's happened, Gina, did you find Heinz?'

Gina shook back the hair that escaped from under her bonnet. 'Looked for him I did, got trains and trams and walked miles it seems, but there's no sign of him. Might be sent back home, the soldiers told me, but they don't know anything for sure.' She shrugged. 'I had nowhere else to go, so I came home.'

'There, have a nice hot cup of tea, Gina. Put the baby down on the floor and rest, you look pale as anything and so much thinner.'

Billy stood in silence, almost to attention, his eyes resting on Gina in sympathy.

'Gina's husband owns the mill,' Rhian explained. 'Heinz is Austrian and he was taken away, supposed to be going into an internment camp.' She glanced at Gina. 'Try not to fret, the war will be over soon. Everyone is saying so, aren't they, Billy?'

'Yes, of course, bound to be. Those Huns can't hold out against the likes of the British Army, not for much longer anyway.'

Gina's eyes were warm with gratitude. 'I did the right thing then, did I? Coming back here, I mean – there won't be no trouble, will there?'

'There'd better not be!' Rhian said quickly. 'Don't worry, people have other things to think about now; there are so many wounded soldiers in town that it's enough to be going on with listening to their tales.' Rhian managed to smile, but Gina still looked uncertain.

'Don't want to bring you no trouble, Rhian – you've got enough to do trying to make a living, I know that.'

'Don't be silly, this is your home,' Rhian said firmly.

Cerianne began to wail and almost without thinking, Gina took the little girl on to her knee. Miraculously, Cerianne stopped crying, soothed as she was rocked in Gina's arms. It was Billy who broke the silence.

'I think you've just solved a problem for us, Gina.' He hesitated over the name and for a moment his eyes held hers. 'We were just wondering who could look after Cerianne while Rhian works in the mill.' He paused and his smile was shy. 'Would you be willing? You're a born mother, I can see that all right.'

190

'Billy, there's clever of you, I never thought of it.' Rhian squeezed Gina's arm. 'Go on, say you'll look after the children and between us we'll have a fair living, I'll promise you that.'

Gina flushed with pleasure. 'Oh, Rhian, are you sure? I'd be glad to mind the babbas – isn't that all I ever wanted in life, to have a big family around me?'

Rhian saw the lines of anxiety ease from her brother's face as she looked at him and they smiled at each other in relief.

'Let's all have another cup of tea to celebrate, is it?' Rhian said lightly, resting her hand on Gina's shoulder.

The days passed quickly and easily, for Gina was good company. Billy visited the mill house every evening, and with this arrangement Cerianne seemed to be content.

Then one morning Billy came early before the dawn had woken the world. He was going away and in the kitchen there was a sombre atmosphere that made Rhian feel restless. Gina lit the fire with swift efficiency and the three of them sat together drinking endless cups of tea. When the children woke, Billy cradled Cerianne in his arms.

The afternoon brought a sudden squall, with rain beating into the river so that the surface dimpled and ripples spread outward in circles.

But as Rhian hurried to the mill, glad to be going to work, a pale sun broke through the clouds and the rain ceased as suddenly as it had started. There were turnovers ready and waiting to be set out to dry and a wind was freshening, coming in with the tide that engorged the river.

She glanced back towards the house where Billy and Gina were still talking softly together, scarcely noticing her departure. They were in the same boat really, alone and bereft though for different reasons. Yet the hurt they had both suffered seemed to make an instant bond of friendship which grew and flowered before Rhian's eyes.

Gina had promised to write Billy a letter each week. 'I can let you know how little Cerianne is getting along and perhaps she can have her picture taken so I can send it to you.' Her voice had been filled with sympathy and for a moment Billy had held her gaze before looking quickly and unseeingly into the flames of the fire which he had stoked right up the chimney.

Rhian carried an armful of turnovers outside and hung them

on the wooden rails, knowing that she must really put her back into the job if she was to earn enough to keep them all. Billy's promise to send money had heartened her, his pay would ease the burden. And she would build up the business, perhaps eventually making them all comfortable if not rich.

She lifted a blanket – heavy and wet from the machine which, like a colander, threw out the excess water – and staggered with it towards the rails.

'Here, lass,' a voice said gently, 'let me help you with that.'

Rhian froze, clutching the sodden wool against her and stared up open-mouthed at the man who was standing over her.

'Mansel Jack!' The name dropped from her lips in a whisper; she felt surprised, almost overawed by his presence.

He lifted the blanket with ease, set it over the fence and then stood watching her, unnerving in his silence. His eyes were dark and penetrating, his crisp hair curling over his brow.

Rhian felt the strength flow from her. She had known Mansel Jack had come to Sweyn's Eye to work, but still she felt he should be in Yorkshire, not standing here on the banks of the river Swan looking as though he would sweep her into his arms.

'You seem a little dazed, lass.' He moved closer but without touching her. 'I'm not a man to let go of an idea once I've made up my mind.' He half smiled. 'You must know I've set myself up in business here, just as I planned.'

Self-consciously she lifted a hand to her tangled hair, trying to tuck it back.

'Don't worry, you look beautiful.' Mansel Jack spoke in a low voice, and when he reached out and touched her shoulder Rhian suppressed the impossible longing to throw herself into his arms.

'And you've dealt with Alfred Phillpot, no doubt?' She forced a lightness into her tone she was far from feeling and Mansel Jack allowed himself a smile.

'That little matter didn't take very long to sort out – he's helping me with my contribution to the war effort.' His eyes searched her face. 'And what about you, is it true you're courting one of the local boys?'

Rhian took a deep breath, feeling the hot colour run into her

192

face. She still felt a sense of unreality, though her eyes were drinking in every line of Mansel Jack's face.

'I think that's my affair,' she said, but her voice was soft.

Mansel Jack smiled ruefully. 'Aye, you're quite right, I've no business to question you.' There was a strangeness in his voice and Rhian glanced at him quickly.

Before she could speak, Billy appeared at the top of the yard. 'Rhian!' his voice was loud and filled with concern and she glanced over her shoulder quickly, sensing her brother's unease. Mansel Jack did not remove his hand from her shoulder, indeed his fingers tightened their hold but Rhian moved self-consciously away, sensing her brother's misgivings.

'Billy, this is Mansel Jack,' she explained quickly. 'I used to work for him in the woollen mills in Yorkshire, but now he's running the munitions factory in Sweyn's Eye.' She didn't look at Mansel Jack. 'This is my brother.'

Billy scrutinised Mansel Jack with unashamed curiosity. There was a stiffening of his shoulders that told Rhian he was not easy in the older man's company.

'A soldier newly enlisted, I'd guess?' Mansel Jack's voice held just the right amount of friendliness. 'When are you off to the front?'

Billy could not conceal his pride. 'I'm moving out with my battalian tomorrow, sir.' It was clear that he recognised the authority in every line of Mansel Jack's stance.

'I envy you. I'd prefer to be an enlisted man rather than work at the factory any day.'

'Every bit as important, sir,' Billy said quickly, placatingly. 'This war's gone on for almost a year now – got to have more shells, haven't we?' Then he looked down at Rhian. 'Bring Mr Mansel Jack indoors for a bite to eat, there's a good girl.' He smiled. 'Not polite to keep a visitor standing out here in the chill wind, is it now?'

Rhian moved towards the house, feeling on edge as though her nerves were pressing through her skin. She had seen how easily Mansel Jack had won Billy over; he was a past master at the game of charm and could coax the best from any man or woman and quell them just as quickly.

In the warmth of the kitchen Gina was seated in the

armchair, a baby on each arm. Her face was falling into lines of quiet composure, though it was clear from the lingering sadness in her eyes that she grieved for her husband.

Mansel Jack seated himself in an upright chair, seeming at home in the small kitchen, holding his hands to the warm blaze that roared and sucked – throwing out heat, then drawing the flames up into the darkness of the chimney breast.

Gina glanced at him briefly, but was forced to centre her attentions on Cerianne who had begun to grizzle.

'This is Mrs Sinman,' Rhian said. 'She and her husband own Spinners' Wharf.' She was puzzled by the sudden intensity of Mansel Jack's gaze. 'Heinz is an Austrian,' she explained. 'He's been taken away to an internment camp – and him loyal to the backbone.'

Mansel Jack spoke evenly. 'Don't be too upset, Mrs Sinman, internees are treated very well in this country.'

The silence seemed to stretch on endlessly and Billy picked up his cap and rubbed his sleeve against the bright badge. Gina moved the babies to a more comfortable position in her arms and it seemed that Mansel Jack was the only one completely at ease.

'Can I get you some tea?' Rhian asked, puzzled somewhat by his manner.

'No, not for me, thank you.' His voice was warm and vibrant. 'But I would appreciate a few minutes' private conversation with Mrs Sinman.' He smiled at Gina. 'If you can spare the time?'

Rhian's bewilderment increased and she sat perfectly still for a moment. It was Billy who, moving with alacrity, broke the uneasy silence which had fallen in the small kitchen.

'Come on, girl, show me the mill.' He smiled at Rhian and took Cerianne in his arms. 'I've always wanted to know how the looms work.'

Rhian marvelled at the way Mansel Jack always got exactly what he wanted. As she rose to her feet and followed Billy to the door, it was as though the charisma of the man reached out and touched her.

'I wonder what he wants with Gina,' Billy said, shifting Cerianne to a more comfortable position on his arm.

Rhian shrugged, 'There's no telling, Mansel Jack isn't one

for confiding his business to anyone.' She spoke offhandedly, but she had been wondering about it herself. She would not admit it, but she felt unhappy to be excluded from the warmth of the kitchen and was disappointed not to be allowed to listen to whatever it was he had to say – they were friends, weren't they?

She saw at once that Billy had no real interest in the mill and had merely been making a polite gesture. He stood staring up at the sky with Cerianne snuggling into his arms and Rhian could almost feel his pain; she knew instinctively he was thinking of Delmai.

She was relieved when the kitchen door opened, spilling warmth over the yard. Mansel Jack's large frame blocked the light for a moment and then he was standing before her, taking her hand in his.

'I'll see you again soon.' His voice was confident and the fingers curling around hers were strong.

'Best of luck to you, Billy!' Mansel Jack moved away to shake her brother's hand. 'I must admit that I'm envious of you.'

He seemed to melt into the darkness, though Rhian could still hear the crisp sound of his boots striking the cobbles.

'Come on inside,' Gina said, her tone breathless with excitement. 'I've got something wonderful to tell you – Mr Mansel Jack is going to find Heinz for me!'

Rhian was the last to move into the light and warmth of the room. She heard the kettle boiling on the hob, felt the heat of the fire on her chilled limbs, but her mind was still in the darkness outside as she imagined Mansel Jack striding away from her, his shoulders proud and his head held at a jaunty angle.

Why had he come here to Sweyn's Eye, she wondered uneasily, for the knowledge of his presence in the town was disturbing. Pull yourself together! she told herself sharply. She was Heath Jenkins' woman now and she must never forget it.

Chapter Sixteen

Sweyn's Eye slumbered in an illusion of peace. Summer had slipped gently by, for russet and gold now splashed hill and dale with rich colour.

With the coming of autumn 1915 the Allied forces had taken Artois and Champagne. The British advance south of La Bassée pierced the German line to a depth of four thousand yards. The village of Loos was captured, as well as the western outskirts of Hulluch.

Honey O'Connor listened to her father reading the news from the *Daily Post*, but her mind was on other matters. She looked across the breakfast table at Morgan; he caught her glance and winked secretly and her heart was warmed.

'You'd better be getting off to the station, my girl,' Stella O'Connor said quickly, rising from her chair and gathering the empty plates into a neat pile. ''Tis getting late, can't you see?'

Honey glanced at the clock on the mantelpiece and its loud ticking in the silence seemed to rebuke her. 'All right, mammy, I'm going in a minute, give us a chance.' She had never explained her sudden decision to leave the Richardson household and take a job in the munitions factory – let sleeping dogs lie, she had thought to herself.

'I'll give ye the back of my hand if ye don't shift!' Her mother leavened the harshness of her words with a smile and dropped a kiss on Honey's cheek. 'Now tie a scarf tight round your head – you don't want your hair turning orange, do you?'

Honey sighed. 'I've told you, mammy, we've got our mob-caps only some of the other girls don't like to cover the whole of their head – that's why their hair is going a funny colour, it's the TNT that does it.'

She stood up, conscious in a proud kind of way of her thick trousers and the loose-cut jacket pulled in by a belt at the waist. This was the uniform provided for his workers by Mansel Jack and it was almost as good as khaki in the eyes of the townsfolk.

'Here, stop dreaming, girl, and take your food. You're thin enough already without forgetting to eat your dinner.'

Outside in the misty morning air, Honey deliberately dawdled, for usually Morgan hurried after her and walked with her from Green Hill to the station, before going off to his shift at the copper works. Today was no exception and they smiled at each other without touching.

'Nice enough day,' Morgan said, clearing his throat self-consciously. Honey smiled up at him – her hair, tied back from her face, hanging rich and gold down to her waist.

'Sure, it's fine,' she replied, a blush heating her skin.

They walked in silence for a moment, each tinglingly aware of the other. Honey searched her mind for something to say, anything that would bring Morgan's eyes to meet hers, but words would not come.

'How are you getting on at the factory?' He spoke in a jerky, stilted way and Honey realised that for Morgan it was difficult too.

'It's hard enough work, but I have friends there now. Katie Murphy's a fine girl and looks after me, sure enough, but it's Janey Jenkins is my best pal.'

Morgan kicked at a pebble, his heavy boots making a crunching sound against the stone. 'I worry about you.' The words came out separately, spaced apart as though he was giving a great deal of thought to what he was saying. 'There have been accidents – worries me, it does.' He was unaware that he was repeating himself, and so was Honey, who felt a warm glow grow inside her.

'I'm careful, sure enough,' she said gently. 'Don't take chances with the gaines, handle them gentle I do, as if they were babies.' She shrugged. 'It's not the fear of an explosion which worries me, so much as the thought of my face turning yellow.' She looked carefuly at her hands; the nails were brownish at the edges and the skin was tinged with yellow instead of pink. 'I use the cream Katie Murphy gave me every

197

night, but it don't do much good.'

'You look lovely to me,' Morgan said softly, 'but I wish you could get some other kind of work; a factory isn't the place for you.'

Honey felt a lightness rushing through her, for this was the nearest Morgan had ever come to revealing his feelings to her. She spoke breathlessly. 'It's much better than working for the toffs up on the hill.'

Just before they reached the station Morgan came to a halt, hands in his pockets, grub-pack under his arm and his tea-can hanging from his belt. He was tall and handsome, every inch a man, and Honey felt the happiness which she experienced whenever she was with him.

'See you later, then.' He smiled and his teeth shone white against the dusk of his skin. The copper was beginning to bronze him, laying its touch upon his face just as it did on anyone who worked it. In a way, Honey thought, he was like her – marked by the job that was his livelihood.

Honey ran then, making up for the time she had spent walking with Morgan, prolonging the moment and not wanting to leave him.

Puffing and blowing, the train had already swallowed up the stream of women whose high-pitched excited voices rose above even the monster's steaming breath.

'Get in here quick!' Katie Murphy hauled Honey aboard just as the train began to move. 'Jesus, Mary and Joseph – cutting it fine this morning, aren't you, my girl?'

Honey sank breathlessly into her seat, squeezing between Janey and Katie and smiling in relief. It would have been terrible indeed if the train had left without her.

'What you been up to then?' Janey giggled at her side. 'Courtin' with that lovely Morgan again, I'll bet a copper-bottomed Toby jug!'

'Hush,' Honey warned, 'don't want anyone else to know. Now you promised me that you wouldn't open your mouth, Janey.'

'All right, only pulling your leg I am, mind. But there's a shine in your eyes that gives your secret away. All the world must know that Honey O'Connor loves Morgan Lloyd.'

'I'll kill you, sure I will, if you don't shut your mouth,'

Honey threatened, but burst into laughter when Janey tickled her waist mischievously.

'What it is to be young!' Katie Murphy moved up a little to accommodate Honey's wriggling body. 'I don't think *I* ever giggled and smirked behind my hands like you girls do today. Sober enough I was, listened to my elders and betters sure enough!'

There was a huge chorus of laughter and Doris, who was already tucking into her grub-pack, pushed at Katie's arm.

'Flighty piece you was, always chasing the boys – had them panting for her, she did,' she winked knowingly at Honey. 'Still panting they are too; can take her pick, can our Katie.'

The laughter subsided into silence as a slender woman in a fine worsted coat and skirt pushed her way into the carriage. Honey stared up in open-mouthed astonishment, wondering if she could believe her eyes.

'Mrs Richardson, sure it is.' She fell back in her seat as the woman glanced in her direction and frowned.

'Will you make some room for me,' she asked abruptly.

There was silence as the already tightly-bunched girls made a space.

'Morning, Mrs Richardson,' Honey said softly. 'It seems you're a working girl now, just like me.'

'So I am.' Delmai Richardson couldn't keep the bitterness out of her voice. 'Patriotism apparently means going out to work in quite unsuitable surroundings.'

It was Doris who broke the sudden silence. 'Oh, hoity-toity then!' The words burst from her lips. 'If'n you'd kept your own babba instead of foisting it on to others, you'd have been able to stay at home in idleness, wouldn't you? We've all heard about you, mind!'

Delmai paled visibly and Honey felt almost sorry for her. 'Hush now, Doris,' she said pleadingly. 'Sure we don't want any bother, now, do we?'

'The likes of 'er can't cause us no bother,' Doris would not be stopped. 'No lady she isn't, runnin' off with one man while married to another. Living tally with Billy Gray, she was. We all knowed that, didn't we, 'tisn't no secret.'

'What I do is no concern of yours,' Delmai said evenly, though it was clear she was shaken and her hands were

199

trembling.

'I think perhaps we'd best let the matter drop, Doris.' Katie Murphy smiled, trying to pour oil on troubled waters. 'Mrs Richardson is doing war work like us and who can ask more?'

Doris leaned forward in her seat, her plump arms resting on big knees. 'What are you doin' then, Mrs High and Mighty?' she demanded. 'Filling shells, is it, or are you working on the lathes?'

Delmai looked at her with dislike. 'I'm an office worker if you must know,' she replied. 'There has to be some administration, even you must realise that.'

'There!' Doris said in satisfaction. 'Safe and snug in the office, she is, and getting her claws into Mansel Jack she'll be next. There's a thing for you!'

Delmai Richardson rose to her feet and moved away to stand in the furthest corner of the compartment, her back to the girl who was tormenting her. 'Don't speak to me, you wretch!' Her voice was hard and cracked. 'You're an ignorant woman and I want nothing to do with you.'

'An' I want nothing to do with you, neither.' Doris would have the last word, even though Katie Murphy grabbed her arm and shook her.

'Now let's stop all this.' Katie's pale skin was rosy. 'We're working together trying to do our bit for the country, how will it help if we quarrel amongst ourselves?' Doris would have said more, but Katie put her palm firmly against the girl's lips. 'Enough!' She spoke quietly but with such authority that Doris subsided, falling back into her seat with her mouth set mutinously.

Later as the clatter of the machinery discouraged all but the most essential conversation, Honey realised she was bone-weary and the day hardly yet begun. She was glad when grub-break came around and she could sit down and ease her aching legs. Janey took her place beside her and held out a thick chunk of bread and a piece of cheese.

'I'll swap you for an apple,' she said, grinning. She edged closer, her coarse trousers rasping against the wooden bench. 'Come on, tell me, has Morgan spoken to you yet?' Janey's eyes were wide with the vicarious thrill of the romance and Honey felt herself blushing.

'Of course he's spoken – sure and don't we talk all the way down to the station?'

'You know what I mean, has he asked you to walk out with him?' Janey bit into the apple, juice running along her chin and dripping on to the thick jacket. Honey averted her eyes.

'Sure and would I be telling you even if I knew what Morgan Lloyd thought about me? Perhaps I'm just a friend because he lives in me mammy's house and that's all.'

'No, it isn't all,' Janey disagreed vehemently. 'He brings you right to the station, doesn't he, and meets you too when he' not working – that's more than friendship, and don't forget I've seen the way he looks at you.'

'Have you really?' Honey asked, excitement flaring through her. Like a thirsty child she longed to drink in any drop of reassurance Janey had to offer, for men were unpredictable creatures. 'Go on, Janey, which way does he look at me? Come on, don't have me on now.'

Infuriatingly Janey took another bite of the fruit, her white teeth crunching into the firm flesh, her lips dewy with juice, her eyes wide with mischief. 'Promise you'll bring me another apple tomorrow and I'll tell you,' she said.

Honey pushed her away. 'I don't know why I bother with you,' she said, shaking her head. 'All you can do is to tease me when I'm deadly serious.'

Janey put her hand on Honey's arm. 'He does feel for you, there's soft you are not to see it yourself.'

Honey put away the remains of the grub-pack, a feeling of warmth and satisfaction filling her. She wanted to think that Morgan loved her, sometimes she could almost believe it. But then when she looked at his well-set-up frame and handsome face, she wondered how he could even notice she was alive.

'The boss is coming – look lively, girls!' Katie's voice was low, but Honey rose to her feet rubbing the crumbs from her jacket and straightening the cap on her head. Mansel Jack was a boss who gained respect without even trying. He stopped at the table, his glance encompassing them all.

'Bad news, lasses.' His hard voice held a trace of softness that was unusual and Honey found herself watching him covertly. He paused as though assessing the quality of the attention he was getting before continuing to speak.

201

'We've received from America a faulty batch of gaines which makes our work more difficult than it already is.' His gaze lingered on Katie Murphy and she nodded slightly, though she did not speak.

'These gaines have a left-handed instead of a right-handed thread. What this means is that the gaines are unscrewing in flight, which is no good at all.' He placed the tube on the table and took up a chisel and a hammer. 'The gaines must be tapped like this – stabbed in two places to break the thread so that they can't unscrew.' He did the work deftly and looked round at the girls who were watching open-mouthed.

'This is a dangerous job, for if a trace of fulminate should be detonated by the blow there would be an explosion.' He put down the hammer and chisel. 'I have chosen you lassies because of your courage and common sense, but I'll say this – if anyone objects to the job, tell me now and you'll be moved to something else with no shame attached.'

Katie pulled at the edge of her collar, turning it up around her face as though she was suddenly cold, but when she spoke her voice was firm.

'We'll do the job all right, sir, you be after bringing us the tools and we'll start right now.'

Mansel Jack smiled his approval and to Honey, watching him, it seemed as though the sun had come out. Suddenly the terrible task they were being asked to perform appeared to be a glorious honour. He waited, his eyes searching the faces of the girls around him, listening for any word of dissent. Finally he turned to Doris, his gaze level.

'I know you have little ones,' he said. 'You may be moved to the lathes or even join another gang if you wish.' Before he had even finished speaking, Doris was shaking her head vigorously.

'Not me, sir, I stick by my friends when there's a job to be done. I won't desert my gang and that's for sure.'

After a moment, he nodded. 'Very well. Now, because of the dangerous nature of the work I mean to set you up in one of the outhouses away from the main factory. I'll make sure you're as comfortable as possible and you'll all receive an increase in your wages. I won't pretend to you lassies, this is dangerous stuff I'm asking you to handle. If any of you has a

202

change of mind, come to me at once.'

When he had gone, Honey felt fear burn inside her. She clasped her hands together to stop them from trembling and was ashamed.

Katie sighed hugely. 'Jesus, Mary and Joseph, what have we let ourselves in for?' She pushed the cap back from her forehead and a stray curl sprang red and gold over her brow.

'Now that the boss is gone, you can all speak out truthfully,' Katie said firmly. 'If anyone wants to drop out, say so now and no excuses needed. You Honey – you're as pale as a blanched nut – anything you want to say to me?'

Honey shook her head and Katie looked at her carefully. 'Think hard now, it's not only your own safety but ours too. If any of you are nervous or feel the job's beyond you, speak up for the sake of the team.'

In the silence Honey stared round at the faces of her workmates, wondering if she was the only one to feel the cold pain of fear. She had never been good with a hammer and chisel – clumsy she was, even with needle and thread – yet how could she speak of her terror when the rest of the girls, even Janey who was the youngest, seemed so calm and composed?

As though aware of her thoughts, Janey caught Honey's arm and pressed it sympathetically. She pulled a wry face and Honey laughed, knowing she was not alone after all.

Honey felt relief flow through her and a kind of strength too. She held her head aloft thinking of the soldiers she had seen maimed and sick, hobbling through the streets of the town. Some of them were blinded and stood on corners selling pathetic bundles of bootlaces. A legless man was carried each day to the station, there to remain playing on his accordion, accepting charity with a face full of suffering. She, Honey O'Connor, was going to do some real work; she would help to win the war and then all the pain and suffering would be over.

Tonight she would talk it all over with Morgan. He would reassure, perhaps even admire her and the thought was like the sun breaking through the clouds on a stormy day.

*

Morgan rubbed at his face with his sweat-rag and the tingling of the copper particles scarcely bothered him now. He was becoming inured to the abrasive burn of the metal on his face and neck, and the sharpness of it in his lungs was no longer such an agony. But he was glad when his shift was over, for he was weary to the bone, yet the thought of seeing Honey sent the blood coursing sweetly through his veins.

'There's a right lecherous look on your face, boyo!' Peter was grinning at him, sweat dripping unnoticed from the end of the nose and chin for he bore the full brunt of the heat from the furnace. *'Jawl*, what it's like to be young – forgotten that bed's for anything but sleeping in, me!'

Morgan smiled. 'And if I believe that, I'll believe the moon is made of English cheese, right?' He straightened his shoulders. 'Well, I'm off home; got better things to do than stand in this hell-hole.'

The air was cool as he left the sheds, the clouds were lowering with the threat of rain and the stink of sulphur hung like a pall over the valley. A gush of sparks from the tall chimneys added to the illusion that this was a place out of hell inhabited by demons with copper faces.

Morgan told himself to stop being fanciful, he must be more tired than he had realised. It was when fatigue overcame him that morbid thoughts haunted his imaginings and his skull became a dark cavern full of horrors. He forced himself to walk more slowly up towards Green Hill, but the feeling of darkness and despair continued to haunt him. He told himself that soon he would wash the stink and dirt of the copper from his skin and sit around a civilised table to eat. And he would be with Honey.

He thought of his father, a prisoner in his bed with only a blank wall for company. The image brought a knife-edge of pain and guilt and he recognised that this then was the seat of all his unhappiness. He had watched his dad die little by little as the weeks passed, powerless to halt the deterioration by one iota.

Now the old man could not even wash himself. Too proud to allow a woman who was no kin to see him naked, he would stubbornly wait until Morgan came home. Sometimes he would have worn stained clothing all day, for he could not always reach for the chamber-pot in time.

The lights from the windows of the little house showered a

welcome upon him and Morgan stood for a moment in the wash of warmth, wondering where he would have been without the kindness of the Irish family.

He recognised that he was in love with Honey and knew her parents would not approve; they would want a good Catholic boy for their daughter.

"'Tis late you are tonight, Morgan boy.' Mrs O'Connor descended the stairs quickly, moving to close the door to the kitchen where the family sat around the large table. 'You'd best go straight up to your old fellow,' she said softly, sympathetically. 'I've had the doctor to him again, but there's little enough he can do.'

It took a few seconds for the words to penetrate Morgan's weary mind, then he was taking the stairs two at a time, his heart pumping in his breast. The sound of his father's breathing was like nothing Morgan had ever heard before. Each breath was sucked in through a mouth which had fallen open, seeming to dominate the drawn grey face. The thin chest rose and fell with each effort to draw in air and Morgan felt himself grow weak with pain and pity.

'Daddy,' Morgan moved to the side of the bed, listening to the harsh sounds of the tortured lungs. 'There's an old cheat you are, falling sick behind my back like that.' He rested his hand on his father's cheek and the old man's eyes flickered open, a little warmth coming to them as Morgan leaned closer.

Fingers thin and trembling reached out for his. 'I thought I'd miss you, boy, but I hung on till you came.' The voice was a faint hiss of sound that drained the last of the old man's strength. Tears rose to Morgan's eyes as he caressed his father's face; the skin was cool and thin, the bones arched upwards, skull-like in the flickering light from the lamp.

Morgan knelt on the floor, longing to pour his young strength into his father's frail body. 'I love you, daddy,' he said and the blue eyes staring up at him kindled with light. His father nodded wearily and then his lids were fluttering, thin lashes coming slowly to rest on cheeks that looked now as though they were carved from old yellow wood.

Morgan raised his fists to heaven in terrible anger, impotent in the face of his father's premature death. And then he was crying harsh sobs that tore and hurt as he averted his face from

205

the still form in the bed that was no longer his father. Silly, inconsequential thoughts ran through his mind and he wondered where he would sleep that night, for he could not share a bed with a corpse.

He became aware that Mrs O'Connor had come into the room, had put her hands on his arms and was urging him to his feet.

'Come on, Morgan, there's work to be done here and you are best out of it.'

Morgan moved obediently towards the stairs and down into the kitchen, where the children fixed him with curious stares for they had never seen a grown man cry before. Honey looked at him for a long moment in silence and then, resolutely, she rose from her chair and came to him, cradling him in her arms. He smelled the freshness of her, felt the silk of her hair against his fingers and was comforted.

*

Funerals were not grand affairs in Emerald Court. A makeshift trestle was nailed together and the deceased set upon it, covered by a shroud. There was little money to be spared for such luxuries as the hire of a hearse, so folks managed without. The funeral of old John Lloyd, retired miner, was no exception. The bearers were the men of the O'Connor family and Morgan in his one good suit walked behind the entourage as befitted the close kin of the dead.

Morgan felt soft rain mingle with the tears on his cheeks as he walked through the mean streets of Green Hill. He looked up at the leaden sky, wondering if life had any meaning at all. He was not aware of the rush of the river as they crossed over the bridge and even the high sloping folds of Kilvey were out of sight, shrouded in thick mist. The walk was a long one, but he scarcely noticed it. He glanced down at his boots, polished so well by one of the little O'Connor girls that the puddles of water spurting up from the roadway met the shiny surface and rolled away again.

At the graveside, he lifted his head and stared across the sloping land to where the docks lay, dull mirrors flung down apparently at random, pewter in the grey light.

Well, he was on his own now, he told himself – free to join

the Army, see the world, do anything he wanted to do. And yet the knowledge was like sawdust in his mouth, for his world had revolved around his father. The simplest tasks like shaving the coarse bristles from the gaunt chin had become a ritual of caring. He had done a thousand things for his dad but had not been able to prolong his life by one minute.

As he listened to the priest's heavy voice, his eyes were suddenly dry. He must not look back, he must go forward but one thing he vowed – if he ever had sons they would never work in the dusty blackness of the pit.

The service over, he turned and followed the O'Connor men to the bar of the Cape Horner. He would drink with them, give them something for their trouble and then he would go back to the little room in Emerald Court and pack up his few belongings, for now there was no excuse for him to stay.

Chapter Seventeen

The rain beat an incessant tattoo on the pavements, washing the streets and houses in a greyness that not even the lamplight or the glow from shop windows could dispel. The heavens seemed to glower over roof-tops, mists creeping between buildings, a close world of drizzle and fog from which there seemed no escape.

Mary Sutton sighed as she stood on the running board of the tram and lifted her ticket machine higher to ease the ache in her shoulder. Why, she wondered for the hundredth time, had she taken the job as conductress? But she knew why – she had harboured some romantic notion of helping the war effort – though surely there were more congenial jobs in which she could serve her country just as well?

It seemed that a restless guilt had been eating at her, for the emporium ran itself, especially now that she had employed old Mrs Greenaway to take charge. Greenie had scarcely changed from the days when she had worked with Mary at Sutton's Drapery Store. There was a little more grey in her hair perhaps, but she had grown in self-confidence and Mary thought that came from working for Heath. Greenie had treated him like a son, crying bitter tears over him when he enlisted. Running his home took very little of her time and she had appeared overjoyed when Mary offered her the position left vacant by Katie Murphy. At first Mary had doubted the older woman's capacity to shoulder so much responsibility, but Greenie had been triumphant, stalking the tea-rooms in a long black dress and keeping everyone in order.

Mary sighed. Almost everyone in Sweyn's Eye was engaged

in some sort of war work and she had not wanted to be the exception. She had been a fool to choose a part-time job on the trams, but now that she was here she might as well do the thing properly and take fares from the passengers, who would just as soon skip off without paying.

Reluctantly, she climbed the metal staircase to the open-topped upper deck where the rain dripped remorselessly from hat-brims, falling on to hunched shoulders and finding secret holes in shabby footwear.

It was almost impossible to work in such conditions, for even as she attempted to write out tickets the ink ran in spidery patterns, defeating her. Angrily she clattered back down the stairs, avoiding the curious looks of the passengers who had not yet paid. She was wet and miserable and her heavy uniform smelled of dampness and moth-balls.

It was a relief when her shift was over. She handed in her tickets and the heavy leather bag of coins and waited impatiently while the checking was done. But at last she was able to turn towards home and, sighing with relief, she made her way towards the waiting tram – pleased to be simply a passenger on the trip up the hill.

It was good to luxuriate in a hot bath before a roaring fire. Here in the peace of her home she could almost believe the war was nothing more than an excuse to make life difficult for people like her. As she rubbed soap over her arms and breasts a frown creased her brow – war was a reality, for Heath was now a soldier in the 14th Welch battalion and might at this very moment be at the front.

Mary was angry that Heath had been accepted into the Army with his record of chest sickness. She thought back to the time when her brother almost died of the lung complaint; it was then that Brandon had shown how much he loved her, sitting up at night with her, caring for Heath with untiring patience and then when her brother was over the crisis, he had taken her into his arms and she had known it was where she belonged.

The bath water ran comfortingly over her body, along the flat planes of her stomach. Mary pressed her fingers there, wondering how it would feel to have life growing within her. The ache for a baby was almost a physical pain; her breasts stood full and proud as though begging for a child to suckle, but in spite of all her hopes it seemed she was still unable to conceive.

She had found it impossible to raise the problem with Brandon, for his eyes would darken and his mouth set into a stern line almost as though she was chastising him. Perhaps he felt that the fault lay in him, she thought with sudden insight.

She dressed in soft cotton petticoats prettily embroidered with rosebuds, then from the wardrobe took a dress of plum velvet, her favourite colour and one that seemed to suit her very well. She brushed her hair back from her face, twisting it up into a bun. Once there would have been a maid to do this for her, but the war had swallowed up most of the young girls and they now worked in factories or on the land. It was only the elderly who were spared ... or the mothers of young children, she thought bitterly.

Hearing the front door slam, she knew with a quickening of her pulse that her husband was home. She hurried downstairs just as he was shrugging himself free of his topcoat and ran into his arms eager for his kisses.

'And how did it go?' He put his arm around her waist, leading her into the drawing-room. 'Still aching from running up and down tram stairs all day?' he inquired.

She smiled up at him, revelling in the clean scent of him, her heart warm with happiness for she loved this husband of hers dearly. 'I'm all right, just sick of the rain, that's all.' She kissed his cheek, watching as he poured them both a drink, realising suddenly that he had something on his mind. She knew at once what he was about to say, and fear gave a looseness to her tongue which she could not control.

'We had the funniest old woman on the tram today,' she began breathlessly. 'Berated some young soldiers for leaving the front and the poor devils were dressed in hospital blue, wounded they were, but she wouldn't listen to their explanations.' She saw from his face then that she had given him the very opening he'd needed.

'We've spoken about this before, Mary,' Brandon said quickly, 'and you managed to convince me that my responsibilities lay here at the works.' He shrugged. 'Now it's not enough for me.' She remained silent, not knowing what to say;

210

she had known this moment had to come and yet now she could not face it. 'Mary,' he took her hand and kissed her finger-tips gently, 'I can safely leave the running of the works to one of the older men.' He paused and looked at her anxiously. 'I'm enlisting first thing in the morning.'

She put her arms around him, her face buried against his shoulder. Although she didn't want him to leave and felt terror at the very thought of him going into battle, she knew instinctively that she must not hinder him. 'There's strange I'll feel without you lying beside me in our bed,' she said softly. Her voice was muffled but she managed to keep back the tears.

'Thank you, Mary, for not making a fuss.' He kissed her mouth gently. 'Don't you think I'm going to miss you? But it's for you I'll be fighting, for peace and freedom, and every day I stay at home I feel more and more like a coward.'

Mary took his face between her hands. 'How long will it be before you have to go?' With an effort she kept her voice steady and Brandon smiled, understanding the expression in her eyes.

'Not long, perhaps a few days or even a few weeks, I can't be sure how much training I'll get.'

Training to hold a gun and fire it at other men, Mary thought despairingly, but she was becoming expert at concealing her feelings. Yet Brandon sensed something of her thoughts because he held her close, kissing her hair.

'Don't make barriers between us, Mary,' he said softly. 'I don't like to be shut out as though I were a stranger.'

'There's daft you're talking,' Mary replied quickly. 'I love you, Brandon, I love you more than I ever did.'

He held her a little away from him. 'But that's not what I'm saying.' His eyes seemed to penetrate into her soul and she wanted to be honest with him, but how could she speak again about her longing for a child, especially now when he was going to war.

'I'm just afraid of being lonely, that's all.' She closed her eyes, leaning softly against him, and his arms tightened round her protectively.

'You'll have something in common with most of the other wives in the town,' he said. 'Mali is alone, has been for some time, you'll be able to keep each other company.'

'Don't worry about me,' Mary replied quickly. 'I have my

store and the work on the trams; there's enough to occupy me, goodness knows.' And Mali has her children, the thought crept treacherously into her mind; Mali was fulfilled, she had a son and a daughter, both children a small piece of their father. What Mary would give to have Brandon's child within her!

'You'll be busier than ever,' Brandon said, smiling. 'I shall expect you to keep an eye on the works for me, no mean feat but you're capable enough, Mary Jenkins.'

She slapped his hand playfully, ' "Mary Jenkins" indeed, I'm a respectable married woman, I'll have you know!'

He inclined his head in acknowledgement. 'And I'm the luckiest man on earth, honey.'

They ate dinner in silence, each locked in their own thoughts. Mary scarcely tasted her food, for misery gnawed at her with the knowledge that soon she would be parted from her husband. It was her punishment, she thought, for greedily wanting more when she had so much already. And yet, was it asking too much of fate to allow her a child – wasn't it every woman's birthright to be a mother?

The meal was almost finished when a letter was brought to Brandon on a silver salver. He took it from the maid with a strange look on his face, then slit open the envelope and took out a thick sheet of paper which crackled in his hand.

'What is it?' Mary asked curiously but Brandon shook his head, continuing to read in silence. Watching the fleeting expressions on his face, Mary felt her heart fluttering in fear; she half-rose from her chair, but Brandon waved her back.

'Finish your dinner, Mary. I'm going into the study – there's quite a lot of paper work for me to catch up on. As for this,' he thrust the letter into his pocket, 'it's nothing to be concerned about.'

She stared after his retreating figure with open-mouthed surprise and took up her glass, sipping the wine slowly, trying to calm herself while questions raced through her mind. Why was Brandon being so secretive about the letter, retreating into his study which was regarded virtually as forbidden territory so far as she was concerned? Clearly he was shutting her out and she was hurt at the rejection.

She moved to the drawing-room and sat twisting the stem of the wine-glass between her fingers, staring into the shimmering liquid with eyes that saw nothing but Brandon's closed face. He had accused her of raising barriers, but that was just what he was doing now.

Eventually she gave up waiting for him and retired to bed. A fire blazed cheerfully in the grate and the heavy curtains hung close over the windows. Mary crept beneath the sheets and lay staring around her as though seeing the brilliant gas-light beneath the opulent shade for the first time. Tears brimmed in her eyes, but she was too proud to shed them. She didn't know why she felt bereft and alone, but it was as though Brandon had already gone away from her.

When at last he came to bed, she pretended to be asleep. She had hunched herself over to her own side of the bed, feeling childishly that she wanted to punish him for acting so strangely. She lay for a long time, wide-eyed, staring towards the pale light that crept beneath the curtains and listening to Brandon's regular breathing. How could he sleep, she thought angrily, when she was so unsettled?

She slid from beneath the sheets and crept silently from the room, feeling like an intruder in her own home as she crossed the landing. On bare feet she padded down the wide staircase and with a cautious look over her shoulder opened the door to the study. She stood in the darkness for a long time, listening to the night sounds of the house, the creaking timbers, the soft tapping of a branch against a window, pausing before lighting the gas-lamp.

The letter lay open on the desk – evidence of Brandon's trust in her – and for a moment her resolution wavered. She had no right to be prying into her husband's affairs, she told herself sternly; if he had wanted her to see the letter, he would have shown it to her. Yet the spidery, feminine handwriting drew her gaze and she sat down at the desk and without touching the letter began to read it.

After a moment, she sank back in the seat, her hands covering her eyes. Yet the words were imprinted on her mind. The signature, 'Mary Anne Bloomfield', was etched on the darkness behind her lids. Brandon's old sweetheart was in town and wanted to see him!

'Snooping, Mary? I thought you were above that!' Brandon was standing in the doorway and Mary turned to face him, trembling and ashamed and yet angry at the same time.

'I didn't mean to spy on you, but why didn't you tell me that Mary Anne had arrived in Sweyn's Eye?'

'Why should I speak of someone from my past?' Brandon challenged. 'I've never delved into your past, have I?'

'That's unjust of you,' Mary said quickly. 'There's nothing you don't know about me. Anyway, why does she want to see you again? Have you met this daughter of hers, is there something I should know?'

Brandon stared at her coldly. 'Don't be foolish, Mary.' He folded the letter and locked it away in the desk, an action that angered her afresh.

'It's too late for that now, I've read the contents.' Mary clenched her hands to her sides, jealousy eating at her so that she wanted to lash out and hurt.

They had become like strangers, she thought as she made her way back upstairs to the bedroom. How had their bright wonderful love become tarnished?

The fault must be hers, she decided, and when the bed creaked beneath Brandon's weight she turned to him, took him in her arms and put her head in the hollow of his neck the way she used to do.

'There's daft I am and me loving you so much that it pains me.' She kissed his mouth. 'I don't give a fig for any other woman, I'm your wife after all.'

He smoothed the silk of her shoulder, his hands gentle and after a moment, his breathing deepened.

'We've something very precious, Mary,' he whispered. 'We must never spoil it.'

Mary closed her eyes against the tears that threatened to spill along her cheeks. He was hers, her very own husband, and no one would ever take him from her.

*

Mary Anne Bloomfield's arrival caused something of a stir in the large houses on the western slopes of Sweyn's Eye. The war had become a long and wearisome matter and ceased to be the highlight of conversation. Any new event was quickly seized upon, for gossip served to lighten the sadness that washed over the houses of the bereaved. There were now so many that it

214

was indelicate to even touch on the matter and so Mary Anne's arrival was given more than its fair share of attention.

Mary was tired of hearing about the subject. She had been looking forward to visiting Mali, had imagined they would talk cosily together and laugh about Mary's work on the trams, discuss their personal troubles in mutual sympathy. But it was not to be, for as Mary entered the elegant drawing-room tastefully decorated in the latest pastel shade of duck-egg blue, Marion Thomas unwound her great length from the depths of a chair and held out her glass to be refilled.

'I hear there's a rival in town for your husband's affections,' Marion smiled knowingly. 'And her daughter too, my dear. What a little beauty . . . and so precocious, as these Americans always are!'

Mary moved towards the fireplace where Sterling, handsome in his officer's uniform, smiled at her in greeting.

'Sterling, you're on leave!' Mary said in genuine pleasure and surprise. 'And looking so well too – how did they let you come home from the front?'

Sterling laughed. 'We are allowed some time off, you know, even though there's a war on.'

Marion Thomas was not easily diverted and, ignoring Sterling, she continued to speak to Mary. 'Goodness, isn't the American girl like your husband, Mary? When I saw them together I just couldn't believe it: the same high forehead and the thick curly hair – there's no mistaking the girl is a Sutton, but which brother is her father?'

Mary resisted the temptation to spin round on Marion and tell her to shut her mouth – not a very ladylike response, she thought ruefully. It was only the risk of spoiling Mali's afternoon tea party that made her remain silent.

She moved to the window-seat where she sat turned away from the chatter of the room, wondering when it was that Marion had seen Brandon with Mary Anne and her daughter. Anger surged through her as she thought of them together and she looking the fool knowing nothing about it.

'There's a scowl likely to bring on the thunder.' Mali sat beside her and patted her hand. 'Come on now, you know better than to listen to that cat Marion, don't you?'

Mary forced a smile. 'You're right, you always did talk a lot of sense, Mali.' Yet her spirits were low and even though she joined the little group of admiring women at Sterling's side and laughed with them at his jokes, she felt cold and lost and there was an ache deep inside her that she could not dispel.

It was on the following day that she saw Mary Anne Bloomfield with her own eyes. The woman was plumpish but dressed in great style, with frills and furbelows decorating her fine velvet coat and skirt. She sat opposite Mary in the emporium tea-rooms, consciously aware that she was the centre of attraction. Her daughter, who looked about sixteen years of age, was slight and pale with an indistinctive cast to her mouth and chin, but the fine eyes and unruly dark hair marked her as a Sutton as surely as if the name was emblazoned across the high forehead.

Covertly, Mary watched the woman she thought of as her adversary, and slowly began to realise that Mary Anne was a voluptuous woman. In spite of her full figure, her skin was fine and her hair silky – falling across her forehead in a most unfashionable but strangely becoming style. Her mouth was full and glossily coloured and her teeth were white and even.

Mary told herself she was being ridiculous, sitting behind an aspidistra plant in her own tea-room spying on this other woman, yet something held her fast. She was fascinated by the woman's extravagant gestures and by the high-pitched American voice. Did Mary Anne know that she was sitting in the store owned by the wife of her former lover, Mary wondered? In her heart she knew that Mary Anne was not the type to do anything without calculating every move first.

'There's soft you are, sitting here like a thief in the night,' she murmured in self-disgust and she twitched the hem of her gown into place and rose from her chair, intending to return to her office.

Her heart missed a beat as she heard the timbre of her husband's voice and cautiously she peered between the large glossy leaves of the plant. Brandon was kissing Mary Anne's fingers and bowing his head to the young girl at her side and even as Mary watched, he took a seat and leaned across the tea cups engrossed in an earnest conversation.

The blood raced into Mary's face and she put up her hands as though to cool her cheeks, controlling the impulse to rush

216

forward and confront her husband. She must not make a scene, she told herself fiercely, that would only help feed the gossiping tongues. She moved forward with a measured tread, her head high and a smile on her lips.

'Brandon, home from work so early?' She leaned forward and kissed his cheek, her hand resting on his shoulder. 'Don't get up, I'll join you. We'll have a fresh pot of tea, please, Greenie,' she said as the older woman hovered anxiously nearby.

'And this must be the Mary Anne I've heard so much about.' Mary's tone implied that there had been a lot of fuss about nothing and Mary Anne's eyes searched her face knowingly.

'And you are Brandon's little wife – and what a sweet, funny way you have of talking, honey.' The tone was friendly but the eyes held nothing but hostility. 'This is Virginia, our daughter.'

The phrasing was calculated to raise the hackles of any woman, but Mary smiled sweetly.

'I can see she's your daughter all right,' she said softly, 'but then I wouldn't know your husband, would I?'

Her words found their mark and Mary Anne could not conceal her dislike. She glared at Mary, her silence acknowledging the fact that there was no husband. The full mouth became a pout as she rose sweepingly to her feet.

'You must excuse us, honey, we have business elsewhere – but don't forget our little arrangement, will you?' Her words were for Brandon, who rose politely to his feet as Mary Anne swept away followed by her silent daughter.

Brandon leaned across the table. 'That was not worthy of you, Mary.' He spoke softly and she looked into his eyes, unable to conceal the pain she was feeling.

'And I suppose it was worthy of you to sit in my own tea-rooms with a woman who once was your mistress?' she asked in a low voice. 'She wanted it that way, Brandon, she arranged it so that I would look the fool before all my friends, can't you see that?'

He shook his head. 'All I see is a woman who is jealous over something that happened years ago. I repeat, it's not worthy of you.'

She rose to her feet. 'Worthy or not, if you meet her again

and make a laughing-stock of me in the town, you'll be sorry.'

His eyes darkened. 'Don't threaten me, Mary.' His voice, though low, carried such force of feeling that Mary was fearful of what he would do next. She turned and walked unseeingly away, and in that moment she almost hated her husband.

Chapter Eighteen

Lightning forked across the hills, cracking the gloomy skies asunder. Thunder rumbled low over the sleepy, early-morning face of Sweyn's Eye like the sound of gunfire, reminding the dozing inhabitants that the country was at war.

Rhian had been awake early, unable to sleep, tossing from side to side in her small bed, feeling alone in her candle-lit room and yet aware of Gina Sinman sleeping in the next room with a child on each side of her. How grateful she was for Gina's company and good sense, for since Heath had been sent to France guilt had ridden Rhian's mind like a nightmare for allowing him to think that she was in love with him.

She went to the mill so early that she needed to light the lamps; in the ghostly glow, the machines normally so familiar seemed dark monsters about to spring and rend. She was being silly and fanciful, she knew, but it was just as well she was up and about early because there was a lot of work to do.

As she brushed back her hair and tied it with a piece of ribbon, she allowed herself a smile. She had every reason to be pleased with herself: at last sales of wool were bringing in a profit. Still, she must not crow too soon, for there was a great deal more to do to put the mill on a solid footing once more.

'And nothing will get done if you stand by here day-dreaming, girl,' she told herself sternly.

She set the mule into motion and watched the slubbings twisting and interlocking the woollen fibres so that they would be suitable for weaving into brightly coloured blankets. She would spend the morning in the mill, she decided, and do her rounds of the houses in the afternoon.

As she worked she frowned in concentration – unaware of the fine lines of her cheek-bones, the slimness of her body and the dark shadows that dusted blue beneath her eyes. She needed to work for when she stopped, her mind would begin to race. When that happened she would be tormented by memories of Heath's love for her, would remember how she had lain in his arms giving herself so readily to his embrace. He had gone bravely off to war, comforted by the thought of Rhian waiting for his return; he was true and honest and did not deserve her treachery. Then, as though to scourge her soul, she would see in her mind's eye Mansel Jack's dark strong face and unhappiness would rise like a blight to encompass her mind.

It was Gina's voice which shattered her concentration. Rhian looked up and smiled as she saw the two children sitting one on each plump hip and Gina smiling as though she had everything in the world that she wanted.

'Shut off that clattering machine, there's a lovely girl, it's time to have a bit of grub before you fall down into a faint.'

The sudden silence in the room seemed to echo Gina's voice and Rhian rubbed at her eyes wearily.

'I am hungry,' she said, smiling. 'I hope there's plenty of food, for I might just start eating the babbas as well.'

Cerianne screamed in excitement as Rhian tickled her plump cheek and clung to Gina as though she had never known any other mother.

Rhian prised her loose and carried the little girl along the coldness of the yard, following Gina back to the house.

'I've got us a nice piece of ham and some cockles and lavabread – you'd better eat it all up, my girl, or I'll be taking offence, mind,' Gina said breathlessly.

Rhian hid a smile; sometimes Gina treated her as though she was a child. 'I'll eat it all up, don't you bother your head about that.'

The kitchen gleamed with cleanliness and warmth and gratefully, Rhian sank down into a chair.

'Look,' Gina said, 'why don't we take Cerianne and little Dewi down to the park for a bit this afternoon.'

'The park? But it's thundering and there's lightning.' Rhian looked through the window, amazed to see that the day had blossomed out into one of sunshine and the birds were singing to usher in the spring.

'You going off your head or something?' Gina said with a smile. 'It stopped raining hours ago.'

Rhian sat at the table with Cerianne on her lap and began to eat hungrily. 'I've got a better idea,' she mumbled through a forkful of bacon, 'why don't we go round the houses selling?'

Gina frowned. 'I don't know, *cariad*, there's still a lot of folks don't trust me, you know. No, you go, good girl. I'll take the babbas down the park on my own.'

'I'm sorry,' Rhian said quickly. 'I know it's hard at the moment, hard on both of us, but we're just beginning to win, Gina. If we carry on like this, I'm thinking of getting a woman in to look after the children so that you can help me in the mill.'

Gina gave her a quick look. 'What woman?' She hugged her son as though unwilling to hand him over to anyone and Rhian smiled reassuringly.

'You know Carrie, who used to come in and "do" for my Aunt Agnes? Well, I thought she'd be ideal. She's a good worker and reliable enough, we can trust her. In any case, we'll only be a stone's throw away should anything go wrong.'

'I suppose you're right.' Gina began to smile. 'It might be nice to work at the loom again.'

'That's settled, then,' Rhian smiled and Gina shook her head at her.

'How sly of you, Rhian Gray, I thought we were talking about "maybe".'

Rhian chuckled out loud. 'All right, maybe we'll definitely get Carrie in to help. I'll see her when I go round with the wool this afternoon.'

Selling on doorsteps was not the easiest way of making money, Rhian found. She had filled two large baskets with hanks of wool in just the right greyish-khaki colour for knitting socks for soldiers, for she had quickly learned that the wealthier women of Sweyn's Eye were delighted to be doing their own little bit to help the war on its way. They paid a good price for the wool too, and Rhian prided herself that it was of the best quality. Some she had double-spun so as to make the wool thicker and the hanks were being bought up more quickly than she could produce them; she could certainly do with Gina's expert help in the mill, she thought ruefully.

221

The hill was rising steeply; the panorama of the sea, the town and the docks was spread out below and it was a breathtaking sight. Rhian paused, feeling her hair drift free of the ribbon which had been holding it and not caring. She was behaving like a gypsy, she thought wryly, so she might as well look like one.

The baskets were quickly emptied and hung on her arms, the handles marking fine patterns against her bare flesh. Rhian sat down to rest, for her feet ached in the heavy boots she was wearing. She really must buy herself more comfortable footwear, for she would be tramping the streets a great deal. Undoing the laces, she eased the boots from her feet, stretching out in a hollow that sheltered her from the gusty sea breezes, a trap for the spring sunshine. She was out of sight of the windows of the fine big houses now. So tired that she found herself becoming soothed and relaxed, she closed her eyes and the sun dazzled orange behind her lids; it was so comfortable that she must rest.

*

The Richardson house was airy and spacious and Mansel Jack stood before the window staring appreciatively into the garden. It was rich with spring blossoms; daffodils strident and yellow grew at random in the lawn and trees fringed the borders of the grounds.

After Yorkshire, Wales was the most beautiful country he had ever seen. But it had another face and one with which he was becoming familiar. He had spent a great deal of time in the heart of the industrial area of Sweyn's Eye; the stink of the copper smoke and the abrasive quality of the dust-laden air had attacked his throat, stinging his eyes, until he became used to it.

Since coming to Wales, he had congratulated himself more than once on having the insight to put his brass into munitions. He had known instinctively that shells and armaments were what the country needed and had been proved right.

He found himself mingling well with the townspeople – the gentry, Doreen would have called them. It was ironic really that she was not here to enjoy the fine company he was keeping.

222

As for Charlotte, she wrote to him diligently, her love flowing from the neat handwriting. He had soon realised that the only feeling he had for her was one of guilt. He pushed aside the thought as Sterling Richardson entered the room with his hands thrust into his pockets, looking handsome and dashing in his uniform.

'Good to see you,' Sterling held out his hand. 'I'm rejoining my regiment today, glad you could call before I leave.'

'I won't beat about the bush,' Mansel Jack said at once. 'It's about the house I'm renting from you – I want to buy it.'

Sterling nodded his head. 'Yes, I think we can come to some arrangement about the property. Let's walk in the garden, shall we?'

For a time the two men strolled through the spring-fresh air in companionable silence. They moved into the arbour where the leaves of the trees grew dewy and green.

'You know, I've been buying up houses rather than selling them,' Sterling said after a time, 'but you're welcome to the house in Meadow Street if it isn't too modest for your requirements.'

'It will do me for now,' Mansel Jack said decisively.

'Good, then consider it settled. I shall make sure you have a bargain, you can depend on it,' Sterling smiled. He was a handsome man with fine features and honest eyes and Mansel Jack had liked him ever since their first meeting at the home of Mary Sutton.

'You know, being at the front gives a man a different kind of perspective,' Sterling said thoughtfully. 'It seemed to me that to build up my empire and my fortune was of prime importance, yet somehow the will to make more and more money has vanished.' He turned on his heel. 'I'd better be getting back into the house, I'm becoming maudlin. I'll say goodbye to you now, Mansel Jack. I need to spend as much time with my family as possible.'

'I understand,' the other responded, smiling warmly. 'I'm just going to walk over the hills – see you on your next leave.'

The two men shook hands, both knowing that there might not be a next time.

Mansel Jack stepped out smartly, feeling the cool of the spring breeze on his cheeks. And yet the sun was shining

223

bravely, a pale sun but warming the land in the sheltered areas between the hill-tops.

He paused for a moment to take deep breaths of the clear air, free here from the abrasive dust which covered the valley. He had a new plan now, one which had been germinating in his head for some time. Wool was in his blood and even though the munitions were a good source of revenue he needed something else in his life. That was why he had made it his business to try to find Heinz Sinman, the owner of Spinners' Wharf, and the news was bad.

Deep in his thoughts, he came upon the little hollow so suddenly that he almost stumbled over the small figure lying in its warmth. He crouched down on his heels, a strange sensation filling him.

Rhian Gray was beautiful to see and a tight feeling filled his lungs as if all the air had been expelled. He saw the way her hair drifted down her shoulders and touched its softness carefully. She was thinner than when he had seen her last and there were shadows beneath her eyes. The lass was working too hard, it was plain enough for anyone to see. Once he owned the mill, he would be sure to take care of her.

As she stirred slightly her thick skirts fell away from her ankles and he saw her feet were completely bare, her toes small and well-formed. He smiled, though there was a strange feeling in the pit of his stomach.

She was a fine young woman, he told himself, who had returned to her native Wales and set herself up to do a job of work with a determination that he had to admire. He would not confide his plans to her, for first he had the unpleasant task of informing Gina Sinman that she was a widow.

He looked down at Rhian's sleeping face, feeling something more than the usual raw urge to have a woman's sweet warmth beneath him. He shook his head, telling himself he was getting soft in his old age; he simply desired her because the day was fine and it was a long time since he had lain with a woman. Yet he could not deny that she had the quality of appearing untouched and untouchable and this appealed to him greatly.

Suddenly Rhian opened her eyes and was looking at him and they stared at each other for a long time in silence. Gradually she became aware of her appearance and sat up, pulling on her boots, trying to brush back the unruly hair that was festooned with small spikes of grass.

'You look very beautiful,' he said softly, 'but you shouldn't go falling asleep on mountain-tops. It rained last night and the grass is probably damp.'

She stood up and even at full height she came only to his shoulder. 'Why were you sitting there, staring at me like that? You'll give me goose bumps,' she said breathlessly.

He ignored her question, amazed at the urge to draw her into his arms and cradle her against him. 'How are you getting along, lass?' He stared pointedly at the baskets and she picked them up quickly, brushing back her long hair.

'I'm doing all right,' she said proudly. Her smile was brilliant. 'I'm so determined that I *make* folk buy from me!'

'Putting to good use all the things you learned at my mill, eh?' he said pleasantly, but she appeared very young and vulnerable.

'Can't I be of some help, lass?' he asked and she glanced up at him, her eyes warm.

'Seems to me you've enough to do with the munitions factory,' she replied, pushing back her hair again.

'Worried about me?' he said, making a move towards her. She swung round the baskets to make an effective barrier between them – not that the look in her eyes wasn't barrier enough.

'All right,' he held up his hands. 'I'm not going to touch you.'

'I know you're not,' she replied shakily, 'for I cannot let you.' She attempted to tidy her hair, but the breeze took the dark red strands and lifted them so that the curls drifted across her face.

'Do you dislike me then, Rhian?' he asked.

'No, of course I don't.' Her eyes were hidden from him now, but her voice trembled.

'Why hold me at bay then, lass? We used to be able to talk.'

She paused for a moment, avoiding his eyes. 'You must know that I'm Heath Jenkins' girl now,' she said at last. 'Going to be his wife I am, when he returns from the war.'

As she began to walk away from him a mixture of emotions raced through him and he was suddenly angry, though he could not have said why.

'Hey, lass!' he called after her. 'For a bride-to-be, you've got a very long face!'

He watched as she stumbled away over the uneven ground, but she did not turn and he stared after her until the small figure was out of sight, wondering at the empty feeling that lay heavy in his gut.

*

Carrie, it seemed, was more than pleased to come to the mill and look after the children. She confided in Rhian how empty her life had seemed, now that she had no one to look after.

'Born to care for folk, I was, and I'm that grateful to you for giving me the chance to be of use again. I'll mind the babbas with the greatest of pleasure,' she said warmly.

'There's good of you, Carrie,' Rhian had been delighted. 'The babies are little monsters on times, what with Cerianne bossing little Dewi, but you'll love them both and they'll love you, I just know it.'

Gina had been reluctant at first to leave her precious son up at the house while she worked the mill, but soon she was transformed, her eyes brighter and her step full of her old verve. And it was with a feeling of happiness that Rhian saw her friend become more confident and assured.

'You're a clever girl, Rhian Gray, you know that?' Gina swung the belt from the fast wheel to the loose and the clatter of the loom died away into silence.

'Now why do you have to throw me compliments that are not deserved?' Rhian was holding up a blanket, struggling under its weight, trying to see if the pattern had worked out as she had planned.

Gina sighed. 'You just get everyone to do what you want – you have a gift for managing people.'

'Hmm, I don't know about that,' Rhian smiled. 'What do you think of this, Gina? Isn't the pattern colourful and won't it sell shawls and blankets like freshly-caught fish?'

Gina stood back and stared at the mingling of red, white and blue fringing, eyes wide. 'There's a good idea for you, now,' she said in admiration. 'Very patriotic of you, my girl. But I can't see the fashionable ladies wearing thick woollen shawls,

226

can you?'

Rhian shook her head. 'No, but they'll buy these warm blankets to send to the front – and as for the turnovers, I'll sell them to all the working women in Sweyn's Eye. We'll wear them ourselves too; nothing like showing off the product, is there?'

'*Duw*, there's a marvel you are, Rhian. Got some good ideas you have – can see you as rich as a queen in no time.'

'Well, for now I'll settle for making a fair living. Come on, my girl, it's back to work for us. Flood the market with these, we will, so that no one else gets a look-in on our ideas.'

Gina frowned. 'Aye, I never thought about that.' She set the loom into motion once more. 'I'll get this turnover off quick and then start on the red, white and blue. We'll show Sweyn's Eye what we're made of!'

Rhian could scarcely hear Gina's voice over the clatter of the machine, but she nodded and smiled, pleased by the eager look on the other's face. That she still grieved over Heinz was clear, for Rhian heard her cry sometimes in the quiet of the night, but Gina's zest for living had returned and Rhian was thankful for it.

The 'patriotic shawls' caught the imagination of the town and soon they began to be seen on the shoulders of the working women from one end of Sweyn's Eye to the other.

But as Rhian had feared, it was not long before Alfred Phillpot was copying the red, white and blue pattern – as she soon learned when she knocked on a door in Canal Street and found Sally Benson's round face sneering at her.

'Got a shawl like that one only better.' She spoke in a sing-song voice, just like a child poking out its tongue and shouting 'sucks to you'.

Rhian stared at her, trying to conceal her dislike. 'Not cheaper, though, I bet a gold sovereign.'

'Yes, cheaper, see. Alfred Phillpot is quicker than you and I've got one of the first shawls he's made, but soon they'll be in all the shops and then your nose will be out of joint.' She closed the door with a snap of finality and after a fruitless tour of the rest of the street, Rhian turned for home.

'The cheatin' little toad!' Carrie said harshly. 'I could kill the po-faced pipsqueak myself!'

227

'Aye, I know how you feel, but how can we stop him?' Rhian sat numbly in her chair and stared into the rosiness of the fire. 'He's got the might of the Co-op Movement behind him and I've got nothing.'

'Wait a minute,' Carrie said softly. 'What about that man Mansel Jack – the one you used to work for? Go and ask him for help.'

Rhian hid her face beneath the heavy fall of her hair, ashamed of the rich colour that came to her cheeks.

'Oh, I couldn't go to him with my problems,' she said softly.

Carrie sighed. 'Perhaps you're right, *merchi*,' she replied, but there was a small smile on her lips. If Rhian would not approach the man there was nothing stopping *her* from asking his advice, Carrie thought; she would see to it this very evening!

Rhian was determined to be at the mill early the next morning, but as she walked along the greyness of the yard she left the warmth of the coal fire behind with reluctance. Gina would join her later when little Dewi had sucked his fill from her round full breasts. Somehow it pained Rhian to witness the breakfast routine; she felt excluded and alone, for usually Carrie was busy feeding Cerianne and everyone except her seemed occupied and involved.

She stared ahead of her now, her footsteps faltering to a stop, unable to believe her eyes. Mansel Jack was leaning against the door of the mill, his hands in his pockets and a smile on his handsome face. From the freshness of his manner, he had been abroad for hours.

'Good morning. Won't you let me inside the mill before this late frost does its worst to my extremities?' He laughed as she blushed, looking down at the key in her hand but unable to set it into the lock. At last he took it from her, his fingers brushing hers and adding to her confusion.

'I understand you need a little support?' he said easily as he moved into the dimness of the mill.

Rhian lit the lamps and tried to gather her thoughts; Carrie must have gone to Mansel Jack and asked for his help.

She took a deep breath and turned to look at him. 'Aye, I suppose I do need some advice,' she said reluctantly.

228

'There, it didn't hurt to admit it, you see?' He smiled, speaking easily, and her colour rose.

'Don't make fun.'

His dark eyes met hers for a brief instant. 'Oh, I'm not making fun of you, Rhian, lass – indeed, I've taken a few hours off from my factory to help you. Now, tell me about the problem you have with this man Phillpot.' He settled himself easily on the long bench seat that ran down the middle of the room and nervously Rhian clasped her hands together. His presence filled the place and he seemed to glow and shimmer, illuminating the dimness.

She shook her head. 'Nothing much to say except that he's stealing my idea of the red, white and blue pattern. He's taking my trade from me and what can I do?'

It was the first time she had asked him for anything and Rhian glanced at Mansel Jack uncertainly, looking away when he would have caught her eye.

'Leave it to me,' he said at last. 'It's a simple enough matter and I'll deal with it – you'll get no more trouble from this Alfred Phillpot.'

She believed him, for Mansel Jack would intimidate anyone. It was not so much his appearance – though he was a big man and strong, with great determination in his face – as his manner, which was enough to freeze over an ocean. But he was smiling now. 'Phillpot's not important, so put him out of your mind. Now, how about coming up to my house this evening for a bite of supper, lass?'

She tensed, drawing herself up to her full height. He rose and stood beside her, not touching her, but it was as though shocks were passing between them. Rhian held her head high and looked into his eyes.

'You know I'm spoken for,' her voice shook. 'And anyway, what would folk think of me, being in your house alone? No, it wouldn't do at all.'

'Damnation, I suppose I'm not thinking straight. You're right, of course.' He rubbed his hand through his fine curly hair and stared down at her with warmth glowing in his eyes. 'But there would be nothing improper about a walk in Brynmill Park, would there?' He smiled then, the charm of his features and the light in his eyes making her feel suddenly

229

breathless.

She backed away from him, on her dignity, her voice more controlled when she spoke.

'Please, just go away and leave me alone. I'm not free, I've explained that to you.'

'All right,' he sounded exasperated. 'I'll leave you alone, there's no talking to a woman who has no spark of humour in her.' He shrugged his big shoulders. 'I thought we had a lot in common, you and me, Rhian Gray – but perhaps I was wrong.'

Rhian wanted to cling to him, to tell him she felt more than simple friendship for him. She would have given anything to walk in the park with him, but how could she when she was promised to Heath?

He left without another word and Rhian stood for a long moment, her thoughts racing, her pulse throbbing. Then she sighed heavily. She must be calm she told herself. 'Forget Mansel Jack!' And yet the image of him and the power of his presence continued to haunt the mill.

Whatever it was that he said or did to Alfred Phillpot, the man stopped producing the three-coloured shawls as quickly as he had begun. Rhian waited for Mansel Jack to call and tell her of his triumph, but she waited in vain for he did not come.

*

Mansel Jack had been pleased to come to Rhian's aid and it had given him great personal pleasure to put the little man from the Cooperative Movement in his place yet again. It had not involved very much effort, just a reminder that he could be exposed as a fraud and then his career would be at an end. Alfred Phillpot had given in at once, smiling ingratiatingly, his narrowed eyes wary and watchful.

'I'll do anything you say, of course.' His reply had been what Mansel Jack expected, but then the man was a windbag who would only try his antics on helpless women.

Calling at the mill house early one morning and hearing the clatter of the loom, he knew that Rhian was at work.

Gina was alone in the kitchen preparing breakfast, and he felt a sense of relief, for what he must say needed privacy. He broached the subject of Heinz' death with care, fearing that she

230

would swoon away in a vapour or become hysterical. He need not have worried, for though gentle she was made of sterner stuff than that.

'You're sure?' she asked, her eyes appealing and he nodded, taking her hands in his.

'I'm sorry.'

Gina drew her son to her and kissed his cheek. 'Then what's to become of us? Rhian can't carry the burden of the mill alone.'

'I have a solution if you want to hear it,' he said, 'but perhaps the time's not right?'

She nodded her head. 'Please speak.'

'I'd like to buy Spinners' Wharf.' He held up his hand when she would have spoken. 'No, hear me out. I'd like everything to continue just as it is, but I could inject much-needed money into the business.' He smiled. 'I'm really being very selfish, for the woollen industry is in my blood and I'd like to see the mill built up to the successful business I know it could be.' He paused. 'By all means take time to think things over, but I would ask that you keep our discussion private for the time being.'

He left the mill and made his way back, pausing to stare at the solid old house that was now his home. He should be concerning himself with his future marriage; Charlotte's last letter had been full of her loneliness for him, and yet there was so much else to occupy his time. He spent his days at the munitions factory, working both in the office and on the shop floor, but it gave him little satisfaction. He simply wasn't needed there; put any good man in at the top and the place would run itself and give him his freedom. But freedom to do what?

The increasing urgency of the war had changed him. Mansel Jack no longer felt it enough to make money, even though his fortune was continuing to grow. He needed a fresh challenge in his life – would owning Spinners' Wharf be enough for him, he wondered.

To think he had once considered marriage to Charlotte Bradley the biggest step he could take. He had a great many years before him, damn it, and was no old man to sit in a corner. But having a wife and watching her do tatting or paint

231

scenery – was that the path he wished to take? He doubted it, for however intelligent and lovely Charlotte was she did not stir him.

The last encounter he had had with Rhian Gray had affected him more than he would have believed possible. With her funny pride and her soft vulnerable little face she had somehow made herself important in his life. He wanted to take her to bed . . . there was no denying that and he did not want to deny it. What bothered him was the fact that he also longed to protect her, to care for her – and that was not possible for had she not told him herself that she belonged to another man? And there was Charlotte who loved him, trusted him . . . what could he do about her?

He must put thoughts of both women out of his mind, cast aside the strange restlessness that gripped him and knuckle down to hard work the way he had done all his life. And yet, teasing at the back of his mind was the possibility that now he might be able to enlist in the Army. More and more men were needed and age no longer seemed to be a barrier. On reflection, the Army might be the best place for him.

Chapter Nineteen

Rain swept from the heavens, shrouding the peaks of the hills above Sweyn's Eye. The sulphurous smoke from the copper works, trapped by the clouds, seeped beneath doors and twisted into narrow courts like prying fingers.

In the Murphy house in Market Street, Katie coughed, grimacing as her mother held out a spoonful of Scotts Emulsion.

'Get it down you, girl. Jesus Mary and Joseph, anyone would 'tink I was trying to poison you!'

Katie dutifully swallowed the evil-smelling medicine and sat at the table crunching a piece of toast in a vain effort to rid her mouth of the fishy taste.

'I've done up your grub-bag, given you a nice bit of bacon and some cheese and bread I baked myself yesterday. Got to keep up your strength working in that factory, so you have.'

Katie drank the sweet hot tea at a gulp. 'The spoon would stand up in this brew, mammy, why do you have to make it so strong?'

'Ah, stop moaning. Put a drop o' gin in it and then you won't notice!'

Katie picked up her bag and shook her head. 'I'd better get down to the station or I'll miss the train.'

Outside in the rain-soaked quietness of Market Street, the sound of an accordion suddenly filled the air. Dai-End-House, a Welshman to the core, was adopting the Irish this morning, playing 'Paddy McGinty's Goat' in a quick breathless way that brought tears to Katie's eyes – which was daft, for she didn't know anything about Ireland except what her mammy had

233

told her.

Still coughing, she hurried down towards the station bending her head against the rain. The last thing she felt like was going to work, but she'd be letting down the rest of the gang if she didn't and what was a little old cough anyway?

'*Bore da*, Katie. Come on, girl, the train's spitting and puffing fit to bust.' Doris dragged on her arm. 'Only kept it back because I bribed Willie the driver with a bit of bread and honey.' They clambered into the nearest carriage, Katie smiling at Doris's effort to make room for them.

'I don't know where Janey's got to, though I caught a glimpse of her earlier, mind – bright in the eye 'cos she'd been out courtin' last night. Daft thing – don't know yet that men only want to get into your drawers.'

The words dropped into an icy silence and Katie became aware that she and Doris were seated in a compartment usually reserved for the clerical workers. It had become an unspoken law that office and factory workers remain apart as much as possible, but this misty wet morning was surely an exception.

Delmai Richardson was seated opposite and she glared at Doris with thinly disguised disgust. It was bad enough that she had been forced to work by Rickie's insistence and by the fact that other women of her station were engaged in the war effort. But to be thrown together with women of such low class was an atrocious state of affairs. The atmosphere grew steadily more tense as the train lurched and lumbered along the line, spitting sparks which the beating rain quickly extinguished.

'There's a way to look at a body,' Doris could no longer restrain herself. 'Got a bit of dog shit on my boots or something, have I?'

Delmai turned her head, her eyes scornful, not deigning to answer. But Doris was alight with righteous indignation, her face red, her hands clenched.

'Thinks you're a lady, don't you, but we all knows that you're little better than a flossie.'

Delmai leaned forward, face flushed and eyes glistening. 'Shut up, you little slut; don't you dare talk to your betters that way!'

Katie murmured to Doris to be quiet. 'Don't let's be having any bother,' she said softly, pulling at Doris's arm. 'Let's just

234

get to work in one piece, shall we?'

'Don't trouble yourself, my dear,' Delmai smiled at Katie as though she was an ally. 'You can't make a silk purse out of a sow's ear.'

Doris was on her feet then – her hands reaching for Delmai's hair, gripping and twisting, her eyes glowing with fury.

'Call me a sow, would you, you *whore*! I'll give you sow! Had two men between your legs that *I* know of, you have, and a babba born out of wedlock, pushed aside like a parcel. I knows too much about you, so don't come the toffee-nosed act with me, Mrs Richardson.' She pulled Delmai from the seat and the two of them went sprawling on the dusty floor, rolling among the feet of the appalled passengers.

'Doris! Jesus, Mary and Joseph, get off Mrs Richardson before you kill her, she's not worth it!' Katie stared at the other women in anger. 'Come on for pity's sake, help me separate them, have you all lost your wits?'

At last Katie managed to prise Doris's hands away from Delmai's hair. Doris sank back in her seat, smacking her palms together in satisfaction.

Delmai was flushed, her hair hanging over her face, her cheek scratched and her lip bleeding. 'I hate you,' she said harshly 'and if ever I can do you harm I won't hesitate, you'll see.'

The train had shuddered to a stop, puffing steam and sparks. Katie became aware that there was a crowd of curious women gathered around the carriage doorway, attracted by the noise no doubt.

A dark shadow loomed into the carriage and Mansel Jack was staring down at the women, his eyes shrewd and missing nothing, his face impassive.

'I won't have any talk about doing each other harm, ladies.' He emphasised the last word dryly. 'There's a war on, men are getting killed every day and here you lasses are fighting like street-cats. I won't have it, do you hear me?' No one dared reply and after a moment, Mansel Jack turned and walked away.

Katie hurried Doris along the platform. 'Why did you let the woman goad you like that?' she asked shortly. 'For goodness' sake, Doris, there's more important things to think about than

235

fighting amongst ourselves, the boss is right enough there.'

'She just gets me all worked up,' Doris said in a low voice. She looked so hangdog that Katie could not help but smile.

'To be sure you're a right scrapper, my dad would be proud of you, I think you must have some of the Irish blood running in your veins.'

A little of the tenseness left Doris's shoulders, she sighed softly and pulled her mob-cap over her tangled hair. 'Wouldn't be a bit surprised. Me mam liked the men; I had lots of uncles when I was small and my sister up in Carreg Fach is as different from me as chalk from cheese.' She made a rueful face at Katie, 'I suppose that's why I count myself lucky to have a man of my own, even though he won't get married and runs off on a spree every now and then.'

'Hey there, you two, wait for me!' Janey was running along the platform, linking arms with Doris and Katie, her small face lit with curiosity. 'What's all this about a fight, then? Is it true you gave Mrs Richardson a pasting?'

Doris blossomed under Janey's incredulous admiration. She smacked her palms together once more and her cheeks glowed. 'I gave her what for, pulled her right down from her pedestal. Thinks she's too good to ride with the likes of us, but I made sure all her mates knew just what she'd been up to.'

Katie sighed heavily. 'Come on, you two, stop blabbering and get to the shed or we'll have a pile of gaines up to our eyebrows, all waiting to have holes hammered into them.'

The long factory was already droning like a hive full of worker bees. The lathes were turning, the tables bristled with upright shells and the women, dressed in trousers and long jackets with mob-caps covering their hair, moved as mechanically as the machines they worked.

'I'm glad I'm not in there,' Doris said quickly. 'I know that working on the faulty gaines is dangerous – well, so the boss says – but I'd much rather be in a little group in our own shed than stuck there with all those clacking machines.'

'Yes, well, we'll all be out on our ears if we don't get some work done,' Katie said loudly. 'I don't want to say it again girls, *move!*'

Katie took up one of the tube-shaped gaines and placed her chisel over the the spot to be tapped, experienced now at breaking the thread. Was there no end to the wrongly threaded gaines sent over by the Americans, she wondered, her brow creased into a frown of concentration. She could hear Doris and Janey chatting and wished that they would pay more attention to the job. Still, Janey was very young and Doris . . . well, she was just Doris who went her own way, worked by her own code of conduct.

She eased her back, standing straight for a moment, and staring round the high-ceilinged shed. There were now three tables in production, for as more and more faulty gaines came into the factory so the work force had to be increased. Katie was in charge of them all and took her job seriously. Glancing round, she saw Honey O'Connor bent industriously over the table, her gorgeous hair hidden beneath the stiff mob-cap, her young face taut with the effort she was making to hammer the gaines in the exact position, for one slip would mean disaster.

Katie smiled to herself. She had seen Honey walking out with Morgan Lloyd – a fine boy, even though he was a Protestant. The two of them were like skittish ponies when together, afraid to break the fragile bond that was growing between them. It was good to be young and in love. She thought of her own first love, William Owen. He had been no good, as her mother had continuously told her. But he was the first one of her life and and under his teachings she had been wild, lying with him in the long grass, letting him have his way with her. And she had revelled in the knowledge of her own sensuality.

She knew he was a 'bad 'un' but she had loved him dearly. When he had been killed, implicated in the disaster of the Kilvey Deep, she had not thought even then of his wrongdoing but had mourned him, believing he would be the only one for her ever. But she had been wrong. She smiled as she thought of Mark, tall and handsome and honest. Her heart swelled with happiness and she wondered how she could ever have doubted that one day she would fall in love again.

But Honey now, she was a different sort of girl altogether. She would take Morgan as her husband and never falter in her faithfulness. Katie put down the gaines she had just finished and walked around the tables, giving a word of encouragement to the women as she went.

237

'Top o' the morning to you, Honey,' she said and the girl looked up at her with a ready smile. Yet there was sadness in the depths of her eyes. Katie frowned. 'Anything wrong?' she asked anxiously and the girl shook her head.

'It's just that Morgan's talking about enlisting in the Army,' she said hollowly. 'Now his dad's gone, God rest him, there's nothing to keep Morgan at our house, you see.'

'I can't believe that,' Katie said gently. 'He seems to be so fond of you.'

Honey looked away. 'I thought so too, but that's what he's saying.' The words were dragged from her and it was clear she was bitterly hurt.

'Have you and Morgan ever talked, *really* talked, I mean?' Katie asked and Honey sighed. Her eyes flashed a little as she lifted her head.

'No, but I thought we had an understanding, I couldn't believe he was interested in me at first, but then he told me that...' her words trailed away as she shrugged her shoulders. 'Ah, well, it's no good me thinking about it all, he's going for a soldier and he says I must understand that he must do what's right.'

A shrill whistle pierced the air and Katie smiled encouragingly. 'Come and have your grub-break with me. Look, it's stopped raining, we'll sit outside and have a bit of privacy. Just let me get my bag.'

The rain had stopped, but small puddles lay like diamonds on the ground. The air was cleaner than in the heart of the town, for the copper works were several miles away and here the fresh breezes rolled in from the sea.

'I don't know that there's much more to talk about.' Honey took a slice of bread from her bag and stared at it without interest. Katie well remembered the time when she couldn't eat because of the love that tore at her insides, so she remained silent as she unpacked her bacon sandwiches.

'I was beginning to think he really cared,' Honey said slowly. 'Sometimes he would look at me in a funny way that made me shivery all over.' She hung her head. 'But then he said he was going to the Army, just casually, as though it meant nothing to anyone but himself.'

'Men are strange creatures,' Katie said after a moment, 'and

238

they think a lot of their pride. They need to fight this awful war, fear they will be branded cowards if they don't enlist.'

Honey looked at her hopefully. 'Perhaps you're right, but what can I do to show him I'll wait for him for ever if need be? I don't want to make a fool of myself.'

Katie took a deep breath. How on earth had she put herself in the role of adviser; she was no great expert on the matters of the heart herself! 'Just ask him to write to you,' she said at last, 'then you can send him little gifts, knit him woolly socks or something – there are more ways than words of saying you love a man.'

'You're right, sure enough,' Honey said, her eyes lit with an inner glow. 'It's so easy, I'm surprised I didn't think of it myself.' She gave Katie a shy look. 'An' you won't be after tellin' anyone about this, will you?'

Katie laughed and licked her finger, making the sign of the cross over her breasts. 'Cross my heart and hope to die,' she said solemnly. Then she rose to her feet, brushing the dampness of the bark from her trousers, coughing a little. 'Come on, we'd best get back inside or there'll be no work done.'

She smiled as she watched Honey enter the shed ahead of her and walk quickly over the cold stone floor towards her table; she was a pretty sweet girl and Katie hoped that everything would work out for her. She paused in the doorway, still coughing, breathing in the freshness of the air that seemed to cool her lungs.

Suddenly, it was as if hell had come on earth. A sheet of flame exploded, snaking with awful brightness across the shed. A terrifying noise roared and crashed about her ears and Katie felt herself lifted from the ground. She could see nothing any more, she could not breathe for the heat that enveloped her. It was as though she was being hurled down a long dark windy tunnel, but there was no light at the end, only a deep impenetrable blackness.

*

The rain no longer swept down from the hills, the air was fresh now with the clouds breaking to reveal the warm face of the sun.

239

Rhian lifted the heavy gardening spade with difficulty and begun to dig the stubborn heavy soil, lifting the late potatoes with more zeal than skill.

Growing food had become a necessity for since the spring, long queues of women had been forced to stand for hours waiting for the meagre allowance of food that was doled out to them by shopkeepers grown shifty-eyed.

Bakers were being inundated with demands for bread, with the result that the price rose from ninepence to a shilling almost overnight. Fancy cakes were a thing of the past and had disappeared altogether from the shelves.

The government advised restraint in the buying of meat, which affected the poor not one whit for they seldom saw meat except bacon and pork which they cured themselves.

Rhian had decided early on to have her own allotment in the unrewarding soil to the rear of the buildings and soon a great many of the townspeople followed her lead.

It was by luck more than skill that anything grew at all in Rhian's patch, but she found she had a new skill and it was gratifying to dig and plant and watch things grow.

Gina had protested at first. 'I don't know why you're bothering, *merchi* – you'll not get much from there, what with all the rubbish running down the stream from the works. Anyway, can't grow our own butter or sugar, can we?'

Rhian's retort had been instant. 'No, but we can bargain, get half a pound of butter for a cabbage. And perhaps exchange potatoes for a pot of honey, for I haven't tasted sugar in weeks.'

But Gina had been clearly worried, feeling that Rhian was carrying enough burdens as it was. 'You've only so much strength, you know; falling sick you'll be, and then what will I do?'

'Stop worrying for a start and get on with the spinning. We've still got plenty of orders for the red, white and blue shawls, haven't we?' She could not know that she had just helped Gina to make up her mind about selling the mill to Mansel Jack.

The business had begun to flourish with a suddenness that startled Rhian. There was not a fortune coming into the mill, but at least enough to keep the women and children in comparative comfort. There was even some left over to have the machines overhauled from time to time.

Nowadays every woman in Sweyn's Eye wanted a shawl or blanket that would show loyalty to the war effort. In the richer homes, the woollen goods were flung lazily over a sofa or even hung against a plain wall. The poorer women bought hanks of wool and knitted red, white and blue pullovers for husbands and sons when they came home from the front. And Rhian glowed with happiness at the success of her venture.

She sighed, knowing the reasons for keeping herself so busy were as much to do with her tangled emotions as the need to earn a living. She had not heard from Heath for some weeks now, yet it was not he who dominated her thoughts but Mansel Jack, the image of whose dark face even haunted her dreams at night.

Her back ached now as she tugged the potatoes free of the soggy ground. She shook away the damp earth and stared with pride at the vegetables that would provide the basis for more than one good meal.

'Ruining your hands, you are,' Gina said, shaking back her fine hair. 'Never be taken for a lady, with your fingernails black with soil and fingers red from washing out wool.'

Rhian felt as though a cold hand had touched her briefly in passing and she shivered. 'I wasn't born to be a lady but a working girl; there's soft you talk sometimes, Gina.'

'Maybe, but come along in now, dinner's nearly ready.'

As Rhian entered the kitchen with Gina still protesting at her side, Carrie held a finger to her lips.

'Hush your clatter will you, girls? I've just got those two little devils off to sleep.'

'My Dewi isn't a devil,' Gina said, half-laughing and Carrie made a wry face.

'He is when he gets the top off the honey-pot and sucks the stuff all over himself. Washed him three times, I did, before his hair was clean – going to have a handful there when he grows up, you are.' Carrie's voice held a touch of pride. 'Be-oo-tiful children both of them and I'll flatten anyone who says different. Here, give me those potatoes, don't stand there dropping mud all over my nice clean floor.'

Rhian scarcely heard her, far off in the distance was an

241

ominous booming which just might have been thunder. She looked up sharply, wondering if anyone else had heard the sound.

'What is it?' Gina asked in a hushed voice. 'Is it a storm starting or what?'

'Probably.' Rhian went to the door and opened it wide, but there was nothing now except the rushing of the stream outside and the calling of a bird flying overhead. Yet a terrible feeling of fear was gripping her; as she moved outdoors and stared across the valley, her mind was repeating the name like a chant: Mansel Jack.

*

It was as though her eyes were glued together. Katie moved her arm, rubbed the blood from her face and sat up. Then she stared round her in horror, for part of the shed looked like a slaughterhouse. Blood stained the walls and dimly she could hear someone moaning.

Experimentally, she rose to her knees and looked down at herself, finding she was unhurt except for a cut on her forehead.

There was a pounding in her head which she quickly realised was the sound of footsteps running towards the building. There had been a bad explosion, she thought distractedly – God, what had happened to all her girls? With a feeling of relief she saw that some of the women were sitting up, scrambling to their feet, faces white with shock.

She placed her folded handkerchief on the cut, which was bleeding profusely, and pulled her cap firmly over it.

Mansel Jack ran towards the shed and their eyes met. Katie shook her head, 'I don't know who's been hurt, not yet.' Together they moved to the pile of shattered wood which had been Katie's bench.

'Christ!' Mansel Jack was pulling at the wooden struts and Katie sank to her knees, waiting, though she didn't know what for. She stared around her, wondering that the explosion had ripped asunder only part of the building. Around the area where she had worked with her small crew there was devastation and, had she not been standing near the door, she would be under the pile of rubble right now.

242

And what of her girls: Doris, Janey? And Honey had just finished talking, telling Katie about Morgan Lloyd – oh, Honey!

Other men had joined Mansel Jack and the small building was crammed with people. Katie could see an ambulance drawn up outside, the horses moving impatiently between the shafts. She stared up at the patch of blue sky she could see through a jagged hole in the roof, wishing she could turn the clock back, stop the dreadful thing which had happened. And yet she felt numb inside.

It was Doris's face she saw first through the pile of splintered planking. Doris was pale, her eyes starting out of her head but appearing to see nothing.

'In shock,' Mansel Jack said firmly. 'Come along, you men, lift her carefully now – that's right, take her to the ambulance.'

Doris seemed to waken suddenly. 'I'm all right, man, there's daft. Not taking me to no hospital . . .' Her voice trailed away tearfully.

'I think you'd best go outside for some fresh air, lass.' Mansel Jack's hand was resting on Katie's arm but she shook her head.

'They're my crew.' Her knees were sore from the hardness of the ground, but she couldn't have moved even if she had tried.

Carefully the men pushed away the debris and then Janey was uncovered. Quickly, Katie closed her eyes, but she could still see the image of the girl who from the chest down was nothing but blood.

But Honey would be all right, she *must* be, Katie thought fervently. Please Mary, Jesus and Joseph, make her all right; she's so young, so pretty, so full of life and she's got a boy who loves her.

There was not a mark on Honey . . . no wound, no blood and her face was set in lines of peaceful repose as though she was asleep.

'Honey!' Katie said quickly, 'Honey, 'tis Katie talking to you. Why don't you answer me?'

Mansel Jack caught her arm and lifted Katie to her feet. And as she watched, a coat was placed over Honey's gentle young face. The hair, so warm and golden and alive, hung free, gleaming and beautiful. Katie began to weep, silent tears running salt into her mouth, and was not really aware of Mansel Jack even when he put his arm around her and held her close to his powerful shoulders.

It was only when she heard other women weeping that Katie realised what she was doing; she was weak, she should be leader here and she was letting her workers down. She straightened her cap and moved out of Mansel Jack's arms.

'I'm all right now.' She stood tall and straight, her head erect, her eyes flashing to encompass the other women. 'Sylvie, I'll work on your table until mine is replaced,' she said firmly. 'Come on now girls, no shirking, the job's got to be done and standing looking at it won't do any good at all.'

She took up a hammer from the floor, seeing that the handle was covered in dry blood. The girls, her girls, had given their lives and she was going to make sure this was not in vain.

'Come on, then, back to work! We'll show the Huns that we're made of stern stuff, just like our soldiers fighting at the front.'

Katie didn't know many Protestant hymns, but there was one that she had heard sung over and over again in times of trouble. She took up some of the gaines, staring unseeingly at them, and after a moment's hesitation the other women followed suit.

Slowly, tremulously at first, her voice soared into the shattered room.

'Abide with me, fast falls the eventide . . .' And one by one, the other women began to sing with her.

Chapter Twenty

Sweyn's Eye slumbered beneath an uneasy sky. Clouds obscured the face of the moon and the sleeping hills crouched silent in the gloom.

Mary stood at her window staring out into the darkness, her spirits low, tears trembling on her lashes. Behind her in the large bed she could hear the even sound of her husband's breathing and wondered in sudden anger how he could sleep at a time like this. It was his last night at home with her, for tomorrow he would rejoin his regiment.

He looked so handsome in his uniform as an officer in the 14th Welch, tall and distinguished, a handsome stranger. The long months he had spent in the Army had altered him and now he was thinner of face, his brow creased in a perpetual frown. And there was an elusive quality about him too, as though his leave was merely a pause in a way of life now become all-important to him.

Tonight they had gone through the motions of making love. She had lain in his arms, held near to his heart, yet she had known – they both had known – that the closeness between them had vanished.

When had the marriage begun to falter? Mary asked herself. She could not blame the arrival of Mary Anne Bloomfield, for the wedge had been there long before that. In her heart she knew the answer: she blamed him for not giving her a child and yet feared that the fault was her own. Impatiently she pushed the thoughts away; she was becoming obsessed – was Brandon's love not enough for her?

The moon slid from between the clouds, silvering the trees

in the garden, turning the small pond into a shimmering jewel. She had so much, Mary thought painfully. She must be grateful, for she had risen above her origins and the terrible grinding poverty of her childhood. She had made a success of her life, owned a big store, married well and for love, so why did she allow discontent to sour everything?

She glanced at the figure in the bed; his broad shoulders were uncovered and his skin was silk in the silver light. She loved him so much, how could she bear for him to go away again?

Wide-eyed, she slid into bed beside him and lay still, staring up at the ceiling. Perhaps she would lose Brandon to this terrible war – the thought was like a blade piercing her soul. Tentatively she reached out and slipped her fingers into his; he stirred a little and she held her breath, not wanting to wake him. Hot bitter tears welled into her eyes, spilling down her cheeks as she turned her face into the pillow.

The early morning light crawled into the bedroom and Mary realised that she must have fallen into an uneasy sleep. At her side, Brandon breathed peacefully and for a moment she felt once more a stinging anger against him. As she rose quickly from between the sheets he opened his eyes, staring up at her; he had the gift of being lost in sleep one minute and the next moment being fully awake. He smiled and gestured for her to come to his side. She obeyed and clung to him, willing herself not to cry. When he smoothed her hair and kissed her closed eyes, his touch though sensuous was a gesture of farewell.

At breakfast, Mary ate little of the crisp bacon with devilled kidneys specially prepared by the cook. She watched Brandon closely and once when his eyes met hers she was shocked to see the eagerness in his face. He *wanted* to go to the war, to be a soldier again. He saw her watching him and reached out to cover her hand with his own. 'Try to understand, Mary, this is something I have to do.'

She sat in the conservatory while he changed into his uniform. Determined not to cry, she held her head high; her mouth was dry but she managed a smile.

'I'll be home on leave again before you know it,' he whispered in her ear. The cloth of his uniform was rough against her hands as she kissed him lightly and moved back a pace, wishing he would go and get the parting over with, yet

246

dreading the moment when he would walk through the door.

'Do you want me to come into town with you?' she asked and in spite of herself, her voice trembled a little.

He shook his head. 'No, Mary, I want to think of you in our home, standing here just like you are now, so elegant and beautiful that I ache with pride in you.'

They clung together for a long moment and then he released her. She stood on the step watching as he made his farewells to the staff, who had lined up on the drive like a guard of honour. Her throat was thick with tears and she could barely keep her lips from trembling. She heard the engine of the car spring into life and then Brandon was climbing in beside the driver, tapping Jim on the shoulder to show he was ready.

Mary raised her arm in one last farewell gesture and then moved back into the house, running up the stairs and into the bedroom to fling herself on to the still warm sheets which bore the scent of him. How could she bear the continued loneliness of being without him?

The sound of the car died away into the distance and Mary closed her eyes, knowing that he was gone from her and not all her crying would bring him back. She wished for a moment that she could turn back the clock a few hours to when she had lain in his arms; why had she withheld a small part of herself? And then the tears came, scalding, painful and she felt the same uncertainty she had known as a child lying in a hovel, hunger and unhappiness a way of life. She had shown courage then and so must she do now, she told herself fiercely. She would throw herself into her work, settle down to the life of a woman whose man was at war as so many other women in Sweyn's Eye had to do. But at least *they* had children . . . the errant thought crept into her mind as she buried her head in Brandon's pillow.

Later when she travelled down into town on the tram, no one would have known from her bland expression that she had spent most of the morning weeping. The town was thronged with people – mostly women, young boys and old men – and Mary realised for the first time just how the war had affected Sweyn's Eye.

Suddenly she felt uplifted and as she entered the emporium, there was an easing of her pain. She had much to be thankful for, she thought soberly.

247

She was greeted at the door of her office by Mrs Greenaway, her face sombre, her eyelids drooping as she twisted her hands together in distress.

'Have you heard about the explosion, Mrs Sutton?' she asked at once and Mary moved into the warmth of her room, shaking her head.

'What's happened, Greenie? I haven't been in town for days.'

Mary sat at her desk, staring at the pile of unopened letters, strangely unwilling to involve herself in the work of the store.

'Down at the munitions factory, like a blood-bath it was, so they say. One of the young girls, Janey Jenkins, was ripped to pieces by the blast – couldn't find enough of her to fill the coffin.'

Mary shook her head, wishing that Greenie would not be so graphic. Her heart sank at this news; although they were only very distantly related, she had lived near the family once, a long time ago when Janey was a baby.

'She can't have been more than sixteen or seventeen, poor child,' she said aloud now, and Mrs Greenaway nodded.

'Aye . . . and that little Honey O'Connor, beautiful girl, sweet as a spring lamb she was, with lovely golden hair – she's dead too, but they say there wasn't a mark on her.'

Mary stared up from her chair, suddenly feeling ill. 'Those were the girls working with Katie Murphy.' The words came out hoarsely and Mrs Greenaway looked at her anxiously.

'Katie's not hurt – well, not too badly – cut on her head, that's all. She was a heroine by all accounts, keeping the rest of the gang's spirits up, carrying on working in spite of the terrible thing that had just happened. Deserves a medal, she does.'

Mary rubbed at her eyes, '*Duw*, there's awful, two young girls killed and for what? But if anything had happened to Katie, it would break my heart.'

'I know, friends for years you've been,' Greenie said softly. 'Katie's like the sister you never had, I suppose.'

Mary sank back in her chair. 'Send for some tea, there's a love.' She pushed the pile of letters away from her with an impatient gesture. 'I don't feel a bit like work today.'

At the door the older woman paused. 'What about the

funeral? I expect you'd want to attend, wouldn't you?'

Mary nodded. 'Will you order some flowers, Greenie?'

The day was one of unreality and afterwards Mary didn't know how she got through it. The thought of returning home to a house empty of Brandon's presence did nothing to cheer her spirits. By late afternoon she was weary and, glancing at the clock, she put down her pen; it might be a good idea to take her tea at the store, she decided.

Suddenly she realised she had not eaten all day and felt hungry. She closed the silver top of the inkwell and rose from her chair, stretching her arms above her head, trying desperately not to think. She didn't want to remember that her husband had gone away or that the awful thing called war was impinging on her life, eating away at the heart of it, destroying everything loved and familiar.

The tea-rooms were crowded and the hubbub of voices was almost a tangible blow. She moved between the damask-covered tables, nodding in greeting to her regular customers, trying to stretch her face into a smile though her jaw ached with the effort.

'Mrs Sutton – isn't it lovely to see you again, honey – won't you join me?'

Mary stared blankly at the American woman seated with her daughter, presiding smugly over the silver teapot like a fat spider, her plump white fingers covered in rings.

'I don't really think . . .' Her words trailed away as Mary Anne interrupted her. 'I've said goodbye to Brandon. Isn't it dreadful that a man like him has to be a soldier? It's scandalous.'

Mary sat heavily in a tall-backed chair, her legs suddenly weak.

'You've seen Brandon today?' She could not help asking the question, even though she knew the other woman was glorying in her bewilderment.

'But of course my dear – you don't think he could return to the front without saying farewell to me, do you?'

Mary took the hot strong coffee that Mary Anne handed her and sipped it without noticing the bitter taste.

'I really didn't think he was obliged to you in any way,' Mary said coldly. 'After all, what happened between you was a lifetime ago.'

Mary Anne glanced meaningfully at her daughter and the girl sank back in her chair, her eyes downcast, her mouth drawn into a sulky pout.

'Yes, but we have such strong ties holding us together; they can never be broken, don't you see that?'

'Mamma!' The young girl spoke sharply, but her mother's withering glance silenced her.

Mary leaned forward. 'Don't try to tell me that this girl is my husband's daughter,' she said, her heart thumping rapidly. 'I happen to know that you ran away with Dean Sutton, and it takes a real slut to play off two brothers against each other.'

Mary Anne drew on her gloves with agonising slowness, smoothing the lacy material over her plump fingers as though the task was the most important thing in all the world.

'Insult me all you like, but I'm not telling you anything that you can't see for yourself, honey.' She smiled dazzlingly and rose to her feet. 'What a charming place you have here – you were most fortunate in marrying a man as well-heeled as Brandon Sutton, weren't you?'

Mary shook her head, pushing down her anger at the injustice in the woman's words. Brandon had been a struggling business man when they had married, while she had wrested a successful living out of selling; but there was little point in telling Mary Anne all that, she wouldn't listen anyway.

Mary Anne rested her hand on her daughter's shoulder. 'One thing I will say, honey, is that Brandon gave me more than he's ever given you.' Her meaning was crystal clear and Mary felt the hot colour rise to her cheeks. Her instinct was to order the woman to leave and never come into the emporium again, but that would be admitting defeat.

She forced herself to smile pleasantly, holding her head high. 'And how many men have you told the same fairy tale to, Miss Bloomfield?' She saw the anger fleeting across Mary Anne's face with a fierce dart of satisfaction and then turned away, walking swiftly towards the door; she felt in need of fresh air.

There was a pain growing inside her as the knowledge of Brandon's duplicity rose uppermost in her mind. She did not give credence to Mary Anne's claim that he was the father of her child because she did not want to believe it. She preferred to believe that Virginia's 'Sutton look' came from Brandon's brother Dean. Yet the fact that Brandon had gone straight from her arms to Mary Anne in order to say goodbye hurt her deeply. Was there anything still between them, she wondered anxiously? There was only one person who might be able to tell her and that was Dean Sutton himself, for he had run away with Mary Anne all those years ago back in America, stolen his brother's fiancée – surely he would know the truth about Mary Anne and her daughter . . . if he could be persuaded to divulge it.

The driver was waiting outside the store with the automobile and Mary's heart missed a beat as it occurred to her that Jim would know where Brandon had gone that morning. The man held open the door for her, his weathered face wreathed in a smile of welcome.

'Finished work early today, Mrs Sutton? Good thing too, you're doing more than enough what with the store and your stint on the trams.' He climbed into the driving seat. 'We're all right proud of you and of the master too – I hope you don't take offence at me being so familiar like.'

Mary sighed and settled back in the cold leather of the seat. 'I'm not doing anything different from any other woman, we all have to do our best in times like these.'

Jim was silent as he negotiated the car through the crowds in the *Stryd Fawr*, heading away from the busy roadways towards the western slope.

'Did you go with Mr Sutton to the station, Jim?' Mary hated herself, yet the question was whirling round in her brain begging to be asked.

Jim tipped his cap back on his head. 'No, Mr Sutton had business to do in town so I just dropped him off. There's smart and distinguished he looked in his uniform – be going to the front with him I'd be too, if I was a younger man.'

Mary Anne Bloomfield had been telling the truth then . . . Brandon *had* gone to see her before leaving Sweyn's Eye. The thought was like a pain inside her.

*

Shortly afterwards, the matter of Brandon visiting Mary Anne was thrust from Mary's mind with startling abruptness when

251

she received the ominous communication. She stared down at the official envelope, her heart freezing in fear, then gazed around the familiar dining-room, giving herself a few moments' respite. At last her fingers tore at the envelope and she forced herself to read the words that leaped out at her. Fragments of them burned her eyes: REGRETS . . . HUSBAND MISSING BELIEVED KILLED . . .

With a moan of pain Mary slumped over the table, but though despair rose in waves to engulf her she could not find relief in tears.

She had little recollection of the next few days and it was a misty, dismal evening when she realised that her life must continue as normally as possible. When she called for Jim to take her out he nodded with his eyes full of sympathy.

'All right, Mrs Sutton, I'm ready – you've only to say the word.'

The silence seemed to stretch on endlessly and it was as though a huge question mark hung in the air. Mary rushed into speech, not wanting Jim to say anything that might hurt her.

'I must go to Market Street, see Katie Murphy. You must have heard about the explosion in the munitions factory, Jim?' She spoke conversationally as though her heart wasn't breaking, and Jim acted as though nothing untoward had happened in the Sutton household.

'Aye, it's all over town. Terrible thing when innocent young girls get blasted into eternity. Didn't have a prayer, for once those gaines explode there's no time to run and hide.' His voice was bitter. 'Place for youngsters is at home preparing for motherhood, not filling shells with TNT. God damn those Huns . . . if you'll excuse the language, Mrs Sutton.'

Mary settled into an unquiet silence, her mind twisting and turning as though a black cloud had settled above her. She must shake herself out of it, she thought painfully.

It would be a good idea to talk to Katie. She would take her some honey and a basket of vegetables from the garden, for at the Sutton household there was no shortage of food. Mary felt she owed Katie and her family a great debt for she had been given shelter beneath their roof, sharing a room with Katie at a time when she needed help most – that was a kindness she would never forget.

Later, as Jim drove her through the silent streets, she found herself thinking of the nursery wing waiting vainly to be used. The rooms were painted cream and blue, with frothy lace drapes on the empty crib. It was a room that was meant to house the future Suttons, but now that must remain only a dream.

Mary sighed and brushed back her hair; it was tied with a dark green bow, for she had been too weary to have it combed and primped into the wide brushed-back style that fashionable ladies were given to wearing.

She drew her coat more closely around her, feeling cold in the mist of the evening.

Outwardly she had changed very little since her marriage, at least in appearance. Her face was still smooth and unlined, her hair held no trace of grey although she was past her thirtieth year. She bit her lip in anguish – now she would never bear the child she so longed for. 'Stop it!' she said harshly. Crying over might-have-beens was of no use at all – where was the courage that had brought her from life in a hovel to the successful business woman she now was?

Market Street was soft under the gas-lighting. The contours of the buildings blurred the windows, gleaming like friendly eyes. Katie Murphy's face lit up when she saw Mary and she drew her into the snug kitchen, hugging her arm in friendship.

'You look pale,' Katie said, studying her anxiously, 'and there's such a look in your eyes – what's wrong, tell me?'

'I'm all right.' Mary couldn't speak of the pain inside her, not just yet. 'I've come to see how you are, *cariad*, I see there's a nasty gash on your forehead from the explosion.'

The welcoming light faded from Katie's eyes. 'Sure, but 'tis little enough hurt compared with the loss of two of my girls.'

Mary clasped her hands tightly, 'I know.' She spoke softly and after a moment Katie nodded her head.

'You'd understand more than most. Come and sit down, me dad's taken mam to visit the O'Connors, to sympathise with them in their grief at losing a daughter.' There was a glint of tears in Katie's eyes and Mary sighed, the bitterness of her own loss heavy within her.

'This war's got a lot to answer for.' Mary knew that she was referring to her own life and now she felt almost compelled to

253

speak. 'It's Brandon,' she rushed out the words. 'I've been informed that he's missing . . .' she couldn't bring herself to utter the words, 'believed killed'.

'Oh, Mary.' Katie hugged her warmly. 'I'm so sorry! What is happening to our little world? Everything's changing, so 'tis, and we powerless to do anything about it.'

They talked softly together, Mary spilling out her sense of hurt and loss and Katie listening with patience and sympathy.

'If only I had his child,' Mary's voice was full of anguish, 'at least then I'd have part of him.

'There, there, 'tis all in the hands of fate,' Katie said in her gentle way.

Mary rose to her feet, suddenly feeling claustrophobic. 'I've got to get on, Katie,' she made an effort to control the trembling of her hands as she drew on her coat, 'but if you ever want to get away from the munitions factory there's always your old job in my store, you know that.'

Mary left the house in Market Street and stood staring around her, breathing in the familiar smell of the place. So much had changed and yet so little, she thought bitterly.

'Go on home, Jim,' she said softly to the driver. 'I need to walk a little.'

Reluctantly he drove away, while Mary stood still in the gloom until the sound of the engine could no longer be heard. Then she made her way slowly along the shining surface of the roadway where pools of light washed down from the lamps, the glow seemingly diluted by the mist. She paused in Canal Street to stare at the derelict laundry that had once been the hub of the area.

It was here she had worked as a young girl, rising to overseer, her endeavours much appreciated by old Mr Waddington . . . God rest his soul.

She thought with renewed bitterness of the way Brandon's father had bought up the laundry and how – hating Mary – he had driven her away from the job she had delighted in. And then as though in poetic justice, one of the long-neglected boilers had blown up, causing such devastation that the laundry had not functioned since.

A cab drew up beside Mary and a tall figure alighted directly in her path, knocking her sideways. She fell against the wall,

feeling the harsh stone graze her cheek, then she was caught up in strong arms. She became aware of dark eyes staring at her and it was a moment or two before she recognised Dr Soames.

'I'm so sorry.' His voice was harsh with remorse. 'I hope you're all right?' He placed a steadying arm around her and suddenly Mary found herself dissolving into tears.

'Hello, what's this then, you are hurt? Look, come inside, let me see to you properly.'

He led her unprotesting into his room, where a fire roared and sucked behind black-leaded bars. Mary sank down on the couch, grateful for the heat that went some way to dispelling the cold within her.

He looked concerned as he rolled his shirt-sleeves above his elbows and then he was beside her. 'Let me help you off with your coat and then I can check to see if there are any bruises.'

She tried to tell him she was all right, but the words would not come. His expression was one of concern as he felt her limbs carefully.

'Nothing broken, thank God! You can call me a clumsy ox if it helps.'

'I'm all right, there's nothing to worry about.' She looked up at him as he knelt by her side and their eyes met and held. The admiration in his gaze was like a balm and she leaned forward almost unthinkingly. His mouth was gentle upon hers and then passion seemed to grow within him as he held her close.

Shakily he would have moved away but she held his shoulders, her grip almost fierce.

'I'd better take you home,' he said carefully but she shook her head.

'No, please, I don't want to go home.'

He drew her into his arms once more and then he was lying alongside her on the couch, cradling her.

The flames from the fire leaped upwards along the walls and ceiling and somehow just being in the small, familiar room was reassuring. That she was in another man's arms did not seem wrong . . . Brandon was beyond solace, but she was not.

She did not even know Dr Soames' first name, but she clung to him with a feeling of relief. Even when his breathing became heavy and his embrace more passionate, still she did not draw away. He was human contact, another being who would help her through the loneliness of the long night, and she felt nothing but gratitude towards him. She closed her eyes and clung to his broad shoulders and was comforted.

Chapter Twenty-One

The roads shone bluey-grey, washed fresh by the rain. Pools of molten gold splashed the cobbles, falling softly from the gas-lamps. Sparks shooting from the plethora of chimney stacks rising to the darkness of the sky crackled and hissed a monster's breath on the night air.

Rhian's footsteps faltered, although she had stepped out from the mill purposefully enough, anxious to speak to Mansel Jack and see for herself that he was unharmed. She had been numbed by the horror of the explosion at his factory and knew deep within her that the death of the two young girls would have affected him badly.

Leaving behind the streets of the town, she began to walk up the hill; she could have taken a tram, but needed time to gather her thoughts together. It was not easy for her to visit Mansel Jack's home, since he might misinterpret the gesture.

As Rhian drew her shawl more closely around her shoulders the fringes lifted in the breeze – red, white and blue, the colours of patriotism. She smiled to herself, for the shawls were continuing to sell well, she was bringing in a steady income and trade was improving all the time. The fact that she now had Gina Sinman's help in the mill made a big difference and they had settled into a good routine. Carrie meantime busied herself with the children, so happy that she sang at her work and her face shone with joy as she saw to the needs of the small boy and girl in her care.

Rhian's heart melted when she thought of Cerianne, her brother's child and so like him that it took her breath away.

And now there was no more time for prevaricating, for she

stood outside the house where Mansel Jack lived and her hands trembled. It was a modest building, plain but solid, with pointed roofs over narrow windows. At the door Rhian almost turned and fled; what words of comfort could she offer him and what made her think he would want to see her? 'Don't be soft!' she said aloud and before she could lose her courage she lifted the heavy knocker.

He opened the door himself and for a long moment Rhian stood on the step looking up at him. Then he moved back a pace and without a word she stepped into the light and warmth of the hallway that smelled of beeswax.

'It's good to see you, lass.' He spoke softly, his eyes searching her face. She met his gaze and was glad she had come.

'I heard about the explosion, I wanted to come sooner but I wasn't sure . . .' She bit her lip, knowing that she was not expressing herself well, but he seemed to understand.

'It's at such times that a man needs friends about him.' He led the way into a small drawing-room where the windows were hung with heavy curtains and the furniture was plump and shabby. Rhian stood near the door uncomfortably until Mansel Jack gestured for her to take a seat.

'The accident has done one thing for me,' he said, standing with his back towards the glowing fire, 'It's helped me make up my mind to leave the munitions and enlist in the Army.' He stared down at her so openly that he couldn't be aware how his words were twisting inside her. Rhian felt as though the earth had moved from beneath her feet, the very light was going out of her life – and in that moment of crystal clarity, she knew that she loved Mansel Jack more than anyone in the world.

'When will you be going?' The words stumbled over themselves and he stared at her, his expression stern. He thrust his hands into his pockets in a swift movement.

'Soon. This war's gone on longer than any of us thought possible and the country needs more manpower.' He smiled and his face was alight, his eyes crinkled, 'They'll even take an old man like me now.'

The look in his eyes took Rhian's breath away. That he was eager to fight for his country was obvious, but how could she bear it knowing he lived in perpetual danger?

'Don't look so grieved, lass.' His words fell softly into the silence. 'Sad, but so beautiful.'

She looked at him quickly, the colour rushing to her cheeks, her throat dry as she waited for him to speak again.

'Forget I said that – I've no right, not with Charlotte waiting at home for me.'

'It's all right, I know you were simply being kind.' The words were drawn from her slowly and painfully. Although he did not touch her, the strength of his presence seemed to enfold her and she wondered fleetingly how it would be to have the love of such a man. But she pushed the thought aside angrily; she too was spoken for, Heath loved and trusted her.

He seemed to sense something of her feelings and took a step towards her, his eyes dark, but she moved rapidly away from him.

'No!' The word was sharp, incisive, brooking no argument.

His face darkened. 'You're right, lass.' He strode quickly into the hallway. 'I'll see you home.'

In the silent darkness of the night, they walked side by side yet separated by an enormous gulf. She longed to reach out her hand to touch him and she knew deep in the core of her being that if she did, she would be in his arms but to what end? A quick roll in the hay would not do for her . . . nor for him either, she thought, glancing up at him.

How she loved him! She stared at the light falling across his strong features and her heart ached with the longing to reach out and touch him. She had never been in his arms, never felt his lips upon hers, yet she knew that nothing could ever match the intensity of her feelings for this man.

Rhian desperately searched her mind for something to say, anything to break the tension of the atmosphere. 'Will you go home to Yorkshire before you enlist?' Her voice was small, falling softly into the silence.

He tipped back his head to look up at the sky and the moon slid from behind the clouds as though at his bidding. 'Yes, I'll need to see Charlotte one last time, my sister too.' His tone was clipped and Rhian felt a coldness settle over her; he was deliberately putting a barrier between them – didn't he know there was no need for that?

'I understand,' she said, but the pain in her voice brought him to a halt. He stared down at her and she wondered for a moment if he meant to crush her in his arms.

'There is no future for us, little Rhian. You are sweet and beautiful, but there are too many barriers.' He smiled. 'But at least your future at the mill is secure, I've seen to that.'

'What do you mean?' she asked quietly, her eyes wide with bewilderment.

'I asked Mrs Sinman not to discuss it, I wanted to tell you myself. I've bought Spinners' Wharf.'

She felt anger drag at her limbs so that she was forced to stop in her tracks. 'You've done what?'

He caught her arm and she stared up at him in disbelief. 'You've bought the mill on some little whim and there's me wanting to make a go of it for Gina's sake.' She took a deep breath, 'Do you realise the hours I've put into that mill, the way I've tramped the streets, coaxing people to buy from me? And it wasn't to make you richer, Mansel Jack, understand that.'

He released her abruptly and her arm felt bruised where his fingers had been. 'Go home, Rhian Gray,' he said flatly. 'You're just overwrought, that's all.'

His words stung and she faced him squarely, her voice low and cold. 'You've taken Gina Sinman's livelihood from her, the business that she and Heinz started together; how *could* you?'

He stared at her with clear eyes, 'I think you're angry because you planned on buying the mill yourself one day.'

She spun away from him and began to run through the darkness, tears misting her eyes. In spite of her anger, she recognised that there was a grain of truth in what Mansel Jack had said. Yet somehow she felt hurt and betrayed and in that moment she almost hated him.

In the mill house, Carrie sat before the fire mending a tiny petticoat, sewing a hem that had become torn. She glanced up and her eyes narrowed as they rested on Rhian's flushed face.

'If I didn't know better, I'd say you've been out on Ram's Tor courting with some fine handsome boyo.' Her voice was low and as Rhian sank into a chair Carrie nodded towards the stairs. 'Little Dewi's been that cross tonight, there's a fuss he's been making – getting his teeth I suppose he is. Hasn't woken Cerianne yet, but Gina's spent most of the night up in the

260

bedroom trying to quieten the boy.'

Rhian was only half-listening as she rested her head against the softness of the armchair, feeling drained and empty.

'What's the matter, *cariad*,' Carrie asked softly. 'Now don't go lying to me, for Carrie knows you better than most anyone, brought you up didn't I?'

Rhian sighed. 'I'm so mixed-up, Carrie, how can I love two men at the same time? It's just not right and proper, is it?'

Carrie shrugged.

'I wouldn't say that. How can I love Cerianne and Dewi so much when neither one of them is my own flesh? Love's a funny thing, not doled out in spoonfuls like medicine. Still, there's doubtless more love you have for one than for the other.'

'But how can I tell which is love and which is just desire for a man's arms around me, Carrie? Perhaps I'm a flossie at heart and not meant to belong to one man only, like the good book says.'

'Rubbish!' Carrie put down her mending and stared at Rhian. 'You are no flossie, you're what I'd call a good girl and if you feel love for two men then bide your time. The moment will come when you have to choose between them, and then you'll know the answer for it will come from your heart.'

Carrie spoke with such authority that it seemed she had experienced the same emotions herself. Rhian watched her covertly, but the older woman's expression gave nothing away.

'*Duw*, I thought them babbas would never get off to sleep,' Carrie adroitly changed the subject. 'Devils they are, the two of them.' Her voice held such warmth that Rhian felt tears burn her eyes. She was sometimes sorry that she was spending so little time with Billy's daughter, but she worked long and hard to make a living for them all and was content that Cerianne did not lack affection. Both Carrie and Gina spoiled the little girl outrageously, making up for the lack of parental love in the child's life.

'There's down in the mouth you're looking, girl,' Carrie said sharply. 'Done nothing but sit there like a wet week since you came in. Where you been, anyway?'

Rhian forced a smile, 'Never you mind where I've been. As

you said, I might have been out courting on Ram's Tor.'

Carrie's eyes were shrewd. 'Come on now, don't hold out on old Carrie, tell me what's on your mind.' She rose to her feet and shifted the big kettle on to the fire.

'There's no need for you to keep asking questions,' Rhian replied impatiently. 'I'm not going to tell you anything more than I have already. I mean it, you know,' she said flatly, 'I'm not going to say any more about myself or my love-life, so you can just forget it.'

Carrie sighed softly. 'I don't mean to be nosey, mind, but I can't abide seeing you so low in spirits. I'm just plain worried about you, that's all.'

'I'm sorry I was sharp,' Rhian said more quietly. 'Just let me be, I'm so tired I can't think straight. It's about time I went to bed.'

'Aye, go on, you look a bit peaky I must say.' Carrie spoke softly. 'Settle yourself in and I'll bring you some hot milk to help you to sleep.'

In the room that she shared with Carrie, Rhian sank on to the bed and kicked off her boots. Her feet ached, indeed her entire being seemed to ache and she knew that the pain had nothing to do with the physical weariness that seeped through her veins.

She drew her thick cotton gown over her head and padded into the other bedroom. There were two cots side by side and at the end of the small room Gina lay on her bed, fast asleep. At first they had decided to put Carrie in with the children because Gina needed to be up and in the mill early, but despite being a good idea in theory it had not worked in practice, because young master Sinman had a voracious appetite and needed feeding every few hours.

Cerianne lay on her stomach, her small bottom jutting above the bedclothes. Her thumb was in her mouth and her breathing was soft and even. She didn't stir as Rhian leaned over and kissed her but Dewi sat up, his hair sticking on end – so much like his father that it was as if Heinz Sinman had been born again.

'Hush, there's a good boy.' Rhian kissed his plump cheek and his podgy fist pressed against her breast as though hoping to find sustenance.

'You're out of luck there, boyo,' she whispered and rubbed

at his fuzz of hair. 'Now lie down, let mammy sleep a while.'

'There's wicked you are, waking my boy like that.' Gina's tone was sleepily playful as she climbed out of bed and took her son in her arms. '*Duw*, like a clock he is, don't miss a minute when his belly's empty,' she smiled. 'Sit by here on the bed, Dewi, mam will get you some hot milk in a minute.'

It was strangely soothing to sit in the room that was silent except for Cerianne's even breathing and the soft sounds of Dewi drinking milk out of a cup. Rhian closed her eyes and leaned against the pillow, feeling weariness washing over her.

'There's a fine pair you are!' Carrie came into the room and placed a tray on the marble-topped wash-stand. 'Left me to rake out the fire and lock all the doors – want mothering, the two of you, don't know what you'd do without me.'

Rhian drank a little of the hot milk Carrie handed her and glanced warily at Gina. 'Mansel Jack's bought you out then?' she asked at last and with a sigh of relief Gina nodded.

'There's glad I am he told you about it.' She paused, 'You do think it's a good idea, don't you, Rhian?'

Forcing a smile, Rhian agreed. 'Of course, the mill can't fail now, can it?'

'*Duw*, I hope I've done the right thing,' Gina said softly, 'but with Heinz gone, I don't see no reason not to sell out. He said we'd be all right, that we'd continue to work as always.'

Carrie filled the sudden silence quickly. 'It's the funeral of those two poor girls tomorrow and about time, too. Don't hold with inquests and the like, get people decently buried is what I say. We must all go to the church, mind,' she added firmly.

Rhian nodded. 'Yes, we'll be there, Carrie, don't worry.' She rose to her feet. 'I'm dead beat, I'm going to bed.'

When she lay beneath the blankets, Rhian stared up at the cracked ceiling and the flickering light from the candle playing over it and tired though she was, sleep would not come.

*

Green Hill woke to a cheerless morning with rain dripping from roof-tops, running along window panes, slipping from sparse-leafed trees as though in sympathy with the occupants of the O'Connor household. The rooms – spotlessly clean and

263

strangely neat – were silent, for even the youngest of the girls felt the grief that hung in the air like a thick heavy perfume.

Morgan had been numb ever since he had been told the awful news. He had watched Stella O'Connor's face, pale and pinched with pain, and heard the words come stumbling from her lips, but could not believe them. Even now on the morning of the funeral, it didn't seem possible that Honey, his lovely gentle Honey, was dead.

He sat in the coldness of his room, pulling on his boots, seeing the rain on the windows and feeling the chill of it penetrate his bones. The one scrap of comfort he had was that she was to go to her rest properly in a real pine coffin, paid for by the generosity of the people of Sweyn's Eye who saw Honey and her friend Janey as heroines.

Morgan stifled a moan. He had tortured himself with thoughts about the explosion, had agonised in his imaginings, seeing Honey's sweetness extinguished and haunted lest she had suffered. They all said she had not – the doctor who had administered a soothing draught to Mrs O'Connor, the undertaker who had deftly measured the slight young form and the nurse who had spent an hour locked with Honey's body. Mrs Benson had spoken to the hushed family with just the right mixture of deference and cheerfulness.

'Your little girl didn't feel a thing, take it from me. There's not a line or crease on her little face, which proves she never knew what happened. Seen people go sudden and in pain, I have, and it always shows.' She had pressed her hands against her sparkling white apron. 'Don't grieve about her passing over, for it was quick and painless.'

But a light had gone from his life and he could never love a woman again, not the way he had loved Honey. He couldn't even share his grief with those who were closest to her, for her mammy had never known for sure exactly how he had felt. As for Mr O'Connor, he was like a corpse himself; he sat in his chair, staring around him with unseeing eyes, unaware even of his other little ones who plaintively begged for attention.

'Morgan, 'tis time you were up and about.' Stella O'Connor was standing in the doorway, her face a mask of tight control, her eyes sunk back in her head from all her tears.

He jerked to his feet. 'I'm ready.' He hated the coldness of his words – why couldn't he hold Stella to him, tell her of his own grief, share with her the pain?

'You're a good lad.' Stella's voice cracked a little, but when her eyes met his and he read her understanding, it was as if some of his burden was lifted.

'I've made you breakfast, try to eat at least some of it for the day outside is ill-tempered.'

The kitchen was cold, for with the coffin next door in the parlour there must not be too big a fire burning in the grate.

The children were dressed, the girls wearing their best black boots neatly buttoned and brightly polished. Morgan had watched Brendan O'Connor work on the footwear the previous night, rubbing and spitting as though his life depended on it. Something to do, they all had the relief of it except himself.

Why had death suddenly forced itself into his consciousness? He had seen his dad die inch by inch and thought it intolerable. But at least he had lived his life, known pleasure and pain. What had Honey known of anything?

A loud knocking at the door startled him and Stella O'Connor pulled off her apron and went to answer it. The hearse stood outside in the roadway and Morgan felt a momentary panic – the fact that Honey was going from him suddenly became a reality.

He was standing staring, open-mouthed, and Stella O'Connor spoke to him twice before he understood the meaning of her words.

'You'll be a bearer, won't you, Morgan?' He nodded, unable to speak and shivering as he followed Brendan into the parlour. One of the men from the undertaker's gently gave directions and then the coffin was pressing against his shoulder. Morgan wondered at the weight of it. The coffin was set next to the one belonging to Janey Jenkins and the two grieving families took their rightful positions behind the hearse as the horses jerked into movement.

Morgan became aware that the streets of Green Hill were lined with people who had come to pay their last respects to the two dead girls. He had never seen anything like it – all the way down to the bridge and over to the left bank of the river, the mourning townsfolk stood to attention.

'Mammy, just look at the canaries!' a child called excitedly and was hushed immediately. Morgan looked towards the gates of the cemetery where, unmistakable because of their yellow-stained faces, stood the women from the munitions factory – the 'canaries' as they were heartlessly called.

'What a send-off our Honey's having, to be sure.' Stella's voice, drifting back to where Morgan walked behind the hearse, was filled with tearful pride. It was clear she found comfort in the display of respect, but Morgan felt cheated and absurdly angry that all these girls and women were alive while his Honey was dead.

Dan y Graig was a cemetery set out on the lower slopes of Kilvey Hill, a large parcel of ground which boasted two churches. Morgan preferred to wait outside in the rain after the cortege had passed under the arched doorway of the larger church and he stared at the marble headstones cheek by jowl with poorer wooden crosses, trying to tell himself that none of this was real.

A piece of ground was ready for Honey, a gash dark and ugly in the face of the earth. What was left for him to want now? He cared nothing for his future, for it was lying wrapped in a shroud inside a pine box.

But somehow he endured the rest of the ceremony, the laying to rest, the unintelligible words and found himself making the sign of the cross as others around him were doing – knowing it for an empty gesture.

Mrs O'Connor began to weep as the heavy soil fell on to the coffin. 'My first-born child, my lovely girl is gone from me and I can't bear it.'

Morgan stood rigid, his face muscles aching with the effort to keep control. He too wanted to cry, to rant against fate, to scrape away the soil and bring Honey back into the light. He watched as the grieving parents moved towards the open gates of the cemetery and then stood quite still for a long time staring at the freshly-dug earth. He did not think or feel, he simply was.

It was only when a pale sun slid from between grey clouds, lightening the graveyard, that he realised he was soaked to the skin. Steam rose from his coat and sighing heavily he turned to leave, knowing he would never come here again. Some might

266

find comfort from tending the burial ground of the dead, but not he.

The crowds which had lined the streets on the way to the cemetery had long ago dispersed and now it was as though Morgan was the only one left in the world. He stared at the docks, at the tall sails which fluttered damply in the sudden breeze and at the steam packets waiting patiently to go out on the tide. It was strange that life could continue as if nothing had happened. He had preferred the rain which had turned the town grey, for it was fitting weather for mourning.

He strode across the wooden bridge, staring down into the swiftly moving river, watching a small branch torn from a tree twist and turn with the current. The river gurgled and lapped towards the banks, running over stones smoothed by many torrents. It must be peaceful to lie under the turgid depths and forget pain . . .

Sharply he drew himself away and moved towards the streets of the town. Sweyn's Eye was as ever bustling with activity. He saw a milkman lift a clanking churn and place it on his cart and heard the sigh of the horse moving between the shafts as though in protest against the heavy burden.

'*Bore da*, Morgan, there's a boy – going to walk past an old chum without a word!' Peter Harries stood before him and there was a world of understanding in the furnaceman's deep-set eyes.

'Just come off shift, I have. *Jawl*, I swear the sheds get more like hard work every day. Didn't expect you to come in today, Morgan. I knew about the funeral of course – there's no need for me to say how sorry I am, is there, boyo?'

Morgan shook his head. 'Don't want to talk about it, Peter, she's gone, nothing more to be said.'

'You'll feel better once you're back at work with your mates. Young you are yet and just buried your dad an' all; life's not easy for some. Want to come for a pint, boyo? Might take the edges away, like, and they say misery needs company.'

Morgan shook his head. 'Not right now, thanks, Peter. Got something to do.'

The furnaceman rested a hand on his shoulder, 'Right you are then, see you in work.' He pulled his cap further down on his forehead and strode away, his tea-can clanking against his

267

side. He was a man who meant well, but he could not understand Morgan's need to be left alone. Peter Harries was perhaps the only one who knew of his love for Honey, but it was not a comfort to talk about her – rather was it a pain shafting through him, a flashing blade that gouged and ripped. He turned off the main street with purposeful stride, his head high.

At the recruiting office the sergeant looked up from behind his desk. His eyes brightened, for volunteers had become few, most of the eligible men having enlisted.

'Well, Morgan Lloyd isn't it, copper worker? What can I do for you then?' He sat back in his chair, his moustache fairly bristling with importance.

Morgan leaned forward on the desk, pronouncing each of his words clearly. 'I want you to send me to the front as soon as possible.'

Chapter Twenty-Two

Soft silver waves washed the rim of the bay like a gentle caress in the stillness of the night. The town groaned and settled into the deep shadows. Even the ever-present stench of the copper works was mellowed by a light breeze and high clouds as Sweyn's Eye slumbered.

Rhian was awake beneath the sloping roof of her room. She turned and twisted in her bed, her eyes hot and dry, her body tense at the prospect of another sleepless night. She could see Mansel Jack in her mind's eye – his eyes flashing, his strong face set and resolute – and could feel the presence of the man reach out to touch her in the darkness. And the thought was a cold, hard reproach, for he was going to war.

Why, she wondered, had she been so angry with him? He had bought the mill with the best of intentions, he had assured her of that. And yet she had believed they were sufficiently good friends for him to have asked her advice on the matter. What then would have been her response? The same anger she had shown when he told her of the accomplished fact, no doubt.

She gave up trying to reason with herself; her mind was jumbled and confused – all she knew was that her whole being cried out in despair, for Mansel Jack had gone from Sweyn's Eye home to Yorkshire.

At last in desperation she rose, knowing that her constant twisting and turning would eventually wake Carrie who slumbered noisily in the bed against the wall. On bare feet Rhian padded on to the landing and paused for a moment, hearing a sound so slight that she thought it might have been only in her imagination. But there it was again – a groan, soft and subdued.

Silently Rhian opened the door to the room Gina shared with the children. There was a rustling of bedclothes as she moved across the floor, carefully struck a lucifer and lit the candle resting in the enamel saucer. Both children were asleep, but Gina was staring up at her with large frightened eyes.

'I can hardly breathe,' she said hoarsely. 'My throat burns like a furnace and there's such a pain in my belly I can hardly bear it. At first I believed it was grief for my lovely Heinz tearing at me, but the pain is real enough.'

Rhian rested a hand on Gina's forehead and found it was dry and hot. Then she held the candle high and took a sharp breath, for Gina's skin was a strange brownish colour and even the whites of her eyes were yellow in the candle-light.

'What is it, what's wrong with me? Am I dying, Rhian, for it feels like it!'

'Hush now, you've got the jaundice, girl, that's all. You know it's common enough for folks who work the wool to fall sick of it.'

'But there's bad I feel, Rhian, and I'm frightened.' She clasped Rhian's hand and stared up at her imploringly. 'What shall we do then?'

Rhian smiled reassuringly. 'I'm going to put a nice cool cloth on your forehead first of all, so you just lie there still and quiet and don't worry.'

She hurried into the kitchen and filled a bowl with water, her mind working rapidly. Tomorrow they would have the doctor round to see Gina; it would be an expense, but a necessary one. Jaundice was not a sickness to trifle with.

Carrie came down into the kitchen rubbing at her eyes sleepily. 'What's wrong, *cariad*?' She sank down into a chair and rubbed at her foot. 'Duw, my bunions are hurting tonight. I bet we'll have rain in the morning.'

'It's Gina,' Rhian said calmly. 'She's got jaundice, I think – at any rate she looks just like a Chinaman.'

Carrie's eyes were suddenly sharp, the sleepiness vanished. 'Now there's a thing to happen, how did she get that then?'

Rhian shrugged. 'It's a disease that sometimes affects those who work the wool, don't ask me why. Take this cloth,

270

Carrie, and bathe Gina's face with cold water while I make her up a potion.'

'Right, girl, I'll do that and then I'll make us all a nice cup of tea. Stir up that fire, *cariad*, it's not out yet; I can see some embers still burning low in the grate.'

Rhian nodded – she should have thought of that herself, for she would need hot water to mix the medicine. She bent over the fire and kindled the glowing embers with a piece of twig, teasing the glow until it became a flame. Carefully she placed sticks and then coals in the grate and soon the fire shimmered and glowed with a life of its own.

Quickly, almost impatiently, she washed the coal-dust from her hands and stared round the kitchen for a moment, trying to gather her thoughts. Meanwhile the kettle began to murmur and hiss as the bottom of the vessel became hot.

The room was almost an unfamiliar place in the silence of the night, with the lamp shedding harsh light and causing deep shadows to crouch in the corners. She suddenly remembered the funeral of the munitions girls and shivered a little, feeling the chill of the stone floor penetrating the soles of her feet. Hastily she pulled on her boots and moved towards the pantry, telling herself not to think morbid thoughts; Gina Sinman was a fine, strong woman who would not let the jaundice get the better of her.

Rhian searched for the small bags of dried herbs which were always hung against the lintel of the door. Snatching them all impatiently from the hooks, she scattered the muslin bags on the table, wishing she had had the foresight to label them before putting them away.

'Hedge mustard, that's what I want,' she muttered as she opened one bag after another, searching for the ragged leaves and hard dried flowers complete with sere and yellow seeds. The strong woody scent of the hedge mustard was unmistakable and with a sigh of relief, Rhian crushed the herb into a small bowl, pouring a little boiling water over it and then covering it with a saucer. Later she would strain off the liquid and the medicine would be ready.

She sighed and sank into a chair, staring into the fire with her hands clasped before her. Once more her thoughts returned to the funeral and her lips tightened, her heart contracting with pity for the two young girls who had died. Janey Jenkins she had hardly known, but she had seemed a warm sunny-natured girl, young and blooming with health; Honey O'Connor had been beautiful, a golden girl with pure, beautiful features . . . both of them too young to die.

How Mansel Jack must have suffered and she had callously ignored his feelings and trampled roughshod through the meeting she had meant to be filled with gentleness. She tried to remember if she had spoken any words of regret for what had happened at the munition works, but could recall nothing except her own bigoted pride which had formed a barrier between them.

At the funeral he had been a stranger in a good worsted suit with a heavy gold watch-chain hanging from his waistcoat. His head had the usual proud lift to it and he seemed not to notice the deference with which he was treated by the other mourners – but then, he was used to it.

He had stood alone and Rhian had longed to go to him, to be at his side, close to him . . . yet how could she? She must be for ever in the background of his life, which was what she found so unbearable.

'She's got the jaundice all right!' As she came bustling into the room Carrie's voice startled Rhian out of her reverie. She removed the saucer from the bowl and the strong woody scent of the herb rose in the steam to greet her.

'There's a good girl,' Carrie spoke warmly. 'Hedge mustard is just the right thing, it will clear the chest and ease away some of the pain – take that horrible hoarseness away too, for I can hardly hear what the poor girl is saying.'

'I'd better strip my bed and we'll put on fresh sheets so that Gina can sleep in with you, Carrie.' Rhian rose and took a strainer from the drawer. 'I'll sleep with the children if you like.'

Carrie shook her head. '*Duw*, there's brave you are, thinking of taking on those two little monsters. But no, you sleep in with Gina and get what rest you can – you're needed to work the mill, don't forget.'

It took the two of them all their strength to carry Gina into the other room. The children slept on oblivious to what was happening around them as Gina sighed a little and clutched at

272

the bedclothes, drawing them up around her face as though for comfort.

'What's going to happen to my baby?' she croaked, her eyes barely open. Rhian sat on the bed beside her and held out a cup containing the liquid from the herbs.

'There's a daft question! Here, drink this, it'll do you good.' She held the cup to Gina's lips, ignoring the look of disgust on her face as the smell rose on the steam. 'Drink it now, do as I say, it'll help to make you better. As for Dewi, don't worry, we won't let the boy starve.'

A glimmer of a smile lit Gina's face, easing out the lines of pain for a moment. 'What would I do without you, Rhian Gray?' she said in a whisper.

In the kitchen Carrie was busy pouring tea and Rhian took a cup gratefully. Her eyes met Carrie's and read the unspoken question in them. 'We'll manage, we'll have to,' she said softly.

'But we're one worker short now,' Carrie was frowning, 'and I'll not be much help because of minding the babbas, though I'll try to come down to the mill and help out when I can.'

'You'll do no such thing.' Rhian sank into a chair and held out her empty cup. 'Any more in the pot?'

Carrie poured the tea, a sombre look in her eyes. 'You'll make yourself sick trying to put up all the orders by yourself – and what good would that do?'

Rhian shook her head. 'I've got an idea,' she smiled. 'What if I ask Doris to work for us? I don't think for one minute that she'll want to go back to the munitions factory.'

Carrie nodded. 'You've got something there. Doris wasn't badly hurt and she's a damn good worker, I'll say that for her. A bit rough-and-ready, mind, we'll have to cover the children's ears when she's around!'

Rhian sank back in her chair and stared at the window where the greyness of dawn was changing to indigo. In the distance the hills were taking shape and the trees became real instead of flat ghosts against the sky. She had spoken with optimism, but her mind whirled with doubts and fears. Though help was necessary, Doris would be another liability, she would require wages, for she had her own family to think of. Rhian wondered sombrely if the output of woollen goods would be enough to carry the ever-increasing burdens she was forced to shoulder.

She sighed softly. 'Let's try to get a little sleep,' she suggested. 'We'll have a busy day tomorrow.'

In the morning Rhian sent Carrie to fetch old Doctor Thomas, for Gina was suffering greatly with pains in her belly and back. In spite of her sickness she managed to feed Dewi by propping him against two pillows, spooning porridge into his greedy mouth.

The doctor was hearty, his eyes faded blue behind his spectacles. 'Seems you've done what's right and proper, my dear.' He addressed his remarks to Rhian. 'There's no miracle that will cure jaundice, just rest and plenty of liquid taken by mouth and perhaps a continuation of the herbal tea.' He smiled a little ruefully. 'Can't do any harm even if it doesn't do much good.'

When he had left, Rhian sat on the bed and took Gina's hand in hers, feeling it hot and clammy to the touch.

'Now you're not to worry, everything's under control. I'm getting Doris in to help us – you know her, the one who used to stoke boilers at the Canal Street Laundry.'

Gina rubbed at her eyes a little mournfully. 'But what does she know about wool?' Her voice quivered with weakness and Rhian's heart melted in pity.

'I'll have her doing the washing and hanging out the blankets and shawls and in no time at all you'll be back on your feet.' Her fingers curled around Gina's as though to infuse some strength in her. The sick woman smiled and lay back on the pillow staring down at her sleeping son, while Rhian leaned forward to tuck the bedclothes around her shoulders.

'Now I'm going to take master Sinman downstairs with me and you're going to sleep, my girl. If you obey orders you'll get over the sickness all the sooner, right?'

Weakly Gina nodded, her eyes already half closed. Rhian lifted Dewi carefully and hugged him close, enjoying the feel of his relaxed body heavy with sleep against her breast. It was a pity that she had so little time to enjoy the children, she thought sadly; she hardly saw Dewi during the day – or Cerianne, her own niece, if it came to that. She sighed for she would be seeing even less of them in the coming days and would need to work even harder to fulfil the orders that were coming in steadily.

'Taking the day off, are you?' It was a little while later and Rhian was pulling on her shawl, tying bonnet ribbons under her chin. Carrie stood watching with a worried frown on her face and Rhian paused.

'I was going to see Doris, but if you think you can't manage the children and Gina, then I'll leave it until later.'

Carrie shook her head. 'There's nothing to stop you going now, so off with you! Of course I can manage – don't be so soft, think you're . . . you're . . .' She gave up her search for the right word and shrugged.

'Indispensable? Of course I'm not, but *you* are.' She kissed Carrie's cheek. 'I won't be long.'

*

Rhian felt the chill of rain in the air as she stepped through the mud and moved past the richly flowing stream towards the cobbled roadway. Mist hung shroudlike over the roof-tops and the peaks of Town Hill and Kilvey seemed to have vanished from sight. The heavy blanket of clouds forced the green smoke from the copper works to hang low over the buildings, penetrating the stonework, twisting sinuously along narrow high-walled courts, burning the eyes and bringing a stinging to the skin from its abrasive dust.

Canal Street had changed, Rhian thought sadly. In the days when she was a carefree young girl working at the laundry, falling in love with Heath Jenkins, it had been a bustling place – the houses tall and elegant with fresh lace curtains at the windows, and the laundry itself the hub of the neighbourhood. Now some of the houses lay forlorn and empty and the Canal Street Laundry was a torn and twisted skeleton. Rhian shivered and walked past the house of Mrs Benson, the midwife, turning the corner into the small road where Doris lived with her two children and her mother.

It was Doris herself who opened the door and the smile of welcome on her round face warmed Rhian's heart. 'There's lovely to see you, *merchi*, come on inside and sit with me for a minute. There's a bit of peace about the place for once, because my mam's taken the children down to the market with her. Glad to see the back of them, I was, wearing me out they were

275

with their noise and screeching.'

'How are you feeling, Doris?' Rhian seated herself on the hard upright chair in the little parlour, though she would far sooner have gone into the warmth of the kitchen and enjoyed the cosiness of the fire.

'All right, see.' Doris had tears in her eyes. 'But it was that terrible, Rhian, like something out of hell itself, when the munitions shed blew up, I thought it was the end of the world and that I'd be playing a harp in heaven or else stoking boilers down below.' She tried to smile but her lip trembled and Rhian saw with a feeling of dismay that Doris was in no fit state to do any sort of work, for the shock was still in her.

'When you feel better, I wondered if you'd like a job down at the mill with me – nothing too hard, mind.'

Doris looked at her and the tears brimmed over, running unchecked down her pale, plump face.

'Thank you, Rhian, I won't say no to that for I need money bad, like.' She stared down at her trembling fingers. 'You know better than most that I don't get nothing from the Prince of Wales Fund – came with me to try for it, didn't you, and them buggers turned me down.' Her shoulders shook. 'Got to earn something soon,' she repeated, 'we'll starve otherwise. Me mam's been doing a bit of cleaning and washing for folks that got in a few shillings, but it's mostly 'cos the neighbours were sorry for us. None of them can afford to keep that up, their bellies are touching their backbones as it is.'

Rhian felt heavy, as though the clouds outside the window had settled over her head. 'Well, whenever you feel strong enough, the job is there waiting for you.' She noticed the way Doris's hands shook and pity welled within her. 'Look, can I do something for you while I'm here? Would you like a nice brew of tea or something?'

Doris's face lit up. 'There's good it is of you to ask.' She had paused for a moment as if the question needed special consideration; she was the same Doris and yet she wasn't, and Rhian was unnerved.

'Aye, all right then, come into the kitchen and you can push the kettle on to the fire for me. My mouth feels dry like a bone buried for a month.' Rhian followed her along the narrow passageway and into the spotless kitchen.

The room was sparsely furnished and the stone floor was covered only by a few rag mats. The heavy table with carved wooden legs was scrubbed white and a rocking-chair with arms rubbed smooth by the years stood before the black-leaded grate. Rhian's childhood had not been one of luxury and yet she had never known such spartan surroundings. In the home of Aunt Agnes there had been warmth and comfort and the little touches that only an adequate supply of money could bring, and she had never thought to question it.

'Now, how many measures of tea do you like in the pot?' She prised the lid from the old bon-bon tin that served as a caddy and looked at Doris questioningly. Doris rubbed at her forehead and bit her lip, frowning in concentration.

'Shall I put one for you, one for me and one for the pot?' Rhian was already spooning the tea out of the tin, her own hands trembling as she set out the cups and did the everyday things that should have been so simple. But it seemed as though Doris could not quite make sense of things; she had no physical hurt, but her mind had suffered somehow during the explosion.

They sat together and yet it was as though a great gulf divided them. Suddenly Doris turned to look at her as though Rhian had spoken. 'Terrible it was, mind, them two lovely girls blown to kingdom come.' Doris twisted her fingers together, forgetting the cup of tea that steamed on the table. 'Not that Honey had a mark on her, but you could tell she was dead – like a light gone out, it was. And Janey . . .' Doris smoothed her skirt over her knees, her hands trembling.

'Please, don't talk about it, Doris, it's too painful.' But Rhian might just as well not have spoken.

'Slaughtered like a pig, she was, split up the middle with her innards falling out.' Doris looked at Rhian imploringly, 'I didn't know what to *do*.'

A loud knocking on the door shattered the silence. 'I'll go, shall I?' Rhian rose quickly, grateful for the interruption, feeling a mixture of guilt and relief.

Mansel Jack stood in the doorway, his large frame filling it. Surprised, Rhian stepped back to allow him in; she had not known he was back from Yorkshire. They smiled simultaneously and Rhian felt foolishly happy. As he moved past her easily and made his way along the passage, it was clear he was no stranger to the house. Rhian followed him, her spirits unaccountably high as she watched him sit down opposite Doris and take her hands into his own.

'Are you feeling better, lass?' He leaned forward, looking into her eyes with the air of an adult talking to a child. Doris nodded and a wide pleased smile curved her lips.

'Rhian came to see me, going to work for her down at the mill I am – won't be short of money then, see?'

Mansel Jack put his hand into his pocket and drew out an envelope. 'That reminds me, here are your wages, Doris. Now, I'll put the packet on the mantelpiece near the clock – don't forget, will you?' He looked at Rhian, asking, 'Where's her mother?'

Rhian shook her head. 'She's taken the children to the market as far as I know.'

He stared down at her, his dark eyes warm. 'Good of you to think of offering Doris work, but you realise she's not strong enough yet?'

'I'm willing to wait,' Rhian said unevenly, staring down at her hands, tinglingly aware of his scrutiny.

'Need help in the mill, do you? Must be doing well.'

Rhian shook her head. 'Gina Sinman's got the wool sickness and I thought that Doris might . . .' Her voice trailed away and she heard Mansel Jack sigh.

'I'd like to get back to the looms myself.' He stood close but not touching her and she found she was trembling. An indomitable strength seemed to emanate from him and she felt he had the power to move mountains if he so chose.

The outer door sprang open, almost torn from its hinges by the two noisy children who hurled themselves along the passageway to slide to a stop in the kitchen doorway.

'*Bore da*, Mr Mansel Jack.' They spoke in unison in a well-rehearsed sing-song while their grandmother, heaving two heavy bags on to the table, smiled respectfully.

'There's good of you to come up here every week, sir – and you so busy – don't know what we'd do without you, though.' She bobbed him a curtsey and her smile was so like Doris's that it was easy to see they were mother and daughter.

'I shall be going away again shortly but there is no need to

278

worry, you'll be well looked after.'

Rhian moved uneasily. 'I'd better go now.' She moved to Doris and took her hand, 'I'll come and see you again soon.'

Doris smiled slowly and frowned in concentration. 'Aye . . . wants me to work for you in the mill, isn't it? I will too, once I'm better.'

Rhian turned away and without looking at anyone in particular made her farewells. She hurried into the street, her boots slipping against the damp cobbles and her mind twisting and turning in a confusion of impressions. Her spirits were low and she had the nagging feeling that she should have come to see Doris sooner, but then she had not realised how deeply the girl had been affected by the blast at the works. Such a terrible experience was enough to turn anybody's mind a little off-balance. Rhian was warmed as she thought of Mansel Jack's kindness; he had made quite sure that Doris received her money even though she was unable to work.

She had almost reached the end of Canal Street when she heard quick footsteps behind her and without turning, she knew that they belonged to Mansel Jack. He caught her arm and smiled. 'Hey up there, lass, not catching a train, are you?' She felt his fingers as though they burned through the thick material of her shawl and carefully she drew away from his grasp.

'No, of course not,' she said slowly. 'There's kind of you to give Doris her pay even though she can't work yet.' The words tumbled from her lips without grace and Rhian drew back embarrassed, hugging her shawl around her shoulders.

He smiled. 'You remind me of a snail.' His teeth were very white and his uncovered hair sparkled with raindrops.

'A snail?' she repeated uncomprehendingly.

'You retreat into your shell the moment anyone comes too close,' he explained.

Rhian began to walk away from the canal, aware of his tallness at her side. She saw a lace curtain twitch and bent her head, pulling her bonnet down over her face.

'Ah, so that's it – ashamed to be seen with me, are you?' he said with a teasing edge to his voice.

Rhian glanced up at him, her eyes reproachful. 'I don't know what you mean, do you have to talk in riddles all the time?'

'Touchy too!' He was openly laughing. 'Afraid of what the neighbours will say – and that's no way to live.'

'I don't give a damn what folks say.' She stopped walking and stared up into his face. 'But I do care about Heath Jenkins and what sort of stories might get told to him. I'm sure you can understand that?'

'And what of friendship, doesn't that come into your life at all?' Mansel Jack was not laughing now, his voice was strong and vibrant.

'There are many kinds of friendship,' she responded, feeling foolish and clumsy, 'but Heath Jenkins loves me and he will make me his wife. He accepts me as I am with all my faults and that's what true friendship is.'

They had reached the edge of the hill now and could see the mill house down in the hollow. A thin mist still drifted upwards, intertwining with smoke from the chimneys, and Rhian could hear the rush of the stream that turned the water-wheel.

Mansel Jack was so handsome as he stood tall and strong, looking down at her, his lean face sober and his dark eyes unreadable. 'I'm coming to help you in the mill. Surely that won't offend the proprieties too much – I want no protests from you, Rhian, I'm speaking as a friend, all right?'

Rhian stared at him, shaking her head in bewilderment. 'But the looms are small, nothing like your mills, and the . . .' Her words trailed away as he put his strong fingers lightly over her lips, silencing her.

'I want to spend my last few days in Sweyn's Eye doing the work I love best.'

Rhian's mouth was dry. 'You've done it then, you've enlisted in the Army?' Her mind was crying out in pain and she wanted to throw herself into his arms, to give him whatever he wanted, for she might never see him again. After a moment, however, she merely nodded.

'All right, if you really mean it, come down to the mill in the morning.' She smiled wanly. 'You'll have to take orders, mind; you may own the mill, but for now I'm the boss and I like things run my way!'

He pulled at his forelock mockingly and Rhian smiled in the

sheer joy of the moment. They seemed so close it was as if all barriers had been swept away; they were simply two people who had reached an understanding, but the glow of happiness went far deeper than that.

And then he had turned away abruptly and without another word was striding down the hill towards the town. Rhian clenched her hands together, resisting the urge to call him back. He was a strange one all right – he had the power to move her and reach into the secret places of her heart and mind. And here she was, feeling light-headed and happy because tomorrow he would be with her in the mill. She told herself she was a fool, yet nothing would dispel the happiness that ran like wine through her veins.

Chapter Twenty-Three

The winter carpet of frost sparkled on windows, dusting the hills with rime. Colder mists were rolling in between the twin hills of Sweyn's Eye, seeming to muffle the Sunday bells. And Mary Sutton sat in her gracious drawing-room before a blazing fire and had never felt so alone in her life.

She was acutely aware of the silence enfolding the big house as she stared down into the garden, her eyes moving to the wide expanse of the sea beyond – it was restless, without colour, like pewter that had not been cleaned.

In her lap was one of Brandon's old letters, in which he assured her he was well but that he was not allowed to tell her the name of the place from which he was writing. He had not enjoyed the sea journey; there had been a sudden gusting wind that had battered the ship, tossing it towards France as though delivering him into enemy hands.

Mary sighed, finding it ironic that he had spoken little of love, but she guessed he had been self-conscious with other men around him. But now her being ached for some reassurance that their love had been good.

Folding the letter away, she put it in the drawer of her desk with trembling fingers. She felt weak and ill; her heart seemed to pump fast in her breast and her head swam as if she was about to swoon. She returned to her seat and stared down at her hands, knowing her sickness was nothing but her conscience playing tricks on her – she was as strong as a horse, had she not always been so?

The door opened and Mrs Greenaway stood uncertainly on the threshold.

'Dr Soames is here. I didn't know you'd sent for him, *merchi*, though pale as a penny chicken you've looked to me lately, with such big shadows under your eyes. Tell him to come in, shall I?'

Mary sat up straighter in her chair, rich colour suffusing her cheeks, but he had to be faced sometime and it might as well be now.

'Yes, tell him to come in, Greenie, it's all right.'

The doctor entered the room quietly, as composed as ever. He was a fine handsome man, younger than Brandon by several years and he had been so virile when they lay together. Mary tore her gaze away from him, washed with a feeling of shame.

'Please sit down, Dr Soames and make yourself comfortable.' She managed to speak lightly, though she knew the crimson was still in her cheeks. He did not obey at once but he moved towards her, taking her hand and raising her fingers to his lips.

'Mary, I've been desperate to see you again and you've been putting me off. Did you think I would embarrass you or perhaps make demands? If so, you mistake my intentions.'

Mary sighed. 'I've been so confused, I needed time to think.'

He sat opposite her then and smiled easily. 'And have you come to any conclusions?'

She nodded. 'What we did was wrong and must never be repeated. I was weak and foolish and I don't blame you at all – indeed, it was all my fault.'

'Don't punish yourself with recriminations, Mary,' he said gently. 'Life's far too short for that.' He paused, 'I'll admit I knew nothing of your grief and I'm glad about that – otherwise I might have felt I was taking advantage of your state of mind. But if you want me to pretend it never happened, then I can't – to me it was a wonderful experience, one I shall never forget.'

Mary bit her lip. 'Don't, please, you're only reminding me . . .' her words trailed away and the doctor shook his head.

'No one will ever know what happened between us for unless you choose to speak out, I never will. But can you not think of me as a friend and please . . . call me Paul, won't you?'

He stared at her, his brow creasing into a frown. 'You look

283

peaky, Mary, why don't you let me take you for a drive? I have the horse and trap today, as Bryn Thomas has no calls to make.'

Mary shook her head; how would it appear to others if she were to be seen driving through town with her doctor?

He seemed to know what she was thinking. 'It would be very proper and natural,' he assured her. 'You know that a doctor is considered above reproach.'

'I suppose you're right.' Mary rose to her feet, realising how much she felt hemmed in by the four walls of the room and by the silence of the day. Lately, Sundays had been so lonely. The rest of the time she had plenty to do – she could keep herself busy enough between the emporium and the work she did on the trams and at night she was so tired that she fell into bed and slept at once through sheer weariness. And after all, what harm would there be in going for a drive with her doctor?

'Greenie, will you fetch my coat please?' Mary called. 'I'm going out for some fresh air.'

Mrs Greenaway concealed her surprise and did Mary's bidding, but it was clear she was torn between approval that Mary was going outdoors and doubts as to the propriety of the occasion.

The mists were rolling away and the sea had lightened, the waves softly tumbling against the crescent of sand that edged the shore. The long encompassing arm of Mumbles Head had become visible, standing out against the sky, dark and craggy.

As the doctor helped her into the chill leather seat, Mary's spirits were suddenly lifted and her gloom evaporated like the mists that had earlier wreathed the seas.

The clip-clop of the horse's hooves on the road was soothing, reminding Mary of the time when she had driven a van around the valleys, selling her shawls to the wives of miners and beginning to make her business pay. She had been happy then, her goal in life to be a successful business woman so that she need never fear a return to the poverty which had dogged her childhood.

Why had she become discontented, she wondered – and why had she allowed her marriage to be eroded by her own selfishness? Look at her now: sitting beside a virtual stranger, knowing in her heart that she was playing with fire. She must

284

stop all this nonsense, she told herself sternly; the young doctor must not be allowed to insinuate himself into her life.

Suddenly she felt a surge of her old determination and strength, telling herself sharply that she had become weak of late – a moaning self-centred woman. She worried about what had happened in her husband's past, torturing herself with doubts about his faithfulness when all the time she had the makings of a flossie deep within her own soul.

'Stop, please, I want to get out,' Mary said suddenly and Paul Soames looked at her in surprise.

'What's wrong?' he asked, his hand resting on hers. 'Do you feel sick or something?'

Strangely enough, in spite of her clearness of mind Mary did feel quite ill. As she stepped down into the road her whole body seemed to tremble; perhaps she was coming down with a chill, she thought, for she had been working in the rain a great deal lately.

'I would just like to walk, if you don't mind.' She stared at him with clear eyes. 'There must be nothing more between us, ever, do you understand?'

He inclined his head. 'If you say so, Mary, but don't be silly about this; let me at least take you home.'

She shook her head. 'No, I'm all right, I can look after myself. I've done so for most of my life after all – and brought Heath up too, come to that.'

The doctor seemed uncertain. 'I don't know, you look a little pale to me, are you sure you're all right?'

And then Mary was not sure at all as she leaned against the rough stone wall at the side of the road and tried to combat the dizziness that was swamping her. A feeling of nausea made her retch and she was suddenly grateful for strong arms holding her as the world spun away into darkness inside her head.

She opened her eyes slowly to find herself lying on a long leather couch. The room was vaguely familiar, but it was only when she turned her head and saw the skeleton in the corner that she realised she was in Paul Soames' surgery. She felt rather than saw a movement and then he was bending over her, his sombre eyes staring down.

'What's happening to me?' Mary whispered fearfully.

He glanced away quickly. 'It's what you've been wanting

for a long time, Mary.' He paused for a moment and his eyes met hers, seeing the dawning understanding in her face. 'That's right, you are going to have a baby.'

She sat up and stared at him in disbelief. 'But how do you know, how can you tell, if I didn't even know?'

'Ask yourself one or two simple questions, Mary. For example, have you been seeing your monthly courses lately? And have the mornings been a little of an ordeal, with a feeling of faintness and nausea just as you experienced today?' He smoothed back his already neat hair. 'Apart from these things there are certain physical indications clear to any doctor and I'm quite certain – I half wish I wasn't, believe me.'

Mary sat up and smoothed her skirts over her knees; her hands were trembling and she still felt slightly sick. Paul Soames helped her to her feet, staring at her quizzically. 'What can I say? I'm as mixed-up as you appear to be.'

She glanced towards the door and he interpreted the gesture at once. 'There are no other patients outside, don't worry.'

Mary's thoughts were tumbling over themselves and she could not form even the simplest of queries. She looked up mutely at the doctor and he patted her shoulder clumsily.

'These things are often a shock at first, but once you've accepted the idea you will be delighted, I'm sure. After all, you wanted a baby, didn't you?'

But not like this, Mary thought in anguish. 'Will you take me home?' she asked, her voice trembling.

He virtually had to lift her into the trap; his hands were strong and supportive and she was grateful for his help. Her mind was scurrying round in circles as she studied the long street of high, narrow houses – staring upwards at the smoke-filled sky, leaning back in her seat, noticing how the leather creaked coldly as she eased herself into it. She could not think, begin to work things out; she needed to get home to her room, close herself in, crawl into her bed and hide from her thoughts.

The doctor did not speak, he simply drove in silence and she was grateful. When they arrived he handed her over to Mrs Greenaway with a few brief words of explanation and then took Mary's hand, though she refused to meet his eyes.

'I'll come to see you soon, Mrs Sutton,' he said formally, 'and in the meantime, get all the rest you can.'

286

It seemed an eternity before she was in her nightgown and alone in the silence of the big bed. As she closed her eyes, tears forced themselves from beneath the tightly-shut lids and the pain that squeezed her heart was almost physical. But at last she slept and in her dreams she was in Brandon's arms, loving him, giving him all of herself, and for a brief time she was happy.

It was dark when she awoke and the moon was silvering the room, casting a glow over the bed that made the white of the sheets appear like snow that had drifted into folds. Mary sat up, her mind clear as she lit the lamp, pulled on her dressing-gown and sat in her chair near the grey ashes of the dead fire. She thought carefully, going over dates in her mind – sifting, remembering – but there was no answer to the question that reared up in her mind. Only one fact stood out plain and clear: she did not know who was the father of her baby.

She had lain with Brandon the night before he had gone to join his regiment. The coupling had been soured with mistrust and discontent – could such a union have resulted in the child she so desired after such a long barren time? Or was it not more likely that her stolen night with a virtual stranger was the occasion when she had conceived?

She bit her lip . . . if so, then she had betrayed Brandon in the most cruel way a man could be betrayed. Clasping her hands together, she wondered if she could pluck up the courage to speak plainly to Paul Soames and if she did, whether he could possibly answer her questions?

And yet slowly the misery began to vanish. Mary wrapped her arms around her still smooth stomach and joy rose within her like great coloured bubbles, shimmering golden and bright and making her breathless with joy. Here within her was the child for which she had pined, the baby she thought she would never conceive! Hot, happy tears poured down her cheeks, so that she gasped with the force of her feelings and softly rocked herself to and fro. 'My baby,' she whispered between her tears.

*

So the days passed in a haze where Mary's feelings fluctuated between overwhelming joy and equally overwhelming guilt. She began to make a reassessment of her life, realising she had

287

loved Brandon as deeply as any woman could love her man and yet had betrayed his memory. This was a fact which she could not alter and so she must come to terms with it.

At first she continually blamed herself for the momentary weakness which had allowed her to give herself to the doctor, yet common sense told her that she had been out of her mind with grief, needing consolation and comfort from contact with another human being. Gradually she came to understand if not forgive herself, deciding at last that what she had done must remain hidden away for ever. The guilt of her betrayal might gnaw at her for the rest of her life, but it was the price she must pay to keep her child's name unblemished.

Now Mary stood on the high platform of the tram, her uniform heavy and uncomfortable, the waist already feeling a little tight. This was her last day as part-time conductress, for she did not think it good for the health of her unborn baby to be rushing upstairs and down in all kinds of inclement weather. She smiled as two soldiers boarded the tram, wearing the blue uniform of the wounded.

'Going to *Parc Beck* are you, girlie?' One of the men smiled down at her and Mary tried to ignore the empty sleeve pinned over his breast.

'There's daft you are, mind, doesn't it say *Parc Beck* on the front there?' She smiled cheekily and the soldier responded by planting a kiss on the tip of her nose.

'*Duw*, there's good it is to hear an honest-to-goodness Welsh voice. I never want to go to "Froggie land" again!'

Mary frowned in confusion and the two soldiers laughed. 'France, girl! Don't you know there's a war on?'

She watched the men take a seat; there was no need to issue a ticket because the wounded travelled free. There was a pain inside her as she thought of Brandon lying buried in an unmarked grave in France – oh, she knew there was a war on, all right.

At the end of her shift she prepared her figures, hoping and praying that the money she had taken would tally with the tickets sold. Sometimes there was a discrepancy and then it worried her that she who was so good with figures should have made a mistake.

When she left the terminus she wandered into the street,

staring at the tram which was swallowing up the waiting crowd and feeling a pang as though there was something lost. Yet she had never set much store by her job as a conductress – it had been merely a way of helping out when there were hardly any men left to do such jobs.

But now she was unaccountably lonely. Although she did not feel like going back to the house yet, she was not dressed for the store and her uniform would be hot and uncomfortable. Suddenly she brightened: she would go to see Katie. They had not talked since just after the terrible explosion at the munitions factory and Mary felt guilty, she had been so wrapped up in herself that she had given no thought to anyone else, nor to how Katie must still be suffering at the loss of her two young friends.

There was a chill wind blowing along Market Street and the stalls clustered together in the square brought back swift, sharp memories of the time when Mary had worked in the market, enduring all sorts of weather as she endeavoured to build up her trade. She remembered the duplicity of Alfred Phillpot who had tried to outwit her, starving her of supplies so that she would be forced to sell her stalls, but she had beaten him in the end.

She frowned, for even now he was bent on provoking her and there was the business of the woollen goods he had bought from Yorkshire, changing the labels so that she believed the articles to be Welsh. Well, Mansel Jack – mill owner from whom Phillpot had purchased – had come down to Sweyn's Eye himself to sort that one out. Strangely enough he had remained to run the munitions factory where Katie Murphy worked and the terrible accident had occurred.

The pungent smell of fish hung on the breeze and Mary wrinkled her nose in disgust. Yet here in this house she had received such hospitality, sharing a curtained-off section of Katie's own room. She sighed, for she had been remiss in neglecting her friend so badly.

Katie was looking much better and the gash on her forehead was almost healed, but there were shadows still beneath her eyes.

'Come in, me darlin', sure 'tis lovely to see you.' Katie took her arm and hustled her into the kitchen where Mrs Murphy sat as usual in her chair, skirts hitched up and knees bare to the heat from the fire. Mary's heart sank – there would be no chance to exchange confidences today. The youngest of the Murphy boys was playing on the floor, running a red-painted wooden tank over the rag mat.

Katie held her hands to her head and frowned in mock annoyance, then pointed to the stairs. 'Come up to my room – we'll not hear ourselves speak down here with that boy making so much noise.'

'Oh, Katie!' said her mother, 'shame on you taking away our company like that, you don't consider your old mammy at all, do you?'

Katie sighed heavily. 'We'll talk to you after, don't worry yourself . . . and how about making us a nice hot cup of tea? That'll give you something to do, so it will.'

Katie's room was different from the time when Mary had shared it and now there was linoleum on the floor, covered with strong tufted mats. The walls had been decorated and the window and bed were hung with good heavy coverings.

'Nothing so posh as your house, Mary.' Katie's shrewd eyes were watching her and Mary shook her head.

'No, but it's very nice Katie – a palace compared with the hovel I was brought up in – and don't you forget it, for I won't!'

'I know that. Come and sit down and tell me what's been happening. I can see in your eyes there's something important you want to say.'

Mary smiled. 'There's knowing you are,' she said, 'far too nosey if you ask me, mind.' She settled herself on the bed and leaned back against the wall, clasping her hands around her knees and wondering how much she was going to tell Katie – her mind buzzed with the need to confide in someone who would understand.

'I'm going to have a baby!' The words fell into the silence of the room and if Mary had expected great surprise she couldn't have been more wrong. Katie merely smiled and brushed back her red-gold hair.

'I knew that the minute I set eyes on you.' Her smugness was infuriating. 'Not that your belly's got big yet, but there's something about your eyes; you can always tell.'

'Oh, can you indeed!' Mary laughed, a little piqued at being deprived of her moment of glory.

Katie put her hand on Mary's shoulder. 'This is something you've been wanting for a long time. I know how much it means to you and I'm so pleased for you Mary, but then you know that. Can I be godmother?'

Mary smiled. 'Yes, but you don't deserve it for guessing my secret without me having to tell you.' She stared through the small window for a moment and saw that the coast of Devon was barely visible through the mists that were rising from the sea.

'Then why aren't you happy?' Katie's words dropped softly into the quietness and Mary did not turn to look at her. She knew she must speak, the words were burning at her and she so needed a friend – one person to whom she could tell her awful secret so that the burden would not be so heavy.

'Katie, I'm not sure that Brandon is the father of my child.' The words fell into a pool of silence and Mary realised at once that she had made a mistake.

'Jesus, Mary and Joseph!' Katie was genuinely shocked.

Mary turned to her earnestly: 'I'd had the telegram to say Brandon was dead . . . I don't know what happened to me then – oh, I can't begin to explain . . .'

The silence seemed to stretch interminably and looking at Katie, Mary felt she was staring into the eyes of a disapproving stranger.

'Mary, how *could* you?' Katie asked, her tone as well as her words holding a reproof. 'You and Brandon were so . . . so right together, I didn't think you could be unfaithful and so soon after . . .'

Mary looked down at her hands as her friend's voice died away. 'Katie, with your past I should have thought you would understand more than anyone.' As soon as the words were spoken, however, she regretted them. Katie had loved William Owen and had lain with him in the hills and been his woman, but it was not until long after he had died that she had turned to another man.

'I'm sorry, forget I said that!' Mary apologised quickly, 'There's soft I was to burden you with all this, there's nothing anyone can do about it.'

Katie stared at her in silence and Mary felt moved to try to explain how it had happened. She had no wish to be at the receiving end of Katie's outraged anger. 'I was unhappy, anyway. I thought that Brandon was interested in Mary Anne Bloomfield again. Indeed, when he was on leave he went to see her.' She knew she was babbling but she could not help herself.

'And so you wanted to pay him back for what you *thought* he'd done? Mary, that's not worthy of you!'

'I didn't plan any of it,' Mary said in despair. 'I can't explain it even to myself.' She rubbed her hand over her eyes. 'Oh, I don't know how it happened – the doctor was kind and I needed kindness just then . . . it was all so easy somehow.'

Katie rose to her feet, her face aghast. 'Mary, you didn't go to bed with the young doctor?' She brushed at her long hair, her eyes wide. 'By the name of all the saints, don't tell this to anyone else – you could destroy that man's whole life, don't you know that?'

Mary bit her lip. This meeting was not turning out at all as she had planned; she had wanted help, advice, reassurance perhaps, but all she was getting was condemnation.

'I'm sorry, I shouldn't have told you.' She spoke in a low voice and then felt Katie move away from her.

'You've behaved like a spoiled little girl, Mary.' She spoke harshly: 'I think you deserve a good hiding, if you must know – not sympathy.'

Mary got to her feet and stared at Katie, suddenly angry. 'All right, if you're going to be "holier than thou" all of a sudden, then I'll go. I'm sorry if I've upset your fine sensibilities.'

She strode from the room and hurried down the stairs, her heart beating swiftly. Barely nodding to Mrs Murphy, who was pouring a cup of tea, she made her way quickly through the kitchen and along the passage out into the street.

Behind her she could hear Katie calling but she didn't stop, hurrying down the hill towards the docklands where she and Brandon had spent much of their time together. Her eyes were filled with tears and though she recognised them as self-pity she could not check their flow. She sat at the quayside, oblivious to the cold air that blew in from the Channel as she stared at the ships waiting to go out on the tide. Katie's attitude had hurt deeply and yet Mary knew the Irish girl was right –

nothing could ever excuse what she had done.

After a time she began to walk back through the town. Her thoughts were still in a whirl and when she found herself outside the shabby house where Doctor Soames had his surgery, she paused – wanting, needing to talk to him.

'Come in, Mrs Sutton.' He spoke formally, but his eyes were warm and Mary felt glad she had called.

She sat in the cold leather seat, staring at the familiar bony skeleton in the corner and took a deep breath.

'A doctor is like a priest, is that right?' The words came out baldly and he looked at her in surprise. 'I mean . . . you can't ever repeat what you hear between these four walls?'

Her tone was desperate and Paul Soames looked at her in concern. 'You can say what you like to me, you must know that, Mary.' He smiled down at her and she averted her gaze. She tried to relax the tenseness in her fingers, stretching them wide and staring at the thick gold wedding ring on her finger.

'Is there any way we can tell who's the father of my baby?' Now she had said it and she glanced at him, relieved to see that he had not recoiled from her.

He shook his head. 'It's very difficult,' he said softly. 'There are ways whereby probability may be decided upon, but nothing we can pinpoint with any certainty.'

'I was with my husband before he left for France – could the child be his?' Mary had to ask the question though the words were torn from her lips.

The doctor shrugged. 'Let me speak plainly, Mary.' He took her hand in his. 'The likelihood is that I'm the father of your baby, don't you see that?' He looked away from the pain in her eyes. 'There is a possibility, a remote one, that you conceived that last time with your husband – but it's not really likely.'

Mary took a deep breath. 'So there's no way I can know for sure?' She met his eyes and read sympathy there as he shook his head.

'I'd advise you to forget this – to go on home, have your baby and enjoy it. If there's anything I can ever do to help, you only need to ask. It would be a privilege and surely I owe you that much.'

She forced a smile. 'You owe me nothing. Thank you for your kindness.' As she rose and opened the door of the surgery a figure moved smartly away and Mary froze into stillness.

'Hello, honey!' Mary Anne Bloomfield smiled enigmatically, her eyes running over Mary's figure knowingly. 'It seems we may have more in common than I first thought.'

The words were innocent enough, but Mary knew without doubt that the American woman had heard everything.

Chapter Twenty-Four

The hum of the mule and the clatter of the loom were like wine to Rhian's senses. Over the last few days she had worked harder than she had ever done in her life, yet a warm feeling of happiness accompanied her labours.

She glanced across the hopper to where Mansel Jack stood, shirt-sleeves rolled above his elbows as he fed raw wool on to the carding machine. The matted wool was evenly distributed to the first group of rollers on the scribbler which, covered in jagged teeth, pulled the wool from one roller to the other until all the fibres were worked loose.

Mansel Jack adjusted the flow of wool and made sure that the doffer scraped off the loose fibres, watching as these were conveyed on an overhead belt and laid broadside on the input to the Scotch intermediate feed, which had much finer teeth and created a uniformity in the wool texture.

He had worked with Rhian for the best part of a week and each morning she feared he would tell her it was his last at the mill, for now the Army had first claim on him.

Becoming aware of her scrutiny, he smiled and as his dark eyes held hers, she found herself moving towards him as though led by some outside force. He stared down at her and her mouth was dry; she looked into his face and knew that in the too brief time they had spent together, she had become bound to him more surely than if the strongest web of wool had entangled her.

Mansel Jack did not speak, he stood over her – a big handsome man, his hair tangled into curls, sweat running down the open neck of his shirt. He was not dressed like a gentleman now, yet there was a quality of steeliness about him still.

The door of the mill swung open and Rhian saw a tall, elegant woman standing framed in the light from the yard. Some instinct told her that this must be Charlotte – Mansel Jack's future bride. She seemed to glide forward, her eyes never leaving his face. When she stopped before him her face was calm, but Rhian could see that the fine gloves were being twisted between slender fingers.

'I had to come,' she said in a slow, cultured voice. 'I want you to release me from my promise to marry you.'

Mansel Jack made a move towards her, but she held up her hand.

'No, please, don't speak. I know I'm doing the right thing.' Her glance encompassed Rhian and there was no malice, only a dignified sadness.

'I have realised for some time now that our lives were moving on separate paths and when you came home to see me, I sensed a change in you. Now, coming here today, I am thoroughly convinced that we were not meant for each other. I have never seen you so happy, not ever, Mansel Jack.' She smiled and her features seemed illuminated. 'All I ever wanted was your happiness,' she touched his arm briefly, 'and I won't be so childish as to fling your ring back at you – I shall keep it if I may as a memento.'

She turned towards the door and with a quick look at Rhian, Mansel Jack followed her outside. He spoke hurriedly, his voice vibrant and though Rhian could not hear what he said, she imagined he would be pleading with Charlotte to stay. A great emptiness filled her as she tried to see the pattern of the wool through a mist of tears.

When Mansel Jack returned to the long room, he stood with his back to the door, staring at Rhian. 'That's it then, lass, I'm a free man,' he said and she could not tell from his tone if he was glad or sorry.

She moved towards him and on impulse rested her head against his shoulder, wanting only to comfort him. She knew she might be inviting a rebuff, but she didn't care.

Slowly his strong arms came around her and she heard his breath, felt it stir the curls on her forehead as her heart tightened. She moved away from him quickly, as though burned, and he sighed softly.

'We'd better get on with our work then, lass.' Rhian nodded but it was some time before she could stop her hands from trembling and concentrate on the pattern she was making in the wool.

It was on the next day that the letter came for Mansel Jack. He came into the kitchen of the mill house and threw it on to the table that was laid for breakfast.

'I've got my orders, ladies,' he said, but his eyes were looking piercingly into Rhian's. 'The day after tomorrow, I'm off to war.'

'*Duw*, we'll miss you right enough,' Carrie said softly. Then as though ashamed of her emotions, she spoke briskly, 'While you are here, might as well do a bit of work then, isn't it?'

Rhian left the room and made her way to the mill, biting her lip to stop the flow of tears. He was going . . . her nightmare had become a reality and she did not know if she could bear it.

Mansel Jack entered the mill and without preliminary took her in his arms. 'Don't look so lost, lass.' His voice was warm and he spoke close to her ear. 'So you do care about me a little, then?'

Rhian turned and was in his arms. 'I've cared ever since the first time I saw you, and all I know is that I can't bear you to go away from me.'

He put his finger under her chin, forcing her to look up at him. 'I do believe I've fallen in love with you!' His tone was one of surprise and smiling, Rhian buried her face in his shoulder. They stood for a moment in a soft silence with arms entwined and Rhian was aglow with happiness. At last she sighed softly and, greatly daring, put her hands on his cheeks to draw his mouth down to hers.

'Rhian, you know I must go away, there may be no future for us.'

'Hush,' she said quickly. 'The time for talking's past.'

His mouth hovered above hers for what seemed an eternity and then his strong lips were like fire against her own. This was the moment she had been born for and she seemed to dissolve, her entire being trembling with love and passion.

He lifted her into his arms and carried her to a corner of the mill where he set her down on a bed of wool that was soft beneath her. She held up her arms and then he was beside her, his hands brushing back her tangled curls. 'You're beautiful lass,' his voice was gentle, 'with those lovely black eyes and the red in your hair – I've never seen anything as fine.'

He kissed her throat tenderly and the warmth of his mouth made her shiver. Then his hand began to caress her, moving softly and sensuously, opening the buttons of her shift with a gentleness of touch surprising in such a big man. Mansel Jack kissed her again, his mouth warm and tender against hers, drawing from her a pure stream of love that was much more beautiful than any sensation she had ever known.

Rhian twisted her fingers in the dark hair that curled on the back of his neck. A slant of sun pierced the gloom and it seemed like a benediction on their love. She knew the pure wine of pleasure when he took her, claiming her with an authority that thrilled and delighted her. They moved together in an embrace that had a magical quality – and she possessed him as surely as he possessed her. They were one flesh, bound together in a harmony of love.

He held her close, their ragged breathing mingled, his heart pounding as if it was inside Rhian's breast. How had she ever doubted their love? He smoothed the hair away from her damp forehead and kissed her gently.

'You're mine now, lass – I've laid my mark on you and no other man but me will ever touch you.' It was a statement and Rhian knew he was right. For good or ill she belonged to Mansel Jack and she would never want it any other way.

Carefully he helped her to dress, buttoning her shift with experienced fingers. But there was no jealousy in her, for Rhian knew with a certainty born of some age-old wisdom that no woman had ever meant what she did to him. He had put his mark on her but she had marked him also – they were bound together now with threads so strong that not even death could sever them. She shuddered slightly and he held her close.

'What's wrong, a goose walk over your grave?' he asked, his lips against her hair.

She wound her arms around his neck, standing on tiptoe to reach his lips. 'I love you, Mansel Jack,' she whispered, her mouth beneath his.

'I know, lass.' He put her away from him gently and they looked into each other's eyes. The mill hummed as though with a life of its own, the spinning mule wound the thread and the carding machine scraped and bit at the wool with relentless teeth.

Rhian looked around almost with surprise and seeing her look, Mansel Jack laughed. He threw back his head and the thick column of his throat was graceful and strong; Rhian realised that she had never seen him like this, unkempt and at ease, so masculine that she felt warmed and protected by his strength.

'You'll come home with me tonight,' he said and once again he was making a statement. 'Gina is much better now and Carrie is well able to care for her and the children.' He touched her cheek lightly. 'This is something I never thought I would say to any woman: I need you, Rhian Gray.'

She bit her lip and felt foolish as the tears trembled against her lashes. But this was the greatest moment of her life and the happiest; she was whole – a woman – and to be loved by a man the like of Mansel Jack was all she could ever want.

He switched off the machines and picked up his jacket and together they left the mill, crossing the yard past the swiftly rushing river towards the house. Rhian paused for a moment and glanced up half-shyly. 'What shall I tell them?' she asked and the colour flew rich and red into her cheeks.

He did not hesitate. 'The truth – that you're coming home with me.' He slipped his arm around her waist and hugged her. 'If you like, I shall say it for you.'

She shook her hair away from her eyes. 'No, don't do that. I'm not a baby.'

He snatched her into his arms so suddenly that she gasped for breath. Laughing, his hair curling around his handsome face, his teeth white and strong and the flecks of green she could see in the brown of his eyes – she loved him so much that it hurt.

*

Rhian hurried silently up the stairs, for she must not wake the children. She peered into the bedroom, hearing the soft breathing that told her both Cerianne and Dewi were well and

299

truly asleep. Looking down at her brother's child, she wondered where Billy was now. Might he meet up with Mansel Jack some time in the future? But the thought was too unpleasant to hold in her mind and she let it drift away as she gently touched Cerianne's soft cheek.

Sighing, she moved into the room she shared with Carrie, standing uncertainly near her bed and wondering what clothes she should take. She would need a nightgown and a clean cotton camisole with matching under-drawers ... and suddenly it struck her as strange that she should be putting clothes into a bag so calmly, preparing to spend the night with a man who had just laid her down in the darkness of the mill and made her his woman.

And yet there had been nothing clandestine about any of it; she belonged to him and they were like two halves of the same fruit. She thought briefly and remorsefully of Heath Jenkins and guilt brought a flush to her cheeks, but she was becoming fanciful – she had made her decision and now, it was time to go.

Mansel Jack had just finished his meal. His strong elbows rested on the scrubbed white table and he looked at home there, as though he belonged.

'Shall we see you in the morning?' Carrie asked smoothly and he arched an eyebrow, smiling.

'I expect we shall put in an appearance sometime during the day, though I won't guarantee it will be very early on, lass.'

Rhian clutched her bag, feeling nervously as though she were going on a great voyage. Mansel Jack rose to his feet and took up his jacket from behind the door, then held out his hand for the bag. Rhian gave it to him and stared around her foolishly, not knowing what to say.

'Well, don't worry about us, mind.' Gina broke the silence, rearranging the shawl around her legs. 'I can see to the babbas fine enough and Carrie will do the cooking for us. You take a rest, my girl, no one deserves it more than you.' It was as if Gina was giving her blessing.

Carrie moved forward then and put her hands on Rhian's shoulders, kissing her cheek before hugging her close in a spontaneous gesture of affection.

'You look after this girl or you'll have me to answer to, mind,' she said, staring up at Mansel Jack with misty eyes.

'Lord, what is this, a wake?' Mansel Jack took Rhian's arm and guided her towards the door and she glanced back just once, aware that her life was at a cross-roads.

The old stone house stood stern and tall, facing west and catching the setting sun's rays so that the long windows seemed lit with an inner glow.

'Here we are, lass, home – at least for the time being.' Mansel Jack unlocked the door and Rhian stepped inside, standing behind him and waiting in the soft darkness as he lit the lamps.

The wash of light illuminated the oak-panelled hallway and the straight staircase of polished wood, carpeted in plain dark jute.

'Nothing very luxurious here, Rhian, as you can see, but it suits me well enough for now.'

She followed him into the drawing-room – heavily furnished and old-fashioned – and watched as if in a dream as he set a light to the fire. She could scarcely believe she was really with him, here in his house. Then she felt her exhilaration evaporating; what was to be her role in his life, she wondered uneasily? It was clear he meant her to live with him until he went to join his regiment. And while she had been in his arms it had all seemed so wonderful. Now, standing in the unfamiliar room, she wondered what on earth she was doing here.

'You look dazed, lass. Take off your coat, settle yourself down in a chair and let me fetch you a glass of porter.'

Rhian obeyed, sitting stiffly in a high-backed chair and feeling at a disadvantage, out of her element and not a little frightened. Suddenly she wanted to be back in the mill house, lying in her own room with Carrie snoring her head off in the other bed.

Mansel Jack came to her, handing her a glass, his eyes warm. 'I know all this must seem strange, Rhian, but I'm here and I'll look after you.' They sat together holding hands, staring into the fire while unaccountably Rhian's feeling of sadness persisted.

Mansel Jack sighed. 'There's some paper work I must do, Rhian,' he said gently. 'I'll try not to be long.'

Alone, she tormented herself with doubts, that he could not love her, she was a working girl. She had come from a good respectable family, it was true, but Mansel Jack was a mill owner and though these last few days he had worked like any other labouring man in Sweyn's Eye, nothing could really change the fact that he was a rich man.

At last he returned and stood staring down at her. 'Come on then, lass, I've been neglecting you.' He took her hands, drawing her to her feet. 'Let's get off to bed.'

The room was cold, for the fire had not been lit. 'Haven't you anyone coming in to see to the house for you?' She spoke almost formally, trying to avoid looking at the great bed which dominated the room.

'No, I've been looking after myself – I'm quite capable you know.' He smiled and pulled his shirt over his head, standing staring at her, his eyes full of laughter.

'What's the matter, Rhian, not feeling shy surely?' He crossed the room in two quick strides and drew her into his arms, kissing her unresponsive lips and slowly warming her with his passion. She clung to him then, knowing that he was her man, that she loved him and that was all there was to it – right and wrong just didn't enter into it.

It was good to lie naked beside him in the bed. His hands were gentle as they stroked her skin and she sighed softly as she moved against him. She must savour this moment, she told herself sternly, for soon Mansel Jack would be out in France fighting the Germans and memories would be all she would have to sustain her.

He wove his magic over her as before, bringing her to such a pitch of joy and ecstasy that it was as though the earth rocked beneath her. They were locked in a world of their own making where nothing existed except their love.

In the morning, Rhian washed and dressed silently and hurried downstairs, determined to make Mansel Jack a good breakfast. She had trouble with the fire, which would not draw even though she fanned the reluctant flames with paper. She bit her lip on a spate of angry words and instead puffed on the flickering fire.

At last she succeeded and with a sigh of relief filled the kettle and set it on the side of the hob. In the deep cool pantry she found a bowl of eggs and one stringy rasher of bacon; her heart melted as she thought of Mansel Jack fending for himself.

By the time he was washed and dressed, she had breakfast on

the table and his smiling eyes met hers so that the colour rose to her cheeks at the message she read in them.

He sat opposite her and she leaned her elbows on the clean linen cloth, watching him eat the food she had prepared. The giving of food was like the giving of love, she thought in surprise – the need was there to nurture and succour.

'Are we going to the mill today?' she asked and after a moment, Mansel Jack stared at her as though not seeing her.

'I'm not going to work today, I have something else planned, but you'd better go ahead and get some of those shawls finished.'

She felt her heart sink; was he tired of her already? 'I almost forgot I'm a working girl, mind,' she said abruptly, 'and can't afford to take days off.'

He made no reply, but helped himself to another slice of bread and smiled enigmatically.

'What is there to laugh about?' The words fell hard into the silence; even now Rhian could not be too familiar with Mansel Jack and felt absurdly shy of him. She knew she was putting him on a pedestal, but she couldn't help herself.

He rose at last. 'I've got to go out.' He looked at her, his eyes compelling, 'I'll see you at the mill, later.' He paused to kiss her lightly and then he was gone; the front door slammed after him and it was as though the sun had vanished behind the clouds.

Rhian walked from room to room. The big house seemed impersonal, not stamped with Mansel Jack's presence except for a coat hanging in the cloakroom in the hall. She held one of the sleeves to her cheek, breathing in the scent of him which lingered in the fabric, sighing softly, not allowing herself to think beyond the moment.

Her day seemed to pass with a strange air of unreality. Rhian found herself tense and unsure and it was only when she lay in Mansel Jack's arms that night that she was truly happy again.

She awoke early in the morning to find that frost had rimed the corners of the window, shimmering like diamonds on the glass panes. She felt cold knowing she was alone and that Mansel Jack had left without saying goodbye. There was no letter, nothing . . . it was as though he could not bear to leave her. . .

*

It was colder than Mansel Jack had ever imagined it could be as he strode along the dank trench, seeing with pity the drawn strained faces of soldiers grown lean, weary and battle-scarred. He had been in France only a week and already had seen enough death and destruction to last him a lifetime.

He remembered something Sterling Richardson had said, how the war changed a man's perspective. It was true and with clarity he realised now that the days he had spent with Rhian had been the happiest of his life. Well, his plans had been made and he felt sure that in due course he would get the leave he had applied for – even the Army had a heart.

A shell exploded somewhere ahead of him in the darkness. A man screamed and, with an oath, Mansel Jack began to run.

*

Rhian had returned at once to the mill and it seemed that everywhere she looked there were memories of Mansel Jack. His presence permeated the building and at nights, Rhian dreamed she was again in his arms.

It was Christmas time now and snow covered the town, beautifying the tall chimneys of the works, lying softly on the banks of the river Swan.

Rhian shivered in spite of the large fire, watching dully as Cerianne and Dewi played with their new wooden toys.

She choked back the tears, knowing she was wallowing in self-pity and yet she simply sat in her chair, staring into the flames and unable to rid herself of the misery that gnawed at her.

The morning air was chill when Rhian awoke to find Carrie shaking her urgently. She sat up sleepily and shivered as the coldness embraced her bare arms.

'I wish you all the joy in the world, *cariad*, but then you know that, don't you? Carrie babbled, 'This man Mansel Jack – he's right for you, it stands out a mile.'

Rhian looked up in bewilderment but Carrie put a finger over her lips. 'Hush, we'll say no more now but just you be calm and happy, for this is the most important day of your life.'

Parcels littered the scrubbed kitchen table and Carrie smiled

304

at Rhian. 'They're for you, presents from Mansel Jack.'

The gown of soft golden velvet glowed in the dimness of the room and Rhian shook her head, unable to speak.

'Here, Rhian, nice hot water for you to wash.' Gina carried an enamel bowl to the table, her eyes glowing with excitement. 'Come on, let's help you to dress! Hurry now, you'll be late, there's a cab waiting outside for you and it's so cold that the poor old horse is frozen stiff.'

'Will somebody tell me what all this is about?' Rhian asked as Gina held a towel towards her.

'Come on,' Carrie was pulling the gown over Rhian's head. 'You'll find out soon enough.'

Rhian stood quite still, her hands on her hips and her mouth set in a stubborn line. She stared at Carrie, who shrugged her shoulders and gave a great sigh.

'All right then, Mansel Jack's home for your wedding – arranged it all before he went away, he did, wanted it to be a surprise.'

Rhian stared at her for a moment in silence, joy vying with anger as she digested Carrie's words.

'Did no one think to ask *me*?' she demanded in disbelief. 'How dare you all go behind my back?'

'Hush now,' Gina spoke in her usual gentle way, 'it was all done with the best intentions in the world; we want your happiness, you must know that.'

'Well, Mansel Jack should have come to me the minute he was home, asked me if I wanted to marry him.'

Carrie laughed. 'And do you?'

Rhian's anger dissolved. 'Yes, of course I do.'

Carrie grasped her arm. 'Right then, let's get on with it.'

The church of St Michael stood on the hill, opposite the square buildings of the school. From the porch, looking downhill, the rolling valleys could be seen shimmering white in the winter sun.

'We're here,' Carrie said, arching her eyebrow in a wicked smile. 'Come on then, don't just sit there, your handsome man is waiting for you.'

Rhian allowed Carrie to draw her beneath the porch of the church and stopped in amazement as she saw the faces of her friends smiling at her. Mark and Katie, both of them resplendent in new clothes, waited for her and Mark held out his arm.

'I'm giving you away, Rhian,' he said softly and then she was being led along the aisle where the winter sun shone through the windows, spilling jewel colours on to the wooden pews.

Mansel Jack was turning to look at her, tall and handsome in his uniform and smiling when he saw her. Then Rhian saw nothing of the staring faces. She moved up the aisle towards the man she loved and as he towered over her, she leaned against him overwhelmed with joy.

The solemn words of the service spilled into the silence of the church and Rhian tried to make herself believe that this was really happening. Mansel Jack must have been planning it for such a long time!

In a low but clear voice she made her responses, promising to love him and cleave only unto him and it was the easiest promise in the world to make.

The wide gold ring slipped easily on to her finger and she looked up at him, her eyes full of tears. The organ music crashed into the silence and Mansel Jack leaned down to whisper in her ear.

'You're mine for keeps now, lass.' He kissed her tenderly and she clung to him for a moment, hiding her face against his shoulder. A deep peace and contentment filled her, for now she was Mansel Jack's wife and there was nothing anybody could do to change it.

Chapter Twenty-Five

The winter snows thawed and the rains fell heavily so that the earth became sodden and heavy. Chill breezes swept down from the skies, sending flannel skirts whipping round the booted feet of the women who walked briskly towards the railway station. Surging like the sea, they left the munitions factory, chattering and laughing – a flock of canaries, as they were called – in trousers and mob-caps.

To the rear of the crowd, set apart by finer clothing and skin unaffected by explosive powder, the office girls walked together, fewer in number and with modulated voices lowered discreetly.

Delmai Richardson was silent, hugging her thoughts to herself. Tonight she would go to Rickie's bed, coax him from sleep, warm him to a passion that she hoped would be fruitful. For Rickie desired nothing more than to have a son, and she desired to stay at home in the comfort of her house and never set eyes on the munitions factory again.

The stink of the explosive powder seemed to impregnate the very fabric of her good serge skirt and crisp cotton blouse, even though she had as little as possible to do with the factory itself. She shuddered as she remembered the accident which had killed two of the girls. For days everyone had been on edge and she herself practically ran past the outer buildings where the workers tapped the gaines.

Her colleagues talked about the bravery of the women who continued working in such appalling conditions day after day, but they were the lower orders after all and were used to such things.

It was good to reach the tram terminus and shamelessly she pushed past a few of the older women, sinking into the chill of the seat with a sigh. She thought again of Rickie's almost obsessional need for a son. The prospect of becoming a mother was not one she welcomed, since she had had quite enough with Cerianne. Her heart seemed to move out of its rhythm for a moment and the biting pain of loss swept over her – a pain that she could not always control. She had been surprised to find that she missed her daughter dreadfully and found her arms achingly empty.

It was an added frustration to know that the child was so close, down at the mill house near the river. Yet she might as well be on the other side of the world, for she was lost to Delmai. She had occasionally toyed with the idea of going to see her baby . . . just to watch perhaps from the other side of the road, not to touch and hold for that would be too painful.

Common sense invariably prevailed however and she usually succeeded in putting the idea out of her head.

But Rickie's constant harping on having a son had at last worn down her resistance and once she had become accustomed to the idea, it was not all that unpleasant. She recognised that her acquiescence owed a great deal to the fact that she would not have to nurse the child herself. No more sleepless nights, and not for her the toil of washing and caring for a baby. She would have all the pleasure without any of the harassment she had endured with Cerianne.

Rickie was already at home and he wrinkled his nose as she entered the drawing-room, an infuriating habit that he had picked up lately.

'I know I smell of fulminate,' she said sharply, 'but then so would you if you worked in the vicinity of the munitions factory. I shall go and change at once. Meantime you can pour me a glass of wine; I need something to refresh me after working all day.'

She saw him frown and knew she had touched on a raw spot. He hated to think of her in dangerous surroundings whilst he sat safely in the office of the Richardson Copper Company. He should by rights be serving his country in France, it was only because Sterling had chosen to go to war and give his brother a role to play in the running of the works that he had been able to save face.

She called sharply to the servants for hot water and hurried to her room, flinging off her clothes. They did indeed smell to high heaven and impatiently she thrust them out on to the landing, kicking off her shoes angrily.

Soon she was warmed and soothed by the comfort of the hot bath-water as she leaned back against the hard enamel, endeavouring to keep her hair free of the steam. If she allowed it to become damp, it would fall lankly on her shoulders and tonight she wanted to look her best.

To her surprise, Rickie entered the room with two glasses in his hands. He pushed the door shut and sat on the dressing-stool, his eyes devouring her. She read desire in them and smoothed the water over her breasts coquettishly.

'Bring my wine here, Rickie.' She spoke the words as though they were a caress and he obediently knelt beside her, his hands reaching towards her. She slapped him away playfully, for she had found it didn't always do to appear too eager. Sometimes she allowed him to believe that he wooed her into a reluctant passion, at other times she played the role of seductress, so Rickie scarcely knew what she would do next. Which was probably why she had kept him from his usual amours with the serving wenches, she reflected.

She stared at him coolly now over the rim of her glass. The wine sparkled sweet and red, reflecting in the water – a fallen shimmering ruby.

Lowering her eyes, she handed him back the glass. 'Will you pat me dry, Rickie?' She sounded a little petulant, but then she needed to avenge the snub he had been so ready to administer when she arrived home from the factory.

She rose with water streaming over her breasts and down the roundness of her thighs, clinging like tears to the curling hair beneath her belly.

His arms enveloped her and he lifted her, carrying her to the bed where he set her down gently.

'Let me love you, Delmai. It will be beautiful, I promise you.' She wound her arms around his neck, feeling roused by the hardness of him pressing against her nakedness, then sighed softly.

'You always do win me over in the end, don't you, Rickie?

309

You know I can't resist you for long.' Making him feel good served a useful purpose, for he was always more vigorous after she had spent time praising him. She felt a sensuous pleasure as his hands roamed over her body. He was no Billy Gray, but then she did not want him to be; she had had more than enough of passion that withered and died beneath the burden of poverty.

Rickie was more delicate in his approach, he did not thrust and plunder, and if his gentleness did not arouse the same degree of ecstasy as did Billy's vigour, then she was content to have it so for there were many compensations.

As her husband came to her, she closed her eyes, clinging to his shoulders and allowing all thoughts to drift from her mind. She was in a bed with fresh clean sheets and silken covers, she was Mrs Delmai Richardson with all the scandal of the past lost in obscurity, thanks to the ever-increasing prominence of the war. In short, she was back where she belonged and nothing must ever again be allowed to threaten that position.

Later when she sat opposite Rickie at the long, elegant dining-table, she smiled at him warmly. 'You were very good tonight, darling,' she said softly, 'and I'm sure your virility will bear fruit. I think tomorrow I shall stay in bed and not go into work.'

Rickie's eyes opened wide. 'But surely, you can't tell yet if . . .' His words trailed away into silence, for his wife had become authoritative of late and he found that she was usually discriminating in her appraisals. She had matured wonderfully and his life had never been more exciting. Now she was a full-blown woman and appreciative of him in every way, as well she might be. So he smiled and agreed that she must stay in bed and rest and that he would indeed ask the doctor to call.

Excitement stirred in him – perhaps his son *had* been conceived, he wanted an heir very badly and Delmai knew it. He failed to see that once his dream became a reality he would be entirely at his wife's mercy, for then she would have a stout stick with which to beat him.

Watching the fleeting expressions on his face, Delmai was well aware of the line his thought processes would be taking. She felt she knew every inch of him and came to the conclusion that he was not too bad a bargain. He was weak, yes, but that

310

was something she could use to her advantage. On the other hand, he was quite good-looking, though his mouth could become sulky if he was denied what he wanted. But their marriage would be a good one, for she would work at it.

She sighed inwardly, knowing that she had had a lucky escape from a life of toil in the Welsh mining valley. It was all credit to Rickie that he had taken her back after such faithlessness – leaving him to live in Canal Street and then running off with Billy Gray. Nevertheless she did not under-estimate her own cleverness; she had made him feel that he was privileged to have her return to his house and to his bed, and so long as she continued to reassure him of her devotion then everything would be all right.

'Penny for them?' Rickie leaned forward to rest his hand on hers and she glanced up at him smiling, her eyes warm with promise.

'I was just thinking how lucky I am to have you for my husband,' she said softly. 'I can't tell you how superb you were in bed, so considerate and yet so passionate.' She turned her hand, curling her fingers in his. 'We must never let anything come between us, Rickie, for I think we both realise that it's our destiny to be together.'

*

It was several weeks later when the early morning light sent rose-coloured pools drifting across the room as Delmai sat up slowly, thankful that she was not due to go to the office. She closed her eyes as a wave of nausea caught her and with her hand over her mouth struggled to control the urge to rush to the bathroom and vomit. At her side Rickie sat up and rubbed his eyes, staring in concern at her paleness.

'What's wrong, Delmai? You're trembling.' He took her in his arms and held her close and she was grateful to him for his kindness.

'It's as I told you,' she spoke almost in awe. 'I was right, I have conceived your child.' She mentally counted the days and her eyes widened. 'Rickie, I must be at least three weeks late, I didn't really think . . .' Her words trailed away and Rickie, smiling, kissed her cheek.

'Well, whenever you tell me anything I believe it and so this comes as no great surprise to me.'

Suddenly weak, Delmai fell back against the pillow and with relief felt the nausea subside. No more up early in the morning, she thought with joy, no tedious train journey and more importantly, no long hours spent over wearisome figures in proximity to the constant smell, not to mention the danger of the explosives.

Rickie rose from bed. 'Would you like some tea, Delmai, can I get you anything at all?' He smiled at her as the enormity of the situation dawned on him. 'I shall not go to work today,' he said with a self-satisfied expression on his face. 'This is the most important event in my life and I'm going to savour every minute of it.'

Delmai returned his smile. 'I'm so pleased Rickie. Come here, and kiss me. And then perhaps we should call the doctor!'

He knelt on the side of the bed and caught her face in his hands. 'The only thing we have to worry about now is that it's a boy,' he said softly.

Delmai looked up at him. 'It's going to be a boy, all right, all our children will be boys.'

He held her close and she closed her eyes, certain that this was to be her punishment: to bear only male children from now on, never to know the love of a daughter.

She felt a tear tremble on her lashes, remembering that she had given up Cerianne so thoughtlessly, needing only to find comfort and security for herself. And since she had forfeited any right to the little girl, they would be for ever strangers destined to remain apart.

'Hey, what's this, you're crying.' Rickie looked down at her anxiously. 'Everything is all right, isn't it?'

Delmai wound her arms around his neck and drew him close to her. 'Of course everything is all right,' she whispered. 'I'm crying because I'm so happy, that's all.'

'Silly little thing,' Rickie said gently. And as Delmai clung to him – feeling the warmth and comfort of the house around her, hearing the bustle of the servants below stairs preparing the day – she knew that if she had to make the choice again, she would still come to the same decision.

312

The morning was chill with the hint of rain in the air and Mary hugged the collar of her coat close about her face. She was late arriving at the store and the bustle of the shoppers and the clink of crockery from the tea-rooms was like a rebuke. She knew her presence was not vital to the running of the emporium, but she liked to keep her finger on the pulse of things.

She took her time climbing the stairs to her office, conscious of the sweet burden she carried though as yet there was very little alteration in her appearance. Strangely she had not been sickly in the mornings, indeed had never felt better in her life physically. It was only at night when conscience reared its threatening head in the darkness that she worried about the possibility of her unborn child being illegitimate.

Mary might have forced her worries out of her mind except for the nagging knowledge that Mary Anne Bloomfield was aware of the situation. For the first few days after leaving the doctor's surgery and seeing the American woman smirking at her knowingly, she had lived in fear of some reprisal. She was sensitive to every glance that came her way, wondering if the scandal of 'Mary Sutton and the young doctor' was being spread about the town.

A soft tapping on the door startled her and she called out more sharply than she had intended: 'Come in, for goodness' sake!'

She leaned back apprehensively against the leather of her chair, half expecting to see Mary Anne, but it was Rhian who stood in the doorway. She really must get a grip on herself, Mary thought worriedly, she was allowing her edginess to show.

'Have I caught you at a bad time?' Rhian asked quickly. 'If so, I can always . . .' Her words trailed away as Mary waved to her to come inside.

'Of course you haven't.' Studying Rhian's face, Mary saw that she was deeply happy and felt envy gnaw at her.

'I must say your wedding came as something of a surprise to me.' Her tone was cold, but she could not help herself. She gestured towards the plush blue chair on the other side of the desk and Rhian after a moment's hesitation sat down.

'I was completely surprised by it all myself,' Rhian said,

shaking back her hair. 'Do you know Mansel Jack didn't breathe a word to me about any of it? The arrangements were kept completely secret. But of course it was exactly what I had hoped and dreamed for.'

Mary pushed a pen absent-mindedly through the blotting paper on her desk. She must not blame Rhian too much – how could she after what she had done herself? And yet she felt deeply for Heath, knowing her brother would take the news badly.

Rhian's face was shadowed. 'We only had a few days before he had to return to the front, but I mustn't grumble I suppose.'

Their eyes met and Mary knew that they both felt the same fear, the same emptiness.

'I was so sorry to hear that your husband is missing, though you must not give up hope at this stage.'

'What regiment is Mansel Jack in?' Mary forced a cheerful note into her voice, watching Rhian as she seemed to square her slight shoulders.

'The 13th Welch,' she answered quietly, 'though I must confess I thought he would have gone home and joined a Yorkshire battalion.'

Mary shook her head. 'Don't worry, he'll meet up with many of his fellow Yorkshiremen once he goes to France. In any case, I think the war has united us all for we face a common enemy.'

She rose from her desk, feeling a sudden anger against Rhian as she thought once more how badly hurt Heath was bound to be by this marriage. 'Let's get out of here and treat ourselves to a cup of tea, shall we?' she suggested with forced brightness.

Rhian smiled. 'I think that's a good idea. I can't be too long though; I have to get over to Doris's house and take her wages to her.'

Mary stood taller than Rhian by a head and, looking down at her, she wondered at the change in her since this man Mansel Jack had come into her life. She was more sure of herself somehow and obviously happy – but did she feel no pity for Heath? Still, there was little point in dwelling on it and Mary had enough to worry about on her own account.

The tea-room was crowded, but Mary always had a table reserved for herself to the back of the room, almost hidden by a

314

plethora of plants set in heavy china jardinières.

'A pot of tea for two, Greenie.' She glanced up at the older woman and watched compassionately as she made her way slowly towards the kitchen; she really should be resting at home at her age. Mary had been forced to release Joanie, Nerys and even Muriel who had worked for her so loyally, so that they could go into more essential occupations.

When the tea was poured and Greenie had taken away the silver tray, Rhian leaned forward with her elbows on the table.

'I've been wanting to talk to you ever since the wedding,' she spoke softly. 'I've been feeling so guilty about Heath; I had to write and tell him what had happened and try to explain, but I haven't received a word in reply. Have you heard anything?'

Mary shook her head. What was wrong with her, all she was doing nowadays was wallowing in guilt; she had even forgotten to write to Heath. It was about time she pulled herself out of it.

'I used to write to Heath several times a week,' she sighed heavily. 'I've sent him parcels of course, like everyone else who has someone at the front, but since . . . well, I've been so upset and unhappy lately.'

Rhian bit her lip. 'Mary, I was right to tell him about my marriage, wasn't I? I know it must be awful for him to get a letter like that when he's already going through hell, but I was afraid he would come to hear of it from someone else and that would be even worse.'

'Don't worry,' Mary said more sharply than she had intended. 'Our Heath is pretty tough, he'll survive.'

'But I feel so guilty. I promised to wait for him and I didn't – couldn't keep my word. There's awful I feel about letting him down like that.'

'No point in feeling guilty,' Mary said quickly. 'We all do things we regret, just don't let it warp your life. It's pointless to go on about it, what's done is done.' She smiled to soften her words and poured more tea, but Rhian was picking up her bag and pulling on her gloves.

'I'll have to go over to Doris's house,' she said quickly and Mary realised her feelings were hurt.

'Do you want some company?' she asked more warmly.

'There's a good idea,' Rhian smiled. 'I'd like that very

315

much.'

Mary sighed. Anything was better than sitting in the office or wandering aimlessly about the shop. She hurried off to fetch her coat, but when she returned to the tea-rooms there seemed to be some sort of argument going on. Mary moved smoothly through the doorway and then her heart began to pound in her breast as she saw Mary Anne Bloomfield confronting Mrs Greenaway who was twisting her small white apron into a ball in her agitation.

'Oh, Mrs Sutton, there you are!' Greenie's lined face relaxed and Mary put a steadying hand on her arm.

'What seems to be the trouble?' She avoided Mary Anne's eyes, but the American woman would not be ignored.

'This servant tells me there are no tables available in there.' She jabbed her finger towards the tea-rooms. 'I'm sure you can find room for me, can't you Mrs Sutton? After all, we have so much in common.'

Mary heard the insinuation in Mary Anne's voice and in that moment felt she hated her. She turned to look at her with a steady gaze.

'You can have my own table, Miss Bloomfield,' she spoke coldly, 'but be careful not to presume too much on my good nature.'

She turned to where Rhian was waiting silently. 'If you're ready, we'll be off,' she said in a controlled voice and Rhian hurriedly followed her out into the street.

'There's cheeky, that woman is,' Rhian said in amazement. 'I'm surprised you didn't throw her out on her fat little head – you would have done once.' She giggled. 'I remember how frightened we all were of you at the laundry – once you got into a temper, we all ran for our lives.'

Mary hardly listened. She was furiously angry, knowing that she couldn't endure Mary Anne's attitude, her blackmail . . . yet just what could she do about it?

Doris was lying back in her chair with her eyes closed, her hair tangled over her face. Her mother bobbed a curtsey to Rhian and Mary, fussing round and offering them chairs, her careworn face creased into worry lines.

'Is she any better?' Rhian asked quietly and Jessie Williams nodded her head. 'She's right as rain at times, but then she

316

takes to wandering in her head, like. Thinks she's back in the laundry sometimes, talks about her old friends a lot as though they are here in the room.'

'Has the doctor been to see her?' Mary asked, staring at Doris and seeing the same strong girl who used to haul coal in the laundry – yet somehow there was an indefinable difference.

'Oh, aye, old Doctor Thomas comes round regular like, he says it's shock and will wear off in time, but I think that thing going off hurt her mind so badly that she can't face the true world any more.'

Mary was saddened by the change in Doris, remembering her as a laughing girl, always good-natured.

'We'd better be going.' Rhian rose to her feet and delved into her bag and Mary moved to the door to avoid causing Jessie Williams any embarrassment. Though Rhian's voice was low, Mary could hear her clearly.

'Here's Doris's pay – and don't worry, the money will be here every week until she's better.'

'That's good of Mansel Jack,' Mary said as they left, drawing on her gloves and shivering in the gusting wind that drove down the length of the narrow street.

Rhian smiled. 'Yes, he has a kind heart even though some might think his tongue is a bit sharp.'

'Best to be outspoken, mind,' Mary said quickly. 'I always found that it paid to speak the truth rather than nurse a grievance.' Her words seemed to hang upon the air as she realised the irony of them.

They walked for a time in silence and then Rhian put a tentative hand on Mary's arm. 'There is something wrong, isn't there, besides your worry about your husband? Are you ill, Mary?' She spoke breathlessly, almost as though she expected a rebuff, and Mary's heart contracted.

'I won't lie to you, Rhian. Yes, there is something wrong but it's nothing I can talk about – not just now anyway.'

'I'm sorry,' Rhian said at once and Mary smiled ruefully. 'Yes, so am I,' she said tersely and then, regretting her shortness, smiled down at Rhian. 'It's nothing really. I expect I'm building a mountain out of a molehill. Anyway, it's freezing – look, your nose is red and your eyes are watering – are you coming back into the store before you go home?'

Rhian shook her head and her face softened. 'No, I won't if you don't mind. I should be working at the mill, getting out some more shawls while the weather calls for them.'

'Of course. I hope we'll get together again before too long,' Mary smiled, 'and let's hope your husband sorts out our problems in France; he seems like a man capable of great things.' She saw the flush of pleasure rise to Rhian's cheeks, she obviously enjoyed having her husband praised and rightly so. What had gone so sadly wrong between herself and Brandon over the years, she wondered miserably; their love had blossomed so promisingly at first. She sighed – now it had come to such a poor pass that she was not even sure if he was the father of her child.

'Are you all right?' Rhian asked, concern in her lovely dark eyes. Mary warmed to her; Rhian Gray had matured from a spoiled young girl into a very nice woman.

'I was thinking about Brandon,' she replied truthfully, shuddering. 'I hate to look at the soldiers coming from *Parc Beck*, some of them with empty sleeves and others maimed in all sorts of ways, it's just horrible.'

'You mustn't think like that,' Rhian said quickly. 'We must hope and pray that Brandon is safe and well somewhere – it does happen, you know!'

'You sound very wise,' Mary said, smiling, 'and of course you're quite right.'

A cold rain had begun to fall and Mary drew up her collar, relieved that they were near the store where it would be warm and noisy and where she would not be alone with her thoughts.

'Won't you come inside, just until the rain stops?' she asked and even as she spoke, Mary became aware of Mrs Greenaway hurrying towards her, waving her arms frantically. She had a heavy shawl thrown carelessly around her shoulders and her hair was windswept.

'Oh, my God!' Mary whispered. 'Something's wrong.' She was vaguely aware of Rhian standing at her side, unwilling to leave her.

'I've just come from Heath's house,' cried Mrs Greenaway, handing Mary a folded sheet of paper. 'I thought I'd best open it – oh dear, there's awful it is!' She began to cry even as Mary unfolded the letter and stared down at the words with

318

disbelieving eyes.

'Mary, what's wrong? Can't you tell me?' Rhian spoke anxiously and Mary turned, a feeling of unreality clouding her mind.

'It's happening to me again,' she could scarcely form the words. 'It's Heath, he's been reported missing believed killed.' Mary felt darkness engulf her and with a sigh she abandoned herself to it.

Chapter Twenty-Six

The war against Germany seemed to be clambering over itself in order to disrupt the natural workings of the town. Sweyn's Eye had become almost empty of its youth. Young men no longer stood on corners with white scarves hung around cocksure throats, and in the parks there were no noisy games of rugby to relieve the dullness of a Saturday afternoon.

Older men took on extra work and the tasks they could not do fell to the women. Even the Sunday services in the many churches and chapels lacked colour and vigour, for most of the true pure tenors were gone, leaving the choirs unbalanced.

Gina Sinman was seated in the kitchen of the mill house, her arms resting on the table and a pen clutched between her fingers. Upstairs the children slept – Dewi, her son, and Cerianne who had become like her own child.

She paused over the letter she was writing to Billy Gray; she had told him that Cerianne was talking like a little demon and that she ate hearty and slept like a top and now there didn't seem much else she could say.

Biting the wooden shaft of the pen, she tasted ink in her mouth and rubbed at her lips with her fingers. She wanted to tell Billy that there were people at home who cared about him, but of course he knew that for Rhian had sent him a parcel of clothes and a supply of Woodbines only last week. And Gina felt she was doing her bit by writing to him – weren't the papers always telling folk to make someone at the front happy with a letter? She frowned and for a moment the words she had written on the page before her were blurred.

Heinz Sinman was gone from her and she would never see

320

him again. Mansel Jack was a man to be believed and trusted and though it was difficult, she must accept that she had lost Heinz for ever.

It seemed that he had never even reached the internment camp. His strong spirit had rebelled at the thought of prison and apparently he had made a run for freedom and been struck down by a bullet fired in panic. But she had no wish to dwell on the manner of his going, the fact remained that her beloved Heinz was dead.

She turned her attention to the letter once more and wrote that Rhian seemed very happy and content in her marriage and that Mansel Jack was a good kind man who would take care of her always. She found she was going on to say that she herself was lonely. Surrounded though she was by kindness and company, she lacked a mainstay in her life – someone who was hers and hers alone. She had her son of course, but she could not tell her heartache to a little child.

The door opened and Carrie came into the kitchen, bringing with her a flurry of cold damp air. 'Have you heard about Heath Jenkins?' she asked, her face a pale glow in the lamplight. Gina sat up and folded the letter, unwilling for any other eyes to see it.

'No, what's happened to him, injured is he?' Gina watched as Carrie shook out her shawl and hung it on the peg on the back door. Her movements were slow, as though suddenly she was giving in to the years which had crept up on her so stealthily that no one had noticed the grey in her hair and the lines around her eyes.

'Missing believed killed.' The words fell like a strange religious chant into the silence of the room.

'There's awful, I expect his sister's heartbroken, isn't she?'

Carrie nodded and stared into the fire. 'I expect so. Make us a cup of tea, Gina,' she asked wearily, tears slipping down her face. 'Empty inside I am and Heath Jenkins was special to me. There's cold I feel, perhaps a drop of tea will warm me up.'

Gina rose instantly and pushed the kettle on to the flames. It was so rarely that Carrie asked for anything that it was clear she was very upset.

'Don't be too downhearted, girl,' Gina spoke softly. 'If he's missing there's no proof that he's not well and chirpy as a

321

cricket, hiding in one of them French haystacks or something. It's not so final, is it?'

Carrie sniffed and dabbed at her eyes with the corner of her apron. 'I suppose you're right, but I've loved that boy these many long years and I can't bear to think of him lying in a ditch somewhere foreign, hurt and frightened maybe . . . oh, to the devil with this war!'

Gina made the tea, her hands trembling. 'Here, have this, there's plenty of sugar in it to bring out the shock.' She sat down and stared at Carrie worriedly. 'What about Rhian? She and Heath Jenkins were very close before Mansel Jack, weren't they?'

Carrie made an effort to staunch her tears, sipping the tea, her lips trembling on the brim of the cup.

'Aye, she loved him too in a way – part of her youth he was, had a passion for him in those days. Might have worked out for the two of them if Mansel Jack hadn't come into Rhian's life. But the right man for Rhian he is, mind, and I'm not saying any different.'

The clock ticked loudly in the silence of the kitchen and the gas-light hissed and popped, sending shimmering patterns of light on to the flagstone floor.

'I've been writing a letter to Billy Gray,' Gina volunteered, trying to take Carrie's mind off the painful subject of Heath Jenkins. 'Only doing my duty, but then I have to admit that I've a special feeling of friendship for Rhian's brother. Hard-done-by he was, what with that hussy Delmai Richardson running out on him and dumping her babba like a sack of spuds. Is it wrong of me to spend so much time writing to another man? I feel it's disloyal somehow to the memory of my Heinz.'

Carrie sat up straighter in her chair and really looked at Gina for the first time since she had entered the room.

'*Duw*, you follow your heart, *merchi* – you're doing a good job, keeping Billy's spirits up, writing to him every week like you do. This war has done funny things to us and we must grab at any little piece of happiness we can. I'm sure Billy loves hearing from you, so write to him all you like and feel proud of yourself for doing him a kindness, that's what I say.'

Carrie was rising to her feet then, pulling her shawl from the

322

peg and swinging it round her shoulders. 'It's no good, I can't sit still. I'm going to see Mary Jenkins; I must talk to her about Heath, for I can't get the boy out of my mind.'

Gina watched her go to the door and shook her head helplessly. 'But it's past eight and getting dark and there's a bit of rain in the wind too.' But her words made no difference, Carrie let herself out and closed the door with a click of finality. After a moment Gina sighed, spread out the letter once more and picking up the pen began to write.

As Carrie hurried through the dark windswept streets, her thoughts were of the past. She remembered with a feeling of warmth the night she had lain in Heath Jenkins' arms; she'd been renting her own little house then and lived quite well on the money paid her by Agnes Gray to do a bit of cooking and cleaning.

Heath had been a bull of a boy, randy as hell and after every bit of skirt in the town. Got his way with them too, if Carrie was any judge. It had been wonderful to be bedded by him, he had youth and vigour and a clean unlined skin and she had gloried in the time she had spent with him.

She hurried through the Strand and up the hill, ignoring the lighted trams that rattled along on the shining metal lines, growling like a beast chained and fettered.

It did not take long to climb the hill, though by the time she reached the brow Carrie was more than a little breathless.

'You're getting old, girl,' she told herself, but she did not believe her own words.

It was a little frightening to knock on the door of the elegant house and at such a late hour, but Carrie stood her ground when a girl in neat uniform stared at her suspiciously from the warmth of the hall.

'I want to see Mary Jenkins.' Carrie stepped inside out of the cold teeth of the wind. 'Tell her Carrie's here and don't stand there gawping, be quick about it.'

Mary was wearing a long robe of deep blue, her hair hung to her shoulders and she looked beautiful even though there were traces of tears in her eyes. 'Carrie, come in and sit by the fire – you look frozen, mind.'

They sat together in the warmth of the gracious drawing-room, for they were old friends and there was nothing uppity about Mary Jenkins even though she had got on in the world.

'About Heath,' Carrie said softly. 'I had to come to see if you've had any more news.'

'Nothing,' Mary shook back her dark hair. 'Only the bald statement that he's missing and that they presume him to be dead.' She clasped her hands together and stared at Carrie with a world of misery in her eyes. 'Just the same cold unfeeling message I received when Brandon was posted missing.'

'But there's something else troubling you, isn't there, *merchi*?' Carrie asked gently. 'There are such shadows in your eyes, would it help to talk about it?'

Mary shook her head slowly. 'I don't know, Carrie. I don't think anything can help me, but I have to talk or I'll die of the weight of it.'

She moved to the door as though to reassure herself that it was closed and Carrie, staring at her, wondered what else could be wrong in Mary's life for she seemed to have more than enough already.

Mary's voice was low and Carrie leaned forward in order to catch every word, for the tense expression on Mary's face showed that she was near to desperation.

'Brandon and me, we had our quarrels but I loved him and I'm sure he loved me. It was all because I didn't conceive his child – I became miserable and picky and I must have been hell to live with.' Her eyes met Carrie's for a moment and they were haunted. Carrie leaned forward and put her hand over Mary's, pressing gently.

'Look, I'm a woman of the world, there's no shame in me for anything I've done. Guilt is a heavy, useless burden, mind.'

Mary relaxed a little. 'I was unfaithful to Brandon – once and only once – but it was enough apparently, because now I'm going to have a baby and it doesn't seem likely it could be my husband's after all the times we've tried for a child.'

Carrie shook her head. 'Don't look so worried, Mary, how many married couples can say they've never strayed? Like it says in the good book, "Let him that is without sin cast the first stone".' Carrie smiled ruefully. 'Something like that anyway – I can't claim to be a religious woman, but there's a lot of sense in that saying.'

Mary bit her lip. 'The worst part of all is that after I heard of

324

Brandon's death, I went straight into the arms of another man – like a cheap flossie, I was, and my only excuse being I was sick with grief.' She paused and glanced up worriedly at Carrie. 'And worse is to come: Mary Anne Bloomfield of all people overheard me talking about it. She's not to be trusted, she hates me as it is.'

Carrie whistled inelegantly through her teeth. '*Duw*, that's a real stunner of a problem you've got there. I'd have told you to keep your mouth shut, 'cos your child would be your own flesh and blood whoever fathered it, but with this dangerous woman knowing all about you – well, that puts a different sort of flour in the pudding.'

'I'm not willing to be at her mercy,' Mary said quietly. 'Mary Anne is the sort who will try to push me to the limit. Already she's exerted a mild form of blackmail, but what can I do?'

Carrie could not conceal her anger. 'Brazen it out, call her a liar if need be – after all she's not one of us, is she? What's more, she's got a past of her own, so who is going to believe anything she says?'

Mary held her head high but there was pain in her eyes. 'And now this news about Heath has just about broken my spirit. Everything seems to be turning sour in my life . . . is nothing ever going to be in order again?'

'There's one little matter you're overlooking, that there's your baby to consider. This is what you've always wanted and it seems you're paying a high price for it.' She paused. 'There is one way out – perhaps you should consider a visit to that nurse, Mrs Benson.'

Mary wrapped her arms around her stomach and sat back in her chair. 'No! I want this baby more than anything in the world.'

Carrie rose from her chair and smiled as though satisfied. 'Then that's it, you'll keep the baby and take the consequences. And after all, the little one might have been planted there by your husband; I don't see how anyone can ever know.' She moved to the door. 'And as for this Mary Anne Bloomfield, take my advice and call her bluff – show what you're really made of, there's a good girl!'

Carrie left the warmth of the house and stepped out towards

325

the roadway, hugging her shawl close round her body. Her heart was heavy with pity for Mary's plight – this strange powerful urge between man and woman had a lot to answer for.

A smile curved her lips – what would she give if only she could partake of the sweet heady wine just once more! She sighed and moved towards the tram stop; the rain was coming down more heavily now and soon she would be soaked and after all, she was an old woman in spite of the fact that her heart told her a different story.

*

The morning air was chill and a cold March wind swept through the streets of Sweyn's Eye. But Rhian was warm and happy in her bed, for she was lying alongside her husband. Given a brief leave before being transferred to another part of France, he had hinted there was something big about to take place and Rhian's heart had raced with fear. But she pushed the unpleasant thoughts away now as she crouched, warm and sleepy, beside Mansel Jack. Her arm was stretched over him, her legs entwined with his; intimacy was so much more than passion, she decided as the mists of sleep cleared from her mind. She had never known that she could love the closeness of a man, the minute details about him from the curling hairs on his chest to the little crease of impatience that sometimes appeared between his eyes.

She snuggled closer to him, knowing a biting fear at the prospect of his leaving her. She put her arms around him and in an instant, he was awake.

'Our last day,' she whispered softly. 'I love you, Mansel Jack.' Without answering, he turned to her, touching her cheek with tenderness. She closed her eyes against the harsh burning tears she had promised not to shed.

It was she who began to move sensuously beneath him, her head back against the sweet-smelling pillows, her eyes closed . . . for she knew she must remember this moment, it might be a long time before they could be together again in this way.

He responded to the rhythm of her, his fingers gentle as they caressed and adored her. Every movement between them was

326

an act of love and when at last it was over Rhian wept as she had never done in her life before.

Wordlessly he held her, allowing her to shed her tears, for they both knew of the emptiness that parting would bring. After a time he rose and disappeared into the small dressing-room; she could hear the normal everyday sounds of him shaving and washing and her tears flowed afresh.

She looked around the room, knowing that it had been a haven for them both. But he was not willing for her to live here alone and in any case she was needed at the mill; there was work in abundance for her and she needed hard work to keep her sane. Carrie and Gina depended on her as well as the two children; once Mansel Jack was gone her life would return to the same pattern as before, yet subtly altered.

She was a married woman now in every respect, she thought proudly, and Mansel Jack was the powerful force that coloured her days. She knew she could love no other man, not now or ever.

When he returned to the bedroom – his face fresh, his hair combed and with small particles of water shining like diamonds in the soft darkness – she smiled at him and forced back the horror which rose to threaten her life with unknown dangers.

She watched quietly as Mansel Jack dressed in his officer's uniform, splendid and handsome and somehow unfamiliar.

'I'll come with you to the station.' She pushed back the sheets and rose from the bed which still bore the scent of him, wondering if all women felt the same pain of parting that now was tearing her in two.

'I'd prefer to take you to the mill and leave you safely there, lass,' he said quietly.

She moved towards him and reached on tiptoe to kiss his mouth. 'Let me have my way in just this one thing,' she pleaded. 'I want to treasure every moment that I can with you. I'll go straight from the station to the mill, I promise you.'

His face softened. 'All right, now get dressed up warmly, I don't want you catching a chill.' When he closed the door the room was suddenly silent and empty, a great vacuum where there was no sound and no light.

She made herself ready with haste, her fingers shaking, her

heart beating swiftly. She must go down to the dining-room, make a pretence of eating breakfast, try to keep back the tears for she would not distress him for the world.

He smiled at her as she entered the room, his eyes warm with approval as he noted her apparent calm. He watched as she placed a piece of bacon on her plate and when she sat at the table he pushed a packet towards her.

'You must pay off the housekeeper for me,' he said. 'Offer my apologies for giving her such a short term of employment.' He smiled into Rhian's eyes. 'But tell her it was my wife's fault, for she worried too much about me fending for myself.'

Rhian reached across the table to touch his hand and their fingers caught and held; she felt tears sting her eyes, tears that she would not allow to fall. It was several moments before she could speak.

'I shall tell her no such thing, for I shall reinstate her as our housekeeper when you are home again.'

She pushed her plate away, knowing she could not eat another bite and seeing that even Mansel Jack had left his plate untouched.

When he glanced at the clock and rose to his feet Rhian felt her being dissolved in fear – the time had come for him to leave the house and go to the station.

'How shall we go? By tram, is it?' She forced herself to speak calmly and Mansel Jack pushed his chair under the table, his eyes meeting hers dark and filled with feeling, though when he spoke his voice sounded normal.

'I have already seen to it, a cab will be arriving at any moment. Come here.'

She went into his arms, feeling the roughness of his uniform against her cheek. His hand caressed the nape of her neck and tears slipped from her eyes in spite of her efforts at self-control. She turned away from him quickly as a loud rapping on the door disturbed the silence of the house.

Surreptitiously she dried her eyes and drew on her coat, holding the large collar up around her face. She pushed a soft velvet hat over her hair and slipped her arm through her husband's as though they were simply going outside to take the air.

The horses' hooves beat a tattoo against the cobbled

roadway and the rain washed down as though the heavens were shedding tears of pain and farewell. Rhian sat upright against the cold leather seat, hearing the creaking and groaning of the cab, feeling the jolt as the wheels hit the cobbles, praying that the driver would rein in the animals between the shafts and make the journey last a little longer.

Her fingers crept into Mansel Jack's warm strong palm and though he did not look at her, she knew by the pressure of his fingers that he felt the bitterness of parting just as she did. She looked at the tall elegant villas on the hill, staring at the blank windows colourless in the rain, forcing her mind to concentrate on anything but the fact that Mansel Jack was going away.

The streets of the town were busy and the narrow main road thronged with vehicles, while on the pavements people hurried along blindly, heads bent against the harsh grey rain.

All too soon the station came into sight and towering above it the hill of Kilvey, looking down as though frowning at the fussy steam trains standing at the platform.

Mansel Jack asked the driver to wait and handed him a generous sum. The man doffed his hat. 'Good luck to you, sir, give them Jerries hell!'

Rhian went on to the platform. Her heart was like ice and she didn't know how she kept walking steadily beside her husband, for her legs were trembling and she felt a great weakness wash over her.

There were several men in uniform and from a carriage further down the platform came the sound of a woman sobbing hysterically. Rhian knew that Mansel Jack would abhor such a demonstration and so she chastely raised her mouth to his and gently he kissed her.

Neither of them spoke for they were beyond words, but his hand was at her waist, pressing her to him.

And then there appeared to be a flurry of activity – the guard was blowing the whistle, doors were slamming and great gushes of steam and cinders flew upwards. Rhian felt a moment of sheer panic, wanting to scream and sob and cling to him, beg him not to go to the war. She stepped away from him, her head high, her neck stiff with the effort she was making to control her emotions.

'Goodbye, my lovely lass.' He spoke softly and she sensed

329

the words rather than heard them. They penetrated her being, lying inside her like precious gems.

'You'll write, won't you?' Her eyes were luminous and Mansel Jack looked away from them swiftly.

'Aye, lass. Now go on home.' He jumped quickly into the train as it began to move, swallowed up as though by a great ravenous monster. She stared at the window and there he was waving his hand as the train gathered speed.

Rhian watched until the sinuous line of the train was a blur on the rain-sodden landscape, and even after it had disappeared from view she stood as though rooted to the spot unable to move.

'Come on missus, no good getting soaked – your man won't want a sick wife to come home to, will he now?' The station-master was old and wise, his eyes having witnessed a great many partings. Rhian nodded and turned her back on the empty line, walking purposefully to where the cab stood waiting for her.

She climbed into the cab that seemed to retain the power of his presence. How she wished she could turn back time to when they were starting out from the house – just to relive the journey to the station, there was so much she could have said to him. And yet she knew in her heart that there was no need of any words, and she rubbed her hand on the leather of the seat beside her as though to remind her that Mansel Jack had sat there next to her.

'Where we goin' to, missus?' The driver hunched his shoulders miserably as rain dripped from his hat down his neck.

Rhian sat up straight, clutching her hands together and holding back the tears with a great effort of will.

'You know the mill house?' Her voice trembled and he gla.ced at her sympathetically, nodding his head.

'I know it, I'll have you there in two ticks. Going to friends, are you? Best not to be alone at a time like this.'

Rhian turned to look at the station. It was grey and lifeless and no one would know the grief and sorrow of the many partings which had taken place on its rainwashed platform.

She alighted stiffly like an old lady and Carrie was there to meet her at the door, opening it wide to reveal a roaring fire

330

that crackled and spat behind shining black-leaded bars. The brass gleamed and a white cloth was spread over the table. Rhian knew that it was all done in an effort to welcome her and so she stretched her mouth into a smile and shrugged off her coat, seating herself in the chair near the fire.

'Gina's taken the babbas out to the shops, just to give you time to settle in all right.'

'There's good of her, I hope the children won't catch cold in this rain.'

'Sturdy they are, the pair of them, and I swear that little Cerianne grows more like you every day.'

Rhian looked up as Carrie brought her a cup of tea. 'I expect there's something of Billy in her too.' Her words were stilted, inane, but she was numb as though she had stood too long in the cold. The tea had no taste, but she drank it anyway to please Carrie who was trying so hard to comfort her.

'Had a letter from Billy we did, just the other day. I'll get it for you,' Carrie offered eagerly, but Rhian held up her hand.

'Not just now, Carrie, but I'd like to know if he's well of course,' she added hastily.

'He's right as rain, *cariad*, says thanks for the parcels and he would like to hear more from us back here at home. Gina's very good, you know – writes to him often, she does – it makes her feel she's doing her duty by Cerianne I suppose, keeping her dad in touch with everything . . .' Carrie's voice died away as she ran out of things to say.

Rhian knew she was making things difficult for Carrie, but her head was buzzing with pain and it was as though she was living in a nightmare world where nothing was real. She could scarcely believe that a short time ago she had lain in Mansel Jack's arms, close to his warmth, had talked to him and touched him and now he was gone.

'*Duw*, Rhian, you'll do yourself a hurt, gripping your hands so tightly together. And those shoulders, look how tense they are – let Carrie rub them for you.'

As soon as Carrie touched her, it was as though a dam had burst. Rhian turned to her, face crumpling into tears, a long cry escaping her lips.

Carrie was on her knees at once, holding her close. 'That's it, *merchi*, you cry it all out and you'll feel better then, I promise

331

you.'

Rhian clung to Carrie's shoulders. 'My husband's gone from me and I can't bear it.'

'It will be all right, I promise you it will be all right.' Carrie rocked her as though she was a child and Rhian wanted to believe her, but in the depths of her soul she knew that nothing would be right until Mansel Jack was at her side once more.

Chapter Twenty-Seven

In the early months of 1916 General Joffre chose the Somme area of France for the joint offensive by the British and French. The actual date was more difficult to arrange, however, for this depended on the Russians and Italians launching a simultaneous attack.

General Brusilov of Russia felt personally that some time after the first of June would be most favourable to his administration. But such preparations took a great deal of time and the war seemed endless for the British soldiers at the front.

By the spring, the air was much milder and the trenches ceased to be the frozen ice-holes which winter had made them. Now the ground was damp and the walls of the trenches crumbled a little more every day.

Above the silent battalion of soldiers just awakening from sleep, the sky was grey streaked with gold as the dawn speared the clouds with penetrating fingers of light.

Morgan Lloyd attempted to ease his cramped toes within the confines of the hard boots and stared around him at the shadowed woods. It was like playing at war, he thought heavily, except that when the guns spat forth in venom there was real blood and the cries of men dying.

He had heard the talk about the battle that was to take place on the Somme. It was all supposed to be kept a deadly secret, but no army could move food, forage, water and ammunition for 400,000 men and 100,000 horses without a soldier in his position making an educated guess as to what was afoot.

Morgan had kept his own counsel as the troops plodded wearily through agricultural lands – skirting small villages, noting plans being made for constructing roads and putting in pumping machinery for water. And all through the increased activity, he made a point of keeping his lip buttoned and his ears open. Indeed all his senses were finely tuned, which perhaps was one reason why he was still alive and a great many of his fellow soldiers were dead.

It was strange really, for he thought daily of Honey O'Connor and the way her young life had been taken by the explosion at the munitions factory. But now those same shells were a means of defeating the Germans – or at least driving them back through unfamiliar foreign territory.

Morgan had reconnoitred on his own and had discovered that the German dugouts were exposed and that the folds of ground close behind the British trenches provided an ideal way of concealing the large numbers of troops and guns which were daily being brought forward.

'Could you use a packet of Woodbines, Private Lloyd?' The voice was strangely familiar and Morgan rose to his feet, putting up his hand in a smart salute, before he recognised Mr Sterling Richardson – copper boss and now Captain in the 14th Welch.

'Not for me, thank you, sir.' He spoke formally, for there had always been a division between the boss and his men even though Sterling Richardson had been known and liked for his sense of *chware teg* – fair play, as the copper men called it. Now with the firm strictures imposed by the Army, any communication between officers and other ranks was almost unheard of.

'Relax, Morgan, I shan't bite you.' Sterling leaned against the crumbling wall of the trench, his eyes shrewd as they rested on the younger man.

'I've been watching you, Morgan. You always had guts – any man who works the copper needs to be hard. I've seen how you behave under stress – you are cool and determined – and I propose to recommend you for promotion to lance-corporal.'

Morgan felt a flash of pleasure. 'That's very good of you, sir, I appreciate it.'

Sterling stared out over the top of the trench, his booted foot resting on the muddy ladder. 'God-awful place to be, a far cry from Sweyn's Eye, wouldn't you say?'

His voice was wistful and Morgan warmed to him. 'Yes indeed, sir, but the sooner the big push forward comes, the better I'll be pleased.'

Sterling looked at him warningly. 'I know you're a bright one and you've doubtless picked up what's going on here, but don't speak of it to anyone.'

Morgan nodded his head slowly. 'You don't have to tell me that – with respect, sir.' He stared at the Captain, feeling it ironic that they might die here together in the mud of a foreign land – and then what good would Richardson's money do him? But he dismissed the thought quickly as unworthy, Sterling Richardson had toiled hard and long to make his profits, had paid his men fair and square and deserved all he had achieved.

Sterling was eyeing him ruefully as if sensing something of his thoughts. 'Death and the muddy fields of France are great levellers,' he smiled. 'Sure there's nothing I can get you – no smokes or woollen socks, nothing at all?'

'I'm all right, sir,' Morgan replied. 'Mrs O'Connor, whom I used to room with, sends me parcels.' But really there was no one back home who cared if he lived or died, he thought bitterly. The only ones close to him were gone: Honey and his father. He disciplined his thoughts sharply, it did no good to wallow in self-pity.

Sterling Richardson was moving silently away and Morgan studied his tall, sinewy frame. This was a man whom he trusted to lead them; he had character and a big share of guts himself. It was lighter now and the savoury smell of hot Oxo filling the air made him realise suddenly that he was hungry and that it was time for breakfast – a small vacuum of time before whatever skirmish was planned for the day took place. He squared his shoulders, adjusted his cap and made his way to the field kitchen.

*

Meanwhile Sterling Richardson strode easily through the trenches, talking to some of the soldiers on the way. He spoke cheerfully enough, but he could not help thinking that all this pushing forward towards the Somme was a waste of time. Even if they were to win the offensive, what would they actually gain except a strip of land that might well be lost again the next day? But it did not do for a soldier to think that way – a man must blindly obey, be honourable at all costs and to hell with doubts and uncertainties.

He pulled back through the lines, watching for a moment as a young fresh-faced boy bent his head over a piece of grubby paper, a stub of pencil in his hand. Sterling felt anger gnaw at him; the lad had been given no time to grow up before being thrust into battle. He moved on – his belly was growling, it was time to eat.

He sighed as he imagined breakfast at home with Mali and their children; he could picture his wife now, her long dark hair hanging over her shoulders, her eyes looking at him as though he was no ordinary mortal. Her letter crackled in his pocket against his heart and although it was foolish, its presence there comforted him. He could see again every word she had written; she was cheerful yet he read her longing for him behind the bits and pieces of light-hearted gossip.

She had told him how her friend Rhian had married Mansel Jack, to the dismay of all the proud mammas in the town who had wanted him for their own daughters. It seemed that Mansel Jack had enlisted and might even now be at the front. A good man to have around, Sterling thought – he was strong and forceful enough to inspire even the most reluctant of soldiers and there was something about him that gave a man complete confidence.

In the makeshift canteen set up in an old outbuilding, his fellow officers were enjoying breakfast. One of them lifted a hand to him and Sterling sat at the wooden trestle table. 'Have a Woodbine, Smithson. I need one to get the stink of the trenches out of my nostrils.'

Smithson was a young newly-commissioned officer and had seen little of the battle so far; yet he was game enough, Sterling decided, watching him strike a lucifer and puff on the cigarette.

'I've just seen one of the men from Sweyn's Eye out there – Morgan Lloyd, good lad he is too.' Sterling took the large cup of tea the mess orderly handed him. 'Used to work for me in the foundry, a strong boy and courageous as well.'

Smithson grimaced ruefully and rubbed his hand through his hair. 'Aye, they're all good lads, more's the pity.'

Sterling shook his head. 'You're right, of course. Heath

336

Jenkins is another local boy reported missing, related by marriage to Captain Sutton. Terrible shock for Mary, both her husband and brother going like that. She's been informed officially of course, but I wrote to her straight away. I hope she got my letter first, it might help break the news more gently – these War Office communications can be so bald.'

Sterling sat back in his chair, listening to the rise and fall of voices. There was even some laughter from the men, a release of the tension which gripped any officer who led his troops into battles from which many of them never returned.

'I wonder what Sweyn's Eye will be like when I get back,' Sterling said musingly. 'Already so much has changed. The women are doing men's jobs and doing them successfully – we'll never hear the end of it, I'll wager!'

He wondered if young Smithson like himself was putting up a façade, and supposed so. Men at the front longed for the comfort of their womenfolk's arms: human contact with someone who cared, a reassurance that the world was not all blood and death and the sound of shells bursting.

Sterling had begun to feel that he had only dreamed Mali, that she must be a figment of his imagination – a beautiful, wondrous image haunting his dreams. She seemed so far removed from him now and yet his love for her was not diminished by one iota.

He felt her letter crackle in his pocket and raised his hand to touch it, for it was a tenuous link with all that was good and clean in life. In some ways it was a reason for him being in this hell-hole. In the worst of the chaos, when all around him seemed to be death and very little glory, he told himself that it was to keep Mali and his children free from tyranny.

'The only one I have to worry about is my mother,' Smithson said quietly. 'Can't say I'm sorry – the way things have turned out, it must be hell having a wife and little ones back home.' He smiled suddenly. 'Though I hear that the womenfolk are coping extremely well and it seems that the mill at Spinners' Wharf is turning out red, white and blue shawls which are selling like hot cakes. God, I wish I was back in Sweyn's Eye at this very moment.'

The two men stared at each other for a moment in silent understanding. So much of the time they hid their fears behind

337

bluster, pretending that everything was under control. It was only occasionally that any of them allowed their real feelings to show.

Smithson rose to his feet. 'Well, I can't sit here all day, I suppose I'd better rejoin my men in the trenches. Poor sods haven't had a good night's sleep in weeks!' He gave Sterling a quick glance. 'I've no confidence in this great push the bigwigs are talking about – all it will gain us is a few hundred yards of worthless woodland.' He shrugged. 'But then, we're not here to think, are we?'

Sterling watched the tall rangy young man walk away and knew that he was right. But it didn't do to dwell on the futility of it all, that only made a man lose heart. He looked round for some place where he could find privacy to write his letter home to Mali.

There was a rough table in the far corner and he moved towards it, feeling in his pocket for his pencil. He stared down at the clean sheet of paper, wondering what on earth he was going to say when all he felt was that he missed her so badly it was as if a part of him had been left behind in Sweyn's Eye.

He knew he must be cheerful and not speak of the horrors of war, but be reassuring. Mali must be allowed to think that he was in no real danger, but was having quite a good time with his fellow officers. He might begin by saying that he had just been drinking tea with young Smithson – it would make her feel better to know he was in the company of men from his home town.

He took her letter from his pocket and surreptitiously pressed it to his lips before replacing it carefully against his heart. Then he began to write with a slow determined script. He would tell her he loved her and needed her, but he wouldn't say that life here was a living hell and he would give anything to be home again.

And what of Heath Jenkins? Should he tell her that the boy was missing? Doubtless she would learn the truth anyway. And how could he phrase the words so that her sweet lips would not tremble in fear that he might be the next? He threw down the pencil and leaned back in his chair, the salt of tears like grit in his eyes.

The sun was warming the small whitewashed bedroom and a cracked ceiling sloped downwards on heavy black beams. Heath opened his eyes a little wider – there was a haze over his mind and he couldn't think clearly. He wondered where he could be and for some unaccountable reason he was frightened.

As he lifted his head a pain shot through his temples so that he sank back against the pillows, lifting his hand tentatively to touch the bandages that covered his brow.

He heard the door creak open, there was the rustle of skirts and a woman was leaning over him, speaking to him softly. 'There you are, you'll be fine now.' She drew the sheets up around his shoulders, her hands gentle and her eyes warm; then she sat at the side of the bed and leaned forward and Heath noticed the way her large breasts strained the material of her cotton frock.

'Who are you?' he asked and as she leaned closer in an effort to hear his words he realised that he was very weak, his voice thin and reedy.

'I'm Margaret,' she smiled reassuringly and her teeth were fine and white. 'I found you in the fields and brought you here in my horse and cart. I thought at first you were past saving, but then I realised you were a strong young buck and would live.'

He tried to think; he was in France, wasn't he, so why was this woman speaking English to him. 'Aren't you a foreigner?' he asked and she shook her head. 'No, I'm from London, but I came here many years ago and married a Frenchman.' Her face became shadowed. 'He's gone now, God rest his soul.'

Heath could see there were tears in her eyes and with an effort he reached out and took her hand. She warmed to him at once.

'I shall bring you some good hearty soup.' She rose and smiled down at him. 'I don't know where you've come from, but I'm going to make sure you're fit and healthy before you leave my cottage.'

Heath was content to lie still, looking up at the patterns of sunlight on the ceiling and hearing the birds singing in the trees outside the windows. He sighed heavily – there were things he should remember, like when he was wounded and where his battalion had gone. There was something else tugging at the fringes of his mind ... a letter from home ... but the memory receded and he gave up the effort, knowing somehow that there would be pain in remembering.

Margaret returned and sat beside him, carefully spooning soup into his mouth. It tasted delicious and it was a good feeling to breathe in the clean fresh woman scent of her and have her so close to him in the wash of sunlight from the window.

He vaguely remembered battles – running up over the top of many trenches, feet slipping, heart racing, rifle at the ready. He smelled blood and heard cries, but then the picture faded and he was safe in the sunlit bedroom once more.

'Where is this place?' he asked and Margaret put down the empty bowl before answering.

'It's near Mametz Wood,' she said. 'Phillip and I lived a solitary life here, but we were content. It was hard at first without him, for my blood was young and flowed like wine but now ...' she shrugged, 'now I'm older and the urges of the flesh no longer trouble me.'

Slowly Heath smiled and memories of his youth came to mind – the many girls he had taken up on Ram's Tor or laid in the grass of Top Meadow. And Carrie, she had been an older woman and more the sweet because of it.

'Perhaps,' he said softly, 'I may be well enough soon to change your mind about that. You're a handsome woman, Margaret.'

She touched his face gently. 'And you are a very sick young man, for shame on you putting naughty thoughts into an old woman's head!' But her cheeks were flushed prettily, her eyes sparkled and she flounced a little as she walked to the door.

'Sleep now, it's the finest remedy for healing wounds that I know. Later I'll come and wash you, change your bandage and make you feel better.' She let herself out of the room and with a contented sigh Heath turned his face into the fragrant pillow and allowed drowsiness to overtake him.

Gradually he grew stronger and the wound on his temple closed up well enough, though there would always be a scar – he could see that by the way the flesh rose in an angry line along his brow.

At last Margaret allowed him to come downstairs to the kitchen. It was good to shave away the coarse beard that had grown and flourished while he lay sick. Margaret watched him, leaning back in her chair, her fine breasts revealed by the low-necked cotton blouse she wore. Her hands were folded in her lap – fine big peasant hands, soothing and gentle hands.

'Why, you're a handsome rascal!' She laughed like a young girl as his eyes met hers. 'I could see you were a fine-built man, but with all that stubble on your chin I didn't know the half of it, did I!'

'And you still don't, my lovely girl.' Heath turned and, taking her hands, drew her to her feet. She made no attempt at resistance; it was clear she had expected him to make advances to her and had decided to welcome them.

Her body was lush against his, her hair soft as he drew out the pins . . . and if there was a tinge of grey among the dark curls, it only added to her attraction.

'You're a beautiful woman, cariad,' he said softly, 'so beautiful that I think the angels must have put you here just for me.'

Her mouth was warm under his and when his hand opened the buttons on her blouse she leaned back and stared up at him with sparkling eyes.

'Let's go up into the bedroom.' As she took his hand and led him up the stairs, he felt suddenly as though this was his first time with a woman.

Margaret was possessed of great passion which had lain dormant since her husband had died. Heath took pains to move slowly, because he wanted her to enjoy him as he would enjoy her. She moaned as he touched the full, naked breasts and ran his tongue over the proud nipples. She clung to him, her eyes moist, her arms around him – caressing, passionate and most of all loving.

'Come to me, I can wait no longer,' she whispered in his ear. He felt the hot sun on his back, the softness of the woman beneath him and knew that he was alive. When he moved to take her she cried out in pleasure, arching her back as though to encompass him entirely. He was lost in a sweetness which had nothing to do with war or death, and joy exploded in him so

341

that he shuddered and cried out a name that was not hers.

She lay beneath him silent, unreproachful, kind, her gratitude bringing tears to her eyes.

'So you have left behind a woman, lovie,' she said soothingly as he buried his face in her neck. 'I would have expected nothing else from a man like you.' She caressed the hair curling on his neck and Heath tried to remember the name which passion had brought to his lips. But there was a warning in his head, a withdrawing, telling him that probing would be painful. So he relaxed and lay back against the pillows, his hand caressing Margaret's shoulder.

'I remember nothing about any woman I left behind,' he said softly. 'I only know that you are here next to me and you are all I could wish for.'

She leaned on one elbow and stared down at him tenderly. 'For however long this lasts, I'll be grateful,' she said solemnly. 'You are a gift from heaven and I shall savour every minute that I have you at my side. I realise that one day soon perhaps you will go back to your army and I shall be alone again, but for now we have each other.'

She slid from the bed. 'Now I shall make us both tea and we shall drink it in bed and then we shall sleep like pigs in the afternoon sunshine.' She smiled at him, her eyes alight and Heath returned her smile, pushing away the nameless fears revived by her talk of the war.

The drowsing days of early May were an oasis of time where nothing existed but making love, eating, drinking and sleeping. Heath became stronger, though his memory was still hazy and he was content for the moment to allow it to remain so.

He awoke one morning before the sun was up to hear a strangled cry from the kitchen. As he sat up sharply, the sound of men's voices rose through the thin boards of the room. He pulled on his clothes and moved stealthily along the landing to stare down into the room below.

He caught sight of uniforms, heard unfamiliar voices speaking in a strange guttural tongue. The hairs on the back of his neck prickled with fear as he realised the men in the kitchen were the enemy. He was about to move back into the bedroom and make his escape through the window when he realised that he could hear Margaret crying.

342

A soldier moved a little and undid the buttons of his trousers – legs open, body thrust forward. He stood over a figure on the floor whose white legs were being held cruelly apart. Then the man thrust downwards, while behind him his comrades urged him on with raucous laughter.

Heath felt a mist rise over his eyes, clouding his brain. These Germans – the hated enemy – were raping and plundering. He was so incensed that the wound on his temple throbbed.

It was Rhian Gray he saw lying there and his memories were flooding back now: Rhian whom he had coaxed out of her fear of men, whom he had loved, telling her that the violent attack by Gerwin Price had not been her fault.

He had convinced her at last and she had lain with him, promising herself to him. But then she had written to tell him that she had married another man. Yet he loved her still and could not allow the men who tormented her to go unpunished.

Enraged, he looked around him for a weapon and saw on the wall a gleaming cutlass. He snatched it up and hurled himself down the stairs.

The first man fell without a sound, blood spurting uncontrollably from the jugular vein. The man astride the woman turned with mouth agape and Heath caught him with the flat of the blade, breaking his nose. He fell to the ground with a harsh cry.

Heath was caught from behind by the two remaining German soldiers, but his strength was that of a madman and the enemy had no hope against him. He strangled the last one with his bare hands while the sound of sobbing filled the silence.

When the violence was over, the mists cleared from his mind and Heath was once again in France. He held Margaret to him, cradling her head against his chest, pity flowing through him as she struggled even in her pain to pull her torn skirt over her legs.

'Hush, everything will be all right. I shall look after you, no one will ever hurt you again,' he said softly and it was as though he was talking to Rhian Gray. But no, *she* had betrayed him, she had married some coward while Heath was risking his life at the front.

'My God!' Margaret was scrambling to her knees. 'There's

343

someone coming – I pray there are no more of the Boches, they'll kill us for sure.'

Heath put his hand over her mouth and drew her with him to the window.

The men outside were British soldiers, he could see the khaki of their uniforms. He felt relief flood through him and then he recognised Morgan Lloyd, who was the lance-corporal in charge of the small party.

It appeared the soldiers were an advance company, sent to reconnoitre the countryside surrounding Mametz Wood. Morgan Lloyd's smile of greeting faded as he stepped inside and an expression of disbelief crossed his face as he saw the unexpected scene of carnage in the small sunwashed kitchen of the cottage.

'*Duw!* There's a bloody sight! What's happened here, man?'

It was Margaret who replied. Clothes torn and face bruised, she saw the young soldier's eyes become shrewd as she stepped forward. He was a quick one right enough and would soon assess the situation, but just to make sure she rushed into speech.

'The pigs of Boches were raping me,' she said through swollen lips, 'and this man came to help me. Tackled them all on his own, he deserves a medal.'

Heath was aware of Morgan looking from the woman to the dead Germans and then back again to Heath. He pushed his helmet back on his head and though he clearly guessed there was more to the incident than met the eye, there was no doubt that the woman had been raped and Heath had indeed killed four of the enemy.

'You're a bloody hero, man,' he said. 'I'm proud to be serving in the same battalion as you.' He held out his hand and as Heath took it, he knew his halcyon days of happiness were over.

'We'll clear up your kitchen for you, missus,' Morgan said crisply, 'and then we shall have to rejoin our own troops.' Quietly he set the men to work and Heath noticed that there was a new strength and confidence about Morgan which would gain any man's respect.

'There'll be a lot of explaining to do when we get back,' Morgan told him, 'so perhaps it's just as well if we go through it now. I can see you've had a head wound – loss of memory, was it?'

Heath nodded wearily. 'Believe it or not, that's exactly what it was. I don't know how long I've been here in the cottage with Margaret, I only know that if it wasn't for her I'd be a dead man.'

'Well, I reckon you've repaid your debt, Private Jenkins.'

Heath did not say goodbye to Margaret, he simply walked away from the cottage without looking back. There was a pain in his head and a sickness in his gut, for he knew that he was no longer the Heath Jenkins who had left Sweyn's Eye with such high hopes. Now a strange and dangerous beast lurked inside his head and he feared it.

Chapter Twenty-Eight

The early summer sun slanted over the roof-tops of Sweyn's Eye, dappling dingy courts, lighting up window corners where copper dust sparkled like gold. It was a dreaming, sunwashed day and the war seemed far away.

In the darkness of the mill house where the soft sun was barely able to penetrate the small round windows, Rhian worked at the loom. The shuttle flew fast as she bent in a graceful arc over the steadily growing pattern of wool. She was mixing new colours – soft violet shades and strong blues – with the traditional biscuit background, and the result was pleasing.

The demand for woollen goods had fallen slightly with the onset of the warmer weather, but the women of Sweyn's Eye still felt it their duty to send parcels to the front and so Rhian was kept busy providing hanks of knitting wool. But sometimes, like today when a strange unhappy mood possessed her, she felt the need to tax her mind with the practical and yet intriguing job of making up new patterns.

There was no need for her ever to work again, Mansel Jack had seen to that, but Rhian could not have endured a life made up of humdrum chores around the house and so she spent much of her day in the mill, occupying herself with her work, frightened of the shadows that haunted her mind whenever she thought of her husband fighting on foreign soil.

The months since her marriage had passed all too slowly and without him, she was empty and lost. But tears did nothing to alleviate the pain of being alone, though she sometimes cried into her pillow at nights with longing for the presence of him, the intangible feeling of strength and love that emanated from

346

him. With him she was complete but without him she felt soulless.

His last letter she kept in the pocket of her apron, reading and re-reading every word. There, amongst the words of love, he had given her instructions for dealing with their finances, told her that pay to Doris Williams must be stopped now that she was improving – generous he was, but not soft.

'Rhian, there's a girl you are. I've been calling you for ages!' Gina stood in the doorway of the mill; at her side and clinging to her skirt was Cerianne, her eyes large as she stared at the machinery.

Rhian switched off the loom and rubbed her hands on her apron.

'Thank God that little tinker Dewi is asleep,' Gina continued. 'He's been getting on my nerves today.'

There was an edge to Gina's voice and Rhian looked at her in bewilderment, seeing suddenly the lines of strain around her mouth and the deep shadows beneath her eyes.

'Come on then, I'm starving.' Rhian kissed Cerianne and the little girl responded by clinging to her with warm plump arms.

Cerianne was growing more like Billy every day, Rhian thought with a catch in her throat. There was little likeness to her mother, which was just as well for Delmai Richardson had not come calling once to see how the little girl was faring.

There was no sign of Carrie in the kitchen and Rhian stood back from the heat of the fire which even on a warm, balmy day was necessary because of the cooking.

'No wonder you're tired, my girl.' She rested her hand on Gina's shoulder. 'The room's hot enough to boil an egg.'

Gina slumped in a chair and sighed heavily, and Rhian leaned over her with an expression of concern.

'What is it, Gina, what's wrong? You look so . . . beaten, somehow.'

'I've just had a row with Carrie. She's gone off in a huff and left her dinner and I just can't cope with it all any longer.'

Gina dissolved into tears, the hands covering her face marred by burns from the oven.

'I've been letting you do too much,' Rhian said remorsefully. 'I'm heartily ashamed of myself – look, why don't you go and lie on the bed with Dewi for an hour?'

347

Gina looked up hopefully. '*Duw*, are you sure you can manage?' The question was asked out of politeness for she was on her feet already, making for the stairs. At the door she turned to look at Rhian, her eyes shadowed.

'It's not just the work,' she said softly, her voice cracking with weariness. 'It's thinking of what's happened to my Heinz.' She put her hand to her breast. 'I feel in here that he will not come back to me, but I can't help harbouring a faint hope.'

Rhian stared at her worriedly, knowing that in her own anxiety and pain at parting from Mansel Jack she had been thoughtless and selfish.

'There's awful I feel,' she said gently. 'I should have realised how you were suffering.'

'It's my spirit that's tired,' Gina said, 'and don't you feel bad, for you've worked like a trooper out there in the mill. You bring the bread into the house as you've always done, and Carrie and me – well, we're grateful.' She shrugged. 'I suppose I just need to get away from the four walls of the kitchen sometimes,' she smiled apologetically. 'Now the weather's good I'll get out more – take the children to the park to see the ducks, they'd like that.'

Rhian felt her throat constrict. 'You've never been strong since you had the jaundice and now you need help with the little ones, that's plain enough.' She smiled cheerfully. 'Look, I have an idea – why don't I see Doris again, ask her to come over a couple of mornings and help with the work? She's been much more herself lately and has been talking again about wanting a job.'

'Aye, it would help,' Gina nodded. 'Carrie isn't as young as she was and her back's been playing her up. I think we could do with another pair of hands around here.'

'That's settled then. You go on up to bed now and have a rest and I'll see to the dinner.'

Gina held out her hand, 'Come on, Cerianne, it's time you had a nap too.' The little girl scrambled off Rhian's knee at once and rested her head against Gina's white apron.

After Gina had gone upstairs, the silence in the kitchen hung like a heavy stone around Rhian's neck. She moved to the door and stood in the cooling breeze that drifted in from the river, wondering how she could have been so blind. Gina was obviously tired and in need of help and understanding.

How would *she* feel, Rhian mused, if she had lost Mansel Jack? She pushed the fearful thought away from her and turned back into the kitchen where the kettle was spitting water into the flames of the fire. There was very little for her to do except keep an eye on the meat cooking in the oven, so she sank into a chair, her hands lying in her lap, and tried to keep her mind still.

Carrie returned within the hour, the basket on her arm full of bread and fruit.

'What's all that you've got there?' Rhian asked in amazement, for food was still scarce.

'There's a nose on you, girl. I have my friends, mind, and it doesn't pay to ask too many questions.' She smiled. 'But I am surprised you haven't missed a couple of blankets here and there, or a couple of pounds of knitting wool.' She glanced round her. 'Where's Gina?'

'I've sent her up to bed.' Rhian leaned forward in her chair. 'I've been so selfish in thinking only of myself and I failed to see how tired Gina's been lately. I shouldn't have been so quick to bury my head in the sand.'

Carrie unpacked the food, shaking her head in bewilderment. 'Jumped down my throat she did, this morning, couldn't understand what I'd done wrong. Of course the babbas were playing her up – well, Dewi was anyway. A proper little boy he is, a right little devil, needs a man's hand really speaking.'

'Well, I've decided to go to see Doris. Mansel Jack has finished paying her wages now she's better, so she'll be glad of a job. She's improved a great deal lately and I'm going to have her come round and give a hand. You remember I asked her before, but she wasn't fit enough then.'

Carrie moved to the fireplace and took up the brown teapot, spilling steaming water into the cold china, swirling it round while all the time her brow was puckered thoughtfully.

'I do try to pull my weight, but I won't deny I've been a mite stubborn what with the pain in my back an' all. Want a cup of tea, *merchi*?'

Rhian nodded her head absently. 'Yes, please.' She leaned

back in her chair. 'Don't worry yourself, Carrie, you always do more than your share and I love you for it. No, we need some help around here, that's the answer.'

As Carrie poured the fragrant tea, she was biting her lip in concentration. 'I suppose Doris will be all right with the children – much better now, I hear, and more her old self, like.'

'Well, later on I'll go into town,' Rhian said decisively. 'Then I shall see Doris and we'll soon have everything sorted out.'

She spoke confidently, but she wasn't so sure of anything if the truth be told. Doris might not want to work for her now, after all she did have children of her own. But negative thoughts would do no good, she told herself sharply; she must stir herself out of her apathy and at least try to do something to improve matters.

It was early afternoon when Rhian walked through Sweyn's Eye, staring at the streets as though she was a sleeper just awakening. The shop doorways were no longer hung about with wares, no boots hung on strings outside the leather shop and the greengrocer's table held nothing but a few tired cabbages.

A man moved past her leaning heavily on a stick, recognisable as a wounded soldier by the blue of the uniform he wore. Rhian glanced away from him, her heart beating swiftly.

She turned towards Canal Street and as she heard the sound of Dai-End-House playing his accordion her thoughts swept back to the days when she was young and had thought herself in love with Heath Jenkins. Those breathless days when she stood at the window of the Canal Street Laundry, her only worry being that Heath might not come to meet her.

How much had changed since then – not least, she herself. She recognised that what she had felt for Heath was not the real iron-strong love she shared with Mansel Jack. And yet there was still a kind of love in her heart for Heath, for he had been her friend since childhood and had cared for her, taking his revenge on the man who had used and defiled her. But now Heath was 'missing believed killed' – how Rhian dreaded those words.

She moved along the narrow cobbled street, seeing the long ribbon of the canal gleaming in the sunlight. The waters were

350

ruffled by the breeze and a barge glided slowly along, harnessed to a horse which moved with heavy deliberation, head hanging wearily.

Doris herself opened the door and smiled widely. 'There's nice to see you – have you brought my money?' She stepped back to allow Rhian into the kitchen and her mother scolded her soundly.

'Hush, girl, there's cheeky you are to Rhian. Come in and sit down by here and I'll make us all a nice cup of tea.'

Rhian smiled. 'No, thank you, Mrs Williams. I have to get back home soon.' She glanced at Doris covertly, seeing that she had gained weight and there was a healthy colour in her cheeks.

'Do you still want a job, Doris?' she asked slowly. 'It's only a few days a week helping to clean the mill house – do you like the idea?'

Doris clapped her hands in delight. 'When can I start? I'm so fed-up with this old place and me mam going on at me all the time.'

'It won't be as much pay as you were getting before,' Rhian cautioned, 'but I'm sure every little bit helps.' She glanced towards Mrs Williams, who was nodding her head.

'There's grateful we are,' she agreed. 'I know Doris needs to get out a bit, especially as her boys are growing up out of the way. She's cooped up by here in the kitchen too much – and her not used to it.'

'Do you think she's strong enough, Mrs Williams?' Rhian asked anxiously and the older women nodded again.

'Oh, yes, nothing wrong with her now – like herself she is, thank the good lord.'

'Well then, that's settled.' Rhian moved towards the door. 'Can you come to the mill house first thing in the morning, Doris?'

'Of course I can. I'll be there as soon as the daylight comes to wake me, don't you bother!'

As Rhian retraced her steps, she wondered if she had done the right thing. Doris seemed well enough, and surely she could come to no harm doing small jobs about the house. It certainly seemed an ideal solution to her problem – killing two birds with one stone, so to speak.

She sighed and strolled down towards the beach where the

351

sea rolled softly into the curving bay and the sky above was cloudless and bright. Moving slowly along the edge of the shore, breathing in the clean salt tang of the air, she wished that Mansel Jack was here beside her, taking her hand in his and towering over her with his great strength. And suddenly she fell to her knees in the softness of the sand and, alone with the sound of the sea laving the beach, she wept.

*

It was some while before Mary could shake from her mind the heavy burden of her grief for Brandon and for her brother. She had remained in her room most of the time, not wanting to rise from bed. Then reason asserted itself and her thoughts clarified as she told herself that she was being weak and self-indulgent at a time when many women in her position were carrying on normally.

She decided that she would go to the store to see for herself how matters were progressing. It was time she took an interest in living again. The day was dry and warm and roses made bright splashes of colour against green lawns as Mary strolled towards the tram terminus, determined to be in good spirits.

It was stuffy inside the swaying car and she pulled at the collar of her silk blouse, feeling breathless and uncomfortable. Her skirts were becoming too tight and needed letting out; she would have to see if Muriel could spare her a little time – the girl always was good at sewing and had helped a great deal when Mary was just starting her business. A smile curved Mary's lips . . . it would be to Muriel she would go for the tiny clothes that would be necessary in a few months' time.

She was grateful to alight from the tram, yet the heat of the street was almost like a physical blow. The pavements shimmered and light seemed to bounce from every surface.

Mary stepped into the comparative coolness of the store's foyer and the soft shiny green of the aspidistra plants set out in heavy china jardinières was a pleasing and refreshing sight. She heard the tinkle of crockery and the rise and fall of voices and knew that the tea-rooms were doing a brisk trade, which was as it should be. Being in no mood for conversation, she skirted the edges of the room, not wanting to catch anyone's eye.

She moved upstairs to her office and sat gratefully at the

desk, closing her eyes for a moment, leaning against the cool leather chair and drinking in the atmosphere of the store. It was a great source of satisfaction to her to know that she had built up the business alone – in that way at least she was her own woman, independent and strong.

And yet without her husband, could she ever be the same again? She had loved him dearly and betrayed him so easily – would it be wrong to give her unborn child his name?

There was an increasingly familiar uneasiness in her, a sense of wrongdoing. And there too was the inherent fear that at any moment she chose to speak, Mary Anne Bloomfield could tear her reputation asunder.

A sudden rapping on the door startled Mary and with a sigh she sat up straighter in her chair.

'Come in!' Her voice was light and controlled and her face expressionless as she faced Greenie's anxious eyes.

'Mrs Sutton, there's sorry I am to trouble you, but there's a bit of bother downstairs – that Miss Bloomfield again.' There was a world of scorn in the older woman's voice and Mary felt her nerves grow taut as she rose to her feet.

'Don't worry, Greenie, I'll come at once.' Mary held her head high as she walked down the stairs, looking neither to the right nor the left. In the tea-rooms Mary Anne was standing in the centre of the floor, her face flushed with the heat, her hair dishevelled and a strong smell of drink hanging over her.

'Can I be of any help?' Mary spoke formally and the room fell silent as all eyes rested on the two women.

'I want a table.' Mary Anne sounded aggressive, her eyes were narrowed as she stared at Mary and her full lips fell into a pout.

'I think you ought to go home to bed.' Mary spoke lightly, but anger was building up inside her. 'I imagine you have indulged in too much wine and in this heat too – not quite the ladylike thing to do.'

Mary Anne's mouth fell open and she stared in astonishment, glancing round mutinously at the discreet laughs which greeted Mary's words.

'Now look here . . .' Mary Anne began but Mary moved closer, towering above the American woman.

'No, you look here. I will not have you making a scene in my

353

tea-rooms. Now please let me escort you to the door.'

'She's nothing but a whore!' Mary Anne cried, trying to draw away from Mary's firm grasp. 'Having a baby and doesn't know who the father is – you ask her!'

Mary felt completely in control of the situation as she lifted her head and spoke clearly. 'Aren't you confusing my situation with your own, Miss Bloomfield?' The laughter rose and she gestured to the doorman to call a cab.

Carrie had been right to tell her to stand up to the American woman, Mary thought in triumph. 'Now you have done your worst and found it has not benefited you in any way,' she said, 'perhaps you will leave – and please don't let me see you round here again.'

'I've not done my worst, honey, not by any means,' Mary Anne said venomously. 'There is a great deal more I can say and do to harm you, make no mistake about it.'

Mary gave her a slight push. 'On your way now, don't forget that I'm not a lady and might just be inclined to give you a good leathering.' She placed her hands on her hips. 'You had your say just now and it's quite clear that no one would believe a woman like you. Now, if you know what's good for you, get into the cab and go away. *Stay* away, do you understand?'

After the cab had rolled away down the cobbled street, Mary stood in the sunshine, taking deep breaths and telling herself not to let the woman upset her. She had done right to face up to Mary Anne, blackmail was cheap and nasty and she would not knuckle down under the threat of it.

'There's proud of you I am.' Greenie was smiling at Mary, her eyes full of admiration. 'You told her what for and no mistake, hussy that she is!'

Mary forced a smile. 'I hope we've seen the last of her.' She paused, noticing that Mrs Greenaway was looking drawn and tired.

'Go on home now, Greenie,' she said gently. 'There's not much left to do here anyway.'

The hours seemed to drag, the afternoon sun was hot and the store was airless. Mary was glad when at last it was time to close and she was free to return home.

As she made her way through the streets, her spirits were at a low ebb and to make matters worse, the trams were so crowded that she had to walk. Slowly climbing the curving roadway in the softness of the summer air, she looked up at the mackerel-bellied clouds and wished for Brandon to be with her under the same sky.

And Heath, her brother – had he lain wounded in some muddy ditch in France? 'Stop it!' she told herself firmly.

At last, with a sigh of relief, she let herself into the coolness of the hallway. She stood quite still for a moment, her heart beating rapidly, her eyes drawn to the letter lying on the hall table.

Slowly she picked it up and took it with her into the drawing-room, standing at the window and staring out into the garden where the flower beds were a blaze of colour and the trees stood proud and heavy with leaves. She glanced at the letter, afraid to open it for it had come from France. Then she moved to a chair, sank down against the cushions and, taking a deep breath, ripped at the envelope with unsteady hands. It took her a few moments to digest the information that her brother Heath was alive and well. His writing was uneven, disjointed, his signature scrawled as though in haste. She felt tears burn her eyes. 'Thank God!' she said quietly.

Mrs Greenaway came into the room, her eyes wide and questioning, and Mary knew at once that she had seen the letter.

'It's Heath, Greenie, he's all right! He was wounded, but not seriously, and he tells me he's going to get a medal . . .' Her voice faltered and tears ran unchecked down her cheeks as Mrs Greenaway crossed the room quickly and held her close.

'There, there, *cariad*, your brother is safe and don't you see what that means?' She dabbed at Mary's eyes with the corner of her pristine apron. 'Why, it means that Mr Sutton could be safe and well too – they do make mistakes, see?'

Mary made an effort to control her tears, rubbing at her eyes and forcing a smile. 'Well, we must keep on hoping, mustn't we? But I find it difficult at times, I must confess.'

'I know you do, *cariad*, and it's only natural, but hope makes the world go round – you know that, don't you?' She didn't wait for a reply. 'Now, let me get you a lovely hot cup of tea and something to eat and then you'll feel better. We must look after you, especially now.'

Mary's gaze followed Mrs Greenaway in surprise for she had said nothing to her about the baby, wanting to hug the secret to herself at least for a time. Then she remembered that Greenie would have heard Mary Anne's accusations – everyone in the store must have heard them, come to that!

She moved to the elongated mirror in its gilt frame and stared at her reflection. Perhaps she was beginning to look a little stout, yet she had thought that the cut of her clothes would conceal the thickening of her waistline.

Mrs Greenaway reappeared almost immediately with a silver tray set for two and Mary looked up at her questioningly.

'The young doctor is in the hallway waiting to see you, so I took the liberty of putting out a cup for him. Shall I send him in?'

Mary was aware that her colour was rising as she nodded her head, turning towards the fire and avoiding the older woman's shrewd eyes. 'Yes, do, that will be fine.' She tried to speak lightly, but in spite of herself her voice shook.

She rose as he came towards her and smiled politely, aware that Greenie was taking her time about closing the door.

'Why have you come, Dr Soames?' The words spilled from her lips as soon as Mrs Greenaway had gone.

He moved further into the room, his eyes resting on her face imploringly. 'I wanted to see you.' He spoke humbly. 'Please don't be angry with me.'

'Sit down,' Mary said shakily, for this was something she had not expected. 'Do have some tea.' She was playing for time, but when she handed him the cup she met his eyes and read the truth in them.

'I've done the most stupid thing, I've fallen in love with you,' he said softly. 'I know it's not ethical or even sane, but I can't help myself.' He reached out to take her hands and Mary stared at him dumbly. Then he leaned forward, brushing a strand of hair from her forehead.

'I know you don't love me, Mary, so don't try to say anything to put me off. Once I heard about your husband being reported missing, I understood what had happened.' He kissed her lightly on the forehead. 'I knew you came to me with grief in your heart, that I was there and you needed comfort. I just want you to know I'll always be there for you, Mary.'

'Dr Soames . . . Paul,' Mary said gently, 'I have a great fondness for you and I am very grateful to you, but I still love Brandon. I suppose I always will, even though I shall never see him again.'

'I know.' Paul Soames moved away from her reluctantly. He seemed to make a great effort to control himself before he spoke again.

'I think it might be best if you went to Bryn Thomas for medical advice in future.' He looked away from her. 'I don't think I would be man enough to see you and the baby and keep my distance.'

Mary swallowed hard. 'I'll respect your wishes, Paul, but is it impossible now for us to be friends?'

Paul Soames walked slowly towards the door. 'If ever you need me or want me, I'll be there.'

Long after he had gone, Mary sat staring into the fire, her thoughts a riot of confusion. 'What a tangled web indeed,' she whispered softly.

Chapter Twenty-Nine

Sterling Richardson sat in the makeshift canteen drinking tepid tea from a chipped enamel mug. Outside the air was heavy, the summer sun hidden behind a haze of clouds. Except for the occasional sound of artillery, it was difficult to imagine that he was in the middle of the battle of the Somme.

And yet he was lucky to be alive, by God! So many of his fellows were injured or dead and Sterling had felt a particular sense of loss when Brandon Sutton had failed to return from one of the futile skirmishes which resulted in victory for no one.

The door of the dilapidated hut swung open and against the sudden splash of light, Sterling found it difficult at first to identify the officer who stepped inside.

'God, it's good to get the weight off my feet.' Smithson sank heavily on to the bench beside Sterling, his face grey with fatigue. Mud spattered his trousers and there was a narrow cut along his cheek. 'This show's a mess,' he said quietly. 'The 38th Welch relieved the men of the 7th division on the front at Mametz Wood, but it looks as though they're failing to hold their position.'

Sterling nodded. 'So I've heard. The heavy rain during the night hasn't helped matters, with men and guns bogged down in the mud.' He took a gulp of the fast-cooling tea and set his mug on the table.

Smithson leaned back in his chair and rubbed his hand wearily through his hair. 'The Germans have come up with a new weapon, the men are calling it the egg bomb. It's easy to handle and can be thrown fifty yards like a rugby ball. Apart from which they have fresh troops coming up to the front, while our men are bone-weary.'

'Talking of weary, it looks as if you could do with a few hours' shut-eye. Go on, get some rest while you can.'

Smithson rose to his feet, his shoulders stooped, his eyes red-rimmed. 'I expect you're right. There'll be a renewed attempt to take the woods as soon as everything's been reorganised and I'll need all my wits about me then.'

Sterling stared into his empty mug. It seemed absurd to be sitting in a run-down building in France, drinking vile tea and talking about capturing a piece of ground as though it was the most important thing in the world. He pushed back his chair and rose to his feet – it was about time he was back on duty.

*

The failure of the 38th Welch to capture Mametz Wood was a blow to the pride of all Welshmen. At 11 am on the ninth of July, 1916, Major-General H. E. Watts relieved Major-General Ivor Phillips at Divisional Headquarters. Orders were given in no uncertain terms that Mametz Wood was to be captured at dawn on the tenth of July.

A large-scale plan of the wood had been prepared, which showed that the ground was roughly divided into three portions. The task of capturing one piece of ground at a time appeared deceptively simple, except to the soldiers concerned.

Heath Jenkins lay amongst the tangle of leaves, his face contorted with fury. 'Think we're blasted pack-horses, they do! These generals just give the order that each man carries two Mills bombs with him, yet we're supposed to be ready to fire if we come upon the enemy unawares. No wonder so many of the 38th were slaughtered!'

Morgan Lloyd shifted uncomfortably in the grass, holding his hand over his eyes and straining to see into the distance. 'How far is Mametz Wood, do you think?' he asked. He felt uneasy in Heath's company, though he could not have said why, but there was a strange light in the man's eyes almost as though a wild animal were trapped inside the lean young body.

Morgan would never forget finding Heath in the kitchen of a French cottage and hearing how, single-handed, he had killed four of the Germans – a proper blood-bath it was, too. Morgan shivered; it was only natural that such an experience would alter a man.

'It's only about a thousand yards from White Trench,' Heath replied. 'I've been here before, you see, I know the terrain.' He paused, trying to clear his thoughts. When had he been in the woods? Was it after he had been injured, when he was found by Margaret? He shook his head impatiently. 'The first five hundred yards are easy enough, almost flat as you can see, but further on the ground drops about thirty-five feet down into a valley – that's going to be a bugger, that is.'

Morgan got to his knees and edged forward, aware of the gun crew to his left panting and groaning as they pulled the eighteen-pounder through the soggy ground.

'I pity the gunners,' Heath said dryly. 'They don't know what they're in for. After the valley there's a steady rise of about four hundred yards. If the Jerries are waiting there, we're all dead men.'

Morgan found that Heath knew exactly what he was talking about. The plunge into the wooded valley was not so difficult for the soldiers, but the gunners needed time to manoeuvre their weapons over the edge of the drop.

'It's a bit of a rest for us at any rate,' Heath said as he lay back in the grass and took out a Woodbine. 'Jesus, I hate this country!' He closed his eyes and thought of Sweyn's Eye – the funny cobbled streets, the little shops that thronged the pavement, jostling with each other for business, the baker's vans smelling of doughy bread hot from the oven . . . and he was homesick.

Then a knife of pain twisted in his gut as he remembered there was no one waiting for him there. Rhian, his woman, the one he had loved all his life, had betrayed him. She had married this upstart from the North, a self-made man who had stolen her away and married her on the sly. Hate poured through his veins like hot, sweet wine as he crushed the Woodbine between his fingers, uncaring of the fact that the lighted end of the cigarette burned his palm. If ever he met this Mansel Jack, he was a dead man!

'Heath Jenkins, wake up!' Someone was shaking him by the arm and Heath uncoiled, snake-like, grasping the man by the throat as a snarl of rage left his lips.

360

'Christ, back down, boyo!' Morgan was sharp, he had a knife to Heath's belly and the cold steel had a calming effect.

Heath sighed heavily. 'Sorry, kid, I must have been dreaming.' He took a deep breath; he must get a grip on himself, for he was behaving irrationally and sometimes was frighteningly aware of his own state of mind. But then a cloud would come down to blot out light and reason and he would be possessed by some monster of dark anger that wanted to reach out and crush.

'Well, don't come it again by here, boyo,' Morgan said levelly, the cold light in his eyes assuring Heath he meant what he said. Not that Heath was frightened of the boy – young and strong he might be, but he would be no match for him. But he was likeable enough, a good Welsh boy, clean and honest and with guts too. Heath rested his hand on his shoulder. 'I've said I'm sorry and I mean it – now, let's forget it, shall we?'

The climb up the hill towards the woods was fraught with danger. Heath felt the hair prickle on the back of his neck, he almost felt the eyes of the Germans upon him – it was as though they had marked him out because he had killed without compunction.

Morgan was breathing heavily at his side and the boy's booted feet slipped on the uneven ground. Heath caught him by his sleeve and held on with almost superhuman strength until Morgan found his footing.

'*Duw*, we're like sitting ducks climbing up by here,' Morgan said heavily. 'I keep expecting the Jerries to lean over the bank up there and shoot us to pieces.'

Heath frowned. 'I suppose we all feel like that, boyo. It's instinct in us – the fight for survival, I mean.'

It was a pity he had not met Morgan sooner, Heath thought; he had had a bit of bad luck in his young life, by the sound of it. Lost his father, then his girl was blown up in the munitions factory. *Duw*, it was a terrible world.

They were almost at the top of the ridge when one of the gunners called out for help. 'Jesus, that's all we need!' Heath said fiercely. 'It's a wonder they don't send a postcard to the Jerries telling them what time we're arriving!'

'Looks like we've all got to give a hand to pull up the guns,' Morgan replied easily. 'I suppose the brass-hats know what

361

they're doing.'

'Then you're a bigger fool than I took you for.' Heath softened his words with a wry smile: 'Give me a good sergeant, a man who knows what's what, and you can keep the bloody officers. All they know about is playing soldiers on a bit of paper. "We'll take Mametz Wood today chaps, looks like a good spot." ' He mimicked the precise tones of the officer in charge and Morgan could not help but laugh.

'You're a strange man, Heath Jenkins,' he said, 'and I'd rather have you with me than against me.'

'Come on, let's get back down this swine of a ridge.' Heath appeared unconcerned. 'I suppose we're never going to get in position if we don't sort out the gunners.'

By 3 am on the tenth of July the troops were in position. The leading platoons of the 13th and 14th Welch were lying just behind a small bank at the top of the rise, the 10th Welch having been scattered behind the spearhead of the attack with orders to advance up the edge of the ridge and await developments there.

'Guess what?' Heath spoke in a low voice, having just reappeared through the bushes at Morgan's side. 'We've had a special message of encouragement sent us from the commander-in-chief – isn't that big of him?'

He saw Morgan frown at the sarcasm in his voice but then, Heath thought, Morgan was new to the game of war – he thought it was death or glory and didn't know of the private hells that lingered in between.

'Well, all I want to do now is get on with it,' Morgan said harshly. His colour was high and Heath knew how he felt. There would be a mingling of fear and pride, a willingness to die for home and country, but it wasn't quite like that out here. Once a man had fought in a few battles he came to see the futility of it all, the ghastly dance to and fro over blood-strewn land, but now was not the time to discourage him.

'That's the spirit!' His words were drowned by a sudden and furious bombardment that tore at the ear-drums and shattered the nerves.

'Some of our artillery are firing their shells,' Heath hissed. 'Let's hope they find their target or we'll get shredded into tiny pieces.'

'Christ!' Morgan was doubled up, his hands over his belly. 'I don't think I can hold myself.'

'Don't worry,' Heath shouted reassuringly. 'Just get behind the bushes there, it's nothing to be ashamed of, we all feel like that from time to time.'

Morgan was all right, Heath thought. He would have plenty of guts when it came to the battle, he was the fighting kind.

The 13th Welch were advancing in waves. Shots were fired and men were screaming, falling, twitching in the mud. Some soldiers lay on their backs, sightless eyes staring up at the leaden skies.

'Come on, Morgan!' Heath yelled. 'We can't let the 13th take all the glory. Come on, we're going over the top!' He held the boy by his sleeve, dragging him forward, stumbling over bodies of their comrades.

Morgan's eyes were alight as he shook himself free. 'We'll show the Jerries, just let me get at them!'

A band of Germans was suddenly facing them, peering with staring eyes over the top of a gaping-mouthed gun. Heath kicked Morgan's feet from under him and the boy fell on to his face, then Heath took careful aim with one of the Mills bombs and blackened smoke muffled the cries of the German wounded.

'Keep down now,' Heath hissed in Morgan's ear. 'The next wave of our men should be no more than a hundred yards behind us. If everyone moves steadily we may yet take this piece of land, though much good it will do us.' And yet Heath could not help the feeling of exhilaration that ran through him – they were slowly but surely gaining ground and the Jerries lay dying at their feet.

He heard Morgan gasp and saw the boy staring with wide eyes at a German soldier who was looking up at him, one sleeve flapping emptily and blood pouring from a wound in his head.

'Kill the bastard!' Heath said urgently, but Morgan was bending forward as though to help the fallen soldier who suddenly had a blade pointing at Morgan's throat. Heath fired at once and the German shuddered as though a chill wind had drifted over him, then he lay still. When his hand fell open, the gleaming knife lay bright against the grass.

'Never trust the enemy, boyo,' Heath said harshly. 'That's

one lesson you have to learn quick, for you won't have any second chance. Come on, don't just stand there, let's get on with it.'

A burly German moved silently out of the trees and Heath drew Morgan into the shelter of the branches. 'Look at Lieutenant Wilson, that's one officer I can respect.'

The Lieutenant was just withdrawing his bayonet from the belly of the big German soldier. Then almost in the same movement, he lifted his arm and with a single shot dislodged a sniper from one of the trees.

'I'd serve behind a man like him any time. Now keep your head low, you don't want it shot off, do you?' Heath pushed Morgan through the undergrowth, staring around him cautiously; so far, some sixth sense that alerted him to danger had kept him alive, but he didn't want to leave anything to chance.

Lieutenant Wilson was instructing his men to dig in and Heath smiled at Morgan triumphantly. 'Well, we've won our little battle,' he said jubilantly. 'The 14th Welch have captured our section of the woods, now it's up to the rest of them to do the same. Come on, Morgan, we'll soon be enjoying a cup of Oxo and a Woodbine.'

The look of exhilaration mingled with disbelief on Morgan's face made Heath laugh and he tapped Morgan on the shoulder. 'Know something? I like you, Morgan boyo.' He sighed and stretched himself out in the grass, uncaring that beads of dampness carpeted the ground. He closed his eyes and within a few minutes was sound asleep.

*

On the other side of the wood, to the right, the 13th Welch were encountering severe opposition.

Mansel Jack, crawling along on his belly, saw that the sun had come up and that it was now almost daylight. He paused, resting his head on the damp earth, closing his eyes against the noise of battle and allowing himself a few minutes to gather his wits.

In his memory he was back in Sweyn's Eye, holding Rhian close to him, kissing her sweet mouth and looking into her young vivid face. It had been hell to leave her behind, knowing

364

he might never see her again, yet if he died tomorrow he would have known real happiness if only for a brief time.

A shell crashing overhead galvanised him into action. He was back in the thick of the war, in charge of a company of men, promoted to Captain by the very force of his personality and leadership. And his soldiers followed him with confidence. He lifted his head and edged forward, waving to his men to keep low behind the scrub.

As he moved towards the front lines and behind the ridge, he saw Major Edwards gesturing to him. 'I'm going to try to take out that machine-gun. It's right at the centre of the hammer head, and if we break through there the men will have a chance.'

Mansel Jack viewed the terrain doubtfully. There would be little cover for anyone venturing over the ridge, yet Edwards was right: the gun had to go.

'Let me tackle it, sir,' he said quickly, but the Major was already gathering his soldiers for the attack.

Mansel Jack shouted the order for his own men to cover Edwards and the sound of exploding shells rang in his ears.

For a moment everything was chaotic, the haze of smoke covering the soldiers who had made the first rush forward. There seemed to be a lull then, a vacuum in time when nothing happened . . . but slowly a few of the soldiers staggered into sight through the acrid smoke. As they tumbled behind the ridge, groans of agony from one man could be heard clearly. Of Edwards there was no sign . . .

Mansel Jack moved quickly over the ridge. The ground ahead of him seemed stark, without cover of any sort. He breathed deeply, trying to still the beating of his heart, expecting to feel the biting sting of bullets in his gut at any moment.

Hearing a sound, he edged forward on his belly. The smoke was clearing and he saw that the enemy gun was out of action – Edwards had achieved his goal. He moved cautiously around the gaping hole where the gun had stood; several enemy soldiers lay still, cast like rag dolls over the shattered earth. At last he caught sight of Edwards, lying face down with a gaping wound in his back.

Carefully, Mansel Jack manoeuvred him away from the

365

enemy lines. The man was heavy and he felt sweat run into his eyes as he eased Edwards on to his shoulder. Then he rose to his feet and ran, twisting and turning like a hunted fox, covering the ground in what appeared to him to be slow motion, as though his booted feet were being sucked into the mud and held there.

Panting, he fell back over the ridge, where willing hands relieved him of his burden. The Major opened his eyes and Mansel Jack read the question there.

'You did it, sir,' he spoke jubilantly. 'You knocked the machine-gun right out of commission! I don't doubt you'll get a medal for this day's work.'

Edwards sighed softly and the life went out of his face. Mansel Jack crouched in the mud beside him, feeling sick to his stomach.

'Major Bond is taking command, sir.' One of the soldiers spoke quietly in Mansel Jack's ear. 'Looks like we're pushing on again through the woods.'

Mansel Jack saw that some of the 13th Welch were already moving forward. But it was clear they were being gunned down mercilessly and it was little short of suicide to continue the thrust. Major Bond was hit almost at once and fell groaning to the ground.

'Wait here.' Mansel Jack gave the order and his men obeyed instinctively. 'Keep down, while I see what's going on up there.'

Something was badly wrong, the Germans couldn't possibly be so close. As far as Mansel Jack was concerned, someone in authority had made a right cock-up of the attack.

'Captain, what's the situation back there at the woods?' Lieutenant-Colonel Ricketts was in command of the 10th Welch, a brave soldier who wanted action. He had been instructed to use his own discretion about bringing up reinforcements, but had no clear idea what was taking place.

'It's a shambles, sir,' Mansel Jack said hoarsely. 'The men are brave enough, but the 13th is rapidly being wiped out. I'm trying to skirt the woods and find out where the Jerries have dug themselves in – they seem incredibly near to me.'

'I shall bring up my men,' Ricketts spoke decisively. 'We shall attack the hammer-head of the German defence, see if we

366

can give your lads of the 13th some cover.'

Mansel Jack watched for a moment as the senior officer gave the order to advance; he was hit almost immediately but didn't falter and his troops were behind him as one man.

By now Mansel Jack had covered a fair stretch of ground; his uniform was caked with mud and his face splattered – though whether with dirt or drying blood he could not tell.

He glanced to the left of the woods and stared in horrified disbelief. 'Good God Almighty!' In his surprise he stood up, staring at the scene before him. The 13th were pressing forward, falling in scores – killed not by the enemy, but from the barrage of shells being fired by the 14th Welch. Mansel Jack moved forward, his one thought to stop the needless destruction of his men.

Meanwhile Heath Jenkins was breathing heavily, around him the men and officers of his battalion. Beside him crouched Morgan Lloyd and in the forefront, ready to lead the attack, was Sterling Richardson.

In Heath's hand was clutched his one remaining Mills bomb, the grenade which would wipe out a man without difficulty.

He rose to his feet, his gaze riveted on the officer coming through the undergrowth. He was waving his hands, ordering a cease-fire, and even through the mud that splattered him Heath recognised Mansel Jack. It was time for the bastard who had taken Rhian from him to pay for his actions!

Heath gritted his teeth and moved forward, the Mills bomb ready in his hand. Mansel Jack would not survive the battle of Mametz Wood and if that meant taking a few innocent soldiers' lives – that was just too bad.

'For Christ's sake, what are you doing?' Morgan was clinging to his arm. 'That's one of our officers out there – stop it, you madman!'

Heath took no notice; he shook Morgan away, hardly felt the weight of him. Carefully he took aim, but just as he was about to throw the bomb he caught sight of Billy Gray, Rhian's brother, alongside Mansel Jack.

Suddenly the world was a kaleidoscope of colour and smoke, then gradually the colours dimmed and a soft darkness encompassed Heath's mind.

Chapter Thirty

The summer sun was low in the sky, the red glow washing the mill house and the swiftly flowing stream with brazen red lights. The gas-lamp on the wharf glimmered faintly, a poor substitute for the sunshine so newly faded.

Rhian closed up the mill with a sigh of relief. She had worked long and hard over the past few days, but with good results: her shawls and blankets with their distinctive red, white and blue fringes were beginning to sell well again even in the heat of July, for the housewives of the town were anticipating the coming of winter.

The business, though small, was successful and she felt she was more than proving her worth, making more than a good living for herself and for the people who depended on her.

Gina was waiting for her at the door of the mill house, her face sombre. 'It's about time you packed in work, you'll be killing yourself, mind,' she said, but her tone was gentle.

'You're not looking too bright yourself, girl, there's big shadows under your eyes that tell me you're as tired as I am. Go on upstairs and rest for a while – I'll call you when the food is on the table.'

From the kitchen came the succulent smell of meat roasting and as Rhian went inside, Carrie looked over her shoulder.

'There's good timing for you, the dinner's just about ready. Doris, get the plates from the hob, there's a good girl.'

Rhian moved to the sink and washed the clinging strands of wool from her hands. As she was drying them, Carrie gave a little cry of annoyance: '*Duw*, there's silly I am, I haven't made the gravy yet, what can I be thinking about? Put the plates back for a minute or two, will you, Doris?'

Rhian moved to the table. 'You're here late tonight, Doris,' she said mildly. 'Won't your mam be worried about you?'

Doris shook her head. 'I've been helping Carrie and she says I can stop and have a bite to eat. Brought her a paper from town, made her sit down and rest I did, she was looking that pale and funny.'

Rhian felt a twinge of guilt. 'That's all right, you're welcome to eat with us.' She seated herself at the table and looked anxiously at Carrie, who was standing with her hands on her back to ease the ache.

'I'm working you all too hard,' she said remorsefully and Carrie frowned.

'Now don't go all melancholy, you're slaving like ten men yourself. Where would we all be if it wasn't for you?'

Rhian closed her eyes, enjoying the moment of peace while around her the tiny sounds of the kitchen soothed her jangled nerves.

The plates chinked as Doris brought them to the table and Rhian heard the hiss of the roast meat as Carrie lifted it from the oven. If only Mansel Jack was home safe from the war everything would be rosy and bright, she thought with a pang of pain.

'When you've had supper, I'll walk back with you to your house. I need some fresh air,' Rhian said, determined not to wallow in misery.

Doris's round face lit up. 'There's good of you, I'm still a bit afeared of the darkness.' She smiled. 'This food looks good; my belly thinks my throat's cut, I'm so hungry.'

'Will you ask Gina if she would like something on a tray?' Carrie asked. 'And be sure not to wake those two little devils – I've had enough of them today!'

Rhian rose and walked slowly up the stairs, avoiding the treads which creaked for she had every sympathy with Carrie's feelings. The two children were lovely and loving, but at the end of a weary day bed was the best place for them.

Gina responded at once to Rhian's light touch on her shoulder, rubbing the tangled hair from her face. Her eyes were clouded and she caught Rhian's hand and held it fast.

'I was thinking about Heinz and I could almost hear him

crying out in pain – oh, Rhian, it's all so horrible!'

'Hush now.' Rhian held her close, patting her shoulder comfortingly, although the words Gina had spoken sent fear shafting through her. 'Come on downstairs now and don't wake the children – supper's ready.'

Rhian shivered as she led Gina back to the kitchen. She tried not to think of the war but it was there; a threatening spectre wherever she turned. It was on the lips of the people who bought her shawls, in the headlines which were flashed in the newspapers and, worst of all, in the shape of maimed and wounded soldiers returned to Sweyn's Eye like faulty goods no longer useful on the battlefield.

'Stop looking so broody and get on with your supper before it goes cold.' Carrie's voice broke into her thoughts and Rhian took up her knife and fork, knowing that her appetite had deserted her.

It was a silent meal, with Gina sitting heavy-eyed in her chair. Carrie gave up all attempts to generate conversation and it was only Doris who made the occasional remark about the goodness of the food, the leanness of the lamb and the bite of the mint sauce.

'*Duw*, I can't eat any more supper.' Carrie took her plate to the sink, her tense shoulders testifying to her emotions. 'Hours I've spent cooking in this hot kitchen and no one is hungry.'

Suddenly, she began to cry. She stood near the stone sink without moving, the tears slipping down her lined cheeks, her face screwed up like a baby in distress. Rhian hurried to her, clasping her in her arms, her own eyes moist.

'Carrie, please don't! We all appreciate what you do for us and we couldn't manage without you.'

Carrie shook her head. 'It's not the damn supper – oh Jesus, help me, I've got to tell you.'

Rhian drew the weeping woman to a chair. 'Carrie, tell me what's wrong.' Her voice was firm and commanding and, surprised, Carrie stopped crying.

'It's all over the newspaper,' her mouth quivered as she fought for self-control. 'News has come through from the Somme . . .' her words trailed away and Rhian bit her lips, half afraid to hear what Carrie was about to tell her.

'There was a dreadful loss of life at a place called Mametz Wood,' Carrie continued unsteadily. 'Ninety-one men missing or killed and two hundred and ninety-seven wounded – and that was only the 14th Welch, the 13th and the 16th were even worse hit.'

Rhian felt as though she was melting in fear. 'Mansel Jack,' she whispered, her mouth dry, her eyes wide.

Carrie was weeping again. 'Heath Jenkins is there and *duw*, there's a feeling inside me that tells me he won't be coming back.'

Gina made a tiny sound. 'Billy's there too. Oh, poor Rhian, your husband and your brother – how can you bear it?'

Rhian straightened, telling herself not to panic. 'Other people have menfolk out there, too,' she said gently. 'Mali's husband is in France, for one. We must all be brave and wait for news, there's no point in jumping to conclusions. Come on, Doris, it's time I was walking you home; your mam will be worrying.'

In spite of her brave words, Rhian was cold and empty inside. 'Perhaps you'll make us a cup of tea when I get back, Carrie.' She spoke firmly and her words brought the older woman's sobs to a gulping halt.

'Aye, I'll do that, Rhian, and I'll say this – you've as much pluck as any soldier fighting in France.'

The streets were still busy even though they were washed by the silver of the moonlight, yet it seemed a lifetime since Rhian had closed the door of the mill and watched the sun going down over the river. She almost wished she could return to that moment, for then she had felt contentment at a job well done and known nothing about the battle of Mametz Wood.

Doris's mother was waiting on the door, her face anxious. '*Duw*, I wondered if someone had kidnapped my girl!'

She drew Doris into the house and Rhian forced a smile. 'She stayed to have a bit of supper with us. I'm sorry you were worried, Mrs Williams.'

'*Duw*, I'm bone-weary too, them boys have given me a dog's life today. I don't think I can go on looking after them much longer, Rhian. Doris will just have to give up her work, that's all.' She turned to her daughter. 'Go on in, you, there's a body waiting to see you.'

Doris hurried away down the long dark passage and Mrs Williams leaned forward confidingly. 'Her man's come back, anyway, says he's going to marry her. Invalided out of the Army he is, but willing enough to find a job, mind.' Her voice became wistful. 'My Doris is so much better since she's been working for you – brought her back to her senses, you have. She's a good girl and deserves a bit of luck.'

'Yes, she does.' Rhian moved away from the lighted doorway. 'Give her my blessing.'

Well, that was that, Rhian thought in resignation. Now she would need to manage her affairs in some other way; perhaps she could get in a young strong woman to work the mill with her and leave Gina free to look after the two children, which was what she most wanted to do. She realised that she was occupying her thoughts with trivia in an effort not to dwell on Mametz Wood and what had happened there.

Rhian turned down Copperman's Row and heard the music from the accordion of Dai-End-House reach out into the night and grasp at her very soul. She stood silent for a moment, staring up at the sky where the stars were appearing like faint jewels in a velvet sky.

In Market Street the doors stood open and from Murphy's fresh-fish shop light spilled in a golden pool on to the pavement.

'Katie Murphy!' Rhian smiled to herself in the darkness. The Irish girl would be just the right sort of person to operate the looms. She was intelligent and quick and had done more than her duty working at the munitions factory.

Katie was seated in the kitchen with Mark at her side, handsome and attentive. For a brief moment, Rhian felt a diamond-sharp point of pain.

'Rhian! Jesus, Mary and Joseph, what are you doing in Market Street this time o' night?'

Rhian was drawn at once into the heart of the Irish family. She found a mug of steaming tea in her hands and smelled the sickly scent of gin as Mrs Murphy poured a drop into her cup.

'Sure I'm glad to see you, but what brings you round here, Rhian?' As Katie smiled, her heavy red-gold hair swung forward over her shoulders in shimmering waves.

Rhian took a deep breath. 'I was seeing Doris home; you

372

know better than anyone that she's not been well since the explosion and she's still very nervous of the dark.'

Katie nodded. 'Yes, I know, but she's been almost herself lately, hasn't she?' She spoke quietly but there were shadows in her eyes. 'Mark keeps on telling me to get out of the factory.' She looked across the room and Mark returned her gaze steadily.

'It can't be soon enough for me,' he said sternly. 'Get out of there, Katie, before you do yourself a harm. It's not just the risk of explosions that worries me, it's the way your skin is becoming stained by the fulminate.'

'Well, in a way this is what I've come to see you about,' Rhian said quickly. 'Doris won't be working for me any more now her man is back and I really need some help in the mill. There's plenty to do and I'm sure you would pick it up quickly enough.'

Mark leaned forward in his chair, his face eager. 'Say yes, Katie; I can't bear to think of you in that damned munitions factory!'

'It's not much money, mind,' Rhian said, 'but there's your food and a few bits and pieces of wool to bring home: blankets that get spoiled in the dying or washing process.'

Katie smiled, her eyes alight. 'I think you've just talked me into it,' she said brightly. 'I'm sick of travelling on that train every day, especially in this heat, and as for the money – sure an' isn't there more important things to consider than pay?'

Rhian sighed in relief. 'Right then, will you start on Monday?' she asked and Katie burst into peals of laughter.

'Saints be praised, she's talking right bossy. I wouldn't know you as the same Rhian Gray who once worked the Laundry, pouting and flouncing if there was too much work to do.'

'I suppose I've changed a great deal since then, but I'm a married woman now, mind,' Rhian said as she rose to her feet. 'Right then, I'll go home and leave you to have some peace.' She moved to the door and Katie followed behind her.

'I'm that grateful to you for thinking of me,' she said softly. 'I've wanted to get out of that factory for a long time now, it's never been the same since Mansel Jack left.' She paused. 'But there didn't seem to be anything else I could do.' She stared at

Rhian, her face wistful. 'Will you teach me the spinning and weaving properly?'

'Of course I will.' Rhian put her arm around Katie's shoulder. 'What good would you be to me otherwise?'

She moved away from Market Street, listening to the sounds of the accordion; as the notes washed like waves through the darkness, the plaintive tune filled her with sadness and she bit her lip as tears rose to her eyes. 'Mansel Jack, where are you?' she whispered and the words were carried away on the soft evening breeze.

Chapter Thirty-One

The platform of the Sweyn's Eye railway station lay washed in patchy sunlight. The rails ribboned away, curving into the distance and gleaming silver against the backdrop of the green hills.

Sweyn's Eye was alive with rumours and stories about Mametz Wood infiltrated like a swarm of bees into humble kitchen and gracious drawing-room alike. It caught the attention of shopkeepers as they scraped maggots from stale bacon to give the meat an illusion of freshness. Women stood in shop doorways with baskets swinging emptily, faces avid with the news that the survivors of the battle were coming home.

At the railway station, clutches of wives and mothers grouped together as though for comfort, yet each one was isolated in her own private hell. Rhian stood apart in a corner of the platform, almost hidden from view. She had argued ceaselessly with Carrie, who had wanted to come with her, but Rhian knew that she had to be alone.

There had been little official news from France and the heartache, the worrying, might be for nothing. But if the train arrived without Mansel Jack on board, Rhian wanted . . . needed to be alone with her grief.

'But, *cariad*, I don't like the idea of you going by yourself and waiting perhaps all day for the train that might not come,' Carrie had said pleadingly.

'Please, let me do this my own way.' Rhian's voice had been firm. 'In any case, I need you to look after the children while Gina shows Katie how to work the loom.'

Rhian had won and quickly she had dressed in a soft cotton skirt and a blouse with a fashionably high neckline. Then she had brushed her hair until it shone and tied it back with a silk ribbon; she must look her best, just in case . . .

She had been trembling as she left the mill house and hurried past the stream, watching as it leaped and spun over smooth boulders to run chattering and sparkling down the slope towards the river. It was a fine, warm, sunny day and as Rhian looked up at the cloudless sky she wondered if Mansel Jack was seeing the same bright fluffy clouds which hung like a lace border on a blue backcloth.

It was only a short walk from the mill to the station and the roadway was crowded with people moving in the same direction, but Rhian saw none of them. Her heart and mind were filled with the hope that today, before the sun moved to the west, she might be in Mansel Jack's arms.

She had moved instinctively to stand behind a hoarding that bore an advertisement for Camp Coffee. Somehow she could not bear to share the uncertainty of the moment with anyone, so she clasped her hands together and kept her eyes lowered. And so it was that she failed to see Mali walk past, her face anxiously searching the groups of people on the platform.

Mali Richardson had spent most of the night tossing and turning in her bed, half afraid to rise in the morning lest there was an official communication from the Army bearing bad news. All she had to go on were rumours; no one seemed to know the truth of what had happened in France and as she dressed to go to the station, she had no idea if she was simply living on false hopes.

Thinking of Sterling, her heart contracted in pain. She longed to see his violet eyes staring down into her face, feel his touch gentle and reassuring, have his arms wrapped protectively about her. She couldn't envisage a life without him there beside her, strong and yet tender, the hub of her existence.

She had kissed the children and hurried towards the roadway. The tram had been crowded with people, mostly silent – staring at each other, drawn together by mutual fear.

Mali had no idea what time the train would come and she didn't care. All she knew was that she would be there and would wait all day if necessary. Somehow, it seemed that being

376

on the station brought her closer to Sterling.

She stood alone at first, remembering how she had almost lost her husband once before in a pit explosion at the Kilvey Deep. Frantically she had searched through the debris and chaos, her belly full with child. And she remembered the pure joy of finding him alive. Surely he had not survived only to die on a foreign field?

'*Duw*, Mali, I thought I'd be the first one here.' Mary Sutton stood tall, her face calm, her bearing one of poise and elegance. Mali wished she could be equally strong, but if she could have read behind the clear eyes, she would have realised that Mary was simply putting up a brave front.

Mary had seen Mali's slight figure with a sense of relief, happy that there was a friend she could talk to. Moreover, there must be some truth in the rumours that the men were being brought home if Mali had come to wait at the station too. Mary had spent a sleepless night, wondering if she could bear to wait for the train and witness other folk's fond reunions. Yet there was Heath to consider – she couldn't allow him to arrive unwelcomed.

'I can't help worrying in case the rumours of the men's homecoming are not true,' Mary said with forced calmness.

Mali's eyes darkened with tears. '*Duw*, I hope and pray they are! You know the old saying that there's no smoke without fire.'

Mary looked down at the slight figure of Mali, witnessing the faith that seemed to shine through her tear-misted eyes like a beacon. There were no dark secrets in Mali's life, no transgressions, no awful guilt to expiate. Her love for Sterling was pure and unblemished and Mary envied her.

The crowds shifted and the patterns of people changed. Voices rose and fell and then there was a sudden startled silence as a train hooted in the distance. The air became charged, the crowds straining to see along the silver thread of the lines. But a guard climbed up on a box and bellowed loudly that the incoming train was simply a local one and would carry only farmers coming in from the country.

Gina Sinman felt like an intruder as she pushed her way through the crowds and found a spot on the platform for herself. She was a widow, she knew that her husband would not be coming home today or ever again. He would never be hailed a hero, for he had been of Austrian blood which was an accident of nature. At heart he was always a Welshman; he had lived and loved among the people of Sweyn's Eye, but in their fear they had rejected him and then he had been sent away to an internment camp and been killed accidentally.

Nevertheless, Gina had felt compelled to come to the station. She had written to Billy Gray faithfully for many months and his replies had been full of gratitude. She knew how he felt and that although they were practically strangers, they needed each other for they had no one else to call their own. And every man at the front needed a woman to care for him, to send him small treats and tell him news of home.

When Gina had asked Carrie to keep an eye on the children for an hour or two, the older woman had looked at her shrewdly.

'There's soft you are, girl – don't go giving your heart away to a man who might not want it. Billy Gray is a wild one, mind – got quite a past, he has – not a bit like your Heinz.'

Gina had felt a momentary anger. 'I'm not looking for a husband and no one could be like Heinz,' she had retorted, 'but I'm sorry for Billy and all I can say is that he's been kind to me and I've grown to like him. You learn a lot about people through their letters, you know.'

Carrie had shrugged. 'All right, *merchi*, don't get your hair off, I'm only trying to warn you.'

Gina had washed and fed the children in silence, her mind darting to and fro as she tried to sort out the emotions that were tumbling through her. She had loved Heinz with all her being, but surely she could offer Billy Gray her friendship – there was nothing wrong in that, was there? In any case, she felt she must come to wait for the train that was bringing the men of Sweyn's Eye home from the war.

She glanced around, feeling alone and isolated, expecting at any moment that someone would charge up to her and challenge her right to be here . . . which was stupid, for no one even noticed her presence.

She saw Mali Richardson talking with Mary Sutton, the two women beautifully dressed as befitted their stations in life. But Gina did not envy them, no doubt they waited as she did with heavy hearts, for shells and bombs were no respecters of persons. She could not see Rhian anywhere, but knew she must be on the platform somewhere for she had left the mill house early.

There was a surge of people behind her and Gina found herself thrust forward almost into the arms of Mary Sutton, who steadied her with a smile.

'There's sorry I am,' Gina gasped, righting her bonnet, 'I hope I haven't crushed your lovely frock.'

'Don't you worry about that.' Mary was looking down from her elegant height and Gina felt small and dumpy in comparison.

'Have you someone coming back from the front?' Mary asked and Gina knew that she was simply being polite. She swallowed hard. 'I'm waiting for Billy Gray. I've been minding his little girl for him up at Rhian's place, just until he comes home.' She was irritated with herself for feeling the need to explain, sure that Mary Sutton wouldn't be the least interested in her reason for being at the station.

'Oh, there's good you are!' It was Mali who spoke. 'I knew that Delmai Richardson had abandoned the little girl and I wondered how poor Rhian Gray would manage to bring up a child alone.'

Gina looked into Mali's open honest face and liked her at once. She might be married to a rich copper boss, but she had not forgotten her origins and still spoke in the language of the Welsh.

'It's true enough,' Gina spoke more confidently. 'Cerianne is such a sweet little child, she's like a sister to my boy Dewi.'

'I have two children,' Mali volunteered, 'a boy and a girl. They take a bit of looking after too.' The women exchanged sympathetic smiles.

'Aye, Cerianne and Dewi lead me a dog's life at times, but they're good babbas really and I can't imagine what I'd do without them. Rhian's got Katie Murphy helping in the mill now, so I can give all my time to the children – it makes things much easier.'

Gina wondered why she was babbling on like a fool, but Mali seemed genuinely interested. Mary Sutton kept looking along the track as though willing the train to come and Gina understood and shared her sense of urgency.

'Katie is a good friend of mine,' Mali said in her soft voice. 'I'm glad she's not working in the munitions factory any longer, it was an awful job for anyone to do.' She sighed. 'I don't know how I can keep talking like this,' her eyes met Gina's, 'I suppose it's because I'm so nervous.' They smiled at each other in complete understanding.

The crowd shifted and moved and Gina found herself separated from Mali Richardson. Their lives had never crossed before, but Gina had been aware of the impact on the town when Mali, a copperworker's daughter, had married the rich copper boss. She had wondered in passing if it was the rich life which lured the young girl away from her own background but now, meeting Mali, she knew that there was nothing grasping or underhand about her.

Restlessly Gina stared around her. She would have to return to the mill soon, for there was a limit to Carrie's patience and she would be none too pleased at being left with the children all day. She sighed and stepped back, leaning against the rough stone wall of the station office; she would give it another half-hour or so and then go home.

Carrie dressed the children with quick, determined fingers. 'There's a soft old woman you are,' she told herself fiercely, 'the only one in Sweyn's Eye not to be down at the station, I'll bet my last penny. Come on, Dewi, get your little hand into your shirt-sleeve now; don't be *twp*, boyo.'

Cerianne was dressed and waiting. She was a good and obedient child and her large eyes looked trustingly up at Carrie. When Dewi began to grizzle, Cerianne took his hand in a motherly way.

Carrie grasped Dewi's other hand firmly and turned to look down at Cerianne.

'Hold on to my skirt now, and don't let go. The streets are dangerous these days, what with all the traffic coming and going. Not like in my young days – quiet it was then, so quiet.'

She laughed out loud at herself, seeing how ridiculous it was to talk to the children as if they could understand. And yet Cerianne had a wise look in her large eyes which made you think she knew just what you were talking about.

By the time she reached the station her feet ached, and to

Carrie's dismay Dewi began to grizzle again.

'*Duw*, I never did meet such a misery as you, boyo. Stop that at once and if you're good, Carrie will buy you some sweeties.'

The station was thronged with people and Carrie pushed her way through the crowds, searching eagerly for Rhian or Gina, anyone who could take responsibility for the children. She was getting too old for such things. Yet deep within her was the knowledge that she was here for one reason only: to welcome Heath Jenkins home from the war.

She had never forgotten that he had lain with her, made her feel like a woman, reached some part of her that was alive to him and him alone. Like a foolish old woman she loved him, a part of her would always love him.

She caught sight of Gina then and thankfully hurried towards her. 'I couldn't keep away,' she said breathlessly, grasping Dewi more tightly as he tried to pull free.

'Come here, Dewi!' Gina swung her son into her arms and he leaned against her shoulder, his eyes already drooping wearily. 'That's right, boyo, you go off to sleep and then we'll all have some peace,' she added ruefully.

Carrie stared along the silent track. 'No sign of the train yet, then?' she asked and Gina slowly shook her head.

'No and nothing's been announced either – we might all have come here on a wild-goose-chase.'

Carrie stared around her, recognising faces amongst the crowd and knowing that a common purpose had brought rich and poor alike to wait through the heat of a summer's day. But where was Rhian? Carrie couldn't see her anywhere. Poor child, how anxious she must be. And yet Rhian was no longer a child, Carrie realised with surprise, she was a woman grown strong and independent. But she shouldn't be alone, not at a time like this – where was she?

Rhian brushed back a curl that had drifted across her forehead and sighed softly. She had seen Carrie hurry into the station with the children, but had chosen to remain out of sight. She was growing more tense as each minute passed and beginning to believe there would be no train, ever. Even as the thought crossed her mind, however, there was a sound of raised voices from people further along the platform. Rhian

381

stood on tip-toe and her breathing seemed to be suspended as she saw the steam from an engine pierce the blue of the sky.

She clasped her hands together, unable to bear the tension, wanting to run and hide her face just as a child would do. She swallowed hard and a tingling sensation filled her as the hoot of the train echoed along the line.

Women were pressing forward to the edge of the platform, but Rhian could not move. She wanted to scream out loud, to fall to her knees and beg heaven to let Mansel Jack be on the train, but she simply stood still, waiting – her mouth dry, her heart pounding within her as though in time with the clatter of the wheels.

A loud cheer rose from the waiting crowds. Someone brought out a huge flag and it fluttered gently in the summer breeze. Carriage doors were opening and Rhian caught her first sight of khaki as a soldier sprang out on to the platform.

Interminable minutes passed while the throng of people began to disperse and those that were left stared with haunted eyes at the spitting, gushing train.

Then Rhian saw Mali Richardson run forward to be swept into the arms of her tall, handsome husband. Mali was weeping openly and Rhian felt her own throat constrict.

A soldier moved past her, solitary and alone, and Rhian recognised the ravaged face of Morgan Lloyd. He was limping badly, but the deepset eyes looked out at the world with bright determination. He stopped and spoke to Carrie, shaking his head, and Carrie turned away in despair like a woman suddenly grown old.

Rhian moved from her corner, her hands trembling. There were hardly any people left on the station now. Glancing to her right she saw Gina who was laughing out loud, staring up eagerly at the soldier who was cuddling Cerianne close in his arms. With a shock of delight she realised it was her own brother Billy and her heart warmed a little as she saw him place an arm around Gina's boy – there was time enough to welcome Billy home.

She hurried along the platform and saw that Mary was just ahead of her, her back stiff, her shoulders tense. Even in her own dark despair, Rhian could feel pity for Mary Sutton.

Mary was breathless with pain and fear. She had watched

382

other couples embrace and her own loneliness and sense of loss were heightened.

'Are there any other soldiers on the train?' she asked the porter in a voice that cracked with strain. 'I'm looking for my brother Heath . . .' her voice died away in disbelief. It couldn't be . . . but it was!

'Brandon!' She almost screamed his name, then stood quite still watching him, unable to believe the evidence of her senses. He had been reported missing and yet he was here, staring at her, his honest eyes looking into hers. In that instant she knew without doubt that she would have to tell him everything; he deserved nothing less than the truth, otherwise Mary Anne's threat of revenge would for ever lie between them.

He held out his arms and like a sleepwalker, Mary went into them, thankful to fate for giving her this moment of happiness as she was held close in her husband's warm embrace.

Rhian had witnessed Mary's joy and now, in fear and trembling, she moved forward. An officer suddenly leaped down on to the platform before her, his dark crisp hair jutting from beneath his cap, his eyes blazing with love as they met hers.

'Mansel Jack!' She didn't remember crossing the space between them; all she knew was that he was holding her, his arms strong, his mouth tender as their lips met.

She was drowning in a mingling of relief and joy, tears thick in her throat. She leaned away from him, drinking in his presence, almost unable to believe he was really here with her.

He touched her cheek with gentle fingers and then hugged her close, burying his face in the warmth of her neck.

Rhian closed her eyes in a rush of joy. 'Come on, *cariad*,' she whispered, 'let's go home.'

The station was silent now, the platform empty. A flag lay discarded, fluttering faintly as though in its death throes. There would be rejoicing in Sweyn's Eye that night. There would also be tears.